A Vampire in Vegas

THE PLANES
BOOK ONE

ELISE NOBLE

Published by Undercover Publishing Limited

v3

ISBN: 978-1-912888-40-5

Edited by Nikki Mentges, NAM Editorial

Cover design by Abigail Sins

www.undercover-publishing.com

www.elise-noble.com

Only a vampire can love you forever...

CHAPTER 1

Vee

It was an unusually cold December night in Las Vegas when my life fell apart for the fourth time. A Friday. And the evening had started out so well...

"Hey, Vee!" The security guard leaning against the wall outside the back door of Club Dead raised his hand in greeting, ash from his cigarette flaking to the ground. "Nice hair."

I smiled. An old acquaintance once nicknamed me Mona Lisa because I'd mastered her tight-lipped, mysterious little quirk of the lips, thanks in no small part to the hours I'd spent in the Louvre.

"Thanks, Darrell." In truth, my sleek bob had ended up a little pinker than I expected, but that was the risk I took shopping for dye—and indeed everything else—on the internet. On the plus side, if people were looking at my hair, they weren't looking at my face. "Got long left on your break?"

"Ten minutes, but I ain't waitin' out here to freeze. Reckon I'm gonna catch Good Omen's first song."

We had two bands playing tonight, with Good Omen

warming up for the main act—Serenity Strange and the Sinners. If the line along the block was anything to go by, the place was packed, and that meant two things—tips and blisters. I could live without both, but I enjoyed my job. When the alternative was sitting at home alone, I'd gladly put up with a few sore toes.

"Where do you want me tonight?" I asked Pandora, the club's manager, as I swapped my tennis shoes for pumps in the break room and carefully refreshed my lipstick. *Focus on your mouth, Vee.* I hated looking at myself in the mirror.

"Can you work the VIP area?"

"Sure. Is there anyone interesting in tonight?"

"Half of the Canyon College football team—as in the ones who are old enough to drink—Dalton Cooper, and that blonde from the purse show. You know, the one where the designers compete to be number-one bag lady? What's her name?"

"I have no idea."

"Damn, I should know it. I'd look it up, but I've been too busy ogling Jerome Keller."

"Jerome Keller is here? Seriously?"

Jerome Keller was Hollywood's latest action hero. Rumour said his Lycra suit wasn't even padded. I'd seen every one of his movies, but I never thought I'd get to meet him in the flesh. Dalton Cooper wasn't bad looking either, even if I preferred rock music to country.

"Yup. His group's got two tables, and they've drunk eight bottles of champagne already."

"Does my hair look okay?"

"Perfect. Knock 'em dead, sweetie."

As I left the staff area, the lead singer from Good Omen leapt off the stage and landed among the crowd, barely missing a beat as the women clawed at him. Some of the men, too—Club Dead was all about equality. I skirted around the edge of the room, heading for the sweeping staircase that led to the VIP area. One of Darrell's buddies grinned as he unclipped the velvet rope to let me past.

"Just yell if they start getting too rowdy up there."

"Always do, Trayvon."

I'd only joined the team at Club Dead eight months ago, but when winter came, I'd increased my hours, and now I worked the night shift six days a week. Eight until four, dusk until dawn. My colleagues had become my family, and on Mondays, my usual day off, I got kind of lonely.

At Club Dead, I was never alone.

Eyes tracked me as I climbed the stairs, and I didn't have to look up to feel the gaze of Lucian Blane, the club's owner. He often stood on his private balcony, hands spread wide on the rail as he surveyed his domain. Of all the men in all the world, Blane confused me the most. A dark aura enveloped him, a presence that rippled through the cavernous building, yet he had a heart.

But enough about Blane. It was time to work. Where was Jerome Keller's party? Predictably, he had prime position at two long, low tables in the far corner overlooking the stage, his entourage draped across leather couches as they waited for the show to start. I'd need to clear some of that glassware so I could serve them more drinks.

But before I managed to get there, Dalton Cooper snapped his fingers at me. "Hey, pink. Running low on beer here."

Good thing he had a pretty face and a sexy voice because he wouldn't have won any fans with his charming personality. Such a shame that fancy packages so often hid disappointing gifts.

"What can I get you?"

"Two American Pilsners and something for the lady. What're you drinking, sweetheart?"

Serenity Strange was sitting next to him, her stool close enough to press her thigh against his. Or was it the other way around? I'd gotten to know Serenity during my time at the club, and she didn't usually go for pretend cowboys, especially rude ones. I avoided the Coopers of this world too. The plain guys—the unmemorable ones—served my purpose much better.

"Just water for me," Serenity said.

"Water? No way. Bring her a glass of champagne."

Serenity gave her head a tiny shake. Rather than cause an argument, I decided to fetch her sparkling grape juice instead. It looked pretty much the same, and I bet Dalton wouldn't notice. Men like him never did.

Down below, the singer from Good Omen jumped back onto the stage, minus his shirt and one of his shoes. Still, he looked as if he was having a good time. I gave Dalton Cooper's order to Kristy at the bar, then went to check on Jerome Keller. American royalty, or so he thought. Someone had even given him a crown, a wonky gold plastic thing that perched atop his scruffy brown hair. The women on either side of me glared when I got close.

"Any more drinks?"

"You'll have to clear this mess away first," one of the harpies trilled, her voice saccharine and her words anything but.

"I'll do that in just a second." *Don't grit your teeth, Vee.*

"Easy, Trixie," Keller told his groupie. "She can't write the order down if she's carrying a tray, can she?"

The woman flicked her hair in a huff and went back to stroking Keller's chest.

"Thanks," I mouthed.

"Used to wait tables myself," he said. "Although not in shoes like those."

I was short, okay? And if I didn't wear heels, I practically got trampled in crowds. Still, I wasn't about to admit to my insecurities, so I did my Mona Lisa thing again.

"Drinks?"

"Keep the champagne coming, sweetheart."

I didn't mind Pandora giving me nicknames, but when Keller did it, I wanted to smack him with my tray. Perhaps because he was looking at my cleavage the whole time.

"I'm anything but sweet, your highness, but I'll get your drinks. Is there a particular brand of champagne you'd prefer?"

"High-end, darlin'."

Darlin'? Gah.

The back of my neck prickled again, and I knew Blane was still up there. I'd only spoken to him a handful of times, and never about anything of consequence, yet still he watched me. Didn't he trust me? If not, I couldn't blame him.

Every other club in Vegas relied on a network of security cameras watching with their beady eyes, and the casinos were worse. You couldn't blink in a casino without someone recording it, and I wasn't fond of being caught on film. Just the thought made me twitchy. But Club Dead's security consisted of a single camera at the front entrance and Lucian Blane.

An hour passed. Good Omen finished their set, and the DJ took over while the tech guys set up Serenity's equipment. My shoes began pinching, and we ran out of Krug Grande Cuvée. The football team drank half of it out of a fancy gold cup they passed around, and the rest ended up spilled on the floor. And me. The quarterback tripped over a cheerleader and threw a glassful over my top, then offered to help me out of it before he keeled over.

"Not now, but maybe later, okay?" I muttered as I dragged him onto a sofa. I never liked to rule out any options. Little Miss Spontaneous, that was me, and he *was* pretty. Perhaps a bit high-profile for my taste, but I made an exception every once in a while.

"What happened to you?" Serenity asked as I stood in the staff bathroom, sponging the sticky mess off my skin.

"A football player who couldn't hold his drink. Are you okay?"

Those dark streaks under her eyes were harsher than her usual stage make-up. Had she been crying?

"Oh, I'm fine." That's what she said, but she'd hesitated for too long before answering.

"Want to talk about it? Did something happen with Dalton Cooper?"

"No." A sigh. "Yes. Sort of."

I thought she might elaborate, but she didn't, just grabbed a wad of tissues, dampened them under the tap, and began wiping the worst of the smudged mascara away from her face. Serenity was beautiful in a macabre kind of way. Black hair, black lips, black dress—the only touch of colour was the red rose pinned in her hair. And her voice... She sang like an angel, but her lyrics were written by the devil himself.

"Anything I can do to help?" I asked.

"Ever fallen into a mess you can't get out of? A pit that sucks you down, down, down until you can't breathe?" Yup, I most definitely had. "Some days, I feel like giving up."

"Don't give up. Never give up. You've got so much to live for—your boyfriend, your music, an amazing career..."

"Me and Joaquin split up."

Oh. Shit. "I'm so sorry."

"Plenty more fish in the sea, right?"

Was that why she'd been cosying up to Dalton Cooper? A rebound?

"Yes, but don't be too hasty. You'll find the perfect man when the time's right."

Her quiet snort suggested she didn't believe me, and to be

honest, I didn't believe me either. But I couldn't exactly encourage her to do something stupid with the King of Country.

"Serenity, just—"

"Here, you missed a bit." She scrunched up her tissue and wiped a sticky patch off my neck. "I need to go."

"Is it time for you to sing?"

"Not for an hour. Blane wants to see me."

"Really? What about?"

Blane rarely spoke to anyone, preferring to issue his orders through Pandora instead. I usually managed to stay out of earshot, but even so, I'd never forget his voice. Deep and husky, yet somehow cold enough to send shivers up my spine. If you looked up the word "intimidating" in the dictionary, there'd be a picture of Blane, glowering out from the page as he lorded over his empire. Pandora would be under "alternate meaning" because she made me nervous as well. Sure, she was always nice, but maybe *too* nice, as if the sweetness was a disguise for her true personality.

"No idea what he wants," Serenity said. "Pandora told me to go upstairs before my set. Can't keep the master waiting."

And I couldn't keep the customers waiting. Besides, I was getting hungry, and I needed to find something to eat. Tonight, the dance floor was heaving with Sin City's great and beautiful, a capacity crowd for Serenity and her band. She'd been playing the club since I arrived in Las Vegas two years ago, but thanks to a series of catchy songs and a viral YouTube video, she'd recently signed a record deal and also made a handful of TV appearances over the past few months. I couldn't see her sticking around the Strip forever. Would Lucian Blane be sorry to see her go?

"Want to grab dinner after we finish?" I asked Serenity. Dinner and a chat had become a habit of ours, and although we weren't super close, Serenity was the best friend I had.

She managed a tiny smile. "Wong Fu's?"

"You bet. I'll call in the order on my next break."

Outside, I glanced up at the balcony, but Lucian Blane had vanished back to his lair. Phew. A smidgen of the tension that coiled around my gut unwound.

"Hey, sweetheart." A sweaty guy in suit pants flicked my hair as I headed back to the VIP area, and his buddies laughed. "Pink. Nice. Does the carpet match the drapes?"

As well as the A-listers on the VIP mezzanine, Club Dead played host to newlyweds, bachelorette parties, socialites, and anyone else who could afford the five-hundred-dollar cover charge to get in downstairs. Unfortunately, that included drunk businessmen with expense accounts.

"Sorry?"

"Huh?"

"I don't understand what you mean." *Please, explain your shitty comment.* "You're gonna have to break that down for me."

"Uh, never mind."

He backed off, melting into the sea of bodies and taking his colleagues with him. Yeuch. Where were the decent men nowadays? Things had really gone downhill since the 1940s. *Come on, there must be at least one delicious guy in the club tonight.* That was a perk of the job, after all. An upmarket establishment like Lucian Blane's generally offered a better range of opportunities than, say, a casino buffet or a hotel bar. Yes, I might have had a rather specific taste in men, but I also had standards, and at least the doormen screened the entrants.

Think that sounds mercenary? Well, in this day and age, it was either eat or get eaten.

I made my rounds in the VIP area, clearing tables, fetching drinks, stopping to chat occasionally, and taking endless photos for the club-goers to put on their Instagram pages. A hefty investment from Lucian Blane had put the club on the map, and lifestyle bloggers kept it there.

The focal point on the mezzanine was a long brushed-steel bar that ran along the far wall, a showpiece beneath strategically lit shelves filled with fancy bottles of alcohol, staffed by bartenders who'd turned serving drinks into an art form. And Blane liked surprises. The club's staff included a troupe of performers who appeared throughout the night—magicians, fire-eaters, acrobats, showgirls... Working there was never dull. I dodged a juggler on my way to the bar, which at that moment had a trio of redheads dancing on it.

"Excuse me, do you work here?"

"Sure do," I said.

The speaker was six inches taller than me, even in my heels, and I stepped back to get a better look at him. Tousled light-brown hair, a strong jaw, and a nice smile, but his eyes looked tired. He hadn't bothered to gussy up either, and technically, his jeans breached the dress code. How had he got in?

"What time does the show start?" he asked.

"You mean Serenity Strange and the Sinners?"

"Yeah, I guess."

Wow, such enthusiasm. "In half an hour. Are you a fan?"

"I'm a fan of sleeping, but my friends decided I needed to get out more."

He waved a hand at a table in the corner, and I recognised Cecily Shepherd and a man I assumed was her husband. I'd never seen her in the club before, but she regularly made the local news for her humanitarian work. Her presence explained how the guy had got through the door—Cecily Shepherd was part of the Las Vegas elite thanks to her father owning two hotels and a golf course in the city.

"Don't worry; she'll only play for an hour. Can I get you a drink?"

"I wouldn't mind a diet cola."

Diet cola? This guy sure knew how to have fun. His drink choice also bumped him right down my list of candidates for a little after-hours fun, which was a shame because I kind of liked him. His honesty was refreshing.

"Sure, I'll be right back. Anything else? Drinks for your friends?"

"Cece's hungry, but she only eats organic food." He spread his hands helplessly. "I don't suppose..."

"Are you looking for hot food?"

"More of a snack."

"We have organic pita chips?"

"Perfect." He flashed me a smile, and I couldn't help returning it. Carefully.

If only all the clientele were as easy to deal with as Diet Cola Guy, my job would be a breeze. Dalton Cooper had thrown a fit twenty minutes ago when I brought him gin without a freaking olive. He'd threatened to leave, and I almost escorted him to the door. Where was he now? His table was empty, and I hoped he'd made good on his offer.

Chips... I needed chips. The upstairs bar had run out, and when I asked Jace downstairs, he just laughed.

"None of this crowd care about organic. Try out back."

I threaded my way across the dance floor. A cowboy trod on my foot and quickly apologised, so I forced a smile even though my toes hurt like hell. *Occupational hazard.* The storeroom was right at the end of the hallway behind the stage, and a chill breeze hit me as I headed in that direction. The rush of cool air was pleasant after the heat of the club, but the fire door wasn't meant to be open like that. Anyone could get in. I slammed it shut, then went to find Cecily Shepherd's organic chips. So many ways to die in this world, and she was worried about pesticides?

The door to the storeroom wouldn't budge when I pushed it, and I swallowed a groan. Had somebody locked it? I shoved it harder, and the *bang* as it hit the wall almost eclipsed my scream.

Almost, but not quite.

Serenity lay on the floor, unmoving, her sightless eyes staring up at the ceiling. A trickle of blood ran across the bare concrete, glistening red under the harsh glare of the strip lights above. *Oh hell, oh hell, oh hell.* I dropped to my knees, checking for a pulse, although I already knew I wouldn't find one. I'd seen enough bodies to know when a person was dead, and Serenity's soul had well and truly departed.

Fuck.

Another scream sounded behind me, followed by several gasps and a man muttering, "I'll call the police."

Double fuck.

What should I do? My friend was dead, and I was right there next to the body. Should I run? Or brazen it out? On the one hand, I knew I hadn't killed Serenity, but on the other, she had two puncture wounds on her neck that looked for all the world as if a vampire had been snacking on the sweet blood within.

And that gave me a problem.

Why?

Because *I* was the only vampire in Club Dead. And if anyone found out, my life was over.

CHAPTER 2

Jack

"Did you hear a scream?" I asked Shep, my best friend, boss, and self-appointed therapist.

He waved at the packed dance floor below us. "Everybody's fuckin' screaming."

"Not that kind of scream." It had sounded like a woman, panicked. "Cece? Did you hear anything?"

Shep's wife shrugged, glancing at her watch again. "Sorry, I didn't. Where *is* Robert? He's over an hour late already."

Like me, Cecily couldn't wait to get out of Club Dead, although any sympathy I might have felt was tempered by the fact that it had been her idea to come in the first place. Why? Because she was determined to raise a million dollars to provide clean drinking water in Africa, and she wanted Jerome Keller to front the campaign. Robert Page, Keller's agent, had agreed to a discussion, but due to scheduling commitments, tonight was the only time all three of them could talk.

Although quite how coherent Keller would be when Page finally showed up, I had no idea. For the last hour and a half, the movie star had been drinking champagne the way I drank coffee—which was to say constantly—and every thirty

12

minutes, he took a trip to the bathroom. Either he had a weak bladder, or a hygiene fetish, or he was indulging in a little extra pick-me-up. It was tempting to follow him and find out, but I worked in the newly restructured CAPERS unit—Crimes Against Persons—rather than Narcotics.

"Maybe Page is stuck in traffic?" Shep suggested. "Why don't you try asking Keller?"

"Because I'd have to fight my way through his harem again, and I'm not sure I'd manage to be so polite this time."

"I love it when you get your claws out, babe."

"See that guy in the blue shirt who just arrived?" She motioned with her head, and Shep and I both glanced in that direction. "He's a reporter with the *Las Vegas Chronicle*. I don't want to see myself splashed across the front page."

"'Socialite elbows wannabe model'? Your father would be so proud."

Yeah, he genuinely would. Maxwell Dorrington pulled no punches himself, which was how he'd risen to the top of the Las Vegas property scene, weathering developer wars and a market crash along the way.

"And that's a perfect reason to steer clear of Keller until Page arrives. Darn it, we should've eaten dinner before we came here."

I glanced over the balcony at the main floor again. Nobody seemed to be running, so maybe my hearing had been playing tricks on me? Or was it the music? The backup singer on this track sounded like a cougar in pain—had I gotten confused?

And speaking of cougars, the brunette who'd "accidentally" fallen into my lap earlier made another appearance, and I slid out of my seat before she could start a conversation. I had no interest in getting laid, despite Shep's best efforts to send women in my direction.

He meant well, but even though he had an IQ in the 130s and graduated magna cum laude with a bachelor's degree in criminal justice, he sometimes displayed the emotional intelligence of a rock. I had no desire to get involved with a woman, not for an evening or a night or even an hour.

Never again.

Shep grinned and gave me a thumbs up, but I shot him a warning glare. *Not interested, buddy.* Cece had her phone to her ear when I headed for the bar in search of drinks and a snack for her to eat. The waitress from earlier had vanished without bringing any chips, and I couldn't see her downstairs either. That pink hair was hard to miss.

Except when I reached the fancy metal bar, the bartender was on the phone, and rather than hanging up, she waved a hand to shush me when I pointed to the soft drinks in the fridge behind her. What was it with the staff in this place? Premier nightspot in Vegas, my ass. Even the worst bars in New York had better service.

"Think you could finish the conversation later? People are thirsty."

The blonde finally hung up. "Sorry, I'm so sorry. Something just happened downstairs."

"What happened?"

A look I'd seen many times before flashed across her face. The momentary panic of a woman who'd said too much.

"Uh, nothing serious. You want a beer?"

"I heard a scream. Is somebody hurt?" When a girl hesitated like that, I knew I was on the right track. "Who's hurt?"

"Sir, please try not to worry."

Sir. So we'd gone formal now? I slapped my badge onto the bar, a gold star identifying me as a detective with the Las Vegas Metropolitan Police Department. Back in New York, I'd progressed to being a first-grade detective. Here, I was just lucky to have a job.

The bartender's eyes widened. "You're a cop? Uh, then you should probably be downstairs."

"*What happened?*"

Her voice dropped to a whisper. "Someone found a body. Out back."

I didn't bother to question her further, just grabbed Shep on my way to the stairs. Cece tried to follow too, but I shook my head and mustered up a smile.

"You should stay here."

"What's going on?"

The good thing about knowing a guy since kindergarten was that the two of you learned to read each other's thoughts. Shep didn't need an explanation to follow my lead.

"Robert Page will be here any minute, baby. We'll be right back, and then we can get dinner, okay? Wanna pick up Chinese?"

"From Wong Fu's? I'd love to, but—"

He blew her a kiss, and a gaggle of women at the table behind fanned themselves. He'd always had that effect on women, which was one reason he'd ended up marrying Cece despite her father's protests. On the surface, having one of the richest men in Vegas as his father-in-law seemed like a pretty sweet deal, but we both suspected that Maxwell Dorrington didn't always toe the line when it came to legalities, and that had the potential to put both men in an awkward position. So far, they'd adopted the "don't ask, don't tell" approach and avoided each other as much as possible.

"Well?" Shep asked as we jogged down the stairs.

"Rumour says there's a dead body around here."

"You're kidding?"

"Wish I was."

"Cece's gonna be pissed. This is my first day off in two weeks."

"If only the deceased could be more considerate."

"Just sayin'."

Days off didn't matter to me anymore, not now that I was on my own. In fact, I appreciated the overtime because anything was better than being alone with my past.

The bartender had said the body was out the back. Did that mean outside? A service alley? The kitchen area? I spotted a door in the corner behind the downstairs bar, which was a circular brushed-steel arrangement with half a dozen staff beavering away in the centre.

"Hey, watch it!"

A girl scowled as I battled across the dance floor, and I regretted not letting Shep go first because crowds always parted for him like the Red fucking Sea. Finally, we reached the door and I shoved my way through it, ignoring the *Staff Only* sign and the security guard who tried to stop me. He followed us along the hallway.

"You can't go through there. This area's private."

Shep turned without breaking stride, badge in hand, and the guard backed off, palms up.

"Where's the body?" I asked.

Wordlessly, he pointed forward. The corridor narrowed as it turned to the left, revealing a hallway spanning the width of the building with doors leading off either side. By my estimation, the left side backed onto the stage where the next act was due to perform any minute now.

The first door on the right led to a kitchen, where a chef was decorating platters of canapés with green shit in the culinary equivalent of "the show must go on." The next door led to a staircase, and the others were closed apart from one at the far end with a dozen people clustered outside it. As I watched, a brunette dressed as a zombie staggered towards us and vomited.

"Safe to say we've found the body," Shep whispered from behind me. "Either that or she's drunk way too much."

It was the former. A black-haired woman lay sprawled on the floor just inside the doorway. Early twenties at a guess, clothing intact, and apart from a neck wound, she looked untouched. I closed my eyes for a moment, remembering the morning I'd seen Angie in the morgue. The ME had tried to clean her up, but I'd never get the image of her broken body out of my head. At least this girl's next of kin wouldn't have the same memory, although that was a small consolation.

"Safe to say we won't be watching Serenity Strange sing tonight," Shep muttered.

"No, we'll have to secure the scene before anyone leaves. Someone should tell management the show can't happen."

"I meant, that's Serenity Strange lying on the floor."

The girl crouched next to her let out a strangled sob, and I recognised the waitress from upstairs. This was where she'd disappeared to?

"Who found the body?" I asked.

She looked up, meeting my gaze with watery green eyes. "I did."

"What were you doing in here?"

Silently, she pointed towards a carton of organic pita chips. Shit.

How long had she been gone? Ten minutes? Fifteen? Stabbing someone in the neck only took a few seconds, and it wouldn't be the first time a killer had stuck around at the scene of a crime to feign innocence. I leaned in closer. *Were* those knife wounds? The holes looked round rather than straight. And where was the rest of the blood? A small dark-red pool was congealing around the victim's head, but it took a lot more than that to bleed out.

"Okay, everyone needs to leave this room. It's a crime scene now."

"But don't leave the club," Shep said. "We'll need to speak

with all of you. Is there somewhere you can wait? A break area? An office?"

A guy dressed as a werewolf piped up, "We have a break area."

"Where's that?"

"At the other end of the hallway."

In an ideal world, we'd want them farther away because the extent of the crime scene was still unclear, but we couldn't send them out into the club because we'd probably never see them again.

"Has anyone touched anything in here?" I asked.

Only the pink-haired waitress spoke. "I checked for a pulse."

"Nobody else?"

The werewolf shook his head, and the others followed suit.

"Could you go and wait in the break area, please, and prevent anyone else from coming this way." Pink Hair moved to go with them, but I stopped her by the door. "I'd like to speak to you first, ma'am."

"Now?"

"If you wouldn't mind."

"Cavalry's on its way," Shep muttered, hanging up his phone. "I'll stay here."

That left me to motion Pink out into the hallway, leaving the coppery tang of blood hanging in the air behind us. The sooner you talked to a witness, the more they were likely to remember. Later, time clouded the details and they started to second-guess themselves, and there was also the risk they'd be influenced by friends and relatives. Their first answers were usually the best, and I took out my notepad to jot down her answers.

"What's your name?" I asked her.

"Vee Pelletier. V-E-E."

"Vee. Is that short for something?"

"Genevieve."

"Sounds French."

"My mother came from Paris."

"Well, Vee, I'm Detective Callahan—Jack Callahan—and I'd like to ask you a few questions if you're up to that."

She looked back at the storeroom, a quick glance. Guilty? Nervous? Or merely remembering the gruesome details? If she'd worked real fast, she could've run downstairs and killed Serenity Strange, but on balance, it seemed unlikely. Thanks to Cece's dietary preferences, I already knew Vee's motive for being in the storeroom.

At this stage, I'd treat her as a witness rather than a suspect.

"I'm fine," she said. "I just can't believe Serenity's dead. I was only talking with her a half hour ago."

"A half hour? You're certain of the time?"

She checked her watch, a cheap thing on a pink band that matched her hair. "Maybe a little longer? She said she had an hour before her set, and she's due on stage in twenty minutes. Was due, I mean." A sob burst out of her. "I can't believe she's dead."

"Where did this conversation take place?"

"In the ladies' bathroom."

"The public bathroom?"

"No, we have one just for staff." She pointed along the hallway, and I recalled seeing a black door marked "Gals" as we hunted for the body. "Someone spilled a drink on me, and I went to wash it off."

"What else did you speak about?"

"Not much." A hesitation. "She seemed upset."

"Why do you say that?"

"Because she was crying."

Yeah, that would do it. "Did she give a reason?"

Vee shook her head, pulling her bottom lip between her

teeth. She quickly caught herself and stopped. Nervous, but for what reason?

"Not really. She mentioned breaking up with her boyfriend, but I don't think that's what made her cry."

"Why not?"

Vee definitely liked to consider her answers before she spoke. That wasn't always a good thing. I wanted the raw truth, not a sanitised version.

"I'm not sure exactly. I guess...after she told me they'd split, she didn't seem more upset than she was before. Like she was over him, and she'd moved on. And she was with Dalton Cooper earlier in the evening."

"Who?"

"The country singer? He had a big hit with 'Girls on the Road.'"

"Never heard of him."

I was more of a rock fan, but I'd sure be doing some research into country when I got home.

"They were together in the VIP section earlier, but I noticed he was gone when I last went upstairs."

"Guy wearing a black cowboy hat?"

"You saw him?"

"Yeah, heading downstairs. He stopped to sign some girl's..." Some girl's breasts. She'd been hammered, and when Cooper groped her, she'd only laughed. I hadn't seen him again after that, which meant his absence was a matter to look into. Surely there had to be security cameras in a place this size? "He signed a girl's skin. Did Ms. Strange mention him when you spoke?"

"I asked her if something happened with him, and she said, 'Sort of.' But it was only a short conversation, and she was trying to fix her make-up at the same time. She said Mr. Blane had asked to see her."

"She didn't elaborate on the Cooper issue?"

"No, and I didn't press her. We were meant to be having dinner together later, so I figured that if she wanted to talk more, we'd do it then."

"And who's Mr. Blane?"

"Lucian Blane. He owns this place."

"I see." If he owned the club, he'd know his way around the maze of rooms out back. "What was her demeanour like? Did she seem worried about the meeting?"

"No, but..."

"But what?"

"Blane doesn't often speak with the staff."

An owner who didn't speak with his staff? How did that work? When I was a cop in New York, I'd worked a few bar shifts at Billy's Bar and Grill to make ends meet, and Billy had been out on the floor every night telling us what to do. A place couldn't run without proper management.

"The meeting was in one of the rooms along here?"

"No, upstairs. Mr. Blane has offices and an apartment above the club."

"Are you aware of any problems between Mr. Blane and Ms. Strange in the past? Serenity Strange is a stage name, right? Do you know her real one?"

"Sorry, I don't. I never heard her call herself anything else, and no, she never mentioned any problems. But Mr. Blane comes across as kind of..." Again she paused, searching for the right word. "Intense."

An intense recluse who was most likely the last person to have seen the victim alive. I knew who was sitting at the top of my suspect list.

"You were friends with Ms. Strange?"

"Friends, yes. But I guess... I guess it was more of a work thing. We often used to have a drink together here after the place closed, occasionally a meal, but we never saw each other outside of the club. I'll miss her." A tear rolled down Vee's cheek, but she didn't seem to notice. "She was easy to talk to, and she never judged people. Sometimes, good people are taken from us far too soon."

Her words hit like a punch to the gut, and an image of Angie popped into my head. Not one of the good ones, but of that final night, those agonisingly slow minutes when I'd held her in the freezing slush of a New York winter street as she bled out in my arms.

Get it together, Callahan.

One year, ten months, twenty-five days, and six hours had passed since she died, and I still felt as though my insides had been scraped out with a rusty spoon. I used to count the time in minutes, and Shep assured me the move to hours was a sign of improvement.

"That's true," I choked out, then steered the subject away from death. Never the easiest thing to do when you were a homicide detective. That I'd let Shep talk me out of quitting was still a decision I questioned every night. "Uh, when you first came downstairs, did you see anyone else around? Hear anything out of the ordinary?"

"No, nobody, and I didn't hear anything but the music." Her eyes suddenly widened. "Wait, I almost forgot! The fire door was open, and I closed it. My fingerprints will be on the handle. It was cold, and I didn't realise Serenity was dead, and I just— What if I ruined some evidence?"

I swallowed a groan. Ruined or not, it wasn't her fault. "You weren't to know. Anyone would've closed the door if it was open. But I'll need your prints for elimination purposes, and I'll also need to take a formal statement. Could you swing by the station tomorrow morning? Say, ten o'clock?"

"I... Uh... Tomorrow morning isn't good for me. I work nights, and I'll be asleep."

"I appreciate it's inconvenient, but I'll try to make it quick. We really do need your prints, Ms. Pelletier."

Vee seemed more unsettled at the thought of going to the station than she did at discovering a corpse. Strange.

"How about I come right now?" she suggested.

"I'm afraid I need to stay here and process the scene, and that'll take several hours."

"Then what if I come tomorrow evening?"

"It's crucial for us to work fast if we want to solve this case."

What was wrong with the morning? Surely anyone would lose an hour's sleep to help solve a friend's murder? The only difference between morning and night was that the station would be busier, and that made me even more suspicious. Was Vee trying to hide something? There was an odd vibe about Ms. Pelletier, and I couldn't put my finger on what. Should I force the issue? As a cop, I could pretty much insist she attend at the time requested, and Shep would back me up. Maybe a clue would shake loose? Then again, if it didn't, I also risked alienating a witness.

Dammit, all I'd wanted was a quiet night off, and now I'd landed in the middle of a case that every instinct told me would be tricky.

What's your problem, Vee Pelletier?

Vee

Dammit, I should've left when I had the chance. Not only was my friend dead, but now a cop unwittingly wanted to kill me too, or at least leave me in agony for weeks. Sunlight and me, we really didn't get on. I wouldn't turn to ash, but my skin blistered and burned and peeled, and no, wearing factor fifty didn't help much.

I had an emergency burka stashed in my closet, but if I wore that, Detective Callahan would surely think that was a bit odd seeing as I was standing before him in hot pants and a bustier, smelling of alcohol. And on the rare occasions I did wear the burka, people kept yelling at me to go back to my own damn country.

If only I could. I missed France, with its history and culture and green fields that stretched to the horizon. I missed the language of my childhood. I missed red wine served by the gallon, ripe cheese, and fresh bread. In 1839, I'd been there when the first steam oven arrived at the Boulangerie Viennoise. I wanted to climb the real Eiffel Tower again, not a half-size replica surrounded by neon lights. But when my creator had fled from America, he'd gone back to Paris, and Europe wasn't big enough for the both of us.

"I honestly do want to help," I told Detective Callahan.

"Then meet me at the station tomorrow at ten."

"It's not that I'm trying to be awkward. I have some, uh, health issues..."

Detective Callahan's expression was a mix of exasperation and forced sympathy. "Sure. Health issues. This can't wait, so how about I come over to your home instead? I can bring a mobile fingerprint scanner and take your statement at the same time."

"Uh..."

On the surface of it, that seemed like the perfect solution, right? I wouldn't have to leave my apartment, Detective Callahan would get what he wanted, and the hunt for Serenity's killer wouldn't get delayed.

But there was just one teensy issue.

Detective Callahan absolutely couldn't see my apartment.

No, I hadn't modelled my home on a Transylvanian castle or anything, and that was part of the problem. Possibly I could come up with a reason for the blackout curtains and the sound insulation, the understated lighting and the cupboards full of peanut butter and canned pineapple—I got cravings, okay?— but there was literally no way to explain how I was able to afford a six-thousand-square-foot penthouse with views of the Strip on a cocktail waitress's salary. My four-poster bed alone had cost thousands.

Yes, it was an extravagance, I realised that, but I didn't get out much, and since I was over two hundred years old—okay, closer to three hundred but I preferred to round down—I'd had plenty of time to build up a cushion of savings and a healthy real-estate portfolio. I'd made good investments. With most acquaintances—my lawyer, my accountant, my agent, tradesmen who visited occasionally—I adopted the snooty persona of a trust fund baby spoiled by Daddy, but that didn't fit with the waitress thing. Trying to explain to the nosy detective why I lived in an eight-million-dollar home and also worked for minimum wage plus tips would be trickier than coming up with a story for my sunlight allergy. Obviously, I couldn't tell him the truth—that my job provided me with company and a regular food source.

No, inviting the detective into my home would lead to him focusing on me and not Serenity, and her murder needed to be solved.

Dammit, now he was looking at me funny.

Quick, Vee, come up with a plan.

"Uh, sure. Can you excuse me a minute? I really need to pee."

Detective Callahan sucked in an incredulous breath, but he couldn't very well ban me from the bathroom, could he?

"I'm not going anywhere."

Stupid, stupid, stupid. I needed to pee? *Merde.* How could I fix this?

The staff bathroom was cordoned off with crime scene tape, so I joined the line for the public one. It snaked right out of the door. The lights in the club were blazing now and drunk patrons milled around, annoyed at being detained by the police. Were they planning to question everyone?

While I waited, I looked for Dalton Cooper, but I couldn't see him, and I had pretty good eyesight. Being a vampire wasn't just about the blood-sucking—in exchange for my freedom and my soul, I'd gotten upgraded senses, a body that healed itself in an instant, and a perky butt for eternity. My ability to judge a man's character? That had come through decades of experience, and tonight, it told me two things: Dalton Cooper was a creep, and Detective Callahan was smart.

I needed to avoid both of them.

Meanwhile, the women in front of me were complaining

about everything from the number of bathroom stalls to the police's stinky attitude to the fact that someone had dared to ruin their vacation by dying.

"It was probably an overdose," a whiny blonde said. "It's always an overdose."

Her friend nodded. "Or a suicide. I went to a party in New York last year, and a guy jumped off the balcony."

A girl dressed in a bridal veil and a white dress that covered nothing agreed with them. "Some people are so selfish. Why do we have to stay? It's not as if we saw anything. We've rented a luxury apartment for the night, and now we won't even get to sleep in it."

The blonde shrugged. "Sleep's overrated."

No, it wasn't. Since I became a vampire, I'd only needed two hours' sleep each night, and finding something to do for the rest of the time that didn't involve going outside was more challenging than you might think. Video games bored me to tears, and there was only so much time I could spend in the gym. Most of my days were spent painting or reading or waiting on my cat.

But hold on, what else had the bride said? They'd rented an apartment? *They'd rented an apartment.*

What if *I* could rent an apartment? As long as I got there by sunrise to close the drapes, it might work...

I pulled my phone out of the pouch on my belt and tapped in my request. *Cheap apartment in Vegas with twenty-four-hour check-in.* By the time I reached the front of the bathroom line, I'd found a suitable place not too far from my own building. There were only two pictures—one of a hideous living room and the other of a bedroom barely big enough for a bed—but it had blinds on the windows and the key was in a lockbox outside. The owner would email the access number at any time of the day or night, so the listing said. It was perfect.

Phew.

I didn't actually need to pee, but I went into a stall and flushed so I didn't look like an idiot, then hurried back to give Detective Callahan my temporary address. Or at least, I tried. A cop blocked my way, and I thought I'd have to go back and wait with the other club-goers until Callahan spotted me and came over.

"Feeling more comfortable?"

"Much, thanks."

"So, about tomorrow morning..." He had a notepad out, ready to write.

"Yes, ten o'clock. I live at 1601 Sunset Tower, and thanks for being so accommodating."

"Sunset Tower, huh?"

I nodded. "The address sounds so much better than the reality."

"Tell me about it."

"You know the place?"

"Yeah, you could say that. We're neighbours. I live on the floor above. The place should've been called the Twilight Zone, not Sunset Tower. Still, it makes my life easier—I can visit on my way home."

He lived in the same freaking building? Shit, shit, shit. Of all the places in Vegas... Was bad luck following me around tonight? What if he decided to pop over and ask follow-up questions? Or borrow a cup of sugar?

I managed a weak, "Great."

"You've just moved in, right? I only ask because the trash chute on my floor got blocked last week, so I had to go down to sixteen, and I'm sure I saw a family of three coming out of 1601. They sounded Mexican?"

Oh, hell. What had I done?

"Literally two days ago. I had to leave my old place in a hurry."

Damn Cecily Shepherd and her weird food fads.

I willed myself to stay calm as Detective Callahan tucked his notepad back into his pocket and checked his phone. At least he'd seemed happy with my vague answer. How long did murder investigations take? A week? A month? Any longer than that, and I'd be forced to redecorate. Or perhaps move to another state.

"Can I go now?"

There was a grocery store on my way home. I could pick up Lysol and hand sanitiser on the way past. Judging by the photos of the apartment, the landlord wasn't too hot on cleaning.

"Would you mind showing me where to find Lucian Blane first?"

Pas de problème. "He's upstairs. Follow me."

I'd only visited Blane's domain twice, once for my interview and once with a message from Pandora, and the staircase was just as dark as I remembered. Black tiles, dark grey walls, and dim recessed lighting. It was almost as if he *wanted* somebody to trip and break their neck.

At the top of the stairs, I pressed the intercom button and waited.

"Yes?"

"Mr. Blane? There's a detective here to see you."

"Show him to my office. Or her?"

"It's a man. Detective Callahan."

A pushy, annoying man whose badge and notepad left me with a horrible sense of foreboding.

The door buzzed open, and the tile gave way to thick carpet, a geometric pattern in fifty shades of grey. Blane's balcony opened up to the left, and his office was second on the right. The door was open.

"In here," I said to Callahan.

Blane was seated at his oversized desk, and he barely

glanced at me when the detective walked in. The office was another study in darkness, but I liked it. No windows. There was a door at the back, but I didn't know where it led.

"Close the door on your way out, Ms. Pelletier."

Dismissed. Thank goodness.

I started along the hallway, but the quiet murmur of voices made me pause. What were they saying? My hearing was more sensitive than the average human's, and I backed up a few steps. Should I eavesdrop? On the one hand, it wasn't any of my business, and I didn't want to get tangled up in a police investigation either, but on the other hand... Why had Blane wanted to speak to Serenity? Had she left any clues before she died? Or worse, had my boss been involved in her murder?

Curiosity killed the cat, but the nine lives thing didn't apply to me. Provided I steered clear of sacred wooden stakes, I had an eternity on earth to look forward to. Centuries of darkness. The question was, did I want to spend any more time than I had to near Detective Callahan?

<h1 style="text-align:center">CHAPTER 4</h1>

<h1 style="text-align:center">Vee</h1>

Oh, screw it—I took a surreptitious look around, and when I didn't see any cameras, I decided to listen for a minute or two and then make a swift escape before Detective Callahan left. Not only was I curious about Serenity's murder, but I also had to admit Blane intrigued me.

While once upon a time I might have had to press my ear to the door to listen, thanks to the curse Voltaire had bestowed on me, I was able to lean casually against the wall twenty yards along the hallway and still hear every word my boss had to say. I just had to pop out my custom-made earplugs and slip them into my pocket first. Now if anyone appeared unexpectedly, I was merely being a conscientious employee, waiting to escort the detective back downstairs once he'd finished. How long did he plan on being in there? Not long, I hoped. I needed to find my new apartment and move in by sunrise. And feed my cat. Muse was a night owl like me, and she got annoyed if dinner was late.

At least Callahan got straight to the point with his questions.

"I heard you spoke to Serenity Strange this evening," he said right after the introductions.

Blane's deep rumble came back. "That's not true."

Really? She'd told me she was on her way to see him, and why would she have lied?

"Really?" Callahan asked. *Mind reader.*

Of course, he didn't truly read my mind. Humans couldn't. That was Voltaire's trick, or at least it sometimes seemed that way, but he was probably living the good life in Paris, drinking fine wine and barking orders at his staff in between refining his control-freak ways and preying on young ingénues. And cursing the philosopher he swore had stolen his name to use as a *nom de plume* several years after they met. A hundred years following François-Marie Arouet's death, Voltaire the first had still been bitter.

"I sent for Serenity, but she didn't show up."

"Did you go looking for her?"

"No."

"Why not?"

"Because there was no need."

"No need?"

"The problem resolved itself."

Problem? What problem? The mess that Serenity had referred to when we spoke? Oh, how I wished I'd asked more questions, probed a bit deeper. Even if I couldn't have saved her, I might have gleaned information that helped to find her killer.

"The problem being...?" Detective Callahan asked.

I felt kind of sorry for him. Interrogating Blane was like a torturous game of twenty questions, and despite Callahan's occupation, I wasn't sure who was in charge during their little exchange. In my experience, Blane had always been a man of few words, but I'd have thought he might be more forthcoming with an officer of the law.

"Dalton Cooper," Blane said.

"Dalton Cooper was the problem?"

"Yes."

Although I'd only met Detective Callahan for the first time two hours ago, I could picture the expression on his face as Blane provided him with obtuse answers. Teeth lightly clenched, his grip tight around that fancy silver pen of his. Most cops I'd come across wrote with a cheap ballpoint, but not Jack Callahan.

"Can you expand on that?" he asked Blane. "How was Dalton Cooper a problem for Ms. Strange? Oh, and can you give me her legal name? I'm assuming she wasn't born as Serenity."

"Her legal name is Lyla Chavez."

"Lyla with a Y?"

"Yes."

"No middle name?"

"Not that I'm aware of."

"Do you have her address?"

"Yes."

A pause. Was Blane deliberately being a dick? Serenity had *died*, and the least he could do was stop wasting police time and answer the damn questions. I found myself hoping that Callahan let him have both barrels, even though I'd be trying to avoid his questions myself tomorrow.

"Mr. Blane, you do realise this is a murder investigation?"

"I do."

"Then you'll understand that time is of the essence when it comes to gathering information. We can keep going back and forth like this, but it'll be a very long night for both of us, and I'd rather be out catching a killer."

Silence reigned, the sound of my breathing deadened by the plush carpet. Why was Blane being so cagey? His evasiveness made him look less like a witness and more like a suspect. Only half an hour after Serenity went to speak to him, I'd found her in the storeroom, her body cooling and her soul departed. Had she changed her mind about going? Did somebody interrupt her plans? Or was Blane lying?

A whole minute passed before he spoke, and the steady *tick* of the silver-edged clock on the wall at the far end of the hallway grated on nerves already stretched by the night's events.

"My lawyer will be here soon. I'll talk after he arrives."

"Why do you feel you need a lawyer? This is just an informal chat."

Yeah, why did he need a lawyer? Surely Detective Callahan only wanted to ask a few questions. Should *I* have gotten a lawyer? Mine only handled property transactions and other contractual issues, and apart from one initial, awkward meeting held in my apartment late one evening, we communicated entirely by email. Perhaps I could ask him for a recommendation, or...

"If you don't know already, you'll find out when he gets here."

Well, that sounded cryptic, and it seemed Callahan thought so too.

"Why would I know already?"

"Because you're here with Cecily Dorrington."

What did that have to do with anything?

"You mean Cecily Shepherd?"

"Once a Dorrington, always a Dorrington."

This got weirder and weirder. And coming from a vampire who'd spent two centuries living the very embodiment of bizarre, that was saying something.

"Not that it's any of your business, but Cece's definitely not a Dorrington."

Another pause, and I imagined Blane shrugging in that offhand way of his. "We'll see."

With the prospect of the lawyer arriving imminently, I had a decision to make. Should I head for the stairs? If I stayed where I was, I'd most definitely get caught and probably be escorted out of the building, but if I stepped into another room along the hallway, that would take me past the point of no return. I'd have no reasonable excuse for being in there.

Three closed doors, and I didn't even know where they led. Offices? Storage closets? A bathroom? I tried the nearest, turning the handle quietly, and it opened a crack, revealing a line of darkness. Not locked, then. Should I slip inside? The sensible, cautious part of me—the girl who'd spent the last century hiding in the shadows—knew I should leave, but dammit, I was curious. What was Blane hiding?

CHAPTER 5

Vee

A bathroom. I ended up in a bathroom because the stubborn part of me couldn't let this go. Serenity—I struggled to think of her as Lyla—had been my friend, and Blane had set the hairs on the back of my neck tingling. What was the worst that could happen? I'd get yelled at? Fired? I didn't need the money, and it wasn't as if he could kill me.

I left the door open a tiny crack and peered through, jumping out of my skin when a shadow glided past. No, not a shadow. A dark-haired man dressed in a black suit, swinging a slim briefcase in his hand as he walked silently along the hallway.

And I mean silently.

Why hadn't I heard him approach? I could detect the tiny footsteps of a mouse on tile if I concentrated hard enough, yet this guy had come out of nowhere. A wraith. A ghoul. Was he Blane's lawyer?

"Joseph Beauregard," he introduced himself. "I represent Mr. Blane. You must be Detective Callahan?"

Yes, the lawyer. Guess that explained the "ghoul" part. I

36

came across a lot of lawyers in the club, and perhaps I just saw them at their worst, but they rarely left a good impression.

"That's right. Now, Mr. Blane—will you answer my questions, or would you prefer we conduct this interview in a different environment?"

"Go ahead, Lucian," Beauregard said. His voice was a little nasal and a lot annoying, the kind of weaselly tone that said he was used to sucking up on a regular basis. There was a hint of a drawl, but it sounded put on, as if he'd picked it up from the TV. "Rest assured, I'm recording the entire conversation so we don't have any misunderstandings."

But Callahan spoke again instead. I tried to fathom out his accent. He'd spent time in New York, for sure, but there was something else that snuck in from time to time too. Something softer. "I'm not sure what kind of misunderstandings you're expecting, Mr. Beauregard. I'm here to talk to Mr. Blane as a potential witness in a murder investigation. Unless he committed the crime, he has nothing to worry about."

"So you say, Detective. What if someone tried to make it look as though I were responsible?" Blane asked. "Serenity died in my club, and I've been involved in some, shall we say, delicate business dealings lately."

"What kind of business dealings?" Translation: are you up to something shady?

Speaking of "shady," my eyes adjusted to the gloom, and I saw that the bathroom I was hiding in was very nice indeed. Black marble, white fixtures, gold taps. A row of unlit candles stood by the sink, and while for any human the aroma of blackcurrant, pear, and cedar would have been tantalisingly pleasant, for me the scent was nauseatingly overpowering. And slightly surprising. Blane bought scented candles? I really hadn't pictured him as the type.

"No need to take that tone, Detective," Blane said. "It's all quite above board, on my end at least. I want to buy a casino. The Devil's Den, to be precise."

Really? The Devil's Den was a smallish hotel and casino just off the Strip, but it had been shuttered six months ago. Financial difficulties, or so I heard. A shame, because I'd hung out there sometimes on my nights off—not to gamble, but to drink cocktails and window-shop the bartenders, who were invariably hot. Occasionally, I got lucky and found a drunken idiot to snack from too. Blane wanted to take it over?

"And?" Callahan asked.

"I'm not the only party interested, but I *am* the only one with financing already in place. I've been pushing to close the deal, and two nights ago, a visitor warned me to back off if I knew what was good for me."

"And who was this visitor?"

"A good question, Detective. The gentleman didn't identify himself. But my main competitor in the deal is Maxwell Dorrington, and his reputation precedes him. Now there's a dead girl downstairs in my club—a girl who was on her way to speak to me before she died—and two cops connected to Dorrington just happened to be drinking in here tonight. Excuse me if I'm a little suspicious of your motives."

Could it be true? It didn't take a genius to work out who Blane was referring to—anybody who read the papers knew Cecily Shepherd was Maxwell Dorrington's daughter, and Callahan had said she was a friend. *Were* the cops involved somehow? After all, it had been Detective Callahan who'd engineered my trip to the storeroom. Had he known what was waiting for me in there?

"I've got nothing to do with Maxwell Dorrington," he told Blane.

"You were sharing a table with Cecily Dorrington."

"Cecily *Shepherd*. She doesn't have a whole lot to do with him either."

Blane's voice stayed calm, level. "Blood is thicker than water, Detective."

"Not necessarily."

"Actually," Beauregard cut in, "blood has a much higher viscosity than water. Although like ketchup, its flow properties change depending on pressure."

Hmm, he was right. Did Beauregard moonlight as a scientist in his spare time?

"Let's get back to the case, shall we? *That's* why I'm here. Why did you want to see Lyla Chavez this evening? You mentioned Dalton Cooper before Mr. Beauregard arrived."

"Yes, I did. I was watching them from the balcony. Cooper had his hand on her leg, and she obviously didn't want it there. Seemed to me that the easiest way to remove it was to send for her."

"So you didn't actually want to speak to her about any particular matter?"

"If she'd shown up, I'd have wished her luck with her set and escorted her back downstairs."

"What happened to Cooper?"

"I had Pandora tell him that Serenity wasn't coming back, and he stormed out two minutes later. Problem solved."

Was it? Or had he merely moved the problem to another part of the club?

Seemed Callahan was on the same wavelength. "You're certain he left?"

"I radioed the doormen to check."

But what if he'd come back? Through, say, the rear fire door? I could still feel the gust of wind that hit me before I found Serenity's body, the chill a premonition. There was security at the front of the club, but not in the alley at the back unless Darrell happened to be smoking a cigarette.

"And what makes you say Ms. Chavez didn't want Cooper's hand on her leg?" Callahan asked.

"She removed it twice, but he kept putting it back. And she was clearly uncomfortable. Any man who's ever paid the slightest attention to a woman could see that." Blane kept his voice light, almost taunting. "Say, Detective, weren't you sitting nearby?"

"I was off duty tonight."

"I see. Protect and serve, but only during working hours?"

"If I'd been aware of a problem, I would have stepped in."

"So your powers of observation let you down?" Blane tutted quietly. "That doesn't bode well for your case, does it?"

Oh, Callahan was *not* amused. He spoke through gritted teeth, his words stilted, and I imagined he wanted to sock Blane in the jaw by that point. I wouldn't have blamed him, either. Serenity was *gone*. Why couldn't Blane quit being an asshole and just help?

"How about we focus on Ms. Chavez? As you so rightly pointed out, she's lying dead in your club, so it would be in your best interests to help us find out who was responsible. When did you last speak to her?"

"Three days ago."

"Not tonight?"

"There was no need. Everything was running smoothly. Pandora's very efficient."

"Running smoothly apart from Mr. Cooper's presence."

"Precisely. And she fixed that. Please, ask her if you don't believe me."

"I intend to. What did you speak about with Ms. Chavez three days ago?"

"Her career."

"I understand she's had some success lately? Started on YouTube and then signed a record deal?"

"That's an overly simplified version. Serenity put in a lot of work in between. The record deal didn't just fall into her lap."

Blane was right—when Serenity wasn't performing, she was writing songs, or rehearsing, or talking to her fans on social media, or doing interviews, or taking meetings. I suspected that was why she and Joaquin had split up. More than once, he'd complained about the amount of time she spent working, and lately, she'd looked more tired than usual. Worn around the edges.

"What exactly did you discuss regarding her career?" Callahan asked.

Blane didn't answer right away. The soft *shush, shush, shush* told me he was pacing back and forth on his plush carpet. Stressed? Nervous?

Finally, he spoke. "We discussed her regrets."

"Regrets? What regrets?"

Yes, what regrets? Serenity was a born performer, a natural. Why on earth would she have regrets?

CHAPTER 6

Vee

I heard the *glug* of a drink being poured, then a quiet gulp as Blane took a sip before he continued speaking. Water or something stronger? I had no idea, but I needed hard liquor myself at that moment.

"Serenity loved singing, but once she got a taste of fame, it proved to be somewhat of a poisoned chalice for her. She's been feeling the pressure for a while now. When we spoke on Tuesday, she asked my advice on her contract—specifically whether it would be possible for her to get out of it."

Was he kidding? Being famous had been Serenity's dream. She wouldn't just give it up. True, she'd been stressed lately, but when we'd eaten dinner—okay, breakfast—together three weeks ago, she'd been looking forward to flying to New York for a week of appearances and interviews with her band. I'd once asked what her biggest ambition was, and she'd said she wanted to play Madison Square Garden to a sell-out crowd.

Then she'd asked me the same question, and I'd had to lie. Why? Because my only ambition was to be human again. But everything I'd discovered over the past two centuries, every story, every snippet of information I'd sought out, said the vampire thing only went one way. So I'd told her I wanted to see a bear in Alaska instead. At least that was vaguely achievable, albeit freaking cold. I should know—when I lived in Alaska, I'd spent many nights sitting on my back deck, hoping for something interesting to happen, but nothing ever did.

"She confided in *you*?" Callahan's voice held a hint of scepticism.

"Don't sound so surprised, Detective. I'm a good listener."

"And what did you tell her?"

"About the contract? I offered to have Joseph take a look if she shared a copy."

"Did she?"

"No. She said her copy went missing when she moved to a new apartment, and she'd have to get a duplicate from her manager."

"Do you know if she asked him?"

"As I said previously, I didn't speak to her after that. But in my opinion, her manager has something of a disagreeable personality, so if she did ask, he probably stalled. I can't imagine he'd have been too happy at the prospect of losing one of his rising stars."

I heard the faintest scratch of a pen on paper as Callahan jotted notes. How did I know it was Callahan? Because Blane had his lawyer recording the whole conversation. I didn't need to take notes either. An above-average memory was one of the few benefits of being a vampire that didn't involve some kind of trade-off. Think having enhanced hearing was a bonus? Well, it was if you never wanted a moment's peace. Immortality? Living wasn't much fun when you'd been in hiding for over a hundred years. And don't even get me started on my insatiable hunger. Sure, I never put on weight, but my grocery bills were no joke.

"Do you have the manager's name?" Callahan asked.

"Sid. I only met him twice."

I'd met him too. Serenity said his arrogance was an asset in the music industry, but I found it unpleasant. Even when he told me that I had lovely eyes, it felt too smooth, a little... sleazy. And he'd been lying, of course. My eyes were my worst feature. Whenever I saw them in the mirror, they always had a weird depth to them, a darkness that reminded me of the horrors I'd seen. Of the evils I'd endured. Voltaire said it was all in my imagination, but he'd lied a lot too.

"Any idea of his surname?" the detective asked.

"No."

"That's okay; we can find it." More scratching. "Can you talk me through your evening? Have you been here at the club all day?"

"No, I was out most of the day, and I got back around nine thirty, right before I saw Serenity with Cooper."

No. *No*, that wasn't true. I'd arrived for my shift five minutes before eight, and Blane had been there. I'd seen him cross the balcony. My boss had a distinctive silhouette—tall and bulky, broad-shouldered, with a ramrod-straight posture and good cheekbones. But more than that, I'd *felt* him. His presence. Blane exhibited a strange pull, like a bodybuilder made from antimatter.

One who carried on lying. "And before that, I ate dinner at Delvecchio's."

"Do you have a receipt?"

Of course he did. The sound of paper being unfolded was no surprise at all. Yes, Blane was the type of man who kept receipts.

"This said you left at seven," Callahan pointed out.

"Yes."

"Delvecchio's is only four blocks from here. Where did you go for the other two and a half hours?"

"I went to see Joseph."

"You met with your lawyer at seven p.m. on a Friday night?"

Beauregard gave a cackly laugh. "No rest for the wicked, Detective Callahan."

Except I knew better. Blane had been at Club Dead earlier than he said, which meant both he and Beauregard were lying. Fancy that—a lawyer who didn't tell the truth. But why? What had Blane been doing that he didn't want Callahan to know about? Or was he simply worried that Callahan was a dirty cop who'd jump on his lack of an alibi and use it to make life difficult?

"What was so important?" Callahan asked.

"Oh, you know better than to ask that, Detective. Any matter we might have discussed is covered by attorney-client privilege."

Callahan let out a sigh that was more of a huff. "And what did you do after you arrived here, Mr. Blane?"

"Checked in with Pandora and took a look around to make sure there were no problems—the usual—spotted Serenity and sent for her, then went to make myself a drink while I waited for her to arrive."

"When you say 'a look,' do you have cameras? Or did you tour the club personally?"

"The only camera covers the front door. I watch from the balcony. Come—you'll find it gives me an excellent view."

"Only one camera?" Callahan sounded incredulous as their footsteps moved in my direction. Clothing rustled, and I took a pace backwards, which was utterly pointless under the circumstances. "What sort of nightclub only has one camera?"

"One owned by a man who values his privacy." The steps stopped right outside. "Cooper and Serenity were sitting over there near the bar. I watched Pandora deliver my message, then Serenity headed down the stairs and made her way across the dance floor to the rear."

"Did she stop to talk to anyone on the way?"

"A few people. She was a sociable girl. The fans loved her, which was one of the reasons I kept booking the band to play here."

"A few… Could you be more specific? How many? And what did they look like?"

"Three, I think. Two men, one woman. No, three men, actually—she also spoke briefly to Trist."

"Who's Trist?"

"A Sinner. The bass guitarist. She tapped her watch and pointed towards the stage, reminding him not to be late, I suppose. Tardiness is a bad habit of his."

"What about the others she spoke to? Did you recognise any of them?"

"Both of the men looked like fans. She signed their shirts. One of them grabbed her arm, but she shook him off and backed away."

If Callahan had been a dog, his ears would have pricked up. "Was she upset?"

"Not on the surface, but women tend to smile as a defence mechanism, don't they?"

"Can you describe these men?"

"I only saw them from above. The one who didn't overstep boundaries was black, slender, wearing a white T-shirt and jeans. The creep was white with thinning brown hair, and he had a suit on. If I had to guess, I'd say he was in town for the big pharmaceutical convention. He had that look about him."

"What, a salesman?"

"No, more that he sampled his own products. Not in my club, though. We're strict about that."

"And the woman?"

"The conversation wasn't quite so amicable. In fact, I'd go so far as to say they disliked each other intensely. Serenity shouldered her out of the way, and the girl shouted something after her. And before you ask, the music was too loud for me to hear what it was."

Dammit, if only I'd been listening myself. *I* could have heard. But on a regular night, I tended to block the noise out, let it fade into one big wall of sound before all the little snippets of conversation drove me insane.

"Description?"

"Blonde. Attractive in a bland sort of way. Little black dress with skyscraper heels. So unoriginal."

"Can you do me a favour? See if any of them are still downstairs, and if they're not, go through the footage from your single, solitary security camera and see if you can spot them coming in? I'll need a copy of the tape too."

"Do you have a warrant?" Beauregard asked.

"Not yet," Callahan snapped back. "But you know damn well I'll get one."

"Well, when you do, my client will be only too happy to hand over what you need."

Asshole.

"For heaven's sake, Joseph... I'll have it ready within the hour." Finally, a touch of humanity from Blane. That fit better with the man I knew—dark, no-nonsense, but not heartless. He hadn't been a bad boss during my time at the club, although I'd been careful never to get too close. "Is there anything else, Detective?"

"Not for the moment, no. Unless you have a bathroom up here that I could use?"

A bathroom? Up here?

Oh. Shit.

CHAPTER 7

Vee

"The bathroom's to your left," Blane told Callahan. "Beauregard will show you out when you're done."

"I'll wait downstairs," Beauregard said.

Should I lock the door? No, that would create more problems than it solved because Callahan would undoubtedly mention the issue to Beauregard and he'd want to know who the hell was using his boss's bathroom.

Blane's footsteps backed away, and I swallowed my groan. My vampire blood made me fairly rapid, but while I might be able to outrun Usain Bolt, no way could I go faster than light. At times like this, I wished I were more like a movie vampire. You know, with an invisibility cloak or the power to teleport? Or perhaps the ability to transform into a bat and hang from the light fixture? But no, the whole vampire thing didn't work that way in real life, and when Detective Callahan pushed open the door and flipped the light on, there was nowhere to hide for anybody but a very tiny contortionist with the ability to fold herself into the equally minuscule cupboard under the sink.

48

"Uh, hi," I whispered.

He closed the door with a loud *click*. Raised an eyebrow. "Well, this is awkward."

"I was waiting to take you back downstairs."

"In the bathroom?" Callahan spoke quietly, his voice dripping with suspicion.

Me? I was dripping with sweat. Another bead trickled down my spine as I tried to think of a plausible story, one that wouldn't make me seem guilty of anything more than gross stupidity.

"I'm not feeling so good. All that blood... Okay, there wasn't actually a lot of blood, but there was definitely a dead body."

"So you came in here to...vomit?"

"Exactly."

He sniffed the air, checking for the telltale smell, and judging by the curious look he gave the candles, he couldn't quite believe Blane's taste either.

"Yet you didn't throw up."

"Guess my stomach's stronger than I thought."

For a few moments, we stared at each other, eye to eye, a foot apart. The temperature ratcheted up another degree. Was this a half-bath or a sauna? I half expected Callahan to drag me out to face Blane and his liar—sorry, lawyer—but no, he just stood there. If I'd been mortal, my heart would have been fast approaching a coronary by the time he spoke.

"Guess I'll be using the downstairs bathroom."

"I'd appreciate it."

"We'll finish discussing this tomorrow."

Oh, hurrah.

He reached past me and flushed, presumably as a cover story, then backed out the door. My knees gave way, and I sank back onto the closed lid. *Stupid, stupid Genevieve.* What had I been thinking? I'd risked my job and perhaps justice for

Serenity by sticking around. But I'd also caught Blane in a lie. The question was, what was I going to do about it? Callahan might have discovered my hiding place, but there was no way I should have heard the discussion in Blane's office from there.

Perhaps I could somehow drop Blane's presence earlier in the evening into conversation tomorrow? Provided I didn't die of mortification between now and the morning, obviously. Or jump straight on the nearest airplane to...well, anywhere except France.

But what if Callahan was dirty? Perhaps I should ask around myself instead? Somebody must know where Blane had been between seven p.m. and nine thirty. What he'd been doing. My investments gave me connections in the real estate industry, and I'd also made some acquaintances in low, low places. It was a necessary evil. I needed to procure spare identity documents so I was always prepared to run at a moment's notice, and I may have had an unregistered weapon or two tucked away, ready for Voltaire if he ever caught up with me. While I might not be able to kill him, there was a chance I could slow him down long enough to make my escape.

I decided to consider my options later. For now, I needed to get the hell out of Club Dead and find my rental apartment before the sun came up.

Muse didn't seem particularly impressed when I dropped a handful of Kitty Krunchies into her bowl, refilled her water fountain, and then hurried into my bedroom to toss some clothes and toiletries into a suitcase. She leapt onto the bed, miaowing, and when I didn't stop to fuss over her, she thanked me by scratching at my silk bedspread.

"Hey! I didn't buy you a deluxe cat tree for nothing, you ungrateful feline. Go destroy that instead."

More annoyed miaowing from Muse, and when I tried to do up my case, she climbed inside and sat there regally, the modern incarnation of Bastet. All she needed was a pharaoh to worship her.

"It's just for a night, Mu. Maybe two. And I bet the club'll be closed tomorrow, so I won't have to go to work."

How long did it take to clean up a crime scene, anyway? And what would happen to Serenity's body? She hadn't been close to her family, I knew that much. Where were her relatives? Who would arrange her funeral? Who would pay for it? I'd be glad to, but funerals weren't cheap, and trying to explain where I'd gotten the money to pay for a casket on a waitress's salary could be tricky.

That was a bridge I'd cross when I came to it. Perhaps I could make an anonymous donation? Problems, always problems... I tempted Muse out of the suitcase with a teaspoonful of caviar, then tugged the zipper closed.

"Stop looking at me that way. You've got an exercise wheel, three litter trays, and an indoor garden. You can cope on your own for a few hours."

Yes, I talked to my cat. Sometimes it was that or go crazy from loneliness. Or perhaps I was already crazy. Who knew? Before I became a vampire, I'd been the life and soul of the party, but now my soul was broken and whether I was alive at all was debatable. Even during my years of hell with Voltaire, I'd had people to talk to most of the time, but now? The last hundred years had been tough. Really tough.

I hurried through my art gallery, shutting off lights as I went. My foot tapped out a staccato as I waited for the elevator. An hour until sunrise, but I hated cutting things fine. *Hated* it. Smoking skin was no joke. Out on the sidewalk, I waved down a cab and gave the driver the address of the nasty apartment. He looked up at the building I'd just left, then turned to glance at me.

"Sunset Tower? You're sure?"

Yes, yes, I got it—there was a world of difference between the two places, but needs must.

"I'm sure."

His shrug said he had his doubts, and quite frankly, so did I. But what choice did I have? Telling Detective Callahan the truth clearly wasn't an option.

At Sunset Tower, the damn elevator had an out-of-order sign stuck to the doors with what appeared to be chewing gum, and I didn't bother to stifle my curses as I dragged my suitcase up the stairs. Good thing I was immortal because I'd probably have died from exhaustion otherwise. *Sixteen freaking floors.* No wonder the rent was so cheap. If the elevator conked out regularly, either Callahan would be the fittest man on earth or his knees would give out.

As promised, the key was in a lockbox beside the door, and I quickly punched in the number I'd received by email, eager to get out of a hallway that smelled faintly of urine and stale beer. Yeuch. The place was every bit as bad as I'd feared, even worse than the tiny apartment I'd stayed in for a month after I escaped from Voltaire. At least that place had been decorated in neutral tones. Casa Sunset had four rooms, each smaller than my closet at home, and the bathroom had a mustard-yellow shower stall that hurt my eyes. Scuffed orange linoleum in the kitchen gave way to a moth-eaten turquoise carpet in the living room, and each appliance came with a thick layer of dust. The worst part? The aroma of marijuana permeated throughout, and I had a cop coming to visit me later this morning.

Dammit.

A quick rummage through the kitchen cupboards turned

up bleach, a bucket, and a mop, but no air freshener. With the sky lightening already, I didn't have time for a trip to the grocery store, so in desperation, I sprayed a generous quantity of Chanel perfume around the place in an attempt to mask the stink, then opened all the windows that weren't stuck shut. Finally, I closed the blinds and crawled into bed.

Did I sleep? Of course not. How could I when yesterday had been a disaster of such epic proportions? For the last fifty years, I'd tried so hard to stay out of trouble. To keep my head down and avoid drawing attention to myself. Before that, back when I'd still held onto a thin thread of hope that there might be a cure for my affliction, I'd taken more risks. Searched out legends, spoken to anyone I thought might be able to help, funded research by a variety of kooks, but to no avail. Now, the light of optimism had faded away into a shadowy corner.

Which brought me to my current dilemma. The sense of pessimism I'd developed over the past couple of centuries left me doubtful that Serenity's killer would be brought to justice. After all, if there were any fairness in the world, Voltaire would have been sent to jail a hundred times over. Or hell. Hell would've made a reasonable alternative.

Who were the good guys at Club Dead? Blane and Beauregard? Callahan and his detective friend? Both sides? Neither? One thing was for sure—I trusted no one but myself.

If I didn't have to work tomorrow evening, I could use the time to ask a few questions of my own, but unless I got lucky, that wouldn't be enough to track down a killer. I needed to find a good supply of information, but where? Should I hang around Callahan and try to learn what he knew? As a cop, he'd have access to suspects and also to any forensic results, but I didn't trust his motives. Would Blane be a better bet? He'd known Serenity personally, and he had connections, but I doubted he'd share his knowledge freely as long as Beauregard was around. If only I were able to go out in the daylight, I'd have had time to shadow both Blane and Callahan, but it was no use wishing for what would never be. I had to pick a target and dig.

But which one? Who would be the most valuable? Blane and his network or Callahan and his badge?

CHAPTER 8

Jack

It was on days like this that I really missed my coffee machine. Three weeks ago, it had gone to gadget heaven with one final death rattle and a hiss of steam, and I hadn't gotten around to buying a replacement yet. Too many assholes, too many dead bodies, not enough time, and Captain Lindsay was riding everyone harder than a two-bit whore on a rodeo bull.

I spooned Nescafé into a mug, topped it off with water, and shoved it into the microwave. Caffeine was the only thing standing between me and falling asleep in the middle of an interview, and I needed to stay awake for this one. Vee Pelletier was one weird woman. First, she hadn't wanted to talk to me today, and then I'd caught her hiding in Lucian Blane's bathroom. If I hadn't provided her alibi myself, she'd have been right at the top of the suspect list, her name underlined twice and highlighted in yellow. But she just hadn't had enough time to kill Lyla Chavez. When I'd gotten there, the blood trickling from the neck wound had already been drying around the edges, and while the ME couldn't pinpoint death to the second, he'd agreed with my assessment that Chavez had been dead for ten minutes or so before Pelletier stumbled across her. And Pelletier had been upstairs that whole time. I hadn't exactly been watching her, but I'd glanced in her direction a time or two. It was the hair. The pink stood out.

And possibly her tits and ass did too, but I wasn't about to put that in my report. Hell, I was annoyed at myself for even thinking of her damn assets.

While the microwave hummed, I pulled the towel away from my waist and bundled it onto the rail in the bathroom. After an hour's sleep and a five-minute shower, I was back on the job. Did I have any clean jeans? I found a wrinkled pair on the floor that passed the sniff test and pulled them on, then unwrapped a new black T-shirt from a plastic package. Laundry had fallen by the wayside since Angie died. Kind of ironic, since I'd met her in a laundry room. One free washer and two people in a hurry. We'd agreed to share, and neither of us had made it to our respective dates that night. Hell, we'd barely made it out of the laundry room and back to my apartment. I'd kidded her that it'd been the sight of her pink thong panties that got me, but we'd both known it was something deeper.

Socks, shoes, gun, badge. I cursed as I scalded the roof of my mouth on the first sip of bitter black coffee. Served me right for forgetting to buy creamer. What was the time? A quarter to ten. Enough time for a slice of toast before I talked to Pelletier again.

Or not.

I dumped the mouldy bread into the trash just as my phone rang. Shep. He'd had roughly the same amount of sleep as me over the last two days, but at least his coffee machine still worked.

"Anything more from the ME yet?" I asked.

Shep snorted. "It's not even ten o'clock yet, and you know

Dr. Rashid isn't a morning person. But I spoke to the roommate."

"And?"

"She reckons Chavez was having man trouble."

"We already knew that—Pelletier said she'd split up with a boyfriend recently."

"No, the roommate—Shelby—she says this was a different guy. The boyfriend was Joaquin, a Latino Chavez met at some dance class, but Shelby says she saw the name Reuben flash up on the screen right before Chavez shut herself in her bedroom and started, well, not yelling, exactly, but she sounded pretty annoyed."

"What did she say?"

"Shelby only heard parts of it, but the gist was that Chavez wanted this Reuben to stop calling, and she also said he wasn't getting a single red cent out of her."

"Are you thinking what I'm thinking?"

"If you're thinking 'blackmail,' then yes."

Blackmail...but over what? Nobody I'd spoken to had hinted at Chavez having any deep, dark secrets. Before I left the club this morning, Blane had identified the two men he'd seen her speak to in the crowd still corralled on the dance floor, and I'd talked with them both. The guy in the white T-shirt was a genuine fan—he'd been pale with shock and quoted Serenity's own lyrics at me when informed of her death.

> *Everybody breathes, everybody dies.*
> *But it's choices, choices, what you do while you're alive.*
> *Fly high, shine bright, fade into the fucking night,*
> *Crash, burn, roar, fight,*
> *And when it's your time, embrace the fated light.*

"She flew high," the guy told me, solemn, almost on the

verge of tears it seemed. "And now she's found the light. Hey, do you think my shirt was the last thing she ever signed?"

From grief to dollar signs in the blink of an eye. Not for the first time, I wished gross insensitivity was an arrestable offence, but it wasn't, and three of the guy's buddies said he'd been with them from the time he got his shirt signed to the moment the club got locked down. The handsy pharmaceutical rep—Blane had been absolutely right about his reason for coming to Vegas—had passed out in a booth between two of his colleagues soon after Chavez pushed him away. Officially, he should've been escorted out, but since he wasn't causing any problems and his friends were spending their annual bonuses on drinks, the bouncers had decided to leave him where he was.

And the woman Blane had seen? She remained a mystery.

"When was this discussion?" I asked Shep.

"Monday or Tuesday. Shelby's almost sure it was Tuesday."

"And did Shelby have any ideas about the blackmail?"

"When she asked Chavez if everything was okay, she laughed it off and said it was just a guy she hooked up with who had trouble letting go."

"Did you check the phone?"

"Shelby has no idea of Chavez's PIN code. I've requested the records from the provider, but we all know how long that takes." Weeks, usually. Sometimes even months. "Did you speak with Dalton Cooper?"

"I spoke with his booking agent." And it'd taken me over an hour to get that far. "Cooper isn't answering his phone, and the agent doesn't have a clue where he is. Said he's probably unconscious in a hotel room somewhere. If he hasn't shown up by the time I've spoken to Vee Pelletier, I'll get Daphne to start calling around."

Daphne. My pet rookie. Captain Lindsay didn't

particularly want me in his department, which was to say that he'd initially told his boss, the Sheriff of Clark County, that I'd only become a detective in Vegas when Nevada froze over. But the sheriff was a regular player at Maxwell Dorrington's monthly poker game, Cecily had finagled me an invite to join them for a few hands, and I'd dropped a pair of thermal gloves on Captain Lindsay's desk during my orientation. Our relationship hadn't gotten any better since. And after I "went out of cell range" during a kidnapping case earlier in the year and shot a sick motherfucker who'd abducted and then molested a four-year-old girl, Captain Lindsay had assigned me a partner. Not so much a babysitter, more of a ball and chain. Daphne had barely scraped through training. Secretly, I suspected she might even have failed, but the department had hired her anyway to meet their diversity and inclusion targets. She also talked too much, regularly lost her handcuffs, and struggled to hit a truck at ten paces on the rare occasions she fired a gun.

Last night when I'd asked Captain Lindsay if there was anyone else available to help with the Chavez investigation, someone a little more competent, I'd gotten a lecture on cost-cutting and crime statistics, plus a reminder that I was "some big-shot detective from New York, so an itty-bitty murder shouldn't be no big deal, should it?"

When I mentioned my sidekick, Shep just laughed. He'd assist where possible—we always helped each other out—but he had his own cases to solve.

"Guess if Daphne strikes out in Vegas, you could have her canvass the whole of Nevada. That should keep her out of your hair for a day or two."

"Today Nevada, tomorrow the world."

"Keep me updated. I've got a spare hour this morning, so I figured I'd speak to Chavez's manager."

"You tracked him down?"

"Via his website. Sid Harber."

"Sid Harber? Sidney Harber? Did his parents really name him that?"

"Who the hell knows? But he just flew in from New York, or so he says, and he's agreed to fit in a chat before his game of golf. I need to check with the airline about that flight. The asshole sounded slippery on the phone."

"If you want to borrow Daphne…"

"Nice try, buddy."

"Figured you'd say that, but could you do me one more favour?"

"Sure, who needs sleep anyway?"

I ignored that. Sleep deprivation came with the job. "Maxwell Dorrington's name came up in my discussion with Lucian Blane. Apparently there's been bad blood between them, and he suggested Maxwell might try to frame him. Blane said they both want to buy the Devil's Den casino."

"Ah, shit. The place that closed down?"

"Yeah."

"And you want me to abuse my family connections?"

"Would you mind?"

Shep sighed. He did that a lot when it came to his in-laws. "I'll ask Cece. She might know something."

"Appreciate it."

I raised the mug to my lips again, but the heat coming off it warned me against taking another sip. Since I only had to go down one floor to talk to Vee, I figured I'd just take it with me. *Genevieve Pelletier.* Usually, I was pretty good at figuring people out—nine years as a cop had that effect on a man—but I'd struggled with her. The pink hair said "extrovert," but her quiet manner and the way she avoided my eyes suggested the opposite. She'd flirted with men in the club, then backed right off if one of them got too close. She said she wanted to help, then threw out obstructions. And rather than scuttle away after she'd shown me up to Blane's office in the early hours, she'd shut herself in the bathroom just waiting to be discovered. What if Blane had found her? Or Beauregard? I couldn't wait to hear whatever excuse she'd come up with for her actions because I sure hadn't believed last night's lame attempt at a story. Hell, had *she* even believed what she was saying?

I had my doubts.

CHAPTER 9

Jack

The elevator was broken again, so I grabbed the bag containing the mobile fingerprint scanner I'd picked up from the station on my way home, jogged down the stairs, and knocked on the door of 1601. Almost instantly, I heard the soft pad of feet on the other side of the cheap wood.

"Detective Callahan?"

Pelletier opened the door a crack, then wider when she confirmed who was outside. I stepped over the threshold, flicking the loose end of the door chain as I did so.

"You should use this. We're not in a great building."

"It's okay. I hear a cop lives right upstairs."

Was that a joke? It was too early for humour. "Sometimes I'm asleep."

"But not last night, huh?" She leaned in closer, no doubt taking in my bloodshot eyes and the dark smudges underneath them. "I'd offer you a coffee, but I see you brought your own. And also I've run out of the good stuff."

Originally, Vee had claimed that she'd be tired this morning, but she looked remarkably well-rested for someone

62

who couldn't have gotten much more sleep than me. Either that or she was good with make-up. I took advantage of her proximity to study her. The hair was still pink this morning, suggesting she'd dyed it that colour rather than wearing a wig, and those big eyes were still a vivid moss-green. Contacts? I couldn't tell, but her eyelashes seemed too long to be real. Angie used to glue extra clumps on for special occasions, even though I told her she was perfect as she was, and she'd known they drove me crazy when she fluttered them.

Vanity seemed to have passed Vee by, dressed as she was in a pair of leggings and a loose T-shirt with a unicorn cantering across it. Her feet were stuck into a pair of sneakers, but she hadn't bothered with socks.

I held up the fingerprint scanner. "So...ready? Your prints will be used for elimination purposes only. We won't keep them on file outside of the investigation into Ms. Chavez's death."

"It's odd to hear you call her that. She was always Serenity. I mean, logically I knew that couldn't be her real name, but..."

"She didn't talk much about her life outside of work?"

"Work *was* her life. She loved singing, performing, writing music. She kept a photo in her wallet of her singing into her hairbrush as a little girl just to remind herself how far she'd come."

Vee moved from the tiny hallway into a gloomy living room. Ten o'clock, and she still had the blinds shut. The furniture was cheap—a chipped dining table with three wooden chairs tucked under it, and a stained couch in shades of brown and orange that clashed with Vee's hair. The only personal item in the room appeared to be a framed photo of a cat on a side table.

"Do you know much about Lyla's family?" I asked. "We're having trouble contacting her next of kin."

The number on her employment records was Mexican,

and when I'd tried calling it, my pidgin Spanish was good enough to tell me I'd gotten an Out of Service message.

"Her mother passed away. She mentioned a brother once, but I don't think they got on well and I'm pretty sure he doesn't live in the US. She said he was trouble."

"Do you have a name?"

"If she ever told me, I don't recall. And I've got a good memory."

"What about her father?"

"She never spoke about him, only her mother. Have you tried asking her bandmates? They probably spent more time with her than anyone else."

I'd spoken to each of them at the club. Invi, Trist, and Lux, their stage names plays on the Latin terms for the seven deadly sins, apparently. Invi from *invidia*, or envy, Trist from *tristitia*—sloth—and Lux from *luxuria*, or lust. Trist had been the last of them to speak to Chavez, and the fact that Lyla had reminded a man named after the sin of failing to take responsibility about the importance of being on time seemed somehow fitting. And none of the trio knew anything about her family beyond the fact that her mother was dead.

"Yeah, I asked them. She told them less than she told you."

"Oh. Perhaps you could try looking at her phone? She might've had a number saved." Vee gave a slight grimace. "Sorry if I'm telling you how to do your job. I'm sure you've already thought of all this."

She was, and I had, but I preferred being taught Detective 101 by a witness over last night's evasiveness.

"We've got her phone, but we don't have her PIN code. We only get ten tries to enter it, and then the device will lock us out permanently."

"It's one-four-seven-eight."

Of all the things I might have expected Vee to come out with, that wasn't one of them.

"Are you sure? I mean, how do you know?"

"She lent me her phone when my battery ran out. And yes, I'm sure that was the PIN code three weeks ago, although she could've changed it since."

"Let me write that down." I always carried a notepad, and even though things were gradually going electronic—the fingerprint scanner being a case in point—I still preferred an old-fashioned pen and paper. *One-four-seven-eight.* "I don't suppose you happen to know a guy called Reuben?"

"Me? No. Or are you asking if Serenity knew a guy called Reuben?"

Was she being smart with me? Or was she just one of those literal people? Daphne could be like that too, unfortunately. Once, I'd asked her to toss a folder onto the captain's desk, and she'd thrown it from the doorway. The papers went everywhere. Which perhaps wouldn't have been so bad if Captain Lindsay hadn't been sitting behind the damn desk at the time.

"I meant Serenity."

"I'm not sure if she *knew* a Reuben, but a man with that name showed up at the club after hours one morning, looking for her. The doorman asked me to let her know, and when I did, she looked confused for a moment, then said she was late for something and left through the back door."

"Late for something? At, what, five o'clock in the morning?"

"I did think it was a bit odd at the time."

"Did you ever see this Reuben again?"

She shook her head. "Sorry. And Serenity never mentioned him either."

"Could you describe him?"

"Mid-twenties, I'd say. Big, but not fat. Muscular, but not big bulgy muscles from the gym, more like he had a physical job. Brown hair that kind of flopped over his forehead, round face, thin lips, and a day's worth of stubble. And he was wearing jeans and a red plaid shirt. I'm not sure about his feet."

"Wow, you're good." Most people wouldn't have noticed half of that stuff, which made me slightly suspicious. "How long ago was this?"

"About a month. Maybe three weeks?"

Yeah, your average citizen would be hard-pressed to remember whether the guy had brown hair or blond after that length of time. Did Vee have extraordinary powers of recall? Or was she lying for some reason? The timeline said she couldn't have killed Chavez, but what if she was covering for somebody? I took a moment to weigh that up. When I'd first seen Pelletier with the body, she'd seemed genuinely upset, and all the staff I'd spoken to at the club said the pair were friends. Gut instinct told me she wasn't involved in the crime, but was she on my side? Or her own? I couldn't afford to ignore the lead she was giving me on Reuben's identity, but nor would I rely on it.

"Would you be able to come to the station later and describe Reuben to a sketch artist?"

"How much later?"

"Say, early afternoon?"

"I could come in the evening. From five o'clock onwards. Or later. Blane sent a message saying the club would be closed tonight."

"Our artist only works until four." She had three-year-old twins, and her husband had run out on her six months ago, so she needed to get home early. "And these sketches can take a couple of hours."

Vee hadn't sat down the whole time we were talking, and now she backed away until she hit the couch with the backs of her knees and stopped short. Just for a second, a faint grimace crossed her face, but she quickly schooled her features into a more apologetic expression.

"Sorry, but I can't."

"Look, this is a murder investigation. I accommodated your request to meet here this morning, but my colleague isn't so flexible. She needs to get home on time for her kids."

"If I could, I would, but..."

"Ms. Pelletier, what's your problem? Don't you want to see your friend's killer caught?"

Perhaps I shouldn't have snapped, but this woman was trying my patience. Once again, she was trying to hinder the investigation. And why the hell had she been hiding in the damn bathroom last night?

So many questions and so few answers. I was determined to get to the bottom of this.

CHAPTER 10

Jack

"Of course I want to see the killer caught! I'd choke the damn life out of them myself if I knew who it was." Pelletier suddenly seemed to realise who she was speaking to. "Uh, I'd never actually do that, I swear."

"Right."

She looked towards the door, but I was blocking her way.

"I...I have a medical problem. Extreme photosensitivity. If I go out in daylight, I break out in hives, which hurts like hell and also means I can't work because who wants to get served cocktails by someone covered in big red blotches?"

Photosensitivity? That was...vaguely plausible. Weird, but plausible. I'd have to consult WebMD because I'd never actually heard of it.

"Why didn't you tell me this yesterday?"

"Because people think it's weird." Guilty as charged. "It's much easier to keep quiet and work nights."

"So you don't go out in the daytime at all?"

"No."

"You haven't tried...I don't know, sunscreen? Wearing a hat?"

68

Probably I deserved the condescending look.

"Trust me, it doesn't help. Look, if you need a picture of Reuben, why don't I just draw you one?"

"We need something good enough to show other witnesses. Put on the TV, maybe."

Not a half-assed attempt by a cocktail waitress. The police sketch artist had been plying her trade for years.

"I can do that, but as you said, it'll take a couple of hours."

"You're an artist in your spare time?"

"I like to draw."

I had twenty people on my list to question, and I could hardly ask for a doctor's note. Right now, Vee was a witness, not a suspect. If I didn't take her up on her suggestion, I'd undoubtedly face the logistical headache of either persuading our artist to come to Vee's apartment or getting Vee to the police station, neither of which were likely to happen until tomorrow. A sunlight allergy? We'd have to wrap her up in a blanket or something.

Oh, what the hell—getting her to try a sketch was worth a shot. Maybe she was a closet Van Gogh?

"Okay, fine." I checked my watch. "It's ten thirty now, so I'll come back at half past twelve."

"Uh, I'll have to do it this evening."

"What? Why? Are you allergic to using pencils during daylight hours too?"

"No, but I don't have any pencils here. Or paper."

She bit her lip, nervous, and my suspicions heightened again. "You're telling me you like to draw, yet you have neither pencils nor paper in your apartment?"

"I moved here in a hurry, and I didn't bring much stuff with me."

"Why'd you leave your old place?"

She hesitated before answering, and if she kept chewing, she wouldn't have much of a lip left.

"Due to unwanted attention from a man." She waved a hand. "And as you can see, I'm still getting settled in, so I don't have much of anything at the moment."

Was she telling the truth? If so, then perhaps I'd been too harsh on her.

"Do you want to put in a report on this guy? Nobody should be harassing women like that."

"Honestly, I just want to pick up the pieces and get on with my life. And that includes finding whoever killed Serenity. It happened at the club where I *work*. What if the murderer's still hanging out there? One of the staff? Or a regular? What if he tries again?"

"That's why we need to get this case solved quickly. Look, if I bring you paper and pencils, will you do the sketch now?"

"Of course."

I'd half expected another objection, at most a grudging acquiescence. Her easy acceptance surprised me. I still couldn't work this woman out. Vee Pelletier was a mass of contradictions—skittish yet oddly determined, poor yet somehow regal.

"Then I'll go to the store. But first, we need to discuss the elephant in the room."

Or rather, the cocktail waitress in the bathroom.

"Oh?"

"Why were you hiding on Blane's private floor last night?"

A blush rose up her cheeks. No, she definitely wasn't wearing make-up.

"I... I'm sorry. I just wanted to know what was going on, and I thought I might be able to hear something."

"From the bathroom? With a bunch of walls in the way?"

"I wasn't exactly thinking straight." Yet she'd held herself together. When I'd seen Angie's body... Fuck. I hadn't been able to function for days. Weeks even. I still wasn't the same person I'd been before her death, and I probably never would be. "But... I guess I figured that if anyone knew anything, it'd be Blane. I mean, he was at the club the whole night, at least the whole time I was there, and he likes to watch what's going on."

Hold on a second...

"Blane was in the club when you arrived? What time was that?"

"My shift started at eight, and I got there five minutes early. Usually, I have fifteen minutes to spare, but my cat ate something that disagreed with her, and there was a mess, and... you don't need all the details."

I glanced around. "Where's the cat now?"

No kidding, Vee turned white. Whiter, since she was pale already. She hadn't meant to tell me about the cat, had she? That slip of the tongue worried her, and I had a good idea why.

"She's, uh, she's sleeping. In the bedroom." Her eyes cut to the closed door on my left. "Yes, she's in there."

"I didn't realise we were allowed pets in this building."

"No, we're, uh, we're not."

I nodded towards the picture on the side table. "That her?"

"Yes. Muse. She's a five-year-old Siberian."

"Relax, okay? I'm not gonna tell your landlord. Someone else here has a dog, and I swear there's a parrot too. I hear it screeching at night."

"Thank you," she whispered.

"No problem." It was a dumb rule anyhow. As long as people cleaned up after their pets, why shouldn't they have them? "So, back to Mr. Blane. Can you talk me through the times you saw him last night?"

"Why? Do you think he was involved?"

Right now? I couldn't be sure. But I did know that either Vee or Blane had lied, and I was inclined to believe Vee. Mostly because I was her damned alibi for the murder, but partly because of Blane's lawyer. Who brought in representation for an informal Q&A? Only a man with something to hide, that was who.

"It's too early to say. But I do want to get a clear picture of everybody's movements during the evening."

"Well, I saw him on the balcony when I got there."

"Are you certain?"

"Well, it was either Blane or someone who looked just like him."

"Did you go into the club through the front door?"

She shook her head. "Not last night, but we're kind of meant to. One of the bar girls got followed into the side alley last month, and there's been that weird guy flashing women around the Strip lately, so Blane told us to use the front entrance when it got dark. But there were so many people on the sidewalk outside..."

I knew about the flasher—he was one of Shep's cases. The media had christened him "the Candyman" because according to eyewitnesses, his dick was shaped like an oversized lollipop. Two dozen women had been exposed to his dubious charms so far, and he was escalating, in terms of both frequency and actions. The last three victims had been groped as well. So far, we had plenty of descriptions of his manhood, but few of his actual face. The witnesses couldn't even agree whether he was old or young. It would sure make for an interesting line-up if Shep ever managed to get a suspect into custody.

"And the back door you came in—is that the one you found open when you went down to get the organic chips?" I asked Vee.

Another nod. "It's also an emergency exit. From the inside, you can push the bar and it opens, but from the outside, you need a pass card. Like this one."

Vee stepped across to the side table and rummaged

through a black leather purse, then handed me a plastic card, white with the club's logo in one corner and her name on a sticker. No photo. Blane could certainly make improvements when it came to the club's security.

"Who gets a card?"

"You'll have to ask Blane. The staff, definitely, and the performers—Serenity had one. But I'm not sure who else."

Chavez's card had been in her purse, which was now on its way to evidence. Her body was in the morgue. The autopsy was scheduled for tomorrow morning, and I planned to attend, probably with Daphne unless I managed to come up with an excuse to leave her behind. Last time, she'd taken one look at the Y-incision and puked on my shoes.

But that was a problem for later. Now, I had a more important lead to follow up—Blane's lie—and that most likely meant another round of verbal jousting with his lawyer. I'd have to get a list of the cardholders and pass it on to Daphne to dig into because I couldn't do everything myself. Unless I asked Vee for help... Not only had she worked at the club for months, but I'd bet she knew her colleagues better than Blane did too. Watching from the balcony like a king was no substitute for actually talking to people, and Vee had given me more information on Chavez than anyone else at Club Dead had offered.

Technically, I wasn't meant to involve civilians in cases, not to that extent, but when I considered the alternative... *A Daphne-induced headache.* Was asking Vee worth a chewing-out from Captain Lindsay? My only goal in life was to get criminals off the streets, and if that meant bending the rules, then to hell with it. If I got fired, I could always work as a mall cop. Spend my evenings watching football and getting lectured by Shep on the dangers of alcohol abuse.

But if I fucked up, I'd also be putting Shep in an awkward position. He was the one who'd pulled strings and gotten me the job at the LVMPD, who'd vouched for me to the sheriff when I left the NYPD under a cloud after punching the asshole who killed my wife. I'd have done a hell of a lot more if half a dozen colleagues hadn't pulled me off him, but... That was my past. The LVMPD was my future, and I wouldn't just be letting down future victims if I lost my job, I'd be letting down my best buddy.

And I had twenty minutes to think about it.

"I'm going to the store for pencils and paper. Do you need anything else while I'm there?"

"An eraser. And a sharpener. And some good coffee if it's not too much trouble?" Vee fished around in her purse again and came up with a hundred-dollar bill. "Sorry, I don't have anything smaller."

"You get a lot of big tippers at the club?"

"Huh?" For a moment, she looked puzzled. "Oh. Yes, I usually work in the VIP section. Once they start drinking, they're quite generous."

They had to be if her wallet only contained hundreds.

"I won't be long, and I'll take your fingerprints when I get back. Don't leave the apartment, okay?"

"I can't, remember? Not until dark."

Right. Photosensitivity... Until today I didn't realise that was a thing. But Vee Pelletier had been full of surprises so far, and I had a feeling I hadn't even scratched the surface of my star witness.

CHAPTER 11

Vee

"Muse, I'm so sorry."

She stared at me from inside her kitty carrier, reluctant to set foot into her temporary new home. I couldn't blame her. That made two of us who didn't want to be in Sunset Tower.

Honestly, I was kicking myself for making that slip-up with Callahan earlier. What if he'd gotten curious and asked to see my cat? He was a cop after all, and in contrast to many of the cops I'd come across, he'd struck me as tenacious rather than apathetic. Good for Serenity, but not so great for me or my sanity.

Or my pussy.

"Here, Mu, I've got Kitty Krunchies. Salmon flavour. Your favourite."

She shrank farther back and hunkered down on her velvet cushion. Perhaps I spoiled her just a little, but since she was the only living creature I could have a deep and meaningful conversation with, that entitled her to some privileges.

And speaking of conversations... My next chat with Callahan had been postponed. He'd called earlier as I was

75

putting the finishing touches on my sketch of Reuben to say that another witness had finally agreed to speak with him, and he couldn't afford to pass up the chance. If I had to guess, I'd say he was talking about Dalton Cooper with an outside possibility of Jerome Keller. Why? The giveaway was his exasperated, "Damn prima donnas," as he apologised for rescheduling, and Dalton and Jerome had been the only big stars in the club last night.

Would he give away any hints about what they said? I'd have been dying from curiosity if I wasn't already sort of dead.

Callahan had promised to call when he was on his way, so I'd risked a visit home as soon as darkness fell to pick up Muse and a few bits and pieces since it looked as if I'd be stuck in this glorious château for another few days at least. On the phone, Callahan had asked for my help with something—said he'd explain when he got here—and of course I'd do anything to get justice for Serenity.

Even scrub mould out of the shower. Oh, what a lovely afternoon it had been. Funnily enough, the landlord had been only too happy to extend my rental by another week.

Now it was eight p.m. Did Callahan expect every witness to be at his beck and call like this? Forty minutes ago, he'd called to say he'd be half an hour, and I was getting hungry. A vampire had to eat. The stove didn't work and the microwave had scorch marks on the top, which meant I'd have to order takeout because I didn't fancy getting electrocuted. While the shock wouldn't kill me, it didn't half sting.

Finally, little cop footsteps sounded in the hallway, rubber-soled boots with a hint of heel-drag, and I hurried to tuck Muse's carrier out of sight in the bedroom. She'd come to say hello if and when she felt like it.

"Sorry about the time." Callahan held up a plastic carrier bag when I opened the door. "Peace offering?"

The delicious aroma of crispy beef and egg fried rice drifted towards me. "Is that Wong Fu's?"

"Shep would disown me if I went anywhere else."

"Shep?"

"Lieutenant Shepherd. Or in this town, Mr. Cecily Dorrington."

Callahan rose half a notch in my estimation. If the way to a girl's heart was through her stomach, Wong Fu's let a man take a shortcut. The satay chicken and pineapple fritters were to die for. And in a moment of sadness, I remembered who'd led me to Wong Fu's in the first place. Serenity. The restaurant might have been open twenty-four seven, but it didn't offer delivery, so she used to go there after her set to pick up our fix of sweet, sweet carbs, and we'd stuff ourselves in the break room before we staggered home.

"I'll get bowls." Assuming this hovel came with some, that was. "Do you want a glass of wine? Or are you still on duty?"

"I'm... Technically, you're a witness; therefore I'm still on duty."

And yet he'd bought me dinner. "I won't tell if you don't."

How by-the-book was Detective Callahan? A few blurred lines could be an asset, but too many, and bent rules folded over into corruption. You think that's harsh? Well, if you'd seen what my creator and his cronies had gotten away with over the years, you'd have a low opinion of the police too. And don't even get me started on politicians.

"I guess a glass wouldn't hurt. Thanks."

Callahan leaned against the wall by the door for a moment, seemingly unbothered by the weird brown stain at ass height. His sigh gave me pause. While I'd been apologising to Muse and shoving essentials into suitcases—yes, I counted the wine as an essential—he'd been out hunting for a murderer. It was late, but I needed to cut him some slack.

In the kitchen, I poured two generous glasses of red. One for me because as a vampire, alcohol only had a fraction of the effect on my body that it did on humans—I could drink the bottle and stay ninety percent sober—and one for Callahan because he needed to relax. Those worry lines belonged on a man twice his age.

"Here you go. And I brought forks to go with the bowls, just in case."

"I'm a chopsticks guy."

"Me too. Well, not the guy part, obviously."

That got me the tiniest smirk. "I'd noticed." He quickly turned serious again. "We should eat. This food's getting cold."

"The table's right over there. Don't put anything greasy on my drawing of Reuben—it took me all afternoon."

He placed the bag on the cheap table—which had seen better days, say, twenty or thirty years ago—and moved to take out the cartons. Stopped. Picked up the sketch pad instead and straightened, holding it at arm's length.

"You *drew* this?"

"No, Pierre-Auguste Renoir stopped by for coffee and gave me a hand."

That wasn't quite as much of a lie as it sounded. Back in the nineteenth century, when Renoir was an unknown and I'd been chained to my creator—metaphorically, not physically— we'd painted together late into the night. Renoir taught me about light and colour, about composition and depth. Voltaire, the man who made me, had allowed me to indulge my creative side while he did the same with his dark side, which was perhaps why my earlier paintings had tended to be quite grim. Francisco Goya once told me he found my work depressing.

"It's...it's..."

"You thought it would be terrible, didn't you?"

"Uh, yeah, I guess I did." At least he was honest. "If you ever quit serving cocktails, I'm sure I could convince the department to hire you."

And open myself up to scrutiny from a bunch of detectives? No, thank you.

"I thought you already had a sketch artist?"

"She's rushed off her feet."

"Well, I'm afraid I'm not interested."

"You could sell your drawings."

I already did that. And my paintings. I'd gone by many pseudonyms over the years, plus employed several lawyers and agents to help me with the logistics. Art wasn't my main source of income—that came from investment property—but it kept Muse in the style to which she'd become accustomed, this week excepted.

I shrugged in response to Callahan. "Believe it or not, I like working at the club." It gave me friends and dinner options, and I wasn't just talking about Serenity's efforts with takeout. And speaking of food... "Shall we eat?"

Callahan passed me a pair of chopsticks. It was weird having a man in my space. Apart from my accountant, who occasionally visited with paperwork, I'd never invited a man into my home for dinner before, and the experience left me off balance. Uncomfortable, even though Callahan was perfectly polite.

"Pork ball?"

He held the container out towards me, and I helped myself.

"Did you order one of everything on the menu?"

"I was hungry. I didn't get a chance to eat anything today. Right now, I'm running on bad coffee and last night's cheeseburger."

"Dalton Cooper kept you busy all afternoon? It was him you went to see, wasn't it?"

Callahan chewed slowly, and I knew he was considering how much to tell me. I suppose it was good that he had ethics, but I still wanted to shake the answers out of him. Finally, he nodded.

"Yeah. The prick kept me hanging around at his agent's office for three hours while he finished another meeting. A *meeting*. Did he think I didn't smell the perfume?"

Yes, the asshole vibes had been strong with that one.

"But you spoke to him?"

"Eventually. He claimed he left the club before you found the body, and he didn't even know Chavez was dead until his agent called him this afternoon."

"Doesn't he watch the news?"

"I suspect MTV's more his thing."

"So you believed his story?"

"We know he didn't leave the club alone. Apparently, there was a bunch of groupies hanging out downstairs, and he took two of them back to his hotel room. I spoke to both girls, and they backed up his story and each other's."

Ugh, what a slimeball. He'd been cosying up to Serenity, only to trade her in for someone who'd put out two minutes later?

"What if he killed Serenity, then picked up the girls before I found her? Everything happened so fast last night, and...and..."

"He doesn't have a motive either."

"Maybe she rejected him and he got upset?"

"Cooper claims he was only talking to Chavez because she owed him money. Apparently, she was meant to have paid him back by now, and he stopped by to—and I quote—discuss repayment options."

Repayment options? Double ugh. I recalled the way his leg had pressed against hers under the table. The drink he'd tried to push on her. It didn't take a genius to work out what alternative Dalton had suggested.

"And Serenity declined his offer. That had to have bruised his ego."

"Maybe, but I figure the two six-foot blondes went a ways toward soothing it. And in truth, he seemed more concerned about the money today. Even asked if he could claim for it against her estate."

Didn't Dalton Cooper ever think of anyone but himself?

"How much did he lend her?"

"Ten thousand bucks, two months ago. Did she mention being short of cash?"

"No." I wished she had because I'd have gladly lent her the money, even if it led to some awkward questions about where I got it from. Far better to fib about an inheritance than to have Serenity indebted to a man like Dalton. Why had *he* lent her the money? To get a hold over her? So he could push her around later? "Did she tell him why she needed it?"

"Said she needed to pay a lawyer to draw up a contract. Which Cooper thought was odd because with all the contracts he's signed in his music career, the other party has taken care of that. Record labels, promoters, venues... Those folks want to put in the small print themselves."

"And he didn't question it? Why would he lend her ten thousand dollars if he thought she was lying?"

"Apparently, because 'that's what friends do.'"

"Friends?" I snorted and almost choked on a noodle. "They sure didn't look like friends to me. I don't even know how they met."

"According to Cooper, they met at a party in New York. Reading between the lines, I'd say he wanted to get into her panties, and he thought a loan might grease the wheels, so to speak. Daphne looked him up on the internet, and rumour says he spent fifteen thousand bucks on champagne in one night last month. Ten thousand bucks is probably pocket change to him."

"Who's Daphne?" And why did I bristle at the mention of her name?

"Daphne's my assistant. She spent most of the day watching camera footage from the club's front door."

"Did she see anything?"

"Not yet. Trouble is, we don't really know what we're looking for yet. The killer's hardly gonna have walked in with a sharpened screwdriver in his hand."

"A screwdriver? That was the murder weapon?"

"I don't know yet. I'm just hypothesising. The autopsy's tomorrow morning."

"We really don't know much at the moment, do we? Only that Serenity's dead and her killer's walking around free." I found my appetite had suddenly vanished. My chest tightened, and I willed myself not to tear up. Why did loss always hit hours later? I hadn't cried about my own death until a whole week afterwards. "I should be eating dinner with her, not you."

"Do you want me to leave?"

"No, I don't. I want you to do everything you damn well can to catch the person who murdered her and make them suffer the way she did."

CHAPTER 12

Jack

Shit. When Angie got choked up, I used to hug her, but that wasn't an option with Vee. I had to make do with words instead.

"I'll catch Lyla's killer, I promise." Although I didn't feel quite as confident as I sounded. Vee clearly liked Dalton Cooper for the job, but my gut said he was a prick, not a killer. "They'll get what's coming."

"Prison." Vee gulped, and I made a mental note to carry a handkerchief at all times from now on. "You mean prison. That still won't bring her back."

"But it will stop the same thing from happening to anyone else. I'm a cop, babe, not the Grim Reaper." Shit. Babe? "Sorry. I shouldn't have called you that, and I apologise if I sounded condescending."

A long moment passed. Vee picked at a spring roll, then got up and walked to the window. The blinds were up this evening, although the view from the sixteenth floor wasn't anything to write home about. A shabby high-rise hotel opposite and beside that, far below, the run-down mall where I'd bought Vee's pencils earlier. Back in New York, Angie and I had lived in a nicer apartment, but with only one income and the thousands in debt I'd run up after Angie's death—funerals were expensive—a studio in Sunset Tower was the best I could afford.

I wished I could have brought Vee dinner under better circumstances. You know, welcoming a new neighbour to the building rather than investigating the murder of her friend. But there we were. Should I break the awkward silence?

"I appreciate everything you're doing." Vee spoke up while I was still contemplating. "Honestly, I do. I just wish there was some way I could help, or speed things up, or...or..."

"Actually, there are *one* or two things you could do to assist." Screw the rules. "How well do you know Ms. Chavez's acquaintances? And what about the other employees at Club Dead?"

"I guess I know most of the people at the club, but Serenity's—Lyla's—other acquaintances... You've probably noticed I don't get out much."

"Anything you can give me gets us a step further forward. I've got a list of contacts from her phone, but there wasn't much in the way of messages or photos."

Only a handful of pictures—arty scenes from around the city and publicity shots of the band—and half a dozen innocuous text conversations, mainly about music.

"Photos? No, there probably wouldn't be many. She dropped her old phone in the toilet a month ago, so she got a new one."

"She didn't back up her data?"

"I'm not sure. But I do know that her insurance was through her old provider and they didn't want to pay for a replacement, so she said to hell with it and went elsewhere. Can you believe they said she'd done it on purpose? Who drops their phone in the toilet on purpose?"

Ah, fuck. Getting the old data would take a warrant and a

painfully long time. And would it even be any use? For a perp to escalate from no recent contact to murder seemed unlikely. I'd start by focusing on the data we *did* have.

"Interesting. Reuben's number was saved in her phone, although there weren't any calls with him in the log."

"She probably deleted the log. Did you try calling him?"

"Yes, but the number's out of service. We'd need a warrant to get his details from the service provider, and right now, we don't have enough to convince a judge."

"But this is a murder inquiry."

"It is, but the way the courts see it, people are still entitled to their privacy. All we have on Reuben is a second-hand conversation."

"Between who? What did they say?"

I repeated what I knew about the conversation Chavez's roommate had overheard. If anything, it sounded even sketchier than when I'd discussed it with Shep earlier.

"And you think the Reuben I saw at the club might be the same guy who wouldn't leave her alone?"

"It's a possibility."

"Maybe that's why she wanted the lawyer? To file for a restraining order?"

"A restraining order's a big step, and lawyers don't come cheap. If a man was harassing her, why wouldn't she call the cops first? You're sure she never mentioned Reuben?"

Vee's lips flattened into a thin line, and her tone changed from helpful to pissy. "I think I'd remember."

Okay, so she didn't like me asking the same question twice. It also meant she was confident in her own recollections, which I had to take as a positive.

"I'll start showing Reuben's picture around tomorrow. Hopefully we'll get a hit. Going back to what you said before, why would Lyla delete her call log?"

"A reporter picked her phone up off the table once, and

before she could snatch it back, he'd thumbed through her call history and some of her photos. A well-known singer had been calling her—I forget which one—and before she could blink, the tabloids reported the two of them were having an affair. They'd only been discussing work, but his wife was furious, and she vetoed the duet he and Serenity had been planning. I think that was Serenity's first glimpse of fame's darker side. Until then, she'd been so excited about the record deal, but after... She was quieter. And she started being more careful about what she kept on her phone."

That went some way to explaining the lack of personal information on Lyla's device.

"Do you know who Gerard is? She phoned him twice the day before she died and once the previous day as well, but when I tried calling, he didn't pick up."

"Sorry." Vee shook her head, then straightened as if a memory had come back to her. "Actually, he might be her hairdresser. Her split ends were bugging her, and she was frustrated because she couldn't get ahold of him."

From split ends to dead ends. I'd get Daphne to keep trying Gerard to confirm, but it didn't sound hopeful.

"How about Shawnn? That's Shawnn with a W and two Ns. We found him in Chavez's contacts, and apart from Gerard and Reuben, he's the only person listed that we haven't managed to speak to."

"An ex. They were dating when I first met her, but I think they stayed friends after they split. I remember her saying that he'd added the extra N to stand out, but now everyone spells his name wrong and he gets really annoyed."

Movement caught my eye, and I swivelled to see a fluffy cat stroll out of Vee's bedroom, tabby coloured with a white chest. Vee had said her name was Muse, right? She ignored Vee completely and darted under the dining table. A second later, I felt her weaving in and out of my legs.

"Hey, kitty."

I reached down to stroke the newcomer as Vee came over and crouched beside the table.

"Careful. Muse isn't normally fond of strangers. She nearly took my lawyer's finger off."

A lawyer? Why did a cocktail waitress need a lawyer? And why had they come to Vee's apartment? I was tempted to ask, but I didn't want to risk upsetting Vee when I needed her help.

"Cats like me. When I lived in New York, we had a Siamese."

She looked up sharply. "We? Sorry, that's none of my business."

Perhaps I *should* have asked about the lawyer. I inwardly cursed my slip of the tongue, but I figured Vee deserved an answer.

"My wife."

"Oh." Vee kept her gaze fixed on the cat. "I didn't realise you were married. You work such long hours, and...never mind."

"I'm not married anymore."

"Right."

"She...she died."

Vee's gasp told me she'd expected a divorce. Why had I told her the truth? I wasn't sure—perhaps because I didn't want her to think I'd wronged Angie or vice versa. I'd loved my wife with everything I had. I still did, and I always would. Sadness washed over me as I thought of the smile I'd never see again. The sweet voice I'd never hear outside my dreams.

Now Vee looked at me, and I wished she hadn't. Other people's pity wasn't as painful as my own heartbreak, but it always made me uncomfortable.

"I'm so, so sorry."

Time to change the subject.

"Let's go back to the case, shall we? I was hoping you could look through the list of pass-holders I got from Lucian Blane. Unfortunately, the security system doesn't record which card was used at any given time, but it would still help to gain an understanding of who *could* have snuck in the back door."

"Sure, of course. Now?"

"No time like the present." I pushed the remains of dinner away, hunger pangs giving way to the yawning emptiness that set in every time I thought of Angie. *Concentrate on work, Callahan.* I gave my head a shake, trying to fight off the tiredness that tugged at my eyelids. Blane's list had almost sixty people on it. The system might have been basic, but Blane swore he kept the record of current passes up to date and deactivated any that were lost or stolen. Then again, he also swore he hadn't been at the club at eight o'clock last night. I'd asked him again, suggesting a witness had seen him, and he'd informed me in no uncertain terms that my witness was mistaken. It was a "he said, she said" situation. And I guess it was possible that Vee's eyes had played tricks on her. The lighting in the club wasn't exactly conducive to an ID parade, and she said he'd been up on the balcony. Perhaps she'd seen one of the bouncers instead?

Daphne had printed the pass list for me, and I'd swung by the front desk to pick it up on my way past the police station. I unfolded it and set it on the table.

"How about we start from the top?"

Pain in my neck cut through my grogginess, and I tried to turn it to the side. Huh. There was something in the way. And what was that weight on my stomach?

My eyes flickered open, and in the dim light, I realised I

wasn't in my bed, or even in my own apartment. My head was wedged against a cushion that smelled faintly of marijuana, and when I reached out a hand, the cat sprawled out on top of me leapt a foot in the air.

Shit.

I'd fallen asleep in Vee's living room.

Where was she? In her bed, I guessed. The bedroom door was open a crack, but I couldn't see anything in the dark, not that I should have been looking. The cat glared at me from the coffee table, annoyed at having her nap disturbed.

"Sorry, sweetheart," I whispered, half to the cat and half to Vee.

How had I gotten onto the couch? The last thing I remembered was sitting at the dining table, covering a yawn as I wrote notes against name number twenty or so. What should I do? Tell Vee I was leaving? Or quietly slip back to my place without a word?

No, I didn't want to wake her.

I spotted the notes stacked neatly on the table and gathered them up. First thing tomorrow, I'd have to apologise for falling asleep in the middle of what was essentially an interview and hope Vee didn't report me to the captain, because I had no idea how I'd begin to explain that little faux pas.

Wait.

That wasn't my handwriting on the first page. I used the flashlight from my key ring to take a better look and found notes had been written against the rest of the names in elegant cursive, detailing each person's role at the club, their length of service, and what Vee thought of them.

Oh, babe.

As I stole along the hallway, I noticed a warmth in my chest. A warmth I hadn't felt for almost a decade. A warmth I hadn't felt since those early dates in New York with Angie.

CHAPTER 13

Vee

I wasn't surprised to find that Callahan had vanished on Sunday morning, although I was strangely disappointed. I hadn't expected to like his company. Having someone in my space usually gave me the heebie-jeebies, but the experience hadn't been as uncomfortable as I'd feared.

How long had it been since I'd shown somebody one of my drawings? I mean in person? Yes, people bought my artwork from galleries, but they didn't know the girl behind the brush. My website didn't have a photo of me, or a biography, not even a hint as to my gender. My lawyer, agent, and accountant had all signed NDAs, and art dealers used my mysteriousness as a selling point, as if by paying an outrageous sum for one of my works, the buyer was somehow indoctrinated into a secret club.

There had been awkward moments last night, like Callahan's revelation that he'd lost his wife and me welling up over Serenity's death, but on the whole, it had been...nice. Would he want to visit again?

"Good grief, Vee."

Muse looked at me funny, but I deserved it. What was I

90

thinking? Last night hadn't been a freaking date. Not that I truly knew what a date was like—before Voltaire turned me, I'd been promised to a French nobleman, a baron from the House of Molinard, and he'd been a pompous ass. Courting consisted of carriage rides where he pointed out his family's property and informed me just how *fantastique* my life would be as his wife. Was it any wonder I'd taken to sneaking out at night to the bars of Mougins in clothes borrowed from my maid? *Beatrice.* She'd been such a sweet girl. I often wondered what had happened to her after I left.

Anyhow, despite spending more than two centuries on this earth, I'd never been on an actual date. Never gone through that rite of passage. Forced marriage? Check. A casual arrangement with a kind but scatterbrained artist? Check. But a proper, romantic date? No. Once or twice, I'd thought of joining Tinder just for the experience, but I'd always chickened out. Not because I was worried I wouldn't like the guy, but rather because I was scared in case I did. If I ever fell in love, a broken heart would be inevitable.

So no, a date was totally off the table, but talking to somebody smart and more-or-less sober without having to carry drinks all evening made for a pleasant change.

I looked around the living room. There was no sign of the notes I'd written, which meant Callahan must've taken them. Good. Hopefully, they'd be of some help. The autopsy was taking place today, wasn't it? I shuddered just thinking about poor Serenity lying cold on a metal slab. Thanks to Voltaire, I'd seen plenty of dead bodies over the years, but not sliced open down the middle with their internal organs scooped out into jars.

"Maybe we should buy Callahan dinner tonight?" I said to Muse. "You know, return the favour? I bet he won't eat much during the day if he's stuck in the morgue."

Miaow.

Did that mean yes, it was a great idea, or no, you've lost your damn mind? More importantly, why was I even considering it? I'd sound like an idiot, asking a cop over for a meal without having a valid reason.

Hmm. A valid reason...

What if I helped with the case in some way?

Yes, that could work. But how?

Reuben. What if I could find Reuben? I knew what he looked like, and I had a laptop. Everyone was on Facebook, right?

Yup, all 3,976 Reubens, and that was just in the Las Vegas area. The top one had a profile picture of a cartoon dog. Perhaps if I wanted company, Tinder really was the way to go?

Oh, come on, Vee. There had to be a way to narrow this down.

Shelby. I could call Shelby. I'd only met Serenity's roommate once, but Serenity must have given her my number at some point because she'd called to invite me to Serenity's surprise birthday lunch. I couldn't go, of course—because daylight—but I'd couriered a gift to their apartment. Just a cheap leather-and-silver necklace, nothing flashy, but Serenity loved it. She'd worn it most weeks.

"Shelby? I'm not sure if you remember me, but—"

"Vee? You worked at the club with Serenity?"

"Yes. I'm so sorry for your loss."

That was the appropriate thing to say, wasn't it? I hadn't had much experience in these situations. Voltaire mostly used to select victims who didn't have close friends or family, and on the rare occasions one of his vampire clan got staked through the heart and actually died, I'd cheered inside as well as feeling a little envious. They were all assholes.

"It was your loss too," Shelby sniffled. "Have the police spoken to you? Who's going to arrange the funeral? I wouldn't even know where to start."

"What about Serenity's family? Won't they do that?"

"I can't find a way to contact them. I guess they're all back in Mexico? And I still have her stuff here, and...and... I can't believe she's gone forever."

"Me neither." I was lying—I'd seen her lifeless body. "I was actually calling about the case. One of the detectives working it lives in the same building as me. Jack Callahan?"

"I spoke with a hot detective. Was that him?"

"I think that was actually Lieutenant Shepherd." Although neither was a hardship to look at. What? I might have been dead, but certain parts of my anatomy still functioned perfectly. "He mentioned a guy called Reuben who wouldn't leave her alone?"

"Oh, yeah. Like a stalker. She said if any guys I didn't know came to the apartment asking for her, I should tell them I lived with my boyfriend."

"Did she say anything else about him? How they met? Where he lived?"

"Nada. She just seemed real tense these last few weeks, ya know?"

I honestly hadn't noticed, which made me feel like *merde* because I should have been a better friend, shouldn't I?

"But you said she'd spoken to a lawyer about Reuben? I don't suppose you caught a name?"

"I can't really remember. Or maybe the lawyer *was* Reuben? The whole thing's blurry. I was texting my boyfriend while she was talking, and he's going through this thing with his boss, so I wasn't paying that much attention. If I'd known it was important..."

Shelby sounded so dejected that I wanted to give her a hug. And I didn't *do* hugs with virtual strangers.

"Don't feel bad. Nobody realised how much trouble she was in."

"Will you call me if you hear anything else?"

"Cross my heart."

My cold, long-dead heart.

Once I'd hung up, I replayed the conversation in my head. *Could* Shelby have gotten mixed up? I opened a search engine and typed in "Reuben lawyer Las Vegas." Four pages of results. That seemed much more manageable. And the best part? Lawyers really, really liked to put pictures of themselves on *their* websites. From the pinstripe suits and eight-hundred-bucks-an-hour smiles of the corporate clones all the way down to the rolled-up shirtsleeves and predatory grins of the ambulance chasers, every attorney in Vegas had a mugshot. Some even had blogs. Behold, the Harvey and Finkelstein annual family picnic. Witness the magnificence of Morten Samuels, who won a six-figure settlement from a glue manufacturer after his client sniffed their product to get high and drove his car off a bridge.

Reuben, it turned out, wasn't a fully fledged lawyer after all. When I finally found him peering from halfway down page three of the "Meet Our Team" section at Broderick, Matherson and Pope, his bio informed me he'd been working as a paralegal in the family law department since July. He looked a little out of place. Every other employee had neatly slicked-back hair and a dead-eyed stare, as if they'd been focusing on a computer screen for a few years too long, whereas Reuben hadn't managed to tame his cow's lick and looked slightly nervous. *Reuben Broderick.* Was he related to one of the partners?

I tried calling the firm to see if they'd put me through, but I got voicemail. Hardly surprising since it was Sunday. Lawyers golfed on Sundays if the chatter I heard at the club was anything to go by. I'd have to wait. On the plus side, at least the discovery gave me an excuse to talk to Callahan again, and that pleased me more than it should have.

CHAPTER 14

Jack

"**M**y wife hates me working Sundays," Dr. Rashid complained. "Damn murderers. Don't they have any respect?"

I waved a hand towards Lyla Chavez, lying on a metal table with a bluish tinge to her skin.

"No. Refer to exhibit A."

"An interesting one, isn't it? On first sight, I thought we'd need an exorcist, not a police officer."

"An exorcist? That's for demons, isn't it? Vampires need silver bullets."

"Oh, yes, yes, possibly you're right."

"Actually, I think the more common method for vampires is a stake through the heart," Daphne said. "Silver bullets are mostly for werewolves. I've been reading up on it, but the instructions on how to kill them are kinda vague."

I didn't like working Sundays either, and I especially didn't like working Sundays when I had to deal with both Daphne and Dr. Rashid. Shep had told me the doc used to work in the emergency room, but rumour said he'd gotten busted down to the morgue after an "incident." Apparently, a

95

patient came in with an eight-inch replica of the Washington Monument lodged in his rectum, and somehow after Dr. Rashid removed it, the thing found its way onto the charge nurse's desk. She hadn't seen the funny side.

"The instructions are vague because vampires don't exist," I said. "And neither do werewolves."

My partner had clearly been watching too much TV.

"What about the puncture wounds? There were a lot of strange people in that club."

"They were just regular people in costumes, Daphne. And *I* was in the club having drinks with Lieutenant Shepherd."

"Did you see anyone with fangs? Or, you know, fake fangs?"

Thankfully, Dr. Rashid piped up. "Sorry to disappoint, young lady, but these wounds are too deep for fangs. You're looking for something longer—a sharpened screwdriver, an ice pick, or maybe a trocar."

"What's a trocar?"

He rummaged in a drawer for a moment and came back with a pointy instrument. "One of these. They're used in surgery. The point makes a hole, then you withdraw the centre of the cylinder and the hollow tube provides an access point for surgical instruments."

Nasty. "Would that suggest the possibility of our killer being a medical professional?"

"He might have been in a medical field initially, but you can buy anything on the internet nowadays." The doctor snapped on a pair of disposable gloves. "Shall we get started?"

We didn't have much choice, did we? Murders didn't solve themselves.

As a cop, I'd been to many autopsies, but they never got any easier. Everyone lying on that table had been somebody's child, somebody's sibling, somebody's parent. Loved and then lost.

Lyla Chavez was no different.

I was almost grateful when Daphne fainted and I had to take her outside to get some air, although this time, I had to concede she did have a good reason for passing out.

"This girl was pregnant," Dr. Rashid had announced.

Thunk. Daphne hit the deck, and my knees went weak too.

Pregnant? Fuck. The revelation made Chavez's death all the more tragic. Two lives taken, not one. It felt like a punch to the gut.

"How far along was she?" I asked Dr. Rashid when I got back to the morgue, minus my sidekick.

"Two months, give or take. Your girl okay?"

"She's not my girl, and yes, I've sent her to sit in the cafeteria."

"Surprised she didn't lose her stomach contents. Speaking of which, Ms. Chavez's last meal was a chicken sandwich. Part-digested, so she ate it three to four hours before she died. There's also some sort of liquid, tea perhaps, with what looks like pieces of dried herb in it. I'd say she drank that more recently. Certainly within an hour of death."

"So someone, what, brought her a drink and then stabbed her in the neck?"

"That's what the evidence says. Except the neck wound didn't kill her. It came post-mortem."

That possibility had crossed my mind. There were only two good reasons for the lack of blood at the crime scene— well, three if you subscribed to Daphne's theory about vampires, which I didn't. One, Lyla had been killed elsewhere and then dumped, or two, her heart had stopped pumping before the wound was inflicted. I'd been inclined to rule out the first option—the killer just wouldn't have had the time for complicated manoeuvres, and with the number of people around at Club Dead, surely somebody would have seen them carrying the body?

"So, how *did* she die?"

"Anaphylaxis. See here?" Dr. Rashid pointed at Chavez's throat. "Her airway's swollen shut. She had an allergic reaction and voila...lights out."

"It's that fast?"

"Well, it's not instant, but I'd guess she took less than fifteen minutes to die."

"Fifteen minutes? Why didn't she call out for help?"

Vee said the door to the storeroom was unlocked when she found the body, so it wasn't as if Chavez had gotten stuck in there.

"See these bruises? Look—wrists, arms, and shoulders. It looks as though there was a struggle just before she died."

The marks were faint, purple tinges on tan skin, shadows behind the tattoos decorating Lyla's arms and torso. Finger marks around her wrists. The splodge of a handprint on one shoulder. Why hadn't I noticed them before?

"I don't remember seeing those at the club."

"Bruises can continue to develop after a person dies. That's most likely what happened in this instance."

So Lyla had been dying—probably had *known* she was dying—and somebody prevented her from getting medical assistance. She'd fought for her life and lost. I felt sick as I realised how close she'd been to surviving—with all those people in Club Dead that night, surely one of them must have had an EpiPen?

"What caused the anaphylaxis?"

"That, my friend, is the big question."

"Could it have been those herbs?"

"I've bagged them for analysis." Dr. Rashid looked up. "The ER's had several cases of anaphylaxis over the past several months caused by traditional Chinese medicine."

"Herbal medicine?"

"Yes. Some kind of injection, if I recall right. Perhaps she tried a natural remedy for morning sickness?"

"She died at night."

"The 'morning' part is something of a misnomer."

If not for the bruises, self-medication gone wrong could have been a plausible explanation, but the stab wounds took her death to a new level.

"That doesn't fit with the other evidence. Can you tell me anything else?"

"About how she died? Not until the toxicology results come back, but you know how things are over at the lab..."

Backed up, as always. Which meant I had to call Shep. He knew Doc Pressley's secretary, and she'd bend over backwards to help him if he needed a favour. He claimed it was his natural charm that made her putty in his hands, but Dorothea was sixty years old and I'd heard a rumour that Cecily's charitable foundation had helped out her sick granddaughter a year or two ago.

When Dr. Rashid began sewing up the Y-incision, I thanked him and went in search of Daphne. She wasn't in the hallway outside, and there was no sign of her in the cafeteria either. Why me? I didn't have time for this. I was about to pull out my phone when I spotted her in the waiting area, kneeling in front of a little girl. Daphne reached into the kid's pocket. What was she doing? During a search, we were only allowed to pat down a suspect's outer clothing, and why the hell was she frisking a five-year-old, anyway?

As I got closer, I saw the girl's eyes were red from crying and quickened my steps, but suddenly she smiled.

"Daphne, what's going on?"

"She found a quarter," the little girl told me. "In my pocket. The magic's true!"

Daphne patted her shoulder. "Guess it must be yours now."

I must have looked puzzled because the girl's mother hurried to explain.

"Your...friend? Colleague?"

"Colleague," I confirmed. Daphne still wore a uniform while I was in plainclothes, which was yet another thing Captain Lindsay hadn't thought through.

"Emily was so scared about going to see the doctor, but your colleague told her there's a magical hospital elf who watches to see which children are being the bravest and leaves them little gifts." She chewed her lip for a second. "I should've thought of that myself."

Daphne's knees cracked as she got to her feet. "This is a real stressful time for everybody. Don't feel bad."

A nurse called Emily's name, and she practically sprinted into the exam room. Seemed Daphne did have some sort of talent after all.

"Sorry," she muttered as we headed for the parking lot. "I just saw the little girl upset, and I... I figured it wasn't a good idea to go back to the morgue."

For once, we agreed on something. "You're good with kids."

"I love kids. I always wanted to be an elementary school teacher."

"What changed your mind?" And was it too late to change it back?

Daphne was uncharacteristically quiet for a moment before she answered. Or rather, didn't answer. "It doesn't matter."

"Yes, it does."

It did matter why she'd passed up the career she'd wanted, a career that might have suited her down to the ground, for one that clearly didn't.

Another pause.

"Promise you won't tell anyone else at the station?"

"We're partners, right?" Unfortunately.

"I guess..." Did she feel the same way about me as I felt about her? That stung more than it should have. "I only applied to the Academy because my father was in the police force, and my grandpa, and my great-grandpa too. And for my whole life, Grandpa's said that law enforcement's in our blood, so we should always have at least one cop in the family. And now that's me."

"What about your dad? He's retired?"

Daphne shook her head. "He died tackling a shooter in the New York Public Library."

What?

For the second time that day, I'd been sucker-punched. Holy shit. Josiah Washington had been murdered right after I joined the NYPD, almost ten years ago now, and even though he'd gotten shot three times, he'd wrestled with his killer long enough to allow backup to arrive. The library had been packed with visitors young and old that day, and he'd prevented a massacre. Afterwards, we'd held a fundraiser for his kid. That was Daphne?

"I should have realised. Your surname... Why didn't you say something?"

"I didn't want special treatment. Or pity," she added hastily, no doubt seeing exactly that in my eyes. "I just wanted to make my grandpa proud."

"I'm sure you have."

"We both know the truth, Jack. I'm not stupid. But Grandpa's sick. He's got a few months left to live, maybe a year at most, and if I can stick this job out until then, I can quit without breaking his heart and go back to school. Study elementary education instead of criminal justice. I'm sorry I'm such an awful partner. I promise I'll try my best until then, but I'll probably keep screwing up. Captain Lindsay's gonna throw a party when I leave, isn't he? You know he didn't want me on his team in the first place? I heard another girl he refused to work with complained about sex discrimination, and so the sheriff decided to assign him a female, any female, so the department didn't get sued."

My brain was still trying to process everything. "Where did you hear that?"

"At the Academy. Everyone was real sympathetic when I drew the short straw."

So much made sense now. Daphne's lack of enthusiasm. Her reluctance to leave the police station and her complete lack of crime-solving ability. Perhaps—although I'd never voice the words—someone at the Academy had looked favourably upon her application because she was Josiah Washington's daughter? And you know what else became clearer? The reason Captain Lindsay had assigned her to work with me. He didn't want me on his team either, and ten bucks said he hoped we'd get sick of each other and quit.

Well, fuck him.

Daphne and her dithering might have annoyed the crap out of me for the last six months, but Captain Lindsay had been an asshole his entire life. Probably in a past life too. And now that I understood the situation, I could deal with it.

"We'll get through this, okay? I'm sorry your grandpa's sick." Did she have any other family? A vague memory told me her mom had died before her dad. "Maybe you could skip the autopsies for a while?"

"Captain Lindsay told me I had to go. He said it was all part of being a cop."

"How about you just spend a really long time in the hospital bathroom? Our secret."

Now she eyed me suspiciously. "Why are you being so nice about this?"

It was a fair question. I hadn't exactly been her biggest fan, nor had I tried to hide that fact.

"Sometimes, it's easy to forget that other people might be going through things that you're not aware of. I should have been kinder to you, and I apologise for that."

"Oh." Surprise with a hint of suspicion. Yes, I deserved that.

"Let's get this case solved, okay? I've got a job for you to do back at the station—some research. There've been several cases of anaphylaxis recently linked to Chinese medicine. Can you see if there was anything hinky reported?"

Because I needed to call Shep and break the news that Lyla Chavez had been pregnant.

~

"She was what?" Shep asked.

"Yup."

"That was a plot twist I did *not* see coming."

"Me neither, but it does make a certain amount of sense. Blane said Lyla was having regrets about her music career." *A poisoned chalice.* "Maybe the baby was the reason why? If she was planning to keep it, then juggling performances and recording and childcare would be difficult. New artists get worked to the bone. It's all promo, promo, promo."

"Plus it gives us one obvious motive."

"A father who didn't want the baby."

"Child support's a bitch. But who was the father? Lyla's ex?"

"That'd be my first thought. I'll have to speak to him again."

Joaquin Gonzalez was the clear suspect, but the news opened up a whole range of possibilities. Who in the industry had invested money in Lyla? If she quit or even took maternity leave, they'd risk losing their capital. But that was assuming she'd told anyone she worked with about the baby. Shelby didn't know, and neither did Vee. Would Lyla break the big news to her colleagues before she shared the secret with her friends? More to the point, did *she* even realise she was knocked up? Two months wasn't far along, was it? That was another question for Daphne. She seemed to know more about kids than I did.

I asked Shep to chase up the lab results, and he said he'd do his best. Something must have caused the allergic reaction, and I'd put money on it being in that tea Lyla had drunk right before she died. We *needed* to find out what those herbs were, and fast.

"Whoever did this, they're cold," Shep said. "They took fifteen minutes to kill Chavez, and at any point they could have stopped and called an ambulance."

Yup. They'd hit the point of no return and just carried on going. "Why the neck wounds, though? There weren't any obvious bruises at the time of death. We might have written the whole thing off as a tragic accident if somebody hadn't gone full Count Dracula on the girl."

"A cover-up?" Shep suggested. "The culprit didn't want us to look too closely at the toxicology results? Maybe they thought we'd take the obvious injury to be the cause of death."

It was a case of contradictions. A famous singer who'd died alone in the city's busiest nightclub. An extrovert who confided in no one. A cold-blooded killer who planned ahead yet panicked in the heat of the moment and stabbed a girl in the neck. None of it made sense.

At least, not yet.

"I guess anything's possible."

"Dorothea's promised to put a rush on those tests. She understands that there's a murderer out there, and if he's killed once, then he could kill again. I do have one small piece of good news, though."

"Tell me. I need good news like a vampire needs blood."

"You can cross the Devil's Den connection off the list. Cece visited her father today, and when she mentioned she'd heard a rumour that he wanted to buy the place, he said the new head of the planning department seemed particularly amenable to him building a casino from scratch on land he already owns, so he's decided to focus on that."

"Particularly amenable? He's bribing the planning department?"

"Cece didn't ask for the details. Neither of us wanted to know. But if Maxwell doesn't want to buy the Devil's Den anymore, then he probably doesn't have a reason to squabble with Lucian Blane."

Shep was right. "Thanks for your help on this."

Now I had to tell Vee about Chavez's baby, and that was a call I really didn't want to make.

CHAPTER 15

Vee

"Why the cryptic message?" Callahan asked. "What information did you find?"

After all my detective work, I'd realised the fatal flaw in my plan. Callahan didn't have to be in my apartment while I broke the news about Reuben. I could simply tell him over the phone like a normal person.

In desperation, I'd sent him a vague text in the hope that he might stop by.

Me: I found some information. I know you're busy, but perhaps you could drop in on your way home?

So lame. As soon as I hit send, I regretted it, and now Callahan was calling and probably cursing me for wasting his time. Why hadn't I simply messaged him the website link?

"Sorry for being so unclear. It's just that I found Reuben."

"You what?"

"I know where he works. Give me a minute, and I'll send you the details."

"No need. I'm on my way over."

"Over where?"

"To your place."

"Honestly, it's easy for me to type out the information."

"Vee, that's not why I'm coming."

Something in his tone made me pause. A heaviness, a sadness that reminded me of my own manner during the decades I'd spent with Voltaire. My throat tightened.

"What happened?"

"I'll be there in half an hour."

"Can't you tell me now?"

"I don't want to upset you."

"Well, you're not doing a very good job of that."

"Shit." I pictured Callahan tilting his head back and taking a breath the way he always seemed to when he got stressed. "It's nothing to get worried over, Vee. Some stuff came up in the autopsy, and I've got a few more questions, that's all. Half an hour, okay?"

Nothing to worry about? Yeah, right. I spent the whole time pacing around the tiny lounge, cursing the fact that I was stuck in a shoebox rather than my penthouse. In Berkshire Place, I had a gym to use if I got stressed, plus my paints and a grand piano if I needed to take the edge off. In Sunset Tower, I had a coffee table to walk around and a cat to trip over. Muse scuttled off into the bedroom after I trod on her tail for the second time, and I made a mental note to order her extra kitty treats as an apology later.

What had the medical examiner found? Drugs? Had Serenity been taking drugs? I'd never seen her dabble. She often used to have a beer in her hand, but a month ago, she'd gone on a health kick and started drinking juice instead of vodka before every set. Said she still wanted to have a liver when she hit forty. Had she slipped off the wagon? The guys in her band weren't exactly squeaky clean—they were called the Sinners for a reason. Had temptation proven too much?

And where was Callahan? He said thirty minutes, but it had been forty-five. By the time he knocked on the door, my nerves had frayed down to the thinnest of threads.

"Did you lose your watch?"

"Sorry." He held up a paper carrier bag. "Peace offering? I didn't eat breakfast, so I had to stop and pick something up. A late lunch."

More like an early dinner. It was nearly three o'clock. Although my body clock was so messed up that I tended to just eat when I was hungry and sleep when I got tired.

"What happened?" I asked again. Maybe he'd answer this time?

Callahan closed the ill-fitting door behind him with the muffled scrape of wood on wood. "Did Lyla ever mention anything about a baby? Or even hint at it?"

"Whose baby?" Slowly, it dawned on me. "*Her* baby? She was pregnant? Oh no, no way."

"Why do you say that?"

"*Was* she pregnant?"

"About two months."

My knees went weak, and I sagged back onto the tatty sofa. Whoever killed Serenity had killed her baby as well. For the first time in a century, I wished Voltaire was still with me. He'd have slaughtered the son of a bitch who murdered my friend and taken pleasure in doing so.

"Poor Serenity," I whispered.

"You really didn't know?"

"Of course not! Don't you think I'd have told you?"

"You'd be surprised by the number of people who withhold information from the police."

"Well, I'm not one of them."

Not in this instance, anyway.

"I had to ask, Vee. You know that. I wouldn't be doing my job otherwise."

"For the record, I had no idea she was pregnant, but hindsight is a wonderful thing. She quit drinking alcohol a month ago, but she said she was detoxing." And yes, it hurt that she hadn't told me the truth. "She probably stopped because of the baby. And before you ask, the only person I can think of who might be the father is Joaquin. Her ex."

"I'm planning to speak with him again."

"What if he killed her because she was pregnant?"

"It's certainly something we'll be considering."

I'd only met Joaquin once or twice, and he'd seemed nice enough. Pretty to look at, but not a whole lot of substance. He worked as a personal trainer in one of the hotel gyms along the Strip.

"How did she die? From the puncture wounds?"

And if so, where the heck did all her blood go? I knew exactly how much blood was in a human body—nine pints for an average-sized woman, twelve pints for a man. A girl Serenity's size could have provided twenty vampires with a satisfying meal, or half a dozen with a veritable feast. I only ever took the bare minimum, enough to stave off my hunger and still let my victim live a long and happy life. Little and often. Voltaire and his band of assholes used to gorge themselves silly and then sit around moaning about the mess they had to clean up. I could still hear him now—*Genevieve, stop whining and help us to move the bodies. They're just shells. Empty husks. They've got no blood left in them whatsoever.*

Speaking of blood, I needed a meal at some point in the near future, and I wasn't talking pizza. I didn't have to drink from a human every night or even every week—once every eight or nine days was sufficient if I didn't overexert myself— but stretch the break between meals too far and I became weak and dizzy.

Callahan shook his head. "The puncture wounds appear

to have been an afterthought. A smokescreen to distract us from the real cause of death."

"Which was?"

"Anaphylactic shock."

Huh? Of all the things I'd considered—suffocation, strangulation, some new strain of vampire I hadn't come across before—anaphylactic shock wasn't a possibility that had sprung to mind.

"Isn't that caused by an allergy?"

"Yes."

"So it was an accident?" Wait. I gave my own head a shake, mirroring Callahan, but it didn't do much towards unjumbling my thoughts. "No, it couldn't have been, not with the damage to her neck. Unless she somehow did that herself, but why would she?"

"It wasn't an accident. She had defensive wounds. Once she began experiencing difficulties, somebody trapped her in the storeroom until she died."

A sob welled up, and I couldn't prevent it from escaping. Hearing what Serenity had gone through at the end... She must have been so scared.

"If I'd only gone downstairs a few minutes sooner, I could have helped her."

"Or you might have been hurt yourself."

Unlikely. At full strength, I could take on an Olympic wrestler and win. I was probably the one woman who didn't mind getting mugged. In fact, I'd been known to enjoy it because the look on an asshole's face when I slammed him head first into a wall was priceless. Don't get me wrong, I wasn't a fan of violence, but there was something decidedly satisfying about seeing a criminal get his just deserts and knowing that I'd been the girl to serve them up. But I couldn't admit that to Callahan.

"What if I'd screamed or called 911?"

"We can't turn back the clock, Vee." He said it with sadness, and I knew he was thinking of his wife. "But we can solve this case. Lyla had what looked like dried herbs in her stomach, and the medical examiner says she ingested them right before she died. Did you see her eat or drink anything that evening?"

"No, but you said herbs? That'd be her special tea. She drinks it before every set because she swears it makes her voice smoother." I swallowed the lump in my throat and corrected myself. "Swore. She *swore* it helped her voice. Throat Saver, I think it's called? She kept it in a pink tin in the break area. I tried it once, and it was disgusting."

According to the package, it contained slippery elm, marshmallow, and fennel, but all I could taste was the liquorice. I hated liquorice.

Callahan cursed under his breath. "If she drank it regularly, it's unlikely to have killed her. Dammit, I was so sure..."

"What if it was a bad batch? Or somebody put something in it?"

"That's a possibility. But we won't find out until the toxicology results come back, and in the meantime, we're left guessing."

"How long will the toxicology tests take?"

"A week? A month?"

"That long?"

"This isn't CSI. There's a backlog. The lab takes forever, and I want whoever did this in a jail cell yesterday."

And I wanted to go back home to my comfy apartment, but instead, I was left camping in a hovel while a murderer walked free. For the millionth time in my miserable existence, I lamented the fact that life really wasn't fair.

"We still have a lead to follow. Reuben."

"You were serious when you said you'd found him?"

"What, you thought I made it up so you'd bring me lunch?"

I'd never seen Callahan flustered before. "Of course I didn't. It's just that Reuben's proven to be elusive, and..." He gestured at the bag he was still holding. "I'd have brought you lunch anyway."

"You would?"

"Sure. If you need anything picked up from the store, just ask. I guess it can't be easy living with your, uh, condition."

My condition. Once again, I was reminded that I was far from normal.

"You'd help out because it's the neighbourly thing to do?"

"Exactly."

Well, that was disappointing.

"That's very kind of you."

"Between you and me, it gets kind of lonely living in a new city." Tell me about it. I had to move every time I started looking too young for my age. "Sometimes, it can be nice to see a friendly face at the end of the day."

"You've got friends, though. What about Lieutenant Shepherd and Cecily Dorrington?"

"Outside of work, they're the only people I know here. I went to school with Shep. Yeah, I meet them for dinner most weeks, but I can't play third wheel every night."

And I couldn't eat dinner with Callahan every night, especially after I moved back to Berkshire Place, but perhaps once or twice a week while the case was still open... His company made staying in Sunset Tower bearable, even if we did bicker a bit.

"If you want to play third wheel to Muse, I can take a turn at buying dinner one night. As you've probably gathered, I don't get out much."

Now Callahan looked at me funny. "*You* want to buy *me* dinner?"

"Why is that so strange? You've bought me food twice."

He took a step back, quickly as if I'd flipped a switch. Uh-oh. "Anyone I've had contact with under colour of authority, I have to tread carefully around. You're a witness in my case. If I accepted gifts, people might say I had power over you that could be misused."

Power over me? *No, I don't think so.* What century did he think this was? Still, I saw how it might look. A jury might say he'd influenced me, and I didn't want anything to jeopardise justice for Serenity.

"What, you think I'm asking you out on a date? Detective Callahan, I merely want to know what's going on with the investigation."

Aw, I'd managed to make him blush. "The investigation. Right."

"What if you just happened to stop by with more questions at the end of your shift, and I just happened to have got carried away ordering takeout, and you just happened to give me an update while we were eating? Would that be okay? Hey, bring your partner if you want." What was I even saying? "The more, the merrier."

I hated myself for pushing Callahan that way. Hated being so desperate for company that I'd lure a cop to my house with food just to converse for an hour. Boy, I really needed to get back to work. Hopefully, Blane would be able to reopen the club tomorrow, and I could find myself someone to eat as well as escaping from this bird box of an apartment. Then my life would start to level out again.

"You probably have more interest in police work than my partner," Callahan said. "I found out today that she wants to become a teacher."

"A teacher? Wow, that's...a change."

"It's a long story." He neatly sidestepped my previous question about dinner and changed the subject. "What can you tell me about Reuben?"

I relayed the details of my internet search and showed Callahan the web page for Broderick, Matherson and Pope. Digital Reuben was still there, smiling worriedly as though he knew what was coming.

"No contact details," Callahan mused. "I'll have to go through the firm's switchboard." He pulled out his phone and tried dialling. "The office is closed on Sundays."

"I know."

"You know? Vee, you shouldn't have tried calling them yourself. You're a witness, not a detective."

"And yet I was the one who found Reuben."

"Touché."

"Sorry."

"I'm grateful for your help, don't think I'm not, but I also don't want you to get hurt. This is a murder case, remember? I'll pay him a visit tomorrow morning."

I wanted to pay Reuben a visit, and soon. I wanted to look him in the eye and ask him what happened with Serenity. Something told me Reuben was important.

But I couldn't go. Not just because Callahan would be annoyed, but due to that little problem with daylight. *Merde*, I hated being trapped like this.

"What about calling the cell company? They might have a record of his home address. You could visit him tonight and save half a day."

"I can't get cell phone data without a warrant. The Supreme Court banned that in the US." Callahan opened up more distance between us. "I'll give you an update tomorrow."

Did that mean he was coming over? Or would he just call? Before I could ask, he was halfway through the door.

"Enjoy your lunch, Vee."

A sub. He'd bought me a meatball marinara sub from Petronelli's, and it was still warm. I set it on a chipped plate beside my laptop while I opened up a new browser tab. It was cute, the way Callahan followed the rules, but thankfully, I'd been living in a grey area for more than two centuries so I'd had plenty of practice at bending them. There had to be a faster way to find Reuben.

Now that I had his surname, I went back to Facebook. There he was—Reuben Broderick. He didn't post much, just the occasional one-line status update and a few thank yous on a handful of "Happy Birthday!" messages dated two weeks ago. The only photo of his actual face showed him posing next to a rodeo horse with a trophy. A petite girl with coppery brown hair stood next to him, and he'd tagged her—Marnie Broderick. His sister? She had the same jawline. Reuben himself looked far more comfortable outside in dusty cowboy boots than he did lawyering in a fancy suit or fidgeting outside Club Dead.

Luckily, Marnie seemed to be more social than her maybe-brother. In fact, the green dot showed she was online at this very moment. Remember that grey area I mentioned?

Jenny Pell: Hi! You're Reuben's sister, right? We haven't met, but I'm a friend of his here in Vegas. I got back from my vacation yesterday and I need to give him his birthday gift, but he's not picking up the phone. Just checking he's okay?

The reply was almost instantaneous.

Marnie Broderick: Oh, he's fine, but he lost his cell again. You'll need to use his temporary number. Give him a hug from me!

She'd attached a screenshot with his contact details, and now I had both numbers as well as his home address. Hallelujah. Logic said I should call Callahan right away, but I knew he wouldn't take me along, not after his little speech earlier. It would be dark soon. What if I paid Reuben a quick visit myself? Callahan would be irked for sure, but Serenity was my friend, dammit, and at least that way I'd be able to see Reuben's reactions first-hand.

What should I do? Sneak over to his apartment? Or do the honourable thing and tell the detective what I'd found?

CHAPTER 16

Jack

"A baby? No way, man. No way."

Joaquin paced his tiny living room, stepping over an empty pizza box and a pair of discarded sneakers as he did so. A hand tore through his messy black hair. Either the guy was Oscar-worthy, or the news of Lyla's pregnancy had surprised him as much as it had me.

He didn't appear to have gotten much sleep since our last chat, and if I wasn't such a fucking cynic, I'd say Lyla's death had cut him deep. The break-up had been her decision, he'd told me. She'd said she needed space, time to focus on her band and her career without worrying about a boyfriend waiting for her at home. Joaquin had offered her the space. Confided that even after she left, he'd hoped she'd change her mind and come back to him someday.

Was he telling the truth? None of the witnesses had come up with an alternate story so far, which meant I gave him the benefit of the doubt.

"She didn't mention the pregnancy at all? Hint at it?"

"If she had, you think I'd have let her walk away? She never came right out and said so, but part of the reason she left was because she didn't want to settle down. I knew it." A faint smile ghosted over his lips, but only for a second. "Sometimes, she said I knew her better than she knew herself. Serenity never imagined herself as a mom, but I was always open about the fact that I wanted kids. I figured she didn't have much of a mother figure in her life to learn from."

"But you did?"

"I got four sisters and a brother. Family means a lot to me. Spent half my life babysitting while Momma went out to work." Another turn. Five more steps. "Are you sure? Sure Serenity was pregnant? There couldn't have been a mistake?"

I believed him when he said he was a family man. Although the apartment was a dump, a small side table near the ratty green couch was clear of clutter, empty save for a cluster of framed photos, a child's painting, and a lumpy clay model that might have been a duck. Joaquin's family plus the fruits of his siblings' labour, if I had to take a guess. No one would have kept something so ugly unless they cared.

"I'm sorry you had to hear it this way. How old are your brothers and sisters?"

"Paulo and Rosaria are twins, both a year older. Silvia's two years younger, and Abril's three years younger than her. Valery was the surprise." I thought I detected a faint grimace, surprising given Joaquin's earlier comments. "She's turned fourteen last month."

"You weren't happy about Valery?"

"She's a great kid, just...unexpected. Papa had gotten the snip three years earlier."

"Ah. And he didn't take it well?"

"Him and Mom had been arguing for a while, but... Is this even relevant? To Serenity, I mean."

Possibly. Joaquin had an alibi for Lyla's murder, but it was shaky. He claimed he'd been right there in the apartment from dusk till dawn, along with his roommate and a young lady named Delilah. But further questioning had revealed that after a brief "hi, how are you?" conversation, Joaquin had made himself scarce while the roommate and his girl watched a movie. The roommate had confirmed the story, but the layout of the apartment, with the two bedrooms opening off the entry vestibule, meant it wouldn't have been difficult for Joaquin to slip out. Hell, if the roommate watched a movie the way I had with Angie when we'd first started dating—which was to say with my eyes closed and my hands busy—a herd of fuckin' buffalo could've stampeded through the damn vestibule and he wouldn't have noticed a thing.

I ignored Joaquin's question and fired back with one of my own. "How did that make you feel? Your mom cheating?"

"How do you think it made me feel?" he snapped. "Papa left. Momma had to work three jobs to support us, and my brother didn't make it to college."

Bingo. Now we had anger. Until that point, Joaquin had only shown grief dulled by the stoicism of a man who expected the worst the world had to offer and usually got it.

"So cheating's something that upsets you?"

"Damn right. And before you ask, I never cheated on Serenity. *Never.*"

He spoke with conviction, but the background check showed he'd taken acting classes before settling on a career as a personal trainer.

"How about the other way around? I hate to ask this, but are you certain you were the father of her baby?"

Joaquin stopped dead. *Dead.* Not even kidding. He froze, and the only sign he was still alive came as his face paled a couple of shades. Fuck, that was hard to fake.

"You okay? Should I call someone?"

He slumped into a chair, and a pile of empty Wong Fu's takeout cartons crumpled beneath him. I swung towards believing his story, and I felt bad for the guy—his life was a mess, both literally and figuratively.

"You think she was seeing another guy?" he asked, his voice barely above a whisper.

"We don't have any evidence of that right now, but it's a possibility we need to consider. Would you be willing to give a DNA sample?"

"Oh, man." The hand scraped through his hair again. It was already thinning, and if he kept that up, he wouldn't have much left to style into what could best be described as hobo chic. "Yeah, I'll give a sample. That *hijo de puta* needs to be in jail. What do you need? Blood? Strands of my hair?"

Joaquin moved to pull a chunk out, and I put up a hand to stop him. No way did I want to contribute towards his impending baldness.

"If you could drop in to the station tomorrow, a lab tech will swab a sample of cells from your mouth."

"That's it?"

"That's it."

And it was. The end of a promising lead, I mean. This was a game of chutes and ladders, and any suspect who agreed to a DNA test that easily—no argument, no threats of lawyering up—practically slid off the board while I was left clinging to a ladder, or worse, scrambling up a chute on my hands and knees while someone shot icy water at me from a fire hose.

"I'll let them know to expect you. Does nine a.m. work?" I finished.

Please, spare me the awkward negotiations I went through with Vee.

"Can we make it the afternoon? I'm training clients from seven till two thirty."

I nodded. The results would take days if not weeks to

come through, but for now, I'd have to focus on other avenues of investigation.

"Did Lyla ever mention a guy called Reuben?"

Joaquin's hands balled into fists. "That's him? That's the guy? I thought you said you didn't know who he was?"

"It's just a name that's come up. Do you know him?"

"Reuben? No, I never heard the name, not from Serenity. Lyla. Hell, it's weird hearing her real name. She mostly stopped using it after she joined the band." Joaquin had resumed pacing, but now he paused mid-step. "*The band*. Was it one of those assholes in the band?"

So there was no love lost between them. "Why do you say that?"

I'd had the same thought myself. By all accounts, Lyla had been focused on her music, which meant time spent writing, rehearsing, touring, and performing with Trist, Lux, and Invi. I hesitated to call them musicians because Shep had played me some of their YouTube videos and they'd sent me reaching for the earplugs, but women seemed to like them, judging by the comments underneath. They'd certainly had the opportunity to knock Lyla up, and presumably the equipment too, but would she have risked complicating things by sleeping with a colleague? My father, God rest his soul, had imparted many nuggets of wisdom over the years, an important one being, "Don't shit where you eat, son."

Had anyone told Lyla the same thing?

"Why? Because once the band started to take off, she didn't have time for anything else."

"Did she strike you as interested in any of the band?"

"Not really, not outside of the music," Joaquin said on a sigh. "Lux had a girlfriend I met a few times, Trist's gay—at least, I think so—and Invi's a miserable bastard. But I was still second best, you know? And who else would it have been?"

"Their closeness irked you?"

"A little. But singing was Serenity's dream, and I'd have supported her. I told her that. I'd have stood by her if she was pregnant too."

And yet she'd still ended things. Why?

"We'll be looking at all the angles. Did any other guys come sniffing around? Fans? Groupies?"

"Well, yeah, but she never reciprocated."

"Did any of them bother her? Upset her that you noticed?"

"Why? You think a fan killed her?"

"As I said—we're investigating every angle." I raised an eyebrow as Joaquin took a step back, presumably to carry on wearing a hole in the threadbare carpet. When the light caught it right, I could see a darker line where he'd been walking. "Could you answer the question, please?"

"She never mentioned a problem, but I didn't go to every show. They went on late, and I start work early."

"No phone calls? Messages? Flowers to her door?"

Joaquin paused mid-stride as something twanged in his brain, one sneaker-clad foot hovering an inch above the floor.

"Not flowers, but someone sent chocolates to the door once. Cheap ones. The kind with the liquor in them, but Serenity had quit drinking so she threw them in the trash."

"How long ago? She quit drinking recently, didn't she?" Right after she got pregnant.

"Like, a month? Six weeks? She said they were from a guy she used to know, someone from her past, but she made a face when she said his name. Sort of screwed up her mouth." He tried to replicate the look and managed a passable imitation of disgust. "I asked if she wanted me to speak to him, and she said it was fine. That she'd deal with it."

"A name?" My palms tingled. "She mentioned a name? What was it?"

"Uh..."

Disgust turned to concentration as Joaquin searched the recesses of his mind. A bottle that once contained Brain Boost Superfood Smoothie lay empty on the coffee table, and I kept my fingers crossed that the blueberries and chia seeds had kept his synapses healthy.

"It began with a J," he said finally. "Same as my name, but pronounced different. One syllable, I think. Jake? Jed? Something like that."

"If you remember, call me, okay?"

Joaquin bobbed his head. He already had my card from my last visit. I'd spotted it on the table in the vestibule as I'd walked in, right where he'd dropped it after I handed it over.

"And that was it? Lyla—Serenity—said she'd deal with it?"

"That was what she said, man."

"Did she seem worried? Tense?"

"More annoyed because she was late getting to the club."

"Can you remember who brought the candy?"

"Some delivery guy on a bike."

"You saw the bike?" Lyla had lived in a second-floor apartment.

"No, but he was wearing spandex pants. Ain't never seen a UPS guy wearing spandex."

I had to agree with that point. "Did you see a logo? The name of the delivery service?"

"Just the spandex. That's all. I only saw him for, like, a second."

How many messenger services in Vegas had spandex uniforms? Probably most of them.

"If you do remember any other details, will you call me?"

"Right away. Promise me one thing—that you'll catch the person who killed Serenity." Joaquin's eyes glistened as the last rays of the afternoon sun filtered through the grimy windows. "She might have been...distracted, but I loved her. I always will. She didn't deserve this."

"Nobody deserves to die."

"What if whoever killed her does it again?"

That was something I didn't much want to think about.

"We aim to prevent that from happening."

Protect and fucking serve, right?

CHAPTER 17

Jack

My phone buzzed with an incoming email as I jogged down the stairs in Joaquin's apartment building. Taking the elevator would have been faster, but when I was eight years old, I'd gotten stuck in one alone for five hours, which kind of put me off elevators for life. Nobody had answered the emergency intercom, my parents thought I was at a buddy's house, and only the stubborn insistence of Mrs. Stranbowski on the floor above—who was determined to get to her book club—had led to my discovery at nearly seven o'clock in the evening. She couldn't manage the stairs with her walking frame, and she'd called the super over and over until he came home from his girlfriend's place to help. I'd been down to my last Life Saver by then, and it was damn near freezing. And now? I wasn't claustrophobic or anything—I just preferred to avoid elevators. Less than ten floors, and I took the stairs. Why invite trouble when you didn't have to?

I glanced at the message and felt that all-too-rare rush of satisfaction as an idea came to fruition.

• • •

Date: Sunday 3 December
  Sender: Reuben Broderick
  Subject: Inquiry

Mr. Callahan,
  Thank you for your inquiry about representation in your child custody proceedings. I'll be in touch tomorrow to schedule a meeting with one of our attorneys.
  Reuben Broderick

Although Reuben didn't have his contact details listed on the Broderick, Matherson and Pope website, several of his colleagues did, and the email addresses were always in the same format—firstname.surname. Since all the lawyers I'd ever known had kept their phones handy, even on the golf course, I'd made a guess at Reuben's address, and it had paid off. The best part? He'd included a cell number at the bottom of his sign-off.

I punched it in, then smiled as the phone rang without going to voicemail.

"Reuben Broderick speaking."

Formal, hesitant. Did he get many calls on a weekend?

On the way over to Joaquin's place, I'd considered how to play it if I managed to speak to Broderick today. By waiting until tomorrow and turning up at his office unannounced, I could maintain the element of surprise and reduce the risk of him running if he felt so inclined, but it would also delay proceedings. The first forty-eight hours in a murder investigation were crucial. If we didn't make progress during that initial window, each day that passed after that both lessened the chance of catching the killer and increased the likelihood of them snuffing out another victim. Every minute counted.

I considered the evidence we'd found so far—that Dalton Cooper had lent Chavez money to hire a lawyer, that Broderick *was* a lawyer, and that Joaquin thought the name of the man paying her unwanted attention began with a J. My gut said that Broderick was a possible source of information, not a suspect.

"My name's Jack Callahan, and I'm a detective with the LVMPD. I understand you might have represented a mutual client of ours in a professional capacity."

"I'm just a paralegal. I don't actually represent clients myself."

"Your firm, then. Her name's Lyla Chavez."

"I'm afraid I can't discuss our clients."

"She's dead. Does that make a difference?"

Broderick's gasp said he didn't watch the news. "Ms. Chavez is dead? Are you serious?"

"Unfortunately. She was murdered on Friday night."

"Friday night? I was in the office on Friday night." The relief in his voice was palpable. "We had a big case to prepare for, and nobody left until one a.m. Actually, it was closer to two."

"That's not why I'm calling. You're not a suspect. But I do have some questions, and it would be easier to speak in person." An interviewee's body language often told me what their words didn't. "Are you free this evening?"

"I guess so. I mean, I need to eat dinner. But as I said, we can't break client confidentiality, even after death."

At this stage, I'd take whatever information I could get.

"We can discuss that when we meet."

"Perhaps we should do this at the office?"

Shit. "That's an option, but would you feel comfortable

waiting an extra day knowing there's a murderer walking the streets of Las Vegas?"

"No, of course not, but—"

"I'm glad we see eye to eye on this. What's your address? I'll come right over."

Don't back out now. I needed solutions, not more fucking problems.

"Okay." Broderick rattled off an address not too far away. "Lyla was nice. And she was *murdered*? I can't believe it."

I could, especially after seeing her brain in a jar on Dr. Rashid's desk. It was always the nice ones who got taken too soon. If all the assholes offed each other, nobody except Captain Lindsay would care and I might even have time for a social life.

"I'll be there in half an hour."

Researching or drafting briefs or fetching coffee or whatever it was paralegals did paid a hell of a lot more than being a cop, that was for sure. Reuben Broderick's building rose into the night sky, a gleaming edifice of glass and steel that made Sunset Tower's brick-and-birdshit facade look like a dystopian horror story. I was in the wrong damn job.

The marble floor of the lobby stretched towards a bank of elevators, dappled in the shade of a forest of drooping ficus trees. I reached out and rubbed a leaf between my finger and thumb. Plastic. The delicate aroma of synthetic flowers drifted among the fauxliage as I wove between pleather chairs, searching for the stairs that fire regulations said must be present. Broderick lived on the eighth floor. Since I'd skipped my last three gym sessions, I had more of an incentive than usual to make the climb.

Unfortunately, that gave me more time to think. Had I

done the right thing in coming back to police work? The highs of closing a challenging case had led me back into the fold like a junkie looking for his fix, but instead of chasing the dragon, I hunted monsters of the worst kind. Once upon a time, Angie had helped me to get through the lows, those all-too-frequent days wasted on chasing fruitless leads and dealing with office politics. I'd lost myself in her.

Now? Now, I was just lost, stuck in a dark pit I couldn't climb out of.

But yesterday evening, I'd seen a chink of light.

"Detective Callahan?"

Broderick had answered the intercom a second after I pressed the buzzer beside the outer door, and now he peered from his apartment, waiting. Keen to help or eager to get rid of me? I moved the edge of my leather jacket so he could see the shield clipped to my belt.

"I appreciate your agreeing to speak with me this evening."

Broderick paused just inside the door, his thoughts transparent. Should he be polite and offer me a drink? Or would that prolong the agony?

"Glass of water?" he finally offered.

"Thanks. Lived here long?"

"Eleven months. Since I moved to the city."

"Oh? Where'd you come from?"

"Just outside Twin Falls, Idaho."

"I thought maybe your father was a partner at the law firm. The Broderick in Broderick, Matherson and Pope."

"Michael Broderick's my uncle."

"Right. How do you like working there?"

"Beats herding cattle with my pop."

So Reuben was a farmer's son. That didn't surprise me. He might have been in Vegas for almost a year, but he still hadn't lost the calluses on his hands, and the way he walked— steadily with a hint of a swagger—suggested he was more at home in a barn than a boardroom. But that didn't mean he hadn't picked up a few tips during his time at Broderick, Matherson and Pope. What followed was the legal equivalent of "name, rank, and serial number." Yes, the firm had represented Lyla Chavez. No, Reuben couldn't divulge the details of the matter, but yes, it had been ongoing at the time of her death.

"Why were you at Club Dead last month?" I asked.

He looked away, eyes cast down towards his bare feet. "Impulse, I guess. I was on my way to the office. She needed to sign some papers, and we'd left messages for her but she hadn't gotten back to us, so I thought I could remind her. She said she always worked late. Or, you know, early."

"Do you do that for all your clients? Drop into their place of work?"

"No. I mean, occasionally we visit them if the need arises." A hint of colour crept up his cheeks. Ah. So he'd been fond of her. "Lyla wasn't like our regular clients."

"I see."

"She wasn't there, anyway. Wait, how do you know *I* was there?"

"A witness saw you."

He nodded, understanding. "The pretty girl with the blue hair?"

Had Vee's hair been blue at that time? Shit, I hadn't wanted to bring her into this.

"I'm not at liberty to discuss the specifics. Did Ms. Chavez show up to sign the papers?"

"Uh, yes. Yes, she did, later that day. And..."

"And?"

Pink turned to red. Fondness to embarrassment. "And she also reminded me that none of her friends knew about her, uh, issue, and she wanted to keep it that way. I think the blue-haired girl must've told her I'd swung by. So you'll understand why I can't break her confidentiality, right?"

"I'm not her friend. I'm a cop."

Reuben gave a helpless shrug. "I'll speak to my uncle tomorrow, see if there's anything more we can do."

I sensed I wasn't going to get any more information from Broderick that evening. While I might have found him, he'd also stuck his boot in my face and pushed me a little farther down the chute.

"You do that. Don't forget this is a murder investigation. We've got no interest in tarnishing Ms. Chavez's memory, merely in trying to catch the man who killed her."

Reuben's head bobbed, and a lock of light-brown hair flopped in front of one eye. "I understand that. I do."

Never did get that glass of water.

What was the time? Eight o'clock, and my stomach reminded me I hadn't eaten for hours. Outside, the neon lights of a diner shone opposite Broderick's building, and I figured I could grab dinner and then fit in another hour or two of work.

Good Eats
Proudly Serving Nevada Since 1965!

Probably at the same scratched metal counter. The diner wasn't just retro, I'd hazard a guess it was original too. No doubt it had been cutting edge in the sixties, but Vegas had grown up around it and now the place just looked tired. Still, it had survived for more than half a century, which meant that the food was good or else it was a front for something. Either way, I was tempted to give it a try.

Unless...

No. No way. I wasn't getting Wong Fu's, and I definitely

wasn't getting Wong Fu's for two. Quite apart from the ethical issues, if I showed up at Vee's door with dinner two nights running, I'd only be one step away from Jed/Jake and his unwanted chocolates. A cheeseburger and fries for one would be fine. Cecily had invited me over for dinner on Friday, so I'd do my penance then with a plateful of organic vegetables. Don't get me wrong, she was a great cook, but when I first moved to Vegas, she'd fed me every night for two weeks and I'd dropped a pants size.

Angie used to curse my rabid metabolism. Every damn month, she'd started a new diet even though she looked perfect, but a week in, and she'd be eating from my plate again. Back then, I used to grumble about it—what man wouldn't when the best parts of his dinner vanished before his eyes—but now I dreamed of losing half my food to the woman I loved.

Six of the eight stools in front of the counter were occupied when I walked into Good Eats—always a positive sign—and although the decor was tired, it looked clean. Until that moment, I hadn't realised how exhausted I was. How many hours of sleep had I gotten over the last three days? Single digits, no more.

"What can I get ya, hun?"

"What does the 'Good Eats Special' come with?"

"Bacon, double cheese, fries, onion rings..."

I tuned out as I caught a flash of pink in my peripheral vision, and it didn't come from the gaudy lights. What the hell? Tell me that was *not* Vee skulking along the sidewalk.

Fuck, it was. That little minx had somehow found Broderick's address because now she was standing right outside his building, staring up at the eighth floor where I'd been only minutes before. Annoyance flashed through me, and I was halfway to the door of the diner before I stopped myself.

Wait a second...

Yes, I couldn't deny it stung that Vee had gone behind my back, but would it really be a bad thing if she asked Reuben a few questions? He'd thought she was pretty, but she was far more than that. Vee was beautiful and *sneaky*. Maybe, just maybe, he'd let something slip if she turned her charms on him.

"You okay, hun?"

I forced myself to unclench my fists and smile at the brunette behind the counter.

"I'll have the special and a black coffee."

And a seat by the window so I could see when my devious neighbour reappeared. I might have stood back and waited while Vee smiled and thanked the guy who held the door open for her to slip into Broderick's apartment building, but one thing was for certain—we'd be having words later on.

Vee

Reuben's building was okay. Not lovely, but a thousand times better than Sunset Tower. The fake jungle in the lobby made me yearn for the lush foliage in my own building. Berkshire Place even had an aquarium. I loved the aquarium. Sometimes in the early hours, I'd settle myself into one of the leather armchairs next to it and just watch the fish. Scuba diving was on my never-to-be-achieved bucket list, along with sunbathing on the beach and seeing the Grand Canyon in all its colourful glory.

The sickly aroma of floral cleaning products made me gag as I hurried past to the elevators. There were occasions when having an enhanced sense of smell was a benefit—when a delicate rosebud became a bouquet, for example, or a mug of fresh coffee turned into sensory overload, or the faintest whiff of smoke meant I could alert a family to a fire that had started in their home. That sure had been a dramatic evening. The firemen had yelled at me when I ran back inside to rescue the cat, but the smiles as I handed him back to his people before slipping quietly into the night meant my efforts had been worth the trouble.

But today? Today, I needed a clothespin to block out the stench.

Right now, it wasn't just my eyes and my nose that were working overtime. Sixth sense made the hairs on the back of my neck prickle as the elevator rumbled its way down the shaft. There wasn't anybody else in the lobby, so why did I feel as if I was being watched?

A shiver ran through me as the doors opened, and when I stepped on board and turned, I took the opportunity to look around. Pedestrians strolled past outside the windows, a tourist posed for a photo in front of the diner opposite, and a cab driver honked at a truck that got in his way. Nothing out of the ordinary.

But the feeling wouldn't go away.

Until the 1950s when I'd discovered a new income stream that allowed me to hide away in luxury, I'd lived by my instincts, and I trusted my gut. Something was up. I wasn't afraid of a physical threat, not today anyway, but the creepy vibe stayed with me as I pressed the button for the eighth floor. I hadn't buzzed Reuben before I tailgated another resident into the building. Would he be home? On a Sunday evening, I figured there was a fifty-fifty chance.

"Yes?"

The apartment door swung open ten seconds after I knocked, and I broke into a genuine smile when I recognised the man I'd seen in the club a few weeks ago. His hair was shorter now, but he still had the same slightly gormless look about him.

"Reuben?"

A moment passed before recognition flickered in his eyes.

"Hey, you're that waitress from Club Dead—Lyla Chavez's friend. You had blue hair before?"

I nodded.

"How did you get in here?"

"A guy held the door open for me. Sorry for the unexpected visit, but I need to talk to you."

"About Lyla?"

What else?

"Yes, about Lyla. Did..." Dammit, I'd never been good at the touchy-feely stuff. Perhaps because death had become a way of life for me. "Did you know she passed away?"

"The cop just told me."

"What cop?"

"The detective investigating her murder."

The niggle intensified. "Did you get his name?"

"Detective Callahan. Brown hair, leather jacket—you probably passed him in the street on your way here."

No, I'd definitely have noticed. And if he'd seen yours truly, he'd have marched me back to Sunset Tower and handcuffed me to my refrigerator. But his proximity explained why I was so unsettled. My subconscious had known Callahan was close even if my conscious mind didn't.

"I didn't see him. Perhaps he went in the other direction?"

Reuben stared at me for a beat. "Uh, why are you here?"

"So I realise we haven't properly met and this is kind of awkward, but Serenity—Lyla..." I sniffled for effect. "She told me that if anything ever happened to her, I should find you and talk to you."

"She did?"

"I was scared, you know, when she started talking that way. And when I pushed for more details, she sort of brushed it off. Said it was probably nothing. We'd had a few drinks, and I thought maybe she was being melodramatic because she got like that sometimes, and then nothing happened so I pushed it to the back of my mind, but now she's dead, and...and..."

I let the tears come. It wasn't difficult to conjure them—I just thought back to the early years with Voltaire, those dark days when I'd tried to slit my wrists over and over only for them to heal before my eyes. A stake through the heart didn't work reliably either, contrary to rumour. Occasionally a vampire got lucky, but Voltaire had watched me fall from a second-floor window onto a sharpened pole, laughing as he sipped wine, and I'd lived to suffer the consequences. My pathetic attempts amused rather than upset him.

"You need to use a cursed stake, *chérie*," he'd told me. "Too bad they all got destroyed in the fire at Cambrai Cathedral."

Voltaire's satisfied smile told me he'd taken up arson as a hobby. "I hate you."

"Strong words, *mon petit jouet*."

He called me his plaything, but that still hadn't stopped him from teaching me a lesson.

When I realised I couldn't end things by force, I'd refused nourishment. Stopped drinking the human blood that gave a vampire strength. At first, Voltaire had tried to force it down my throat, but I'd batted the cups away and scratched his face, which had healed faster than my wrists, leaving smooth, pale skin behind. But eventually, he tired of fighting and simply locked me in the basement. First, I waited for him to reappear, but when he didn't come, I waited for death. For nothingness. But it never came either. I grew weaker and weaker until I was nothing but a frail carapace dragging myself along the floor, but my heart just wouldn't give up. My lungs kept snatching ragged breaths even as I begged them not to. And after three months of hell, months that felt like years, Voltaire finally returned.

"Drink," he told me, holding out a crystal goblet.

Half-delirious, that was the moment I finally broke. I snatched the glass of still-warm blood and poured it into my mouth. My body might have regenerated in minutes, but when I followed Voltaire up the rickety wooden stairs, I wasn't the girl I'd been before. Genevieve 2.0 was weak and full of loathing, both for myself and for the man who'd made me that way. Trapped in a nightmare. Trapped *with* a nightmare. It had taken me years to finally break free and learn to accept myself as best I could. Genevieve 3.0 still hated to drink from the living, but I gave them a taste of myself in return. A sweetener, if you like.

Why hadn't I simply walked out into the sunlight, you ask? Well, I'd tried that too. And it turned out even UV couldn't kill me; it just hurt like hell. Everything blistered. *Everything*. Even my *eyeballs*. And sunlight was the one thing that I couldn't heal from in a hurry. It had taken two months, gallons of blood, and several thousand smug reminders of "I told you so" from Voltaire before I'd recovered.

I forced a smile for Reuben through my tears. "Look at me —we've barely met, and now I'm crying outside your door."

"I guess you should come in."

He stepped back and opened the door wider. How much had he told Callahan? Was I wasting my time? Probably, but I figured I may as well take a chance. I owed Serenity my best effort.

Inside, Reuben's apartment was nice but not fancy. Functional. That was a good word. Off-white walls, a beige carpet, a sofa facing a TV tuned to the news, and a dining table covered in papers. It looked as though he'd brought work home with him. The place smelled vaguely of fast food, and a glimpse of a bare kitchen through an open doorway to my left led me to suspect Reuben wasn't much of a cook.

"So, you were friends with Lyla, huh?"

"Yes, except she was always Serenity to me. Nobody called her Lyla."

"Right. I think she told me that once."

"I suppose with you being her lawyer, she'd have wanted to stay formal."

"I wasn't actually her lawyer. That was my uncle. I just helped out with her case."

Oops.

"Even so, she seemed really impressed with everything you did for her. She said you went above and beyond." Such as dropping in to visit her at work. "And it was you she told me to speak to."

He preened a little, and I imagined he didn't get many people singing his praises. How far would flattery get me?

"I'm glad she was happy with my work, but we have this thing called attorney-client privilege." Oh, rats. "Even after a client dies, we still can't disclose information about their affairs."

"In that case, I'm sorry to have disturbed you. I guess maybe Serenity—Lyla—I guess she didn't realise that or she wouldn't have sent me." But rather than heading toward the door, I slumped onto the sofa. "Did you know her for long? Or aren't you allowed to tell me?"

Reuben fidgeted a bit, no doubt weighing up his options. Should he throw this virtual stranger out of his apartment so he could get on with his work? Or do the gentlemanly thing and comfort a distressed woman? As I'd hoped, manners won out and he took a seat in the armchair opposite.

"I first met Lyla around six months ago. How about you?"

Six months? That was when her career really began to take off. It would have made sense for Broderick, Matherson and Pope to have represented her on a contractual matter, but Reuben's bio said he worked in family law. What family was she having trouble with?

"Six months, huh? It was eight months for me, but it felt like so much longer."

"She sure made an impression when she walked through the door at work. Most clients going through..." What? *Through what?* "Through what Lyla went through are older."

Dammit, why couldn't he just tell me?

Not for the first time in my life, I cursed a lawyer. Had Reuben been taking lessons from Blane's buddy Beauregard?

CHAPTER 19

Vee

Take a deep breath, Vee. What was that phrase I'd learned in England? Ah, yes—softly, softly, catchee monkey.

"I guess whatever the problem was, Serenity didn't let it affect her work. Did you ever hear her sing live?"

Reuben shook his head. "No, I never did. Wanted to, though. She said she'd get me tickets to one of her gigs, but then *my* work..." He waved towards the papers on the table. "Work always wins."

"Sometimes, there are benefits to being a lowly cocktail waitress. Not many, but..."

I laughed when Reuben laughed. That was a trick I'd learned at the club—establish rapport, and I got better tips. I didn't actually need the tips, but I liked the challenge.

"There's been a time or two when I've considered going back home to work on the ranch."

"A ranch? With horses? I've always dreamed of galloping a horse across the prairie at sunrise."

"Ever sat on a horse?"

"Once when I was little, but that feels as if it was centuries ago."

Back when women rode side-saddle, in fact. Champignon, my childhood pony, had been a stubborn beast who'd thrown me so many times my mama forbade me to ride him. But I still snuck out to the stables whenever my nanny's back was turned. Ten-year-old me had been a daredevil.

"If you want to give it another try, I'd recommend Cloud Creek Ranch. It's not too far from here."

Even if it were on the doorstep, a visit would still have been out of the question. And we were getting off topic. I needed to bring us back on track.

"Lyla told me about a place that did camel safaris. We were gonna go one day, but..." I threw in another sniffle for good measure. "But now we never will."

"Let me get you a tissue. Uh, do you want a drink?"

"Thank you. And yes, please. I'm really sorry about this, all the..." I waved at my face. "I'm such a mess, but I don't have anyone else to talk to. I just miss Serenity so, so much."

"Water? Coffee? Something stronger?"

Yes! "Do you have any wine?"

"Red or white?"

"Whichever you prefer."

Because while alcohol would barely affect me, it might well loosen Reuben's tongue. All I had to do was keep him talking for long enough to let down his guard.

And it seemed that Reuben was lonely too because once he started speaking—and drinking—I thought he'd never stop. Work was forgotten as he sipped his way through one, two, three glasses of white. He really had liked Serenity. Maybe even in a slightly unprofessional way, although it seemed he'd never crossed any sort of line with her. I let the conversation meander from Reuben's upbringing on the ranch to shows in Las Vegas to restaurants to Muse and her antics, but every so often, I brought us back to Serenity and slipped in a question or two. And in return, he let little snippets of information escape.

"I'm surprised she wasn't more bitter, you know?" Reuben said. "Most women in her position are *really* bitter."

Bitter? Why would Serenity be bitter? That was an interesting choice of word. Whenever I engaged a lawyer, I was usually either dotting the i's and crossing the t's or a tiny bit angry. "Bitter" suggested that Serenity's resentment had been building up over time. But who had she been upset at? I knew it was a man—Reuben had referred to Serenity's problem as "he" soon after his second glass of Sauvignon Blanc.

"That was Lyla—sweet all over."

"Sweet, yeah." Reuben hiccupped, then giggled. Oh dear. "She lit up the offish when she walked in. Even our receptionisht loved her, and Marla can be...well, I shouldn't shpeak ill of her, but...uh, *dragon*..."

"It's okay, I get it. When I was in high school, I worked in an office over summer vacation, and we had a receptionist just like her. Only smiles for her favourites, right?"

Reuben tried to nod in agreement, but rather than moving up and down, his head wobbled about like a bobblehead doll's. Uh-oh. Perhaps we were reaching the limits of his alcohol tolerance. His hair flopped over his forehead, and when he tried to push it back into place, he jabbed himself in the eye instead.

"Ow."

Ah, crap. I needed to get a move on if I was going to get the answers I needed.

"Lyla would have been a star, but she was still so down to earth. And kind too. She once noticed a fan getting pushed around and stopped her set to help."

"Thatsh...thatsh nice."

"And now *I* want to help *her*. She deserves a dignified

send-off, but Detective Callahan mentioned that the police can't trace her next of kin. Do you know who I could call?"

"Nobody. There's nobody."

"Her brother?"

"What brother?"

So he wasn't the source of the problems, then. "Her father?"

"Huh? She never... She never..."

"She never what?"

"I swear, if I'd thought he was dangerous, just...just..."

Reuben keeled over, and I only just caught his wine glass before it hit the floor. Good old vampire reactions saved me again. A soft snore rumbled out of him, and he hugged the cushion against his chest. Dammit. I'd been so, so close.

Still, I was further forward than I had been before—I'd ruled out Serenity's brother, and when I'd mentioned her father, Reuben had looked genuinely confused as well as a bit...droopy.

But who did that leave?

Who did Reuben think wasn't dangerous?

And who *was* going to arrange her funeral? Nobody had mentioned taking responsibility. If it was going to fall to me, I should start making arrangements, and the prospect left me hollow. Not for the obvious reason—I'd be saying goodbye to a friend—but because I'd spent years daydreaming about my own funeral the way other girls dreamed of their wedding. We always wish for what we can't have, right? I didn't even want a fancy affair, just a plain wooden casket and a simple goodbye. Barber's "Adagio for Strings" playing as I was finally lowered into peace. A granite headstone with a short epitaph.

HERE LIES GENEVIEVE ÉLIANE PELLETIER
LOVE TODAY
FOR TOMORROW, EVERYTHING MAY CHANGE.

What would Serenity have wished for? It was hardly a subject I could have brought up in one of our after-work chats over Wong Fu's, was it? *Hey, Serenity, do you want to be buried or cremated?* I pondered the options as I carried Reuben into his bedroom and tucked him under the quilt. Would he remember our conversation? Hopefully not. The last thing I needed was a curious paralegal asking questions about why *I'd* been asking questions. His snores grew louder as I did the washing-up and tossed the three empty wine bottles into the trash. A fourth was still half-full, and that went into the refrigerator, although it deserved to go down the sink. Another problem with my life—I'd spent a hundred years in France, and Voltaire had turned me into a wine snob. He might have had his faults—many, many faults—but he did know how to pick out an excellent vintage.

"*Au revoir*, Reuben," I whispered as I clicked the apartment door shut behind me.

Although I'd rather it were *adieu*. I didn't particularly want to see Reuben again, but knowing my luck, he'd show up at the funeral.

The funeral... Serenity wouldn't have wanted a dreary affair. Perhaps a splash of colour, rock music rather than classical. If I begged, would Wong Fu's help with the catering?

My stomach grumbled, reminding me that I hadn't eaten dinner. I was hungry in more ways than one. Tonight, I needed regular food, but at some point in the next day or two, I'd need to find a human to sip from as well. My strength was ebbing. I'd noticed it when I picked Reuben up, and hauling him into bed had left me red-faced and panting. Plus my canine teeth were elongating. Soon they'd be noticeable.

The lights of a diner twinkled opposite the apartment building, and I was tempted to order a burger and fries rather than making a detour on my way home. Perhaps onion rings too. High cholesterol wasn't an issue—there had to be the occasional perk to eternal damnation.

But I kept walking because for some reason, this neighbourhood left me twitchy. That creepy-crawly feeling was back.

Why?

"Busy evening?"

I jumped a foot in the air as Callahan's lips brushed my ear. If I'd been human, that little stunt would have given me palpitations.

"What the hell…?"

He looked so damned pleased with himself.

"Question too difficult for you?"

"How dare you sneak up on me like that?"

"It's my job."

"What, scaring people to death?"

"No, catching witnesses when they deliberately interfere in an investigation."

Oops.

"I have no idea what you're talking about. I just stepped out to eat, and somebody at the club recommended this diner."

"Really? I'd recommend it too. You know why? Because I was eating dinner there two and a half hours ago when you walked into Reuben Broderick's apartment building, and the food was delicious."

Oh, crappity crap. Busted. And Callahan's triumphant expression said he knew he'd boxed me into a corner.

"Would it help if I apologised?"

"Babe, the only thing that would help is you telling me exactly what Reuben told you. I saw you smiling when you walked out of his building. You got something."

"Not much."

Callahan folded his arms. "Spill it."

"Over dinner? I truly am starving."

"Fine. I'll join you for a drink, but you're buying this time."

"Of course."

After being caught, it was the least I could do. I'd quite happily fork out for the good wine too, but somehow, I doubted the alcohol trick would work on Jack Callahan.

CHAPTER 20

Jack

Vee sashayed off down the street, and I couldn't decide whether I wanted to kiss her or throw her in jail. For her own good, of course. Having a witness investigating a case while a killer was still on the loose would cause all kinds of trouble. And if Captain Lindsay found out, I'd be sharing a cell with her.

Although now that I thought about it...

Get your mind out of the gutter, Callahan.

Vee held up a hand, and three seconds later, a cab swerved across two lanes of traffic and screeched to a halt in front of her. The only person I'd seen get a ride faster was Cecily, and that was because she usually had photographers following her and the cab drivers slowed out of curiosity.

In New York, cabs hadn't been a concern. People walked places in New York. In Vegas, everyone drove everywhere, including me, but tonight I was in a police-issue Ford and using it to take a witness out for dinner might be seen as improper. Hell, just taking a witness out for dinner was shady, whichever way we got there. Appearances mattered, especially in Captain Lindsay's book. But to hell with it. I wanted to

148

solve this case, and Vee Pelletier was my best asset right now. I'd pick up my car later.

In truth, I was a little surprised that Vee didn't own a vehicle. She seemed to have a somewhat steady job at Club Dead, and if she worked the VIP section regularly, she probably made more in tips than most. Had she ever learned to drive? Or perhaps she'd been scared by an accident?

"Where do you want to eat?" Vee asked.

"I already ate, remember?"

"Right."

She gave a soft giggle. Was she nervous? I hoped so—she should be.

"You know La Nostra Casa?" she asked the driver.

"Everyone knows La Nostra Casa."

Not quite everyone. "No relation to La Cosa Nostra, I hope?"

"It means 'our house.' But Carmelo—he's the owner—he's distantly related to the Gambino family."

Great, as if eating dinner with a witness wasn't bad enough, our host was connected to the Mafia. Part of me wanted to get the hell out of the vehicle, but curiosity made me keep my mouth shut as the driver wove through traffic. Vee stayed quiet too. Trying to come up with a good excuse?

"You don't drive?" I asked to break the silence.

"Uh, no."

"No licence?"

"I have a licence."

"But no car?"

"I don't go out much. There's a bus that goes right from my building to the club."

I had to admire her response. An explanation without an outright answer. The little hesitation at the beginning told me she was lying, or at the very least, she was leaving something out. *Did* she have a car? I made a mental note to abuse my computer privileges later and check.

The cab pulled up outside an Italian restaurant—not one of the glossy, buzzy, touristy places, but a dark storefront with red velvet drapes covering the front window. Dim light filtered out around the name written in an arch on the glass. What were they using in there? Candles?

Yes, it turned out. Fat, half-melted candles lit the centre of every table, assisted in their efforts by tasselled lamps mounted on the walls. Scarred wooden tables sat between gilded chairs and banquettes that matched the drapes—faded and old fashioned—but the place was packed. All locals, by the sound of it.

"The decor's not much, but who cares when they serve the best pasta in Vegas?" Vee murmured as a hostess came to seat us.

"Same table as usual, Signorina Genevieve?" The grey-haired woman looked at least seventy, but she moved with the energy of someone a third of her age. Her red lipstick matched the rose tucked behind one ear. "You two are...together?"

Her brows pinched, and I took that to mean Vee didn't often bring a guest to dinner.

"If you don't mind, and yes."

The hostess led us to a cosy table near the back, one in a quiet corner screened by a potted palm. On the plus side, none of my colleagues were likely to see our tête-à-tête. The problem? If the hostess's ear-to-ear grin was anything to go by, she definitely had the wrong idea about the purpose of this dinner. That was confirmed when she practically ran to the kitchen after she seated us. Her stage whisper would have been heard in the back row.

"Carmelo! Genevieve has a date!"

"Perhaps we should've gone to Taco Bell," Vee muttered. "This is gonna be awkward."

Ouch. Was the idea of dating me that bad? Not that I *did* want to date the pink-haired troublemaker, but...yeah. I held out hope that she was just a big fan of tacos.

"So, about your little excursion tonight..."

"I did what I had to, okay?"

"You interfered in an ongoing investigation."

"You'd have done the same if it was your friend who'd died."

Probably, but I couldn't admit that. I was meant to uphold the law, not encourage other people to bend it.

"You don't know that."

"Oh, really? Well, I know you got nothing from Reuben."

Ouch again.

"Tonight was just a preliminary chat. I'm going through the proper channels, and tomorrow, I'll speak to his boss at the law firm."

"I thought you said it was crucial to work fast if we wanted to solve the case?"

"Yes, I did, but—"

"So I was only taking your advice when I went to speak to Reuben. And as you keep reminding me, I'm a witness and not a cop, which means I don't need to follow the rules. If I want to drop by to visit an acquaintance, I'm perfectly entitled to. Besides..." She gave a coquettish little smile. "Sometimes, unorthodox methods bring the best results."

Oh, no. No way. Surely she hadn't...? Vee hadn't slept with Reuben, had she? I recalled her red cheeks when I first spotted her on the sidewalk outside his building. Her slight breathlessness. Fuck.

Yes, we needed results, but the thought that Vee had been so desperate for justice that she'd resorted to prostituting herself... Screw the lawyers and their rules. *Lawyers and their rules.* Had Reuben known why Vee was there when he'd taken advantage of her? Because surely that had to be some sort of ethics violation?

"Are you okay?" I asked Vee.

She gave me a strange look. "Of course. Why wouldn't I be? I didn't do anything I haven't done before."

Shit, that didn't make it better. My anger at Vee for going behind my back slid away. I barely knew a thing about her past —how bad had it been?

"Babe, I—"

"Let's add some romance," the hostess announced, setting two heart-shaped pink candles beside the stumpy church-style one. "And our chef sends complimentary spinach-and-artichoke bruschetta. Have you two known each other for long?"

"Only a few days," Vee said. "But—"

The hostess clutched both hands over her heart. "Ah, young love. Are you ready to order? Do you want your usual?"

"Yes, please. But, Rosetta—"

"I will ask the chef to grate truffle over the top. You know what they say about truffle, don't you?" Just in case Vee didn't, she added a wink and told her anyway. "It's an aphrodisiac. And what can we get for your *ragazzo*?"

I hadn't opened the menu and I wasn't even hungry, but that didn't seem to matter.

"The tagliatelle with pesto... Yes, I will bring that. The basil, the pine nuts... With an appetiser of honey-glazed figs. And that red wine you like, Genevieve."

"Wait, I—"

But the hostess was already gone, and I had to laugh. "So, you eat here a lot?"

"Two or three times a month. Sure beats cooking. I tried making pasta myself once. Bought one of those little machines to roll it out and everything, but it turns out you need four hands, and also Muse loves playing with raw spaghetti."

"You still have the machine?"

What was I even saying? Inviting myself over to make pasta was the worst idea in the history of bad ideas.

Luckily, Vee shook her head. "My current apartment doesn't have much space."

"Where did you used to live?"

"Why does that matter? I thought we were here so you could interrogate me about Reuben?"

It was telling that she'd rather discuss tonight's activities than what had come before. I'd humour her—for now—but perhaps I'd also do a little digging. Genevieve Pelletier intrigued me like no other girl since...since Angie. Now, that was a sobering thought.

And a very, very dangerous one.

Angie had been a straight shooter, what you saw was what you got. Vee? I'd barely scratched her surface, and if I did probe any deeper, I suspected I'd find a spider's web of cracks.

Tonight, it was safer to stick to the plan. Forget the rest.

CHAPTER 21

Jack

"Right. What *did* you learn during your little chat with Reuben?" I asked Vee.

"That the person causing problems for Serenity was a guy. Family, because that's Reuben's area of expertise, but not her father or her brother. Whatever was going on, she started taking legal advice six months ago."

"And?"

"He didn't strike Reuben as dangerous."

"And?"

"And that's everything. It's still more than you got."

Vee slept with the guy, and that was all he'd given her? Hell, if she got naked and turned her charms on me, I'd dictate an alphabetised summary of every case I'd ever worked. Which was why I absolutely had to keep my pants on around her.

"Let's start at the beginning. Talk me through everything he said. And think about his body language—were there any points when you struck a nerve with your questions?"

"I was careful to avoid nerve-striking. At the beginning, he shut me down pre-emptively by citing attorney-client privilege, so I had to slide my questions in when he wasn't really concentrating."

Like when Reuben was sliding something else in? Vee was one calculating little vamp.

"So—"

"Here's the wine," Rosetta announced. "And a special surprise for you. Carmelo! *Vieni qui!*"

A man not much younger than Rosetta shuffled towards us, holding a... Oh, fuck... Was that a violin? As he played the opening bars of "Innamorata" and everyone in the restaurant turned to stare at us, I wanted to crawl under the tablecloth. So much for keeping a low profile. Several people got out their cell phones and started videoing as Rosetta joined in.

"Back in Italy, she was an opera singer," Vee murmured. "Sorry about this. I've never brought a man here before, and I don't think I ever will again."

I smiled stiffly while Rosetta warbled through both verses, but it still wasn't over. No, when she'd finished, she grasped our hands and squeezed.

"Don't look so nervous, *caro*. Our Genevieve won't bite."

Vee choked on a mouthful of wine and started spluttering. Rosetta grabbed a napkin while I thumped Vee on the back, and some asshole was still fucking filming. Next time, I'd put Vee into my car, ethics be damned, and we'd go home via the drive-through.

"You okay?" I asked her.

"Fine, totally fine. The wine just went down the wrong way."

Vee's eyes were watering. The chef appeared with a glass of iced water, and the guy with the phone moved to get a better angle. Fuck that. I pushed my chair back, took six strides, and snatched it out of his hand.

"Hey!"

"Have some respect."

"That's private property. I'm calling the cops."

"Firstly, I am a cop, and secondly, you're gonna struggle with that since I've got your phone." I deleted the offending video, then scrolled through a few others. "So you like looking up girls' skirts, huh?"

His turn to splutter. "Those aren't mine."

"This isn't your phone?"

"No, it is. I, uh, downloaded them from the internet."

"What's your name?"

"Are you really a cop?"

I showed him my badge. "Your name?"

"Dusty Theobald."

"Well, Dusty, it's your lucky day. Since I've got company, I'll let you off with a warning. But if I ever hear of you filming a woman against her will again, I'll put in a word for the prosecution. Don't bother finishing your meal—pay the check and leave."

By the time I'd erased another twenty clips, Dusty's horrified date had stormed out, and he'd thrown fifty bucks onto the table.

"Don't forget to leave a tip."

I wasn't sure the staff at La Nostra Casa deserved a fucking tip, but I figured Dusty was more of a prick than the guy with the violin. I handed his phone back and watched as he hightailed it through the door as well.

This evening was cursed.

"How do you feel about McDonald's?" I asked Vee as I took my seat again.

"I'm beginning to see the appeal. But not tonight. When I tried to tell Rosetta that we're not *together*-together, she just said we make a lovely couple and the chef's whipping us up chocolate ganache bomboloni for dessert. And since those are my favourite and he only makes them on special occasions, I'm not going anywhere until I've eaten at least four."

"So you want me to play along with this charade?"

"If you leave, I'm fairly sure he'll still make them for me out of sympathy, but it might invite some awkward questions."

"These had better be damn good donuts."

"You'll stay?"

"I can think of worse ways to spend an evening. But if anyone heads this way with another instrument, I'm going to the bathroom."

"I'll be right behind you." After a pause, Vee broke out in a genuine smile. "I guess if this *was* a real date, we'd look back on the evening and laugh. I honestly thought you were gonna arrest that guy."

"Oh, I was tempted. But then I'd have spent the evening doing paperwork, and that's even worse than being serenaded by a waitress with a lousy sense of timing. Besides... Never mind."

"Besides what?"

"It doesn't matter."

"Are you sure? You look kind of...haunted."

Sometimes when I let my guard down, I forgot my poker face. Ironic, considering we were in Las Vegas.

"Tonight just reminded me of my first proper date with my wife, that's all."

"Because you went to an Italian restaurant?"

"Because it was a disaster."

"In what way?" Vee took a sip of wine, this time without coughing, and stared at me over the rim of the glass with those big green eyes. "Actually, you don't have to tell me. Not if you don't want to. But I'll always listen if you want to talk."

I didn't mention Angie often. Only to Shep and

occasionally to Cecily. Nobody else in Vegas had met her. After she died, the department sent me to a shrink, but it had been more of a box-ticking exercise than a genuine attempt to help. By the third session, I'd come to understand that alcohol did a better job of dulling the pain, and I hadn't gone back for the fourth.

But now here I was, two thousand miles away with a very different woman. Did I want to dredge up the past? When the alternative was to let the memories die along with Angie's light, I realised I should take Vee up on her offer to listen. Angie and I had always said that when one of us passed, we didn't want the other to be alone. I'd just always assumed it would be me who died young.

"We went to a Mexican joint near the gallery where Angie worked."

"An art gallery? Which one? Did she paint?"

"The Spectra Project. She was a sculptor, but she also curated exhibitions there."

After a moment's pause, Vee's eyes widened. "You were married to Angelina Callahan?"

Now it was my turn to be surprised. "You've heard of her?"

"Yes. I mean, I've heard the name. Sometimes I browse art exhibitions on the internet. In the summer, when I can't go out much. And there aren't so many museums here in Las Vegas anyway, not like in New York." Another pause. "Your wife was very talented."

What a small world we lived in. I suppose I shouldn't have been amazed about the art connection given Vee's talents in that department, but still... It was a shame the two of them had never met. Angie would probably have liked Vee. And I wouldn't have given her a second glance if Angie were still alive, but she wasn't, and now I didn't know how to feel.

This was *not* a date. It was more of a business meeting.

"Yes, Angie was talented." Not commercially successful, but she'd taken metal and stone and wood and glass and turned them into beauty. A labour of love. When she'd put her mind to something, she poured her whole heart in too. "But she was also fun, which was perhaps the only reason we survived our first official date."

"What happened? Were there any violins involved?"

"No, but two of the kitchen staff got into a fist fight and it spilled out into the restaurant. Me and another guy pulled them apart, and I ended up with a black eye. So I'm sitting there with a bag of ice on my face, thinking things couldn't possibly get any worse, when this redhead storms over and starts whacking me with her purse. The candle falls over and sets fire to the tablecloth, and a girl at the next table throws a jug of ice water over us to put out the flames. Angie's wiping her eyes, but she still gets up and pulls the bitch off me, and they end up rolling around on the damn floor."

"Who came out on top?"

"Angie. That was the moment I fell in love with her."

She'd sat on the redhead and grinned up at me, triumphant, as she fished an ice cube out of her bra. I'd nearly asked her to marry me on the spot. Except the redhead had started screaming bloody murder and a bunch of my colleagues arrived because someone had called them about the fight. *That* was awkward.

"Why was the redhead yelling at you?"

"She hadn't worn her glasses that night, and she got me confused with another guy. Her friend's fiancé. She thought I was cheating on a girl I'd never even met."

Vee began with a smile, which turned into a giggle and then a full-on fit of laughter.

"You're right," she choked out. "That *was* worse than the violin."

"What's the worst date you've ever been on?"

The laughter stopped dead.

"I don't date."

"Not at all?" Common sense told me not to pry, but I just couldn't stop myself. "Never?"

"No."

"Why not?"

"I'm not exactly relationship material."

"Because of your medical condition?"

Surely the right man would work around that? Go out during the winter, spend more time at home in the summer. Alter his sleeping hours a little. This was Vegas—there was plenty to do at night.

Vee merely shrugged. "Partly."

Partly?

"Here are your appetisers," Rosetta announced, setting two plates on the table. That woman really did have the worst timing ever. "And we have glasses of Prosecco, on the house. Let me top off your water."

When Rosetta disappeared, Vee turned her attention to her glazed figs. Thanks to the generous portions at Good Eats, I was still full from earlier, so I picked at mine as I searched for a way to steer the conversation back to where we'd left off without coming across as an asshole.

"So..." we both said at the same time.

"You go first," I told her. Better to be gentlemanly than nosy, even if I was curious as hell.

"We were talking about Serenity? I remembered something else Reuben said."

Nice subject change. Truly. I was impressed.

"Go on."

"Reuben described her as bitter. So whatever was going on between her and our mystery man, I think it had been festering for some time. But it was weird—Serenity never acted bitter towards anyone I saw her with. The opposite, in fact. So who was she upset at?"

"Bitter? That was the word he used?"

"Yes. And I'm stumped."

Family law. A man. Not her father or her brother. *Bitter.* Holy fuck.

CHAPTER 22

Jack

I pulled out my phone, scrolled to Daphne's number, and dialled.

"What are you doing?" Vee asked. "Who are you calling? What's happened?"

"Do you know who gets bitter? Ex-wives." A female voice answered on a yawn. "Daphne?"

"Hey, boss."

"I need you to look something up for me. Get hold of someone at the Office of Vital Records and find out if Lyla Chavez was ever married. Check outside of the state too."

"Married?"

"Yeah, married. Rings, flowers, a cake."

"Wow, okay. I'll do that right now."

"Married?" Vee echoed as I hung up. "Serenity wasn't married. She had a boyfriend."

"So did my mom when she split from my dad. And she was as bitter as hemlock."

Vee reached out to cover my hand with hers. "I'm sorry to hear that."

"Don't feel too sorry for Dad. He had a girlfriend. That was why she left him in the first place."

"It's not your father I care about."

Vee cared about me? That was…unexpected. And slightly concerning. But my hand didn't get that message, and my fingers twined with hers all of their own accord.

"It happened a long time ago."

"Are they happy now?"

"My dad passed away. My mom? I'm not sure she knows how to be happy. She's one of those people who's never content with what she's got."

"I'm so sorry about your father."

So was I, but we'd grown apart after my parents' divorce, and although it filled me with guilt to admit it, his death hadn't hit me as hard as Angie's.

"It happened over a decade ago."

"Still, I'm sorry. And your mom—you don't get along?"

I shrugged. My mom had brought me up, and I'd always love her, but life was easier when I didn't see her much. The last thing I needed was the weight of her expectations sitting on my shoulders.

"Our relationship's complicated. What about your parents? Do they live in Vegas?"

"They died."

Ah, shit. I gripped her hand tighter. "I'm so sorry. Was it recent?"

Vee shook her head. "I've had time to get used to being alone."

I was almost relieved when Rosetta arrived with the main course. Her eyes lit up when she spotted our joined hands, but Vee didn't let go, and neither did I. *She was alone.* Her parents were dead, she'd just lost her friend, and she didn't have a partner to support her. How was she holding it together? I'd fallen apart completely after Angie's death, and I'd had people to lean on.

Vee might not date, but she could probably use a friend. And we *were* neighbours.

"If *you* ever want to talk, I'll always listen."

She drained her wine glass and poured herself another before she answered.

"I appreciate that. Are you ready to try the pasta? I swear you'll never want to eat Italian anywhere else, violins or no violins."

Hint taken. I extricated my hand and wound tagliatelle around my fork. Vee was right—grocery store pasta couldn't compete, nor pasta from any of the other restaurants I'd eaten at in Vegas. Her "usual" appeared to be spaghetti carbonara, but it looked yellower than the version I was used to.

"Organic egg yolks and no cream," Vee said when I commented on it. "And they use guanciale—cured pork cheeks—instead of regular bacon."

"Do they do takeout?"

"Officially? No. But in the summer when the days are long, they'll send food over in a cab."

See what I mean? People could adapt to Vee's needs.

"Maybe you could sweet-talk them into making dinner for us one day? I could pick it up."

"I thought you weren't interested in having dinner with me? We have to tread carefully, you said."

"Is a man allowed to change his mind?"

"I guess."

"We'll have to keep it quiet for the moment. The case and all that."

"Right."

"Friends?"

"Friends."

"Just don't go behind my back and start questioning witnesses again. Talk to me, okay?"

"Okay. I'll talk to you, but if I think I can get better results, then we'll have to come to a compromise that allows me to get involved because I want Serenity's killer in jail. Or a casket—that option works for me too."

"I won't risk your life."

"I'm tougher than you think."

Unlikely. I thought Vee was hella tough. I didn't doubt her strength or her tenacity, not for a second, but I still wouldn't put her in harm's way.

"And I'm a cop. It's my job to keep you safe."

"I won't do anything stupid."

"You mean anything *else* stupid? Promise you won't visit Reuben again."

"It wasn't stupid. I got answers."

"It was risky. What if Reuben killed Lyla?"

Silence.

"If we find another witness, we'll come up with a plan together, okay?"

"*When* we find another witness."

A shadow fell over me, and I groaned out loud. Our favourite hostess-slash-waitress-slash-entertainer was back.

"You didn't like the food? You only ate half."

"I wasn't expecting to come here tonight, so I already ate one dinner before this. And apparently, I still have to eat bomboloni. I hear they're the best."

Rosetta beamed at me. "*Si, caro.* I'll put the rest into a box. You can take it with you."

I managed four bomboloni; Vee got through half a dozen plus a large cappuccino. How much time did she spend in the gym? She ate more than any girl I'd ever known, but she was still slim.

"Excuse me a moment?" she said. "I need to use the bathroom."

"Sure."

While she was gone, I checked my phone. Nothing from Daphne yet. Could I be right? Did Chavez have a husband nobody knew about? Or an ex-husband?

I finished my wine, and I had to concede that Vee had good taste. Out of interest, I picked up the wine list. How much did it cost? Maybe I could get a couple of bottles myself? I worked my way through until I spotted the Tenute Silvio Nardi Brunello di Montalcino right at the end. What the fuck? A hundred and twenty bucks a bottle?

There must have been a mistake. But why hadn't Vee said anything? I stuffed the wine list into the holder and sat back. No matter what I'd said earlier, I'd planned to split the check, but I wasn't made of money. Then again, neither was Vee. Was she?

"Hey." She touched me on the shoulder. "Ready to go?"

"Rosetta hasn't brought the check yet."

"No need, I already paid on my way back."

"You did?"

"That was what we agreed."

"Right." I slowly got to my feet. "Thanks for dinner."

"You liked it? The food, I mean? The whole serenade thing made me want to crawl under the table."

"Yeah, I liked the food. The wine too." I held the door open for her, the bag of leftovers clutched in my other hand. "It was kind of...acidic? But good."

"That's the tannins. You get that taste from a good Brunello. Uh, I learned about wine at the club."

No mistake, then. Vee had known precisely what she was drinking. Waitressing must pay a hell of a lot better than I thought. If I had that kind of spare cash, I'd move to a better apartment, especially if I was trapped there all day, every day, but who was I to judge someone's priorities? Vee...she intrigued me.

Outside, she did her cab trick again. After half a bottle of wine, I'd have to leave my car where it was until the morning, so I climbed in with her.

We'd only gotten a hundred yards when my phone rang. *Daphne.*

"Got any news?"

"You were right! How do you do that? Actually, forget it. You're a detective. Okay, okay, I had to search for a while, but I found the record. Lyla Chavez—same date of birth—married Jeb Moutree in California five years ago."

Vee's gasp said she'd heard the news. Impressive in itself since *I* could barely hear Daphne speak over the traffic outside.

"We need to find this guy."

"I'm on it. He made a court appearance for DUI in Barstow three years ago, and I'm checking for a current address."

Barstow? That was only two hours away. Close enough to interfere in Lyla's life in person as well as through a lawyer.

"Call me when you find it. I don't care how late it is. If Moutree's still there, we'll visit him tomorrow."

"Both of us?"

I tamped down a sigh. Captain Lindsay would complain if I kept leaving Daphne behind, even if we were both happier with that arrangement.

"Both of us."

I hung up and turned back to the woman I'd much rather have by my side. If the rules allowed it, obviously, which they didn't. At least if I went to see Jeb Moutree in daylight, I wouldn't have to worry about Vee sneaking along uninvited.

"I can't believe Serenity was married and she didn't tell me."

"Hey, she didn't tell anyone."

"How well did I really know her?"

"Better than most people. If she was consulting with a lawyer, she was most likely seeking a divorce. She probably hoped it would all just go away."

"I never even heard her mention Jeb Moutree's name. Not once." Mental note: Vee was an excellent eavesdropper. "What time will you visit him tomorrow?"

"During the day. Don't even think about it," I warned.

Vee thunked her head back against the seat. "I hate that I can't do more."

"Remember what we said about interfering in the investigation? Let me do my job."

"Will you tell me what happens?"

I shouldn't, but I would. "Yeah, I'll tell you."

In Sunset Tower, I headed towards the stairs while Vee stopped in front of the elevator.

"I'll take the—" we both started, then laughed.

"You don't like elevators?" she asked.

"Not much. And I also ate two dinners. But I'll go with you in the elevator tonight."

"No, I'll take the stairs."

"Vee..."

"I'm taking the stairs. Even if you take the elevator, I'm taking the stairs."

Stubborn as a fucking mule. Angie had been the same, and I'd both loved and hated that about her.

"Fine, the stairs."

Seventeen floors, but at least it saved me from going to the gym. And I could take a break on sixteen when I saw Vee into her apartment. If we made it that far. By the tenth floor, her face matched her hair plus she was breathing hard, and I began to get worried.

"Let's ride the rest of the way."

"I'm okay. Just not...just not feeling so good today."

Another floor, and things only got worse. Vee looked as if she was in shape, so eleven storeys shouldn't have left her puffing like a racehorse. Was she sick?

"Vee..." I grabbed her hand when she tried to carry on without me. "Wait."

"I'm—"

"You're not okay."

Oh, screw it. I scooped her into my arms, and either she was lighter than she looked or I was stronger than I thought. I used to carry Angie home that way after nights out, and we'd both collapse onto the bed when we got home. And then we'd... *Don't think about that, Callahan.*

I kicked open the door out of the stairwell and headed for the elevator, grappling with both Vee and the bag of leftovers from La Nostra Casa.

"Push the button, babe."

She folded her arms. Pretty as a picture, and Vee didn't just channel one mule but a whole damn herd of them.

To this day, I don't know why I did it. I shouldn't have. But I leaned in and nibbled her earlobe, then ran my tongue along the edge of her ear. It was the wine. It had to be the damn wine.

"Push the fucking button."

She pushed the button.

"Thank you."

I didn't put her down until we reached her apartment door, and even then, I had to fight to keep my hands away from her ass. If I hadn't been a cop and she hadn't been a witness, I'd have done my utmost to get her out of the little purple dress she was wearing, and her underwear too. But instead, I gripped the doorjamb and tried to talk myself out of throttling Reuben Broderick. He'd taken what I wanted. What I couldn't have. And to him, Vee was probably just another piece of tail.

"Get some rest, Vee. If you still feel like shit tomorrow, go to a doctor."

"It's nothing."

"You can't be sure of that. Take it easy, and I'll call you in the afternoon."

There was a moment. A moment when I could quite easily have kissed her. But a plaintive miaow came from the living room, and I took a hasty step back as the spell was broken. Saved by the cat.

"Good night, Jack."

"Sweet dreams, Vee."

CHAPTER 23

Vee

What a disaster of an evening. First, Callahan had caught me sneaking out of Reuben's building, and then I'd made the mistake of going to La Nostra Casa. Rosetta had only been trying to help, but all I'd wanted was a quiet dinner, and then she brought the bottle of Brunello without me asking. Worse, I'd accidentally blabbered on about tannins when Callahan mentioned it.

Had my excuse that I'd gleaned my knowledge of wine at the club been plausible? I sure hoped so. And thank goodness I'd managed to intercept the check before he realised how much a bottle of good Brunello cost. Explaining that could have been a tad tricky.

And the awkward moments had only continued when we'd gotten back to Sunset Tower. Why had I insisted on climbing the stairs? Usually, I saw my stubbornness as a good quality, but Voltaire had always warned me it would be my downfall. And tonight, it very nearly had been, quite literally —if Callahan hadn't picked me up, I'd probably have taken a tumble because my legs had been about to fail me. And why the hell had he licked my ear? Had he been *that* drunk?

"Muse, I'm an idiot."

She didn't disagree, just stared at me and back towards her food bowl. It might have been full of Kitty Krunchies, but it wasn't the fancy ceramic dish she favoured at Berkshire Place, and Muse was a snob.

"It won't poison you."

Miaow.

My phone vibrated with a message from Blane. Him texting so late at night wasn't a surprise—he lived his life in darkness the same way I did, although in his case, it was out of choice.

Blane: Club's open again tomorrow. Can you work 8 - 4?

Oh, thank goodness. I didn't usually work Mondays, and an eight-hour shift would exhaust me, but Club Dead was the best hunting ground for my next meal. I could scout potential targets without getting hit on constantly, and when I helped a drunk tourist back to his hotel room in the early hours, well, I was just doing my civic duty.

Me: That's fine.

Muse miaowed again, and this time, she gave her water bowl a disgusted glare. Usually, she drank chilled Evian from a fountain, and room-temperature water made a poor substitute. I'd tried running the faucet, but she merely turned her nose up at it and slunk away.

What was the time? Almost midnight. I'd be safe outside for another six hours.

"Want to go home, Muse? Just for a little while?"

I took her haughty expression as an affirmative.

Callahan's earlier question about my driver's licence reminded me that I should take my car out for a spin. Otherwise, the battery would go dead, and I didn't need that hassle right now. Who knew when I'd need to make a quick getaway? I could sleep in my own bed for a couple of hours, then head out for a drive before the sun came up. As long as I didn't exert myself too much, I'd be okay.

Plus driving aimlessly helped me to think.

I *needed* to think.

That moment at my door with Callahan had been intense. Even though my soul was diseased and my body had let me down and my mind was frazzled, I'd still felt it—a weird connection that made my blood heat and my skin prickle. Which was even stranger considering what I'd learned earlier in the evening about his past.

I was still mulling over what it all meant when I opened Muse's carrier in the foyer of my penthouse forty minutes later. Angelina Callahan's sculpture dominated the space, a glass-and-metal hummingbird that hung suspended on a steel wire. As it twisted slowly to face me, it flung a rainbow of sparkles over the white walls.

I'd fallen in love with the piece the moment I saw it at the Spectra Project. Rarely did I go to galleries, but that month's exhibition had been themed as Night into Day, so the VIP launch party started at midnight. I'd been living in the Upper East Side in those days, back before I'd spotted one of Voltaire's cohorts sniffing around Tribeca one chilly November evening and fled the city. Voltaire might take a trip to New York, but he'd never go to Vegas voluntarily. Too loud. Too garish. *Uncouth, ma petite épine.* He'd always called me his little thorn. The thorn in his side. But even when I'd begged, he'd still refused to set me free.

Anyhow, I'd seen Angelina's hummingbird, and I'd bought it in a heartbeat. We'd sealed the deal over a glass of champagne. Then we'd spent the rest of the evening setting the world to rights and discussing our favourite artists, past and present. One of my paintings had been in the show too, and she'd gushed over the composition, but I'd told her my name was Jenny, so she'd never made the connection between me and VV Pelham.

At the end of the night, she'd suggested meeting for dinner. Would I have gone if I hadn't left New York? Maybe. Angelina had possessed a beautiful soul, a light that shone out of her. No wonder Callahan missed her so much. Now that I knew her fate, I felt the loss too.

Fate. She was a cruel mistress.

Somehow, my connection to Angelina, however fleeting, made the moment I'd shared with Callahan all the more wrong. His heart belonged to her. I'd got the runner-up's prize —a narcissistic Parisian sociopath who belittled my every move, raged when things didn't go his way, and slept with the living behind my back.

And a cat. I had a cat. As Muse skulked around the penthouse, I scrubbed out her water fountain and refilled it, then put fresh Kitty Krunchies into her preferred bowl. She was gonna be pissed when I took her back to Sunset Tower before dawn. Thankfully, her claws couldn't do me much damage, but from my past experience, that only seemed to irk her more.

The irrigation system had kept the plants healthy, and I sifted through the mail as I ate a peanut butter and pineapple sandwich, tossing the junk into the recycling box and stuffing the rest into my purse to deal with later. My paints were calling to me, but tonight, I had to ignore their lure. Only three hours left—three hours to sleep, drive, grab some extra clothes, and ride back to purgatory.

Let the countdown begin...

<h1 style="text-align:center">CHAPTER 24</h1>

<h1 style="text-align:center">Jack</h1>

"It should be somewhere on the left," Daphne told me, comparing a printed map to the satnav unit on the dash. "There, just past that crooked tree."

According to the DMV, Jeb Moutree now lived in Heron's Rest, California. The small town was an hour farther away from Vegas than Barstow, and we got delayed on our trip by a traffic accident. By the time we arrived downtown, which was basically one street and a couple of bars, I'd have sold my soul for a pair of earplugs. I'd never been on a long road trip with Daphne before, and it turned out she talked. *Constantly.* A recap of what she'd found out about Jeb Moutree quickly devolved into a running commentary of landmarks, accompanied by the kind of pointless facts that would make her a winner at Trivial Pursuit.

Ooh, look, there's the road to the Mojave National Preserve, home to the largest Joshua tree forest in the world. Great for hiking. And did I know that the average person would walk five times around the equator in their lifetime?

No, and nor did I care at that moment. I was more concerned with finding Jeb Moutree and asking what had been going on between him and Lyla Chavez. Did he know she was dead? The story had been all over the news. And even if he'd managed to miss it, wouldn't someone in his family have called? Or how about his friends? Did they know he'd been hitched to an up-and-coming rock star? It wasn't the kind of thing a man kept quiet.

I'd phoned ahead, and a deputy from the Heron's Rest Substation had agreed to meet us. When I'd mentioned Moutree's name and said I needed to speak to him regarding a case in Vegas, there had been a pause followed by, "Guess that don't surprise me." Apparently, Jeb was well known to the department.

The sun was shining as we pulled into the parking lot of the substation, and when we got inside, we found Deputy Collins waiting with coffee and carrot sticks.

"My wife put me on a diet," he grumbled.

In my opinion, that wasn't necessarily a bad thing. His shirt strained at the buttons, and when he sat down at his desk, the chair creaked ominously. The extra weight couldn't be good for his health. Daphne and I took seats opposite. Some detectives might have asked their questions over the phone, but I always preferred to meet people in person. Shep accused me of being a control freak, but I'd been stung early in my career when other people took shortcuts, so I called it being prudent.

"What can you tell us about Jeb Moutree?" I asked.

"Jeb's a pain in the department's ass. His cousin too."

"His cousin lives in Heron's Rest?"

"Skeeter Moutree rode into town 'bout a decade ago. Got arrested three days later, give or take."

"What for?"

"Public intoxication. Got so drunk he fell off his horse right in the middle of Main Street."

"When you said he rode into town, I didn't think you meant literally."

Deputy Collins guffawed and chomped on a carrot stick. "Skeeter's one redeeming feature is that he knows horses. Works out on Bud Lightfoot's ranch, when he remembers to show up, that is. Drives Bud crazy, but Skeeter's one of them horse whisperers. Last year, he worked his magic on a wild mare Bud's foreman wanted to shoot and turned her into a prizewinner."

"How about Jeb? Does he work on the ranch too?"

"Naw, that's too much effort for him."

"Does he work at all?"

"So he claims. It's one get-rich-quick scheme after another for him. He tried selling some cider vinegar cure-all, then magnetic bracelets, and one time he had a bunch of kids assembling dollhouse furniture for him to sell on the internet. Never amounts to much. In between times, he does odd jobs around town, but mostly he just causes a ruckus. We got a couple months' respite when he found himself a girlfriend and took a job over in Barstow, but it wasn't long before she came to her senses and Jeb fell back into the gutter." Collins pointed out of the window. "Right outside there."

"Convenient."

"That's what we said. Jeb Moutree spends more time in the drunk tank than in his own bed. Probably thought he was comin' home."

Why the hell had Lyla Chavez married an idiot like Jeb Moutree? By all accounts, she was a hard-working, personable type, and judging by the way she'd clawed her way up the ladder in the entertainment industry, she didn't suffer fools gladly.

Could we have got this wrong?

"You mentioned a girlfriend? It's our belief that Jeb Moutree was married."

Collins almost choked on a carrot stick. I thumped him on the back while Daphne fetched a plastic cup of water from the cooler two desks away, and once he'd stopped spluttering, he shook his head.

"Married? Jeb? Naw, I doubt that. Who would marry him?"

"All the details match," Daphne said. "Names, dates of birth. He put his occupation down as 'entrepreneur,' which also jibes with what you just said. The wedding was five years ago. Lyla Chavez was twenty-one, and Moutree would have been twenty-three."

"Five years ago, you say?" Collins half rose from his chair, gripping the edge of his desk. "Hey, Johnson," he hollered at another deputy on the other side of the room. "When did Jeb Moutree up and leave the time before last?"

"Right before the incident at Dixie Hart's seventy-fifth birthday party. Remember we were all mighty glad to have the extra space in the drunk tank?"

Deputy Collins nodded along. "And Dixie turns eighty next week. Let's hope we don't have a repeat."

"What happened?" I asked.

"Dixie and her friends got sloshed on illegal moonshine she brewed in her summer house, and they all lined up along Main Street to moon passing traffic. We had to arrest them for their own safety."

"Fifteen of them," Deputy Johnson said. "One of the ladies groped my unmentionables when I lifted her into the back of my patrol car."

Rather them than me. But the timeline fit. "What happened with Moutree five years ago? You said he left?"

"Told Carol Ann at the Mighty Barrel Saloon that he was off to make his fortune. We didn't see him for at least three months."

"I take it he didn't make his fortune?"

"When he came back, he was driving a new truck, and he splashed the cash around in town for a week or two before he ran out of money and went back to his old ways. But he didn't say nothin' about gettin' married. You say the girl was called Lyla Chavez? Ain't never heard that name around here."

"Her stage name was Serenity Strange."

Collins gave a low whistle. "That singer who died? You reckon she was his sugar momma?"

Honestly? No way. If a lady was that desperate for company, surely she'd buy a dog instead? Or a cat. I thought of Vee—she spent a lot of time alone due to her medical condition, and she'd picked Muse over a man.

"I don't think that's a likely scenario. Any other theories as to where he got the money?"

"I figured it was drugs. Like I said, Jeb was always after a fast buck, and a couple of runs down to Mexico could've made him enough cash to buy the truck."

"Was he smart enough not to get caught?"

Deputy Collins mulled that over for a moment before nodding. "I'd say so. Jeb Moutree's not stupid, just lazy. If he laid off the alcohol and got himself a proper job, he might be able to make something of himself. Why are you looking at him? You think he was involved with the Chavez case?"

"Possibly. I'd like to find out where he was last Friday evening."

"You don't think he killed her, do you?"

I shrugged, non-committal. "Somebody did. I take it you don't see him as a suspect?"

"How'd she die?"

"Anaphylactic shock."

"And yet you're investigating it as a murder?"

"We don't know what caused the anaphylactic shock, and Ms. Chavez also had a stab wound to her neck."

Another pause.

"What are your thoughts?" I asked him.

"Jeb Moutree's an asshole, but I've never heard of him being violent. And he's one of them vegans, or at least, he used to be. One time, he was selling animal-friendly shampoo door to door. My wife bought a bottle. Said it wasn't bad."

"I'm not sure veganism and murder are mutually exclusive."

Collins's turn to shrug.

"Can you show us where to find him?"

The deputy checked his watch. "If he's not at home, he'll be in the Mighty Barrel."

"At eleven o'clock in the morning?"

"Yup. C'mon, we can take my car."

CHAPTER 25

Jack

There was no sign of Jeb Moutree in the Mighty Barrel Saloon, but the girl behind the bar said he'd been there until the early hours.

"He'll be at home," she said. "Unless he passed out on the way there."

Lyla sure had picked a treasure, hadn't she?

At first, we thought he wasn't home either. We picked our way along the cracked front path and Deputy Collins knocked on the front door once, twice, three times to no avail, but then Daphne peered through the grubby window of the dilapidated bungalow.

"He's on the couch," she said. "I'm not sure if he's... Oh, he just moved his arm."

Collins hammered on the door again. "Moutree, get your ass out here."

Finally, Jeb rolled off the couch and stumbled across the living room. A few rattles and a *thunk*, and he fumbled open the front door, then clutched at the door frame for support. Daphne stared at his hairy legs in disgust—somewhere, he'd lost his pants, and his boxers proclaimed him to be the "pussy monster." Not a good look on any man. I wanted to apologise on his behalf and then offer bleach so she could wash out her eyes.

"What'd I do?"

From Moutree's garbled words, it wasn't clear whether he was being belligerent or he genuinely couldn't remember. Either way, his breath stank of stale whisky, and the pink tinge to his brown eyes suggested his blood was eighty proof.

"These detectives want to ask you some questions," Collins told him.

I stepped forward. "I'm Detective Callahan from the Las Vegas Metropolitan Police Department, and this is Officer Washington. We're here to talk about your wife."

"My wife?"

I stayed quiet and watched him carefully. First, he seemed confused, but then his eyes widened a fraction and he straightened an inch.

"You mean Lyla?"

"Unless you have any other wives we don't know about?"

"Whatever she told you I did, I didn't do it."

"Why would you think she told us anything?"

"'Cause she..." Moutree hiccuped, then went into a coughing fit. "She doesn't want to give me my fair share."

I noted he used the present tense. Was he a great actor, or did he really not know Lyla was dead?

"Fair share of what?"

"Our assets."

"What assets?"

"In the divorce. My lawyer says I'm entitled to half of our marital assets, but she wants to keep it all."

Was he serious? Moutree wanted half of everything Lyla had worked so hard for over the last five years, and in return, she'd get a share in a rusted pickup, some moth-eaten furniture, and... What were those boxes stacked up in the hallway? Slim-Plan Supershakes according to the label.

"When did you last live together?"

Now Moutree shifted from foot to foot. "A while ago."

"Do you have a TV?"

I couldn't see one, but there was an empty side table near the couch.

"What does that matter?"

"Just answer the question," Deputy Collins instructed.

"I needed money for my new business venture, so I pawned it. Wanna buy a case of slimming shakes?" Moutree focused his watery eyes on Collins. "Might help you to lose that spare tyre."

The deputy clenched his jaw, and I quickly moved the conversation on.

"So you haven't seen the news for a few days?"

"I bin busy." Busy drinking? "Don't watch the news anyway."

"Then I'm sorry to be the one to inform you, but your wife passed away."

I watched as the emotions crossed Moutree's face. It took a good ten seconds, but shock came first. Either Moutree was a great actor, or the revelation caught him unawares. His mouth opened and closed again. Then his eyes flicked up to the right, followed by feigned sadness. And I say "feigned" because I knew what it was like to lose a wife. The heart-stopping moment where the bottom dropped out of your world and air wouldn't go into your lungs. The darkness that fell. The brief moment of hope that the person tasked with breaking the news was wrong, that you were stuck in a nightmare. The tears that wouldn't stop. The words that stuck in your throat.

There was none of that from Jeb Moutree. No, he swallowed once and gave his head a little shake, then his surprise turned to curiosity.

"Bummer. How'd she die?"

Wow. Out of the corner of my eye, I saw Daphne's fists clench. If there hadn't been witnesses, I might have socked him myself.

"You're not upset?"

"Yeah, well, of course I'm upset. We were married, weren't we?"

"Where were you on Friday evening?"

"Why?" Realisation dawned. "Wait, you don't think *I* did it?"

Based on his reactions so far, I was around sixty percent sure he didn't, but I was one hundred percent certain Jeb Moutree was an asshole. If I could make his life uncomfortable, I'd do it with pleasure.

"You had the most to gain."

"What? No, I didn't. How's she gonna pay me alimony if she's dead?"

For a second, I thought I might have to handcuff Daphne. She took a step forward with her mouth twisted into a snarl, and I cut her a warning glance. Now wasn't the time.

"That's your wife you're talking about, not a cash machine."

"*She* was the one who left."

"Can you answer the question? Where were you on Friday?"

"What day is it today?"

For goodness' sake. "Monday."

Moutree began counting on his fingers. "Friday… Friday… I picked up a bunch of shakes in the morning, then I had a sales event in the afternoon."

"A sales event?"

"At the school. Most of the moms could stand to lose a few pounds."

In a room full of assholes, Jeb Moutree would stand cock and balls above the rest.

"Witnesses?"

"Yeah, loads of them. Jolene Cummings from the hair salon bought three cases."

"I know Jolene," Collins said. "We can speak with her."

"What time was that?"

"Like, three o'clock? End of the school day."

"And where did you go after that?"

"Probably the Mighty Barrel."

"Probably?"

"Yeah, I went there."

"How late did you stay?"

A shrug. "Who knows?"

"What did you do on Saturday morning?"

"Helped my cousin with the horses at Bud Lightfoot's ranch. Skeeter Moutree. You can call him, he'll tell you."

I'd admit to being disappointed that Moutree had an alibi. He deserved to be locked up, if for no other reason than giving men a bad name. What the hell had Lyla Chavez been thinking?

I decided to try a different tack. "Five years ago, you got a new truck. Where did you get the money?"

Interesting. Was that a flash of fear in his eyes? "Why do you even care?"

"Humour me."

"I won the lotto. You gonna arrest me or what?"

If I thought I could possibly get away with it, I'd have done it in a heartbeat, but Captain Lindsay would have torn me a new one.

"The jury's still out on that. How did you and Lyla meet?"

"In a bar in San Diego. We were both new in town, and a mutual acquaintance introduced us."

"What took you to San Diego?"

"A job opportunity."

"What kind of a job opportunity?"

"Does that matter? It was five years ago."

I saw what Deputy Collins meant about Jeb Moutree being smart underneath the veneer of stupor. The more questions I asked, the more awake he became and the sharper he got. And his defensive tone most likely meant the job was shady. San Diego was down near the Mexican border, so perhaps Collins's assumption that drugs were involved was correct? I backed off a fraction. The last thing I wanted was for Moutree to get a lawyer involved, and he already had a law firm on call thanks to the divorce.

"Whirlwind courtship, eh? I hear you weren't gone from town for long."

"When you know, you know."

True.

"Who asked who out?"

A shrug. "I needed a roommate, and she needed somewhere to stay. After that...things just happened."

"When did you last see Lyla?"

"In person? Couple months ago."

"Where?"

"At my lawyer's office. Do I need a lawyer today?"

Shit. "I don't know. Do you?"

"I ain't done nothin' wrong."

"Did you have a big wedding?" Daphne asked. "How many people came?"

"Twenty-seven."

"Ooh, just a small affair, then. I'm getting married myself next year, and there's so much to plan, isn't there? What kind of cake did you have?"

What? Daphne wasn't getting married. No, she was up to something, but since she didn't seem to be doing any harm, I let her run with it. At least it would turn Moutree's thoughts away from his lawyer.

"A three-tier vanilla sponge."

"Nice. We're having a fruit cake, but we can't decide on live music or a DJ. What would you suggest?"

"We had a live band called Chase the Storm. They sang covers."

"Oh, wow. How did you find them?"

"Uh… I'm not sure. Look, I'm done answering your questions. I'm a grieving man."

"I just have one more." He tried to slam the door, and I blocked it with my foot. "Was Lyla allergic to anything?"

"What? Yeah, painkillers, or so she claimed. She used to moan like hell when she got a headache."

I moved my foot, and the door slammed in our faces. I had to take a hurried step backwards to avoid getting my nose broken, and Collins chuckled behind me.

"Told you he was an asshole. Guess you'll want to be checking out those alibis?"

"Yes, we sure will."

CHAPTER 26

Jack

Jolene Cummings clearly remembered Jeb being at the school on Friday afternoon. He'd been selling his wares out of the trunk of his car, three cases for the price of two, at least until the principal gave him an earful and moved him on. Jolene was also pissed. She'd followed the instructions on the shake package to the letter and put on two pounds in three days.

"It might be water retention," Daphne suggested.

"Jeb Moutree's an asshole."

I was beginning to sense a recurring theme.

Bud Lightfoot recalled Jeb being at the ranch on Saturday morning but said he didn't show up until nine o'clock.

"Dunno why he showed up at all," Bud said. "He didn't do no work. Just sat around on a hay bale, smoking, so I threw a bucket of water over him." Bud pointed at a *No Smoking* sign nailed to the wall of the barn. "Idiot don't understand fire hazards."

"I'd have been tempted to do the same thing," I told him.

"Skeeter, he's okay, but Jeb Moutree's an asshole."

Jeb's unexpected appearance at the ranch sounded a little like a contrived alibi to me.

"Why do you think Jeb came to the ranch if it wasn't to work?"

"My wife puts on a good spread for breakfast. He probably ran out of cash for groceries again. Wouldn't be the first time."

Unfortunately, that also seemed plausible, but interestingly, the barmaid at the Mighty Barrel wasn't absolutely certain that Jeb had been there on Friday night.

"We were packed, so I didn't notice, but he was probably around," the barmaid said. "He's here most nights. Some of the regulars'll know for sure. Can I get you an early dinner while you're here? We've got pulled-pork sandwiches on special today."

"Why not?"

We had to eat, after all.

While we waited for our food, I stepped outside to call Vee. I'd promised to give her an update, and I was also worried about her.

"How are you feeling?"

"Not too bad," she said, but her voice didn't sound as strong as usual.

"Did you go to the doctor?"

"No need. It's probably something I ate."

Not last night's Italian, because I felt fine. Or Saturday's Chinese. And I hadn't seen Vee eat at all on Friday night. Still, I couldn't force her to seek medical attention, and did she even have health insurance?

"Just let me know if you feel worse, okay?"

"Okay. How are things going with Jeb Moutree?"

I gave Vee a quick rundown, wishing I had more positive news. "I hoped he'd be our culprit, but it doesn't feel right."

"Could he have hired somebody else to do the deed?"

"Not unless he paid them in slimming shakes. His home's one step above a cardboard box, and his truck muffler's held on with duct tape."

"Sometimes appearances can be deceptive."

"The deputy we're working with says he's too lazy to hold down a job for long, and he spends most of his spare time drunk."

"I guess that doesn't sound hopeful." Vee yawned. "So we're back to square one."

"Every case has its setbacks. If you're tired, make sure you get an early night."

"I can't. Blane's opening the club again this evening."

"You're not going to work?"

"How else will I eat?"

"I'll buy you dinner." Shit. The words just popped out. "If we get the witness interviews wrapped up quickly, I can make it back to Vegas late tonight."

"Thanks for the offer, but I'm still going to work. Honestly, I'll be fine after a nap."

There was that stubbornness again.

"Promise me you'll take care of yourself."

"I promise."

How many times had I had this exact same conversation with Angie? All those late nights in her studio, the times my shift patterns meant I couldn't pick her up and she stumbled home in the morning after falling asleep on her battered old couch. The night she'd finished a piece in the early hours and skipped outside into the arms of a mugger. The desperate call over the police radio. Her blood, red splatters on melting snow.

"Get a cab home. I'll pay for it."

"The bus goes right—"

"Get a fucking cab, Vee. If Moutree didn't do this, there's still a killer walking around."

A pause. "Okay, I'll get a cab. But I'm paying for it."

That was a compromise I had to accept. "Thank you."

"Call me tomorrow?"

"I'll bring you breakfast."

What was I doing? I wasn't sure, but I didn't have time to consider it because the waitress was calling me inside to eat. Daphne and Collins were already tucking in. I squirted ketchup over my fries, then took a bite of my sandwich. Not bad.

"What were those questions for?" I asked Daphne. "Why the imaginary fiancé?"

"Just a hunch. You were married, right?"

"What's that got to do with anything?"

Thinking about Angie was painful enough. Talking about her was ten times worse. But Daphne refused to give up.

"How many people went to your wedding?"

"I'm not even sure. We started off with a list of thirty or so, but some of them brought plus-ones, and there were a couple of kids. Angie took care of the invitations."

She'd made the cards herself, each one a little piece of her soul, handwritten with painted flowers on the front. Fuck, I missed her.

"What kind of cake did you have?"

"No idea." I'd had more important things on my mind, like getting Angie naked. "I don't think I even ate any of it, but I'm pretty sure it was white. Why does that—" Suddenly, Daphne's questions made a modicum of sense. If I didn't know that stuff, why would a jerk like Jeb Moutree remember those answers? "Ah. I see."

Seemed Daphne was smarter than I'd given her credit for. But what did Jeb's responses mean?

"See what?" Deputy Collins asked.

"My friend Melanie fell in love with a Mexican guy working in San Diego," Daphne explained. "And when he wanted to apply for a marriage-based green card, they both got interrogated by an immigration officer. Melanie found a whole list of possible questions on the internet, and they spent weeks going over them before they attended their interviews. I helped them to practise. Roberto had no idea how many people were at their wedding either before we counted them all up. Melanie was in charge of the invites."

"And those marriage questions were on the list?" I asked.

"Yup. Did Jeb's answers sound rehearsed to you?"

"Absolutely."

"Sure did," Collins agreed. "I got no idea what cake my wife picked out either."

"So when Moutree said he won the lotto, maybe he meant the green-card marriage lotto?" Daphne suggested. "I googled it. Immigrants pay middlemen twenty thousand bucks for a marriage package. That includes the spouse, the wedding, an apartment for a few months, and coaching to get through the interview."

That would explain a lot. Jeb's caginess. His lack of compassion. And when his wife had begun to make a name for herself, of course his natural desire to make money by doing no work whatsoever had kicked in. Lyla would have been stuck between a rock and a hard place—green-card fraud was illegal, and she couldn't admit to what she'd done without risking not only her career, but also her home and her freedom.

And worse, it cemented Jeb's claim regarding a lack of motive. He'd had little to lose by getting pushy in the divorce, and Lyla had had *everything* to lose. The more famous she'd become, the worse it would have gotten. If anything, she'd been the one with the motive for murder. Coupled with Jeb's alibi...

"Daphne's right, and Jeb isn't our man. We'll button down his whereabouts in the interest of completeness, but we'll do it quickly because we need to get back to Vegas and hunt for the real culprit."

And I had to ask the lab to check Lyla's blood for painkillers.

~

Tracking down the witnesses took hours, mainly because Jeb Moutree had left the Mighty Barrel early on Friday to pal around with rejects from the Heron's Rest branch of Alcoholics Anonymous. Their twelve steps took them from the parking lot to the nearest liquor store. We found them drinking by the river, and it took most of the evening for them to sober up enough to answer questions coherently.

Deputy Collins offered to find us motel rooms for the night, but I couldn't get Vee out of my head. I catnapped in an empty office while Daphne finished the paperwork, then we drank a couple of coffees each and headed back to Vegas. At least traffic was light. And thankfully, Daphne snored the whole way rather than talking.

After I'd dropped Sleeping Beauty back at her apartment and waited until she was safely inside, I headed to Club Dead. The temporary closure didn't seem to have affected the crowds. The place was busier than ever, perhaps due to all the ghouls visiting to see what the fuss was about. Groups of tourists dotted the sidewalk opposite my parked car, taking pictures of the tattered crime scene tape still hanging from the lamp posts.

If Vee was working to the same schedule as before, she'd finish at four a.m., and it was a quarter to four right now. I'd dropped her a text, checking she was okay, but there was no reply. To be honest, I didn't expect one. She wouldn't hear the phone over the music, and she was probably busy serving last-minute drinks and helping VIPs to not fall down the stairs.

And also shovelling them into cabs. At a quarter past four, she half carried a man out the front door and did her waving-down-a-cab trick. The guy was drunker than the crowd in Heron's Rest, and Vee looked...fragile. I was halfway out of the car to assist when I realised she wasn't just helping him into the cab, she was getting into it with him. What the...? She was into hook-ups? In the back seat, he leaned in and kissed her, and she wrapped an arm around his neck, pulling him closer.

My blood turned to ice.

I knew I had no right to feel the way I did—I'd been the one to tell her nothing could happen between us, after all—but jealousy paid no attention to logic. Damn, it hurt seeing Vee with another man. And not just any man, but one who seemed to care more about getting into her panties than about her feelings. The fucker was mauling her. Why didn't she stop him? Part of me wanted to pull the cab over for some imaginary transgression, to lock the prick up for acting like a horny frat boy, but Vee was an adult. I had to respect her decisions, even as my heart puckered in my chest. I watched them drive away.

Fuck, I needed a beer.

CHAPTER 27

Vee

My skin tingled as I ran from the cab to the front entrance of Sunset Tower. Whew. That had been cutting it close. The sun was starting to glimmer over the horizon when I dashed inside.

No need to take the elevator this morning. I felt great, and just a tiny bit buzzed from the alcohol content in Leonardo's blood. At least, he'd said his name was Leonardo. I was fairly sure he'd lied, same as he'd lied about being single. The pale band of skin on his ring finger had given the game away.

Did I care? Not really, not when it was a matter of survival. And I don't mean surviving literally—I couldn't starve to death—but keeping my life in Vegas. I was happy there, and in order to stay free, I had to look like a regular human and not a zombified skeleton. I'd spent three nights in prison at the beginning of the last century, and that was quite enough.

Thankfully, I hadn't even needed to sleep with Leonardo the liar, despite him bragging about his sexual prowess for the entire evening. When we got to his room at the Tropicana, he'd necked back three miniatures of whisky on top of the drinks he'd poured down his throat at the club—mostly doubles, since I'd been making them—and then passed out before I even took off my underwear. I'd waited ten minutes until he started snoring, then given him a prod. No reaction.

As a vampire, my saliva contained an analgesic that numbed a person's flesh as soon as I bit into it. Voltaire used to keep human girls as pets—he probably still did—and one of them had told me that a vampire bite felt like a hard pinch, just for a second, and then nothing. The girls hadn't even minded their living arrangements. Voltaire exhibited a magnetic pull to every female except me, and whenever one pet died, there were a dozen others waiting to take her place.

Leonardo had barely stirred as I drank my fill. A slight twitch, that was all, and he quickly got comfortable again. Practice meant I didn't spill a drop. When I'd finished, the wounds healed in a minute or two, leaving only smooth skin behind. *Sloppiness is a sin, ma petite épine.* Through trial and error, I'd found that if I dribbled a little saliva into the holes, they closed up even faster.

When I walked into the apartment, Muse miaowed at me, a cross between "I'm hungry" and "Where the hell have you been?" and I tossed her a salmon-flavoured treat before I skipped through to the bedroom. Then I took a moment to text Callahan.

Me: Got news! Will tell you over breakfast.

I'd have time for a couple of hours' sleep before he arrived with food, and then I could update him on what I'd found out at Club Dead last night.

The scratchy buzz of the intercom woke me up. Callahan? No, he'd knock on the door. I stumbled out of bed and picked up the phone, almost tripping over Muse on the way.

"Hello?"

"Ms. Pelter?"

Close enough. "Yes?"

"I have a delivery for you."

"Really? Where from?"

"From Furniture World."

Oops. What time was it? Ah, rats—nine thirty. I'd slept for longer than I thought.

"Come on up." I turned to Muse. "Our stuff is here!"

Perhaps it was silly ordering new furniture for a rental apartment, but I had plenty of money, and when a woman was forced to stay inside all day, every day, the walls started to close in. Even the opulence of Berkshire Place felt like a prison at times. Sunset Tower was more of a coffin, and contrary to any rumours you might have heard, I did *not* want to sleep in one of those.

Muse was distinctly unimpressed when the men carried in my new sofa, a bed, a dining set, two nightstands, and a credenza. Perhaps she'd be happier when her new kitty tree arrived? Or perhaps not, since that meant we'd be staying in Sunset Tower for at least another week. I'd spoken to the landlord to extend the rental period and asked if he'd mind me updating some of the fixtures and fittings, and although his words had been grudging—"I suppose that would be okay"— his tone said he was rubbing his hands together in glee.

I hadn't ordered particularly fancy stuff. If Callahan dropped by, I didn't want him to wonder how I'd afforded the makeover, so I'd bought cheap flat-pack furniture, veneer rather than solid wood, fabric rather than leather. The sofa had even been discounted. Now that I saw it in person, I understood why. The website showed it as a pale lemon colour, but in reality, it was more mustard. Yeuch.

And that wasn't the only problem. The delivery left me with an apartment full of furniture and no room to swing a hamster, let alone a cat. I should have arranged for somebody to take the old stuff away first, shouldn't I? Sure, I was back at full strength, but strength only got you so far when you were trying to manoeuvre a box spring in a tiny apartment. What I needed was longer arms.

The entry phone buzzed again, and I cursed under my breath.

"Yes?"

"It's Benito with your groceries."

Fantastique. Another thing I hadn't thought through. Out of habit, I'd ordered my groceries from the same store I always used, and it never occurred to me that the same delivery driver would service both Berkshire Place and Sunset Tower. I mean, they weren't even that near each other. Benito was a gossip—he knew my neighbours and their transgressions better than I did—and now I had to come up with a believable explanation for moving from a swanky penthouse to what was basically a hovel.

"Come right up."

An excuse... An excuse... Staying with a friend? It would have to be a boyfriend because there was only one bedroom. Awkward. Research for writing a novel? Sort of like method acting? No, that wouldn't explain the new furniture. What if I claimed to have bought the apartment to sell on? Flipping homes was big business nowadays.

Two minutes later, Benito knocked on the door. I'd more or less decided to tell him I was cat-sitting for an acquaintance who was in the process of fixing the place up. Muse wasn't fond of strangers, so Benito had never gotten a good look at her at Berkshire Place. When the furniture guys showed up earlier, she'd fled into the bathroom, and she was still hiding in there.

"Hi, if you could just— Oh."

It wasn't Benito. It was Callahan, complete with

bloodshot eyes, a day's worth of stubble, and a bag from a nearby café.

"Uh..."

"Genevieve?" Benito called from along the hallway. "You moved? This place, it's..." He wrinkled his nose. "Not so nice."

Ah, *merde*.

"I'm kind of hoping it's not permanent."

The groceries were stacked onto a cart in sacks—one hundred percent recycled paper—with the name of the store emblazoned on the side. The most expensive supermarket in town. If Callahan hadn't been looking at me funny, I might have facepalmed.

"Where do you want the bags?"

"In the kitchen, please. Uh, if you can get in there."

"New furniture? What happened to the stuff you had before? Your grey couch was, what, three months old?"

Stop talking, Benito.

"It was easier to leave it behind. A fresh start, you know? Perhaps you could just put the groceries right here? I'll stow them away."

"I'm meant to do that. You paid extra for the platinum service, remember?"

Right, plus I always tipped him well, so of course he'd want to help. I hastily fished a twenty-dollar bill out of my purse, handed it over, and started unloading the cart myself.

"Here you go. Thanks a lot, and I'll see you next week."

"Wait, wait, I can carry the bags. Say, where's that pretty glass bird? Tell me you didn't leave *that* behind?"

"It's in storage." I attempted to herd him out the door. "Have a nice day."

Finally, Benito took the hint, flashed me one last smile, and sauntered off along the hallway with his cart, whistling. That left me with Callahan, and he didn't smile at all.

"Busy morning?" he asked.

"A little."

"I'm surprised you've got the energy after last night."

Why would he say that? Surely he couldn't know I'd had less than three hours' sleep?

"What do you mean?"

"You went back to work, didn't you?"

"Yes, yes, of course. Work. Did you get enough rest? You look kind of...tired?"

More than tired. Slightly hung-over, and also a tiny bit annoyed.

"We had a long drive back, and we didn't leave until midnight."

"How did it go?"

"Jeb Moutree's alibi checked out. What's your news?"

"Do you want coffee? I ordered a nice Colombian blend."

The beans were grown and roasted on a family-run plantation near Manizales, and each bag came with a handwritten note from the person who'd picked the contents. Pablo was my favourite—he always drew little cartoon characters at the bottom. I probably paid an extra five bucks for each of the notes, but I didn't really care. They made me smile. And I'd picked up my French press when I went home the other night. I'd have preferred my Jura machine, but I could neither fit it into my car nor explain its presence in this crappy apartment.

When Callahan didn't answer, I nudged one of the grocery sacks with my foot. "It's in here somewhere."

"I need to get to work."

He took a step forward, tossed the bakery bag onto the dining table, and retreated to the doorway. Then checked his watch. He'd never checked his watch like that before.

"Oh, uh, okay." Why was he being so cold? He'd been fine on the phone yesterday. "So, I asked some questions at the club last night, and Madeleine said she noticed there's an ice pick missing from the drawer in the staff break area. She wanted to use it to score through the tape on a box of chips. I searched the drawer myself because I remembered seeing it in there too, right at the back behind the teaspoons, and it's definitely gone."

Now Callahan perked up a bit. "An ice pick? The search team took four from behind the two bars, but nobody mentioned one in the staff kitchen."

"I'm not even sure why it was there. I've never known anyone to use it except Madeleine, and it wasn't fancy like the ones at the bars." Those were topped by antique bronze skulls with jewelled eyes. "The handle was plain silver."

"I'll look into it."

He turned to leave. No goodbye, no smile, no small talk. What had I done?

"That's not all. Carlene—one of the waitresses—lost her door pass a couple of months ago. She didn't want to risk Blane getting angry, so she just borrowed her roommate's because they always work the same shifts, except last night, her roommate went home sick, and Carlene asked to use mine instead. Those passes open the back door."

"Does she have any idea where she lost it?"

"Nope. Maybe at the club, but you don't need it to get out at the end of a shift, so she's not sure. She could have left it in a cab, or dropped it on the street, or even misplaced it at home."

"Means, motive, and opportunity," Callahan muttered. "Potentially hundreds of people had the opportunity, but nobody we've identified so far has a good motive."

"What about the means?"

It took a special kind of callousness to kill a person. I knew that all too well.

"Were you aware Ms. Chavez was allergic to painkillers?"

"She was?"

That was an automatic reaction because Serenity had never mentioned any allergies whatsoever. But then I recalled a day soon after I started working at the club. She'd been lying on the sofa in the break room with her eyes screwed shut and her hands wrapped over her head, covering her ears. "I offered her Advil once when she had a headache, and she said she never touched the stuff. But she didn't tell me it made her ill. Where did you hear that?"

"From Jeb Moutree. They lived together for three months."

I was beginning to realise just how little I'd really known Serenity. We hadn't hung out at each other's apartments or anything, but we'd spent plenty of time talking in the early hours. She'd been my closest friend, but I clearly hadn't been hers. And perhaps I was making a habit of misjudging people? After two dinners with Callahan, I'd begun to think of him as a friend too, but today he was businesslike. Stand-offish.

"Serenity had a lot of secrets, didn't she?"

"Yeah, you think you know someone..." Callahan nodded towards my new sofa. "What's with all this?"

"I thought I'd treat myself to some furniture that didn't smell like stale tacos, but now I need to get rid of the old stuff. I don't suppose you know of a service that does that?"

"You're not gonna put it on eBay?"

"I think I'd have to pay somebody to take it away, not the other way around."

"There's a family moved in next door to me, and they'd be grateful for it. Mom and two kids."

"Really? It's not very nice."

"Anything's better than nothing, and that's what she has right now. She left her ex-boyfriend in the middle of the night with her belongings in a trash bag. She's terrified he'll find her, and every time my phone rings, I worry it'll be her begging for help."

"Well, of course she can have the furniture, but I'll need a hand to carry it to the elevator. Would you help? Or would she?"

If not, perhaps I could ask Benito? He struck me as a man who'd assist with manual labour if the price was right.

Callahan sighed, long and resigned. "I'll help you this evening."

"Shall I order dinner?"

"Thanks, but I'll pass."

Why was he acting this way? Granted, my experience with men was limited—after Voltaire, I'd tended to avoid them for the most part—but were mood swings a regular feature? I began to regret buying the furniture. Deep down, I knew I'd only considered sticking around at Sunset Tower a little longer because of a certain upstairs neighbour, and if he was going to be a dick...

"Is something wrong? You seem distant today."

"Why would anything be wrong?" He softened infinitesimally. "I've got a lot going on at work, that's all. See you later."

Aaaaaaand he was gone.

CHAPTER 28

Vee

"Blane wants to speak to you," Trayvon said as he moved aside to let me up the stairs to the VIP area. The club was packed again. Blane hadn't lost any business, that was for sure.

"Any idea why?"

Trayvon shrugged. "Just said to tell you as soon as you got here."

Blane couldn't know about my little visit to his bathroom, could he? I'd been careful to leave everything exactly as I found it, and I was sure Callahan wouldn't have given the game away, even if he was still being weird. He'd helped me to shift my unwanted furniture upstairs earlier, but every time I tried to start a conversation that wasn't directly related to the case, he'd changed the subject. When I asked whether he had a busy week coming up, he'd requested a screwdriver, which he then didn't use. When I suggested ordering an early dinner for both of us later in the week, he remembered he had to call a colleague, but thanks to my stupidly sensitive ears, I'd been able to hear both sides of the conversation. He'd waffled on about fingerprint analysis while a robot recited movie times at the nearest theatre. My heart ached, even though it had no right to. I'd lost a friend I'd never truly had in the first place.

The family upstairs had seemed nice, though. Marianna, the mom, was around my age—as in twenty-six, not two hundred and change—with two young children. Three-year-old Lola and one-year-old Pablo. Until I donated my old stuff, all three had been sleeping on a camping mattress Callahan had bought her. The apartment was almost empty, but she'd tried to brighten it up with drawings on the wall, mostly her little girl's, plus a few nice abstracts I suspected were hers and the odd scrawl that might have been Pablo's. I'd managed to take a look in the kitchen too, and the cupboards were almost bare. Benito would have another delivery to make tomorrow morning.

Tonight, I slipped through the crowds, skirted around a contortionist twisting herself into knots on a raised platform, and made my way to the VIP bar. Kristy was already working there, her face painted with its usual sugar skull. I'd worn a blood-red corset and a short ruffled skirt with thigh-high black-and-white striped stockings. The corset clashed with my pink hair, so I'd tucked it up under a black wig, a short bob.

"You look cute," Kristy told me. "Blane wants to see you."

"Right now?"

"Well, he didn't exactly say, but I got that impression."

I swallowed a groan. It wasn't that I didn't like Blane, nor that I was scared of him, but the man made me uncomfortable. And then there was the fact that he'd lied about his whereabouts last Friday evening.

"Love your make-up. Which tables need service?"

"You're not going to find Blane?"

"I'll go when it quiets down."

"I don't think that's gonna happen."

"Which tables?"

Kristy gave me a *"you're making a mistake"* look, but she pointed to a group who'd claimed four sofas and two tables near the edge of the mezzanine. Mostly guys, but there were half a dozen girls sitting on laps, wiggling in time to the music. We had a DJ tonight, no live band, but the floor was still heaving. A pair of acrobats on aerial silks kept the patrons entertained.

"What can I get for you guys?"

My smiles didn't come quite so easily these days, but I made the effort. Good tips were a point of pride. Plus anyone willing to drop four hundred bucks on a bottle of champagne deserved a friendly server rather than a misery guts.

"Three bottles of Veuve Clicquot and one of those plates with the Italian snacks."

"The antipasti platter?"

"Yeah, that."

"And some pita chips," the blonde on his knee added. "Low-fat ones. Do you have organic?"

Merde. What were the chances one of my colleagues had brought a package or two up from the storeroom? Not good, I feared. I should have gone to see Blane instead.

"Sure, we have organic." The smile got harder to hold. "I'll be right back."

Just in case, I checked behind the bar, but there were only lightly salted potato chips plus pretzels. We didn't have much storage space upstairs, and hardly anyone ordered the pita chips. My heart weighed heavy in my chest as I fought my way across the main floor, went through the *Staff Only* door, and trudged along the quiet hallway.

"Could you prepare an antipasti platter?" I asked the chef on my way past the kitchen.

"Coming right up."

The fire exit was closed tonight, the red eye of the

electronic lock glowing in the dim light. *Had* somebody snuck in from outside to slay Serenity? Or had her killer been in the club? Worse, what if they were *still* in the club? I'd thought I was prepared to come back to work, but now I found myself staring at my colleagues with suspicion, jumping at every shadow or sudden movement. And *I* was more or less immortal. How must the other girls be feeling?

I shoved the storeroom door and got a horrible sense of déjà vu when the bloody thing wouldn't open. The hairs on the back of my neck prickled as a dark, foreboding dread washed over me.

"Looking for this?"

I squeaked and spun around to find Blane leaning against the wall, a key dangling from his fingertips. I hadn't heard him approach. Not a single footstep, and instead of feeling relief that it was my boss standing there instead of a mad ice-pick murderer, I shivered as chill ran up my spine. How did he move so quietly?

"Do you make a habit of scaring your staff?"

"You were meant to come and see me."

"I'm busy working. Or at least, I would be if you hadn't locked the door."

"I thought securing that room would be prudent in light of what happened. If you'd obeyed my order, I'd have given you a key."

Obeyed his freaking order? He sounded like bloody Voltaire. He wasn't... He couldn't... What if Voltaire had learned to shape-shift somehow? I took half a step forward, but my foot hovered in the air. Blane's eyes were different, a rich golden brown instead of Voltaire's pale grey. Coloured contacts?

No, no, if Blane were Voltaire, he'd have spirited me straight back to Europe, not toyed with me for eight months in Las Vegas of all places.

"I was going to come to your office later," I said. I wanted to add "you arrogant dick" onto the end, but Blane was my boss, and he paid my salary even if I didn't technically need it. A ready source of food was more important to me than making my feelings known.

"How about now?"

"Why?"

"Because I'm asking you nicely and I don't particularly want to have this conversation in the corridor?"

"What conversation?"

Blane waved a hand back the way he'd come. "Please."

He took out his phone and dialled. "Kristy, could you take over the big group near the railing for Vee? I'll send Emilio up with the food."

Then Blane raised an eyebrow, turned, and walked away. I followed. I didn't have a good excuse not to. He wasn't so quiet this time, the *tap, tap, tap* of his leather-soled shoes like thunderclaps in my ears.

Blane was a conundrum. I didn't understand him, but I knew there was something not quite *right* about him.

Upstairs, Beauregard was already in Blane's office, lazing in a leather chair to the side of the desk, his legs stretched out in front of him. The lawyer wore socks decorated with tiny snowmen. Didn't he realise he was in Nevada? I hadn't gotten a good look at him before, just a fleeting glance as he glided along the hallway the night of Serenity's death, and now that I had the chance to see him up close, the uneasy feeling in the pit of my stomach only intensified. Beauregard didn't speak, just watched me the way a lion might watch an injured gazelle. And his eyes were dark. Not only in colour, but in character too.

Despite my strength, despite the vampire blood that flowed through my veins, I felt threatened.

"What do you want?" I asked.

Instead of answering, Blane sauntered over to the credenza beside his desk and poured himself a drink from the crystal decanter.

"Want one?"

I shook my head. I didn't even know what the amber liquid was. Scotch? Or possibly cognac, which was Voltaire's tipple of choice and consequently something that made me gag.

"Joseph?"

"Why not?"

Was this a power game? A move designed to leave me fidgeting near the door while they took their time? Because I wasn't playing. No, I dropped into a visitor's chair in front of the desk, arranged my hands in my lap, crossed my legs, and waited while Blane made himself comfortable in his high-backed leather swivel chair.

"You're paying me by the hour, you know."

Beauregard barked out a laugh, then hastily shut up when Blane glared at him.

"I'm aware of that, Ms. Pelletier. And I'm paying you by the hour to serve drinks, not to ask questions."

"Questions?"

I tried to act innocent, but I was guilty as charged. I *had* spent a little too long yesterday evening doing Callahan's job instead of my own.

"Yes, questions. About ice picks and door passes and... teabags? And also about me."

Ah. So this was what the meeting was for. I'd ruffled Blane's feathers. Who had told on me? I thought I'd been discreet, but obviously not discreet enough. Mental note: Blane had spies everywhere.

How should I phrase my reply? Obviously, I knew Blane had lied, but the only reason I knew that was because I'd eavesdropped on a private conversation. Admitting what I'd done would only annoy him more.

"I got curious. The police asked me a whole lot of questions, and one of the cops mentioned you hadn't been here on Friday evening." Sorry, Callahan. "But I thought I saw you, and I wasn't sure whether I was mistaken, so..."

"So you thought you'd check up on me?"

Deep breaths, Vee. Blane couldn't hurt me.

"Serenity was my friend. If you were here and you saw something, you should tell the investigators."

Blane glanced at Beauregard, and unspoken words passed between them. Finally, the lawyer shrugged as if to say, "Up to you."

"I was here, but I didn't see anything relevant. Don't you think I'd have told them if I did? I cared about Serenity too."

"So why did you lie?"

"Because..." Blane swirled his drink and took a sip. "I came back early because I got a report that Saint Anthony was here."

"Who?"

Not the actual saint, surely? Unless one of Voltaire's ancestors had somehow gotten involved, Anthony of Padua had died in the thirteenth century.

"He's a local pharmaceutical supplier. Coke, mainly."

Oh, now I understood the reference. "Saint Anthony, patron saint of lost souls?"

Blane half smiled, seemingly pleased that I'd got the joke.

"That's right. I don't tolerate drugs in Club Dead. Anthony's aware of that, and he'd also been told before that his presence wasn't welcome here. This time, I needed to deliver a stronger warning."

Translation: Blane had skipped the main course so he could hotfoot it back to the club and beat up a drug dealer.

Ever since I'd started working at Club Dead, there'd been a strong anti-drugs policy. Anyone suspected of taking illegal substances was promptly ejected by security, and all the staff had been told to report concerns directly to Blane. So his explanation actually sounded plausible, and I guess I could understand why he didn't want to explain his actions to Callahan.

"Don't worry; Anthony's still alive," Beauregard told me. "The bruises are probably fading by now."

"That's good," I said automatically, then quickly shook my head in an attempt to impart some sense into myself. "No. No, not good. You should call the police, not take matters into your own hands."

"If they did their job properly, Saint Anthony would be sharing a cell at High Desert State Prison, not enticing my customer base into hell. And you'd better believe that if I find out who killed Serenity before the LVMPD does, the only thing left of the perpetrator will be bleached bones and a doomed soul."

A doomed soul? Was Blane a preacher now? An eye for an eye, a tooth for a tooth? Although I'd sworn off murder since leaving Voltaire, the prospect didn't horrify me. Did that make me a terrible person? Or was I merely staying true to my heritage?

"I'm not sure whether I should wish you luck, or...?"

"You can go back to the bar now, Genevieve."

Conversation over: dismissed. When I didn't move quickly enough, Beauregard got to his feet and opened the door for me, then gave me a wink as I walked through it.

"Nice outfit, Vee."

Urgh. I ignored him and hurried along the hallway, conflicted. Not over whether Beauregard was a sleaze or not—the answer to that was clear—but over Blane's confession. He'd injured one man and might kill another if nobody stopped him. There was a possibility he'd been bluffing, but I didn't think so. Should I tell Callahan? This time yesterday, I probably would have, or at least framed it as a hypothetical situation and asked for advice, but he'd been really off with me today. I wasn't sure how he'd react, and I certainly didn't want to see my boss go to prison. Maybe I'd be better off just keeping my mouth shut?

CHAPTER 29

Vee

"**M**use, can't you keep still for longer than thirty seconds?"

She glared at me in that imperious way of hers. I spoke five languages, and while Cat wasn't one of them, I could hazard a reasonable guess at what she was trying to say: *Why the hell are we still here?*

"I'm sorry, little one. I know this place is small."

Muse's tail twitched. I'd been trying to draw her, just quick sketches, but every time I got halfway done, she began mooching again.

"I don't want to be here either."

At least, I didn't think I did. If you'd asked me the same question early yesterday morning, I might have given a different answer. Sure, the apartment was pokey and it still smelled funny and the downstairs neighbours shouted at each other in the early hours, but it had been bearable because I'd thought I had a friend. Maybe even...preferable?

Gah! What was wrong with me? After I'd escaped from Voltaire, I'd sworn off relationships for life, but in only five freaking days, my happiness had somehow become dependent on whether Callahan smiled at me in the morning. And right now, it was eleven a.m. and he hadn't even replied to the text I'd sent at seven thirty.

Perhaps it was grief that had sent me off the rails? Last week, I'd lost the closest thing to a friend I had, in sudden and devastating circumstances. Surely it was only natural that I'd want to fill the void? Muse and her haughtiness didn't cut the mustard, and who else was there? Nobody.

I sagged back onto the sofa—the new, comfortable-yet-hideous sofa—pleased that I'd worked out what the problem was. My strange attraction to Callahan was nothing but misplaced grief. Psychology 101. Hmm... Psychology... Perhaps when things settled down, I could take a course online? Another degree? The internet had changed my life. For decades, I'd spent my days learning from books, then radio came along and I used to get up early to listen to lessons broadcast over the airwaves. Radio was followed by TV, and cassettes, and CDs, and finally the holy grail of virtual classrooms: Zoom. I had bachelor's degrees in science, humanities, and the arts, although my study of genetics hadn't shed any light on how I managed to be both dead and alive at the same time. Or how I could stop my skin from blistering at the merest hint of daylight.

Somebody knocked on the door. I hadn't been expecting anyone, and my pencil skidded across the page, leaving Muse with the feline equivalent of a handlebar moustache rather than whiskers.

Had Callahan decided to drop by? No, he rapped on the door confidently, and the *tap, tap, tap* of this morning's visitor was hesitant, timid even. A delivery person? No—Muse's kitty tree wasn't due to arrive until after lunch, and besides, a courier would buzz up from downstairs. Unless they were early and a neighbour had let them in? This was why I liked living at Berkshire Place—the concierge took care of this stuff, leaving me free to do...well, nothing really.

I put down my sketchbook and went to open the door.

"Marianna?" Callahan's nextie stood there with Pablo on her hip, Lola hiding behind her legs, and a paper carrier bag from Gourmet Nation hooked over her free arm. Good. Benito must have delivered her groceries this morning. "Is everything okay with the furniture?"

"Yes." She nodded, her gaze fixed on the floor. "And I think... Did you send me food? I asked Jack, and he said it wasn't him, and I don't know anyone else here, so..."

Busted. "I thought maybe you needed a hand."

She burst into tears. Ah, *merde*. What had I done wrong? Was she a vegetarian? Perhaps I shouldn't have ordered the *filet de bœuf*, but it was always delicious, and I'd thought Marianna might like it too.

"I'm sorry," she sobbed.

I grabbed a handful of tissues from the box on the credenza, but when I held them out, she shrank back, seemingly on instinct. That poor girl.

"Why are you sorry?"

"F-f-for being such a mess."

The door opposite opened, and a neighbour I'd never met before poked his head out. "Keep it down, would ya? Some people are tryna sleep."

He slammed the door before I could retort. That asshole! He'd been playing music until three a.m., and now he had the gall to complain? I had a sudden urge to borrow a subwoofer from Serenity's bandmates and play heavy metal at eleven o'clock every single morning.

"Why don't you come in?" I asked Marianna.

After a tiny hesitation, she stepped over the threshold, Lola following. Now what? I wasn't used to having visitors. With Callahan, it had been easy—mostly we'd talked about the murder case, and in those moments of awkward silence, he'd always known what to say. Marianna just stared at me.

"Uh, would you like a cup of coffee?"

She held out the bag. "I...I just wanted to thank you, for the furniture and the food. My ex-boyfriend, h-h-he always said I was t-t-too emotional."

A gift? She'd brought me a gift? I took the bag and peered inside. No, she'd *made* me a gift. A dark chocolate cake covered in gooey icing. I *loved* chocolate cake. The only thing better was pineapple upside-down cake with peanut butter on the side.

"Wow, you didn't have to do this."

She only shrugged, unable to meet my gaze. Without Callahan around, Marianna was even shyer than yesterday. I got the impression that she was as off balance with the situation as me, wary, but also incredibly sweet because Benito didn't start delivering until eight and the first thing she'd done after he arrived was to start baking for somebody she barely knew.

"It's my abuela's recipe," she told me.

"How about I make us both drinks?"

"I didn't want to disturb you. I just..."

"You're not disturbing me, not one bit. I was doodling, that's all. Why don't you take a seat?"

She didn't answer, but she did perch on the edge of the sofa with Pablo on her lap. Lola hopped up alongside, her feet dangling in the air because she really was a tiny girl.

"How long have you lived in Sunset Tower?" I asked as I spooned coffee grounds into the French press.

"Three weeks. Nearly four. Are you new here as well?"

"Relatively. Do you take sugar?"

"No sugar."

"What about drinks for Pablo and Lola? I have, uh, green

tea, regular tea, elderflower cordial...” What did kids even drink? “Water, milk, orange juice...”

“They both like milk, but Pablo isn't very good at drinking from a cup yet. Sometimes he dribbles.”

“Don't worry, I have a cloth.”

I made the drinks, but in the absence of a tray, I had to carry them through to the living room two by two. I also cut slices of cake for everyone, but when I put the plates down on the coffee table, Lola stared in horror.

“No, no, no!”

Marianna tried to console her. “It's okay, *changuita*. It's not the same cake. Shh, shh, I promise.”

What was the problem? I had no idea, but I took the plates straight back to the kitchen. When I returned, Marianna looked as miserable as her daughter. What should I do? I was at a loss, but thankfully, Muse took charge of the situation and jumped onto Lola's lap—a minor miracle because not only was she usually wary of visitors, she also wasn't fond of being petted. But she curled up and purred as Lola scritched her head.

“Is Lola okay?” I asked Marianna. “Are *you* okay?”

“I shouldn't have made the cake. I shouldn't have, but it's my favourite, and I thought maybe Lola had forgotten.”

“Forgotten what?”

Marianna's voice dropped to a whisper as Lola cuddled the cat. “Her father, he... Lola used to love the taste, chocolate with cream filling, so she always used to ask for more, more, more. And one day, her father heard her and told her no, and when she kept asking, he covered a slice in chilli flakes and made her eat the whole thing. I tried to stop him, but I...I couldn't.”

“That's barbaric.”

“It was life.” Marianna took a shuddering breath. “But we're here now. This is much better.”

"How did you get away? I mean, it couldn't have been easy with the children." *Merde*, that was a rude question. "Sorry, I shouldn't have asked."

"It's okay. The more people who talk about these things, the easier it will be for others. The actual getting-away part was easy—I mixed Benadryl into his beer and snuck out—but I had nothing. Nowhere to live, no family, and only the ninety bucks he had in his billfold."

"What about friends?"

She shook her head no. "It's hard, living with a man like that. He alienated all my friends in Escondido, and when we moved house, I wasn't able to make any new ones. Even now, I still get the looks. *Why didn't she leave sooner?* That's what everybody thinks, I know it. But until you've gotten involved with a monster, it's hard to understand. They're like onions. Every layer you peel away, they make you cry more."

I'd refused to give Voltaire my tears. He deserved nothing from me.

"Why did you choose to come to Vegas?"

"I wanted to go to Portland, but the bus was cancelled, and I was panicking in case Miguel came after me, so I just got on the next one that came along. Twenty-two hours later, I was standing on the Strip with two little ones and twenty bucks in my pocket." Marianna focused on her lap. "Those were the worst days."

Coffee turned into lunch. Marianna went upstairs to get food for Pablo while I made microwave risotto for the rest of us. Now that Marianna had started talking, she seemed happy to carry on, although she was still timid. When the delivery man buzzed up with Muse's kitty tree, she nearly jumped out of her skin. Shards of glass flew everywhere as her drink hit the floor.

"Sorry! I'm so sorry!"

"It doesn't matter one bit. Honestly. Just keep the children and Muse safe while I answer the door, okay?"

I cleared up the mess, Marianna did the washing-up, and then we built the kitty tree together, although Muse was less interested in her new toy than in her new playmate. I'd never seen her be quite so friendly before. And by the time our three guests left that afternoon, I felt as if maybe, just maybe, I might have made another friend.

One step forward, two steps back.

Callahan was still being weird with me. He showed up at six o'clock on Wednesday evening carrying a bag from Petronelli's, but when I opened the door, he hesitated, leaning against the doorjamb with one hand in his pocket.

"Hey."

I smiled because one of us had to. "Hey yourself."

"You said you had more news?"

"Do you want to come in and hear it? Or shall we chat in the hallway instead? I should warn you, the guy opposite really doesn't like people talking above a whisper."

"Why? What did he say?"

"He told Marianna off for crying."

Callahan's mouth flattened into a thin line. "Want me to bust him?"

"Can you arrest him for being a jackass?"

"No, but if we look hard enough, I'm sure we can find a valid reason."

"Serenity's case is the priority."

Callahan stepped inside and closed the door behind him. "Despite what you might have heard, men *can* multitask."

I already knew that. Voltaire had spent years acting charming with others while simultaneously driving me crazy. But instead of saying so, I just pointed at the bag in Callahan's hand.

"Are you staying for dinner?"

"I wasn't sure whether you'd be expecting company."

Normally, I'd have laughed at the suggestion, but after today, I hoped Marianna might come over occasionally. I'd enjoyed having her there. She was different from Serenity, but easy to talk to in the rare moments when she relaxed.

"Nobody's coming over tonight, no. Want to try out the new dining table?"

Callahan sighed. Was the idea of having dinner with me really that wearing?

"Sure, why not?"

"Shall I open a bottle of wine?"

"I guess I could have one glass."

I'd bought some cheap wine especially for him. Not paint stripper, but twenty bucks a bottle rather than a hundred and twenty. After a brief battle with the corkscrew, I poured two generous measures. After all, he hadn't specified what *size* of glass.

"Here you go. Did you make any progress today?"

"Not really. So far, all the fingerprints at the club have come to nothing. Nobody has a good motive other than the father of Lyla's baby, and we don't have the DNA results back yet. Plus I picked up a new case—an assault over in Meadows Village. I spent most of the day at the hospital. It was nasty, Vee. Be careful out there."

"The assault was on a woman?"

He nodded, and I felt bad that I'd been peeved the whole day because he hadn't gotten back to me quickly.

"I'll be careful, I promise. My news probably isn't important. I just wanted to let you know that I talked to Blane last night, and he admitted he'd been in the club earlier on Friday evening. But he said he was only there to scare off a coke dealer and didn't see anything suspicious."

Callahan put his head in his hands. "You shouldn't be questioning suspects."

"*Is* Blane a suspect?"

"He was at the club, and he lied to me. Perhaps to you too."

Okay, so Callahan had a point. "I didn't just walk into his office and start interrogating him. I asked some of my colleagues if they'd seen him last Friday, and he heard about it and called me in."

"That's worse. If he's involved, he's not gonna like that you're poking around. Vee, I get that Serenity was your friend and you want to see her killer in jail, but you've gotta leave this to the professionals."

"But you just said you're not making any progress."

"I'd rather make no progress than see another woman I care about in the morgue."

Huh?

"You...care about me?"

Was that an actual blush from Callahan?

"We're neighbours. Friends too, right?"

Friends? That was it? I mean, I always knew it couldn't be more, but it was still disappointing to hear him put it into words.

"Right."

"So don't go questioning Blane. I'll talk to him again myself."

"Could you leave out the Saint Anthony part? He'll know for sure it was me who told you."

"Saint Anthony? That was the dealer's name?"

"Nickname. Nobody would call their child that."

"You'd be surprised. I once arrested a guy called Ninja Quest, and that was the name his momma gave him."

"You're joking?"

"I'm not, I swear. And Shep got into a foot chase with a hooker called Phelony Rapp. Phelony with a P-H, Rapp with two Ps."

"And were her parents charged with child abuse?"

"Unfortunately not, but they should have been in every possible way."

And just like that, we were friends again. But only friends. Callahan dropped by most days that week, sometimes only for a few minutes, but there was no hint of the cosiness we'd shared at La Nostra Casa. He didn't call me "babe" again, although I did get promoted to "buddy" one time when a friend called to ask where he was. I'd basically been friend-zoned, and I wasn't quite sure how to feel about that. I'd always wanted friends, but even though I had two now, plus a new stove and microwave, I still wasn't entirely happy.

Did I say two friends? Yes, because Marianna kept showing up too, usually with some kind of baked good. I wasn't going to say no. And she admitted that she got lonely as well. Callahan was checking into support groups for her, but until she found help with childcare, she was stuck scraping by on government assistance and charity in Sunset Tower. I'd looked after the two children one morning while she went out to buy art supplies for me and extra diapers for Pablo, which worked out well for both of us, but I couldn't offer to do that permanently. Not when I'd be leaving soon.

Because I would be leaving soon, wouldn't I?

Nearly two weeks after Callahan had dumped me firmly into the friendzone, I was totally confused. Life at Sunset Tower hadn't turned out to be as bad as I'd feared. On the minus side, the apartment was cramped, the walls were paper thin, and the neighbours on my floor weren't particularly nice, but Callahan had got one of his colleagues to pick the jackass up for soliciting, which allowed me a small measure of satisfaction.

And on the plus side? I had Marianna and Callahan to talk to.

"Muse, what should I do?"

Muse glared at me. She'd been sulking for the entire afternoon, ever since she'd chased a fly across the living room and ended up skidding into the wall. When she tried that trick at Berkshire Place, she had the space to slide gracefully across the floor until she hit a rug. But Muse loved Lola. Her life wasn't all bad. And I could buy a new rug.

I was torn. On the one hand, I liked having company, but on the other, I missed my real home and my old life. Evenings in the hot tub looking out over the city, my art gallery, coffee from the Jura, long drives in the desert on my nights off. If I stayed at Sunset Tower, would I grow to resent the place and the people? Leads on Serenity's case had fizzled out, so I had no good reason to stay.

And if I stayed, leaving would only get harder. And I *would* have to leave at some point, no matter what. There were only so many years I could stay the same age without arousing suspicions, and Callahan was more observant than most. Was it better to get it over with?

Living in limbo was hard. What should I do?

CHAPTER 30

Jack

"You're buying the drinks tonight," Shep told me as we prepared to leave the squad room late on Wednesday evening. It had been a long, long shift.

"I caught the Meadows Maniac and made you look good, so shouldn't you be the one opening your wallet?"

"How does that square with you telling me I had to buy donuts for the whole department on my birthday last month?"

Okay, I had to give him that one. Truth be told, I'd never understood the office-birthday tradition—having to spend half a day's salary on treats, including vegan and gluten-free options, only for other people to eat them. The day I turned thirty, I'd been called into a meeting with the captain right after I arrived at the station, and when it finally ended, only crumbs were left.

"And besides," Shep continued, "you might have been the one who cuffed the Maniac, but you had help with the catching." One corner of his lips twitched. "Are you gonna call Whitney?"

A neighbour of Whitney Pruitt, the Maniac's intended

victim, had dialled 911 when she heard a noise in their shared yard. I'd only been five minutes away when the call came through, but by the time I got there, Whitney—who happened to be the Nevada ladies' taekwondo champion—had basically handed the guy his nuts in a carrier bag. A recycled-paper carrier bag, judging by the size-too-small "Save the Planet" T-shirt she wore. All I'd needed to do was Mirandize the asshole. He even held out his hands for the cuffs. And afterwards, when Whitney had finished giving her statement, she'd not-so-subtly given me her phone number too, a move that hadn't escaped Shep's notice.

Back in the days when I used to play the dating game, I'd never thought of myself as having a type. But if I did have a type, Whitney wasn't it. Call me picky, but I liked my women to have less testosterone than I did.

And just lately, it seemed I'd also liked my women to have pink hair, expensive taste in wine, and an aversion to sunlight.

Two and a half weeks since we first crossed paths, and I still couldn't get Vee out of my head. When I first met Angie, I felt as if I'd been hit by a train. With Vee, it had been different. More like getting run over by a steamroller. A little trip and she'd caught my foot, then I'd been helpless as she gradually sucked in the rest of me, from the moment we'd shared in Lucian Blane's bathroom to that ridiculous dinner at La Nostra Casa. When I saw her climbing into the cab with that prick from the club, she'd crushed my heart, and over the past two weeks, she'd flattened me completely.

I'd tried to stay away from her.

I'd failed.

When I went out to buy lunch on my days off, I found myself picking up food for her too. When I watched TV late at night to help myself sleep, I wished she was lying next to me. And when I jacked off in the shower, I imagined it was her hand stroking my cock instead of mine. Man, I'd lost my fucking mind.

But every time I saw Vee, I only wanted her more. The woman had dug her claws into me, and she didn't even know it. But I wasn't Vee's only fan. She was being so damn sweet to Marianna as well. Yesterday, they'd been cooking together while Pablo slept in his stroller and Lola drew pictures at Vee's dining table, a dozen fat crayons spread out in front of her. Vee's kindness reminded me of Angie's. Collecting waifs and strays had been one of my wife's favourite activities, everything from an elderly stray cat to the homeless man she'd helped to clean up and get a janitorial job at the Spectra Project.

"No, I'm not gonna call Whitney," I told Shep.

"What about Ramona?"

Ramona—Dr. Ramona Livingston—was a good friend of Cecily's and had been dropping hints for months. Had I tried that new Italian place on East Flamingo Road? Was I a Raiders fan, because she had a spare ticket? And ooh, she'd just happened to bake a whole extra coffee cake one weekend. Ramona was also a urologist at MountainView Hospital, and while the passion she showed for her work was admirable, I didn't need to hear about urinary tract infections over dinner. Even Cece admitted that Ramona never got through a whole evening without bringing up genitals in some form or another.

"I'll pass on Ramona too."

"Why? Still too soon, or because you're hooked on Genevieve Pelletier?"

Ah, fuck. Why did Shep have to be so damned perceptive? I glanced around the room—probably something to do with him being a detective.

"Shh."

He lowered his voice a smidgen. "You're not denying it?"

What was the point? He'd know I was lying.

"Vee? She's not interested."

"But you are?"

Persistent as well as perceptive. Shep was a mosquito among men.

I shrugged. "What does it matter? Even if I was, we couldn't get involved. She's a witness in the Chavez case. If my lips so much as touched hers, I'd jeopardise a future prosecution. Plus Captain Lindsay would nail my nuts to the wall."

"He can't." Shep grinned and dropped his voice to a whisper. "Not after he got caught tickling an informant's tonsils with his dick last year."

I nearly choked on my own damn tonsils. "He *what*? Where did you hear that?"

"I didn't hear it, I saw it. Late at night in the back of his wife's Buick. We'd had a report of a car driving slowly around the neighbourhood, and I saw a vehicle parked in a disused service alley, so..."

"Holy fuck."

"Bleached my eyes out afterwards, buddy."

"Does he know you saw?"

"He knows for sure that *somebody* saw. And I'm pretty sure he knows it was me, but he's never had the guts to ask. Every so often, I make a joke about Deep Throat in a meeting and watch him choke."

"How'd you know the woman was an informant?"

"At the time, I didn't, but I got a good look when I shone the flashlight. Then a month later, the Debra Stringer case blew up, and I realised she was Stringer's personal assistant. You remember it?"

"The Mojave Madam?"

Prostitution was illegal in Clark County, yet Stringer had managed to make millions providing "services" to everyone from politicians to pop stars. By day, she'd taught computer science part-time at a local high school. It was a great cover.

Who would ever have suspected that sweet, grey-haired Ms. Stringer designed an app allowing men to order their kinky fixes at the push of a button while simultaneously harvesting their credit card details?

"Yeah, that's her."

"And Captain Lindsay's side piece was the whistle-blower?"

"Rumour says she saw the walls closing in and decided to cut herself a deal. All of which means that the captain won't say anything if you do cross a line with Vee. And Pelletier's hardly tangled up in a criminal enterprise. She found the body, that's all. What's she gonna say on the stand? That she saw nothing and heard nothing? And we know she's not a suspect because we're her alibi."

"She saw Lucian Blane in the club that evening when he said he was at a restaurant."

"Is *he* a suspect?"

A good question. He didn't appear to have a motive for Chavez's murder. At first, I thought he might have gone too far when he'd spoken to Saint Anthony, gotten a little enthusiastic with his fists, but although I hadn't managed to track down the dealer myself, I *had* met several people who'd seen him since Chavez's murder and he was apparently alive and well.

"Not a likely one, but I still won't risk Chavez's killer walking free."

"Well, in that case, you know what you have to do?"

"Enlighten me."

"Solve the case. Then make sure you wait a few weeks before you bring Vee to any departmental cookouts, and nobody'll care."

"Oh, sure, just like that. Solve the case. It's already going cold."

"Buddy, you had one of the highest clearance rates in the NYPD. You solved the unsolvable."

"I had a lot of luck. And did you miss the part where I said Vee isn't interested?"

"How do you know? Have you told her how you feel?"

"Not really," I confessed. "But I might have mentioned that witnesses are off limits to detectives. And then I saw her outside the club with another guy."

"A boyfriend?"

"I don't think so. She hasn't said a word about him since."

"So you've still been seeing her?"

I slumped back into my chair, thanking my lucky stars that the squad room had emptied out. "I might have dropped by occasionally." A pause stretched between us. "Okay, most days."

Rather than telling me I was an idiot as I'd expected, Shep dragged his own chair over and took a seat next to me. "Guess we'll be skipping the drinks tonight."

"Why?"

"Because if the only way you can make a play for Vee Pelletier is for us to solve the case first, then we need to read through the whole file again." Shep cut his eyes sideways and flashed me a sly smile. "Unless you'd rather go for beers at Club Dead?"

In answer to his question, I turned my computer back on. Seeing Vee now would hurt more than it helped because Shep was right—I needed to crack this case before I made a move, and do it quickly. If Vee got serious with another man, the dull ache I still carried in my chest would bubble over like a volcano all over again. The thought of moving on hurt as well, but I knew Angie wouldn't want me to spend the rest of my life alone. That was the kind of person she'd been. She'd always said her soul was happiest when those around her were happy too. And if our roles had been reversed and she was the one left behind, I'd have smiled down as I watched her heart heal.

"Cece won't mind you working late?"

"She wants to see you happy as much as I do." Shep smacked his head. "Now I sound like a fuckin' girl. Get the damn case file, bro."

I reached for the mouse, but before I could click the right folder, an email notification popped up in the corner of the screen. Seemed we weren't the only people working late tonight.

Lyla Chavez's lab results were back.

CHAPTER 31

Jack

According to the toxicology report, the liquid in Chavez's stomach contained liquorice, slippery elm, marshmallow, and fennel—a match for the Throat Saver tea Vee had mentioned previously. Then there was ibuprofen. Again, no big surprise. After Reuben's comment, I'd half been expecting it. The report estimated that three or four tablets of a generic brand had been dissolved in the tea. But then came the interesting part. The lab had also found traces of mifepristone and misoprostol.

Holy fuck.

Shep leaned closer, elbows on my desk. He'd found a package of candy in my drawer, and now his breath was minty fresh.

"What the hell? Aren't those abortion pills?"

His shock mirrored my own. Had Lyla Chavez been trying to get rid of her baby?

"I believe so."

"Well, shit. Did she take them, or was she given them?"

That, folks, was the sixty-four-thousand-dollar question.

"She didn't even tell any of her close friends about the

baby, let alone discuss a termination. But she mentioned breaking her recording contract to Lucian Blane. Why would she have wanted to take a step back if not because she was pregnant? Looking after a young child wouldn't have been easy if she was trying to tour and record new music and give interviews as well."

"That would suggest she wanted to keep the baby."

"Exactly."

I picked up the phone. Since Doc Pressley had sent the report just a few minutes ago, he must still be working. Although he wasn't a detective, he'd often helped out in the past when I needed technical questions answered, and he'd gained more insights into drugs during his years in the lab than most cops would during a lifetime in the field.

"Doc? It's Jack Callahan." I put the phone on speaker so Shep could listen too.

"Thought I might get a call from you. Ms. Chavez had a most interesting final meal."

"We'd already guessed about the tea and the ibuprofen. Her husband said she was allergic to painkillers, so we're working on the assumption that the ibuprofen could have caused the anaphylaxis that killed her. Does that fit with your findings?"

"Indeed that's possible. Such severe reactions are rare, but not unheard of. She could have been dead within fifteen minutes."

So it looked as though we'd found our cause of death.

"And the mifepristone and misoprostol? Can you tell if those were taken at the same time as the ibuprofen? Were there any traces of coating or capsule left?"

"Both drugs appeared to be dissolved into the liquid. My opinion is that the pills and the tea were mixed as one cocktail. A tragedy in so many ways."

"She wouldn't have taken the ibuprofen herself," I said.

"So if somebody had the opportunity to add that to her tea, they could easily have added the other pills too."

"Oh, yes. Those were almost certainly given to her by a third party."

"You're sure? How can you tell?"

"Because mifepristone and misoprostol should ideally be taken twenty-four to forty-eight hours apart. If Ms. Chavez had intended to terminate the pregnancy herself, there was no reason for her to take both together. It would only have increased the risk of failure."

A chill ran through me. The motive was clear now. Someone hadn't wanted that baby to be born.

One nasty murder had turned into a double homicide.

"Thanks for your help, Doc."

"Good luck with the case, Detective."

I hung up. Shep looked at me, slowly crunching on a Life Saver.

"Five minutes," I said. "Five minutes, that's all it took for the case to be turned on its head again." It had already happened once before, when we'd found out that Lyla had been pregnant in the first place. But then every lead had petered away to nothing. "Plenty of people would have benefited if Chavez lost the baby."

"Lucian Blane's back on the suspect list. Serenity Strange was a big draw at the club."

Blane wasn't just back on the list, he was at the damn top. I'd been trying to speak with him for the last two weeks, but his slimeball of a lawyer kept giving me the runaround. And I'd admit to getting distracted by the Meadows Maniac. Four attacks in two weeks had made the rapist the more pressing problem for the whole—understaffed—department.

"The boyfriend's another possibility. He wasn't the father —DNA testing proved that—but if he already knew that and wanted to take out the competition..."

"Then there's her manager and the band members. The Sinners. Maybe one of them decided to commit the ultimate sin? They'd all have been better off if she kept singing. Serenity Strange was a rising star."

"Didn't the manager tell you he had no idea she was pregnant?"

"Yeah, he did. Chavez had made an appointment to see him the Tuesday after her death—his PA confirmed that—so she probably planned to break the news then. Plus Harber has an alibi—he was hosting a dinner party with his wife at home in New York that Friday evening. Did you know he married the heiress to a frozen food empire? Anyhow, there were ten witnesses, and I spoke to three of them."

"You said you were going to check with the airline Harber flew to Vegas with as well?"

"Turned out he rented a private jet, but yeah, I checked. No dice."

How the other half lived...

"Thanks for doing that. The band, though—they were at the club. But all three say they had no idea about the baby, and they swear there was no band meeting, which was how they usually dealt with important news. I got the impression that although Serenity Strange and the Sinners came as a package deal, it was more of a business relationship. Strange was the star, and they were the backup. Friendly, but not too friendly, if you get what I mean."

Shep nodded. "It was a friend who killed her. Someone with a shred of compassion, at least."

"Why do you say that? They stabbed her in the fucking neck as she was breathing her last."

"Because although they did the shittiest thing in the world, they tried to take the pain away with the ibuprofen, even though that was what ultimately led to her death. Miscarriages hurt like hell."

The way he hesitated before the last sentence... The pain that leaked out on the final word... Fuck.

"Cece?" I whispered.

Another heartbeat, and he gave the slightest nod.

"I'm so sorry, buddy. I didn't realise..."

"Neither did we until it happened. The baby, it wasn't...it wasn't planned." Shep swallowed and glanced away. "But we would have loved it with everything we had."

I gave his shoulder an awkward squeeze. "Did it happen long ago?"

"Nine months. Cece's still cut up about it in private, but she's had plenty of practice at hiding her feelings."

With Maxwell Dorrington as her father, she'd needed it.

"Want to take a break? Pick this up tomorrow?"

He shook his head. "Nothing'll change. And I want to catch the sick fuck who stole two lives as much as you do. I'll speak to the captain tomorrow, get clearance to work overtime on this."

"I'd appreciate that."

Shep managed a faint smile. "Got to catch us a killer, and you've got to get your girl."

I took a deep breath and tried to steer my thoughts back on track. "Speaking of getting things, where would a person get ahold of mifepristone and misoprostol? Aren't they available by prescription only?"

A medicum of internet research showed us that yes, the drugs were only available following a consultation with a doctor, and even then, strict criteria had to be met. But as with most drugs, there was a thriving black market. Dubious websites offered both pills, no questions asked, but with that came two risks for our culprit—an electronic trail of the transaction, plus the possibility that the drugs might be fake. A recent study indicated that ten percent of all pharmaceuticals sold worldwide were counterfeit, rising to fifty percent for those purchased online. If the killer had gone to the trouble of locating the medication and slipping it into Chavez's drink, he'd have wanted to be sure it would work. And I believed it was a "he." Sure, there was a tiny possibility that a spurned lover of the baby daddy could have been out for revenge, but how would she have found out about the pregnancy? No, I couldn't see it. The other motives were more straightforward. Occam's razor said we'd focus on the men first.

And that included our elusive drug dealer. We knew Saint Anthony had been in the club that night. What if he'd been making a prearranged delivery?

"We need to find out exactly what kind of pharmaceuticals Saint Anthony sells," I said. "I heard coke, but does he have any sidelines?"

"Have you asked the narcotics division?"

"I asked them where I might find him. At the time, I wasn't too interested in his product range."

"But I take it you didn't find him?"

"The guy's a ghost."

"Know where he lives?"

"The last time he was booked, he gave an address on Fremont Street, but he's moved on. People say they see him around downtown, but I haven't been able to get a lock on him."

"Does he own a vehicle? We could put out a BOLO."

That was something I hadn't checked. Until now, Saint Anthony had been a loose end rather than a serious suspect in anything.

"I'll take a look."

Saint Anthony's real name was Anton Hardy, and according to DMV records, he owned a fifteen-year-old navy-blue Honda Civic. A clunker, much like Anton himself. He stared back at me from the photo on his driver's licence—

shaggy hair crying out for a barber, sallow skin, and sunken eyes that had seen too much. According to the date of birth, Anton was twenty-seven, but he looked a decade older.

I sent out the BOLO alert, then a faint memory niggled at me. Something about Vee and a car? The details slowly came back—before that disastrous trip to La Nostra Casa, Vee had told me that she had a driver's licence, but then she'd evaded the question when I asked if she owned a vehicle. Before I could stop myself, I'd typed her name into the search box. Technically, we weren't meant to run personal searches, but everyone did it and Shep had gone to get coffee, so he couldn't tell me what a dumb idea it was. With hindsight, I wished he'd stuck around.

Because only one result showed up for Genevieve Pelletier.

And when I saw it, I had no idea what to think.

CHAPTER 32

Jack

"Are we stopping for coffee?"

Too damn right. "Do bears shit in the woods?"

"Well, I guess they must, but have you ever actually seen a bear poop?" Yes, I was stuck with Daphne again. "I went hiking in Yosemite last year, and the rangers warned us to watch out for black bears, but I didn't see any, and now that I think about it, I didn't see a single pile of poop either."

It was too early for this. Okay, so it was nine a.m., but I'd only gotten four hours' sleep, and despite Shep and me spending half the night out looking for Saint Anthony, the search had been fruitless. Everyone we'd spoken to said he was "around," but nobody had more precise information.

Which left Daphne and me heading to speak with Joaquin Gonzalez, the ex-boyfriend. Although on paper he made a reasonable suspect, my gut told me he wasn't the one. Still, Captain Lindsay had given me a long lecture on how gut feelings weren't admissible in court, so until we found evidence either way, Gonzalez was a lead that needed following up. And as Angie had always told me, it was better to be doing something than nothing.

None of the other suspects on the list were available to speak with this morning. The Sinners were doing an interview with a vlogger, Saint Anthony appeared to be a vampire in that he only came out at night, and I'd already arranged to meet Lucian Blane at the club later. Shep would come with me for that, although it was kind of tempting to sic Daphne on the man and let her irritate a confession out of him. Even if he hadn't murdered Chavez, no way was the man whiter than white. And his lawyer buddy gave off bad vibes too.

Daphne had offered to take a turn behind the wheel today, which was a nerve-racking experience because she drove two inches from the kerb at all times. In the few short months I'd known her, she'd lost three side mirrors and come too close for comfort to more pedestrians than I could count. This morning, she paused at a traffic light, and I took the opportunity to breathe. Then I noticed the sign outside the building next to us, and the air stuck in my chest.

Berkshire Place.

Where had I seen that name recently?

Ah, I remembered. Last night, when I'd looked up Vee's DMV record. She'd listed herself as living on the eighteenth floor. I craned my neck and quickly counted. The penthouse? She'd lived in the fucking penthouse? *Oh, how my angel has fallen.* Berkshire Place was luxurious, a monument to money, the kind of edifice where you took off your boots on the sidewalk before stepping through the revolving door. White marble lined a lobby filled with half a rainforest. Uncomfortable-looking leather couches were scattered between the trees, although this month, a ten-foot-high tree decorated with silver ribbon and baubles took centre stage. Ah, shit. Christmas. It was less than a week away, and I still hadn't written a single card. I sure could use the services of the concierge seated behind the curved desk in front of the elevators. He looked bored out of his mind as he guarded the residents against undesirables.

Who the hell did Vee used to date? She'd told me that she left her last home because of a problem with a man, right? Was he an entrepreneur? A trust fund baby? A celebrity? How did *anybody* afford an apartment in Berkshire Place? Legally, I mean. Cecily's father could find the money, but he was shady as fuck.

As Daphne moved off, I felt another pang of pity for Vee. Not only had she lost her friend recently, but she'd also lost her home. Had the bastard kicked her out with nothing? Moving from an opulent penthouse to the dump that was Sunset Tower was a spectacular fall from grace, and yet somehow, Vee had remained upbeat. I had to admire her strength of character.

Would I see her tonight? I wanted to. The only place I'd seen her last night was in my dreams. By the time I'd finished traipsing into alleys and drug dens with Shep, it had been kissing four a.m. and Vee had arranged to share a cab home with another waitress. At least, I hoped it was another waitress. I couldn't forget that morning when I'd seen her ride away with a drunk party boy, his hands all over her. He seemed to have disappeared from the scene, but... *Don't think about it, asshole.*

I rubbed my eyes, desperate to stay awake until we reached the drive-through. The search for Saint Anthony had been a gigantic waste of time so far, and all I had to show for it was a bruise on my shin where an addict had kicked me plus a severe case of sleep deprivation.

My phone buzzed. Vee? I'd messaged her an hour ago to say good morning. I fumbled the thing out of my pocket and nearly dropped it into the footwell.

Vee: Have you seen the TV this morning?

No, I'd rolled out of bed, pulled on the first set of clothes that smelled good enough to last another day, and staggered out the door.

Me: What's on TV?

I hit send but didn't wait for an answer. I dialled Vee's number instead. Partly because talking would be quicker than typing, but mostly because I just wanted to hear her voice.

Damn, I was gone for this woman.

"What's on TV?"

"Good morning, Detective Callahan. Lovely to hear from you. How are you today?"

Shit. "Sorry, babe. Sleep well?"

Babe? Dammit. Too late, I remembered where I was, and now Daphne was looking at me funny.

"I slept fine until Muse decided to chase a beetle in the early hours. She knocked a vase off the credenza and gave me one hell of a scare. Anyhow, the TV... That slimeball's on the news, saying how much he loved Serenity and that he misses her terribly."

"Wait, wait. Which slimeball?"

"Her so-called husband. I can't imagine her ever being married to that man. He looks drunk. Why would he do this?"

Why indeed? From what I'd seen of Jeb Moutree, money talked.

"Twenty bucks says he's setting himself up to inherit her estate. Playing the grieving spouse."

"Can he do that? She was trying to divorce him."

"Who knows? I'm not a lawyer. I hope not."

But I was very much afraid that he could. Laws weren't always just.

"Isn't there anything we can do?"

"Unfortunately, being an asshole isn't a crime. If it was, we'd need a lot more prisons."

"What if he *had* committed a crime? That's the main reason I'm calling. I might have seen him at the club."

"Recently?"

"The night Serenity died. There was a guy... He didn't look exactly the same, but similar. Longer hair, stubble, fatter cheeks, blue eyes rather than brown. All things that can be changed. I know you said Jeb Moutree had an alibi, but I think maybe he was there."

"Are you sure about the day?"

"He trod on my foot as I walked across the dance floor to fetch Cecily Shepherd's organic pita chips, and did he apologise? No. And I also remember he was wearing nearly the same shirt as Dalton Cooper. Black with white embroidery and tassels on the chest. Except Dalton's cowboy gear clearly came from a designer label while the man downstairs looked as if he belonged in it."

"Cowboy gear?"

"Yes, jeans and leather boots as well as the shirt."

Ah, fuck. *A cowboy.* What did Skeeter Moutree look like?

"Can you sketch a picture?"

"Sure, I'll do it right away."

"Thanks, b— Vee."

I hung up and closed my eyes. Could Skeeter Moutree really have been at Club Dead that night?

"Is there a new lead?" Daphne asked. "Or did you get a new girlfriend?"

"Yes and no, in that order."

"*Babe*?"

"Slip of the tongue."

I didn't miss Daphne's quiet snort. She didn't believe me, and I couldn't blame her for that. She *was* training to be a detective, after all.

"So, what's the new lead?"

"We need to find out if Skeeter Moutree has an alibi for the night of Chavez's death."

"*Skeeter* Moutree?"

"That's what I said. When you were watching the video footage from the camera at Club Dead, the one over the front door, did you see a man wearing a black shirt with white embroidery and tassels on the chest?"

"That singer? The one who said he lent money to Chavez? Cooper?"

"No, another guy. Similar shirt, jeans, cowboy boots."

Daphne shook her head. "I don't remember anyone else. But he could have been wearing a jacket." Or come in through the back door. "Members of the public have been submitting their own photos through the online portal, like, hundreds of them. Want me to take another look?"

Yes, and I needed to call Deputy Collins and ask for a favour. Two favours, actually. A picture of Skeeter Moutree and a review of his whereabouts on that tragic Friday night.

"Head to the station. We can visit Joaquin Gonzalez tomorrow."

CHAPTER 33

Jack

"Do you want me to stay?" Daphne asked.

I checked the clock on the squad room wall. Seven thirty. Daphne looked as tired as I felt, but I'd napped for an hour on the battered leather couch we kept in the corner for that very purpose while she worked through lunch. I hadn't missed the Tylenol she'd been swallowing like candy all day either, or the slight grimace each time she tried to straighten. She hadn't said anything, and no way was I about to broach *that* conversation, but I suspected she suffered from bad period pains the way Angie used to.

"Go home and get some rest. And good job today."

She flashed a half-smile. "Thanks, boss. Same time tomorrow?"

"I'll message you after I've talked to Lucian Blane."

It had been an interesting afternoon. First, Vee's sketch had dropped into my inbox, quickly followed by a mugshot of Skeeter Moutree. The two bore a remarkable resemblance.

Then Daphne and I had spent hours combing through photos of inebriated businessmen, girls dancing, and Good Omen—the Sinners' support act. Plus the arty shots of cocktails, tableaus of Club Dead, and at least fifty covert pictures of Jerome Keller. Vee's cowboy appeared in the background of two of the images. The first was too blurry to be of any use, but the second was either Skeeter Moutree or his twin.

We were ready to drive to Heron's Rest and turn the thumbscrews when a call from Deputy Collins stopped us. Checking Moutree number two's alibi was a work in progress, but Bud Lightfoot, Skeeter's boss at the ranch, confirmed he'd looked worse for wear on the Saturday morning following Lyla Chavez's death. Details of Skeeter's whereabouts on Friday evening were hard to come by, mainly because he was out of town today and couldn't answer any questions. According to Bud, he'd gone to pick up a horse from Wyoming and wasn't due back until tomorrow night.

But Bud did come up with an additional snippet of information, one that threatened to derail the investigation yet again. After Skeeter's last bender, he'd crashed his truck into the gate at the Lightfoot ranch, and Bud had given him an ultimatum. Dry out or get out. Skeeter quit drinking and started going to church. The local pastor had taken him under his wing, and not only had Skeeter substituted religion for alcohol, but he'd also fallen hard and fast for the pastor's daughter, although she didn't quite feel the same way. *Yet.* Skeeter was determined to clean up his act and win her over, so Bud claimed. But the most significant point in that little tale? The pastor was fiercely against abortion. If Skeeter had embraced his teachings as Bud Lightfoot thought he had, no way would he have dropped those pills into Serenity's drink.

"But that boy won't stay out of trouble," Deputy Collins scoffed when he told me. "Not long-term. He's a Moutree. It's in his blood."

"How about lately? Any recent problems?"

"I guess it's been a few months since we had to bring him in."

"What are your thoughts on the pastor?"

"If he found out Skeeter tried to terminate Ms. Chavez's pregnancy, he'd run that boy out of town."

"We'll still need to speak to Skeeter."

"Bud's gonna call me when he gets back."

We had little choice but to wait. The other option was to chase Skeeter all over Nevada, Utah, and Wyoming, and he'd be back in California before we'd even begun to coordinate with local law enforcement. With every passing day, this case stretched my patience thinner.

At least I wouldn't have time to dwell on the things I couldn't change this evening. Shep would be here any minute, and Blane had agreed to see us at nine o'clock. The Sinners were on the bill at the club tonight in their first gig since their lead singer's death. According to Cecily, who seemed more clued in to these things than the cops, a guest singer would front the band—Keira Michaels, a peppy blonde who'd come second in a TV talent show last year. I'd looked her up on YouTube, and her style didn't seem to fit with the Sinners' at all, but who was I to judge?

"Ready to go?" Shep asked.

I looked up as he walked into the squad room. Instead of his usual attire of jeans, T-shirt, and sport coat, he'd changed into a suit that probably cost more than his monthly cop salary. Being married to Cece had its perks. Although sometimes, I thought Shep put more effort into his appearance than she did into hers.

I waved at my own clothes—flannel slacks, a button-down shirt, a leather jacket, and work boots. "I thought I was, but now I'm not sure."

"If we're going to Club Dead, I might as well look the part."

"Think of me while I'm stuck on the other side of the velvet rope."

"Just wave your badge. They'll let you in."

"You sure know how to make a guy feel good about himself."

Shep only snorted. I couldn't complain because firstly, he'd always lend me a good suit if I needed to borrow one, and secondly, he'd called a car from the service Cece used. Ten minutes later, we climbed out in front of Club Dead.

"Get to the back of the line," a guy yelled at us as we headed straight for the Amazon standing beside the door with an iPad. The blonde woman was over six feet tall, and she had muscles that put most men's to shame. Her "don't mess with me" expression meant everyone gave her a wide berth, including her fellow sentry.

"Are you on the list?" she asked.

"Detectives Shepherd and Callahan for Mr. Blane."

She turned away for a moment and spoke into her comms set, then came back with what might have been a smile. "Somebody will meet you next to the bar."

Somebody? She showed no signs of elaborating, and her attention was already focused on the next person in line. I caught Shep's eye, and he shrugged.

"We *are* detectives," he said.

Inside, the bass threatened to shake my teeth loose, and I recognised Good Omen on the stage. The lead singer's shirt hung in shreds as girls clawed at him, but he didn't seem to mind. A glutton for punishment, I glanced up at the VIP area. Vee was working tonight and were it not for the small matter of a murder investigation, I'd have veered left and climbed the stairs to say hi. As it was, I had to make do with a glimpse of pink hair as she crossed the mezzanine.

The crowd of heaving bodies parted, and I spotted Beauregard standing alone by the bar. I wasn't surprised to see him, but I *was* a little irritated. His presence meant Blane was unlikely to give us any straight answers. We'd probably wasted a trip.

"Lawyer," I mouthed at Shep, and he rolled his eyes.

Beauregard was the only person in the entire place wearing a tie, and I suspected he was drinking club soda rather than any kind of alcohol. Had he been born with that stick up his ass, or did he receive it as a graduation gift? When we got closer, he caught my eye, then turned and walked towards the door marked *Staff Only*, expecting us to follow.

"Arrogant fucker," Shep murmured as we got into the—thankfully soundproofed—rear hallway.

Just for a second, Beauregard stiffened in front of us. Had he heard Shep's comment? He couldn't have. Shep had barely spoken loud enough for *me* to hear, and Beauregard was ten metres ahead. Still, the man offered a thin smile as he opened the door that led to Blane's private quarters. Voices drifted in our direction as we climbed the stairs. We weren't the only visitors?

As if he'd read my mind, Beauregard provided an answer. "The Sinners will be leaving shortly. Their set is about to start."

Shame. We could have killed four birds with one stone.

Blane and the band were sitting in a private lounge behind the balcony. Keira Michaels was there too, perched on the arm of a couch, looking more like a cheerleader than a rock star. If she stuck around, would the band change their name? Angel and the Sinners?

I had to assume the huge glass window that overlooked the dance floor was double-glazed because the room was mercifully quiet. The group had been there for a while judging by the number of empty beer bottles, plates, and glasses that littered the coffee table. Blane's leather-soled Oxfords rested on the polished wood too as he reclined in a leather armchair, wine glass in hand, not a care in the fucking world. He glanced across as we arrived but finished his conversation—something about set lists—before he bothered to get up.

"Detectives. How can I help?"

"You can wait for us in your office while we speak to these gentlemen. And lady."

He'd made us wait, now we could make him wait.

"They're due on stage in five minutes."

"We'll make it quick."

Blane stared at me for a beat, then shrugged and strolled out with Beauregard scuttling along behind. A dog following his master. I wasn't sure which of the pair was worse—the lawyer, or the man who paid him.

CHAPTER 34

Jack

"Have you arrested anyone yet? For...for...you know?" Trist asked from his seat next to Keira.

Out of the three band members, he'd been the most upset in the initial interviews. There had even been tears. Invi had seemed even more miserable than normal, and while Lux expressed the right sentiments, he'd also wondered out loud what the loss of Chavez would mean for the Sinners' future. Could he have had the same thoughts about the singer's pregnancy? Nothing in Lux's background suggested murderous tendencies, but our chat had still raised a red flag. If I had to write a list of the likely suspects right now, he'd be on it, along with a combo of Skeeter and Jeb Moutree and Blane as a wild card.

"Not yet. But we're looking at a few leads." I let my gaze wander to the door Blane had just walked out of. What reaction would that get?

Invi was the first to pick up on it. "Lucian Blane? *He's* a suspect?"

I shrugged. "I'm not at liberty to disclose any names."

"No way, man. They always got along."

250

Trist leaned to the side and looked out the door. Checking that Blane really had gone? "But he's kind of...I don't know...dark?"

"He's all right," Lux said. He lived up to his nickname—every item of clothing he wore had a designer logo on it. "Kind of a prick sometimes, but he's giving us a chance without Serenity. Most of our other gigs got cancelled."

"Headline act too?" Shep asked.

"He's always given us breaks, ever since we got together. Our first paid gig was here."

"Probably because he already knew Serenity," Trist supplied. His real name was Chad, so I could see why he'd changed it. "Chad" didn't exactly scream rock 'n' roll. "She used to work at his casino. As a hostess."

Casino? Blane had mentioned trying to buy the Devil's Den, but not that he already owned a similar establishment.

"What casino?"

"Not one of those flashy places on the Strip. She said it was more of a private club for high rollers."

"Why didn't you tell me this before?"

"I-I-I guess I didn't think. Her death... I couldn't..." He cast his eyes to the floor. "Sorry."

"Is it important?" Lux asked.

"I'm not sure." We'd gleaned precious little information about Chavez's past, or Blane's for that matter. "But it's information we didn't have before, and any clue might lead to your friend's killer."

Keira spoke for the first time. "I used to waitress at a weekly high-stakes poker game. Some of those rich guys are real creepers. They hate taking no for an answer."

The kind of men who might get a girl pregnant and then try to cover it up?

"How long did Chavez work there?"

Shrugs all around.

"I never even knew she *did* work there," Lux said as his phone vibrated on the table. He checked the screen. "We need to get on stage before there's a riot downstairs."

"We'll need to speak to you all again. Tomorrow?"

The three of them looked at each other, and then Lux answered. "We can talk in the afternoon. Where? My place? We don't wanna get seen going into the precinct. It'll be all over the internet before we can do damage control."

"What happened to 'no publicity is bad publicity'?"

"My place?" Lux repeated.

I'd agree to that. Better to have the band cooperate than balk at the interview location and get lawyers involved.

"Can you do any earlier? First thing?"

"Not if you want us awake."

"Later? The evening?"

"We're playing a Christmas party for some hotshot football player. His girlfriend's a fan."

Speaking of Christmas and girlfriends, I needed to buy a gift for Vee. Not that she was my girlfriend at the moment, but I had hope.

"I can speak with these guys if you're busy," Shep offered. I'd filled him in about Skeeter and my potential trip to Heron's Rest on the drive over. One advantage of taking a limo instead of a cab was the privacy screen. Okay, and the drinks cooler, the heated seats, and the TV.

"Thanks, buddy," I murmured, then turned back to the band. "Two o'clock?"

Lux nodded, and the other two men shrugged.

"Me as well?" Keira asked.

"Did you know Ms. Chavez?"

"I met her a couple of times. We have—had—the same manager. And if somebody's targeting female singers, I want to do everything I can to help."

"Then we'd appreciate you attending too."

"Are we done now?" Trist asked.

"I have one more question before you leave—are you familiar with a man known as Saint Anthony? We believe he was here on the night Ms. Chavez died."

Surprisingly, it was Keira who spoke up. "Oh, sure, I know him." Then she clapped both hands over her mouth. "Uh, I totally don't buy his products or anything. I've just, uh, seen him around. At parties."

"He's a dealer?" Lux asked. "We don't do drugs."

"We're not looking to bust anyone. We only want to confirm whether he was here, and if so, who he spoke to."

"He's about your age," Shep supplied. "Small guy, brown hair."

"We don't know him, right?"

The other two band members shook their heads. Without a better description or a recent mugshot, it was difficult to dig any further. I'd seen pictures of Anton Hardy with a goatee, without a goatee, with long hair, short hair, a gold chain, a sloppily knotted tie, a suntan, pale white skin, and everything in between. What had he looked like three Fridays ago?

"Do you need to speak with Ant?" Keira asked.

"I've been looking for him for two weeks."

"Try Harmony."

"Harmony?"

"The karaoke club?" Shep asked.

Keira bobbed her head. "It's Jojo Hill's birthday today. She's having a party."

Was I meant to know who Jojo Hill was? "And you think he'll be there?"

"You swear you won't bust the place?"

"I can't speak for the narcotics squad, but if they get a tip, it won't be from me."

"Keira, hurry up," Trist called. "We're meant to be on stage now."

"Yeah, sorry." She headed for the door but paused for a second and turned. "Ant always goes to Jojo's parties."

We followed the band out, but when they turned towards the stairs, we headed for Blane's office. He'd started on the hard liquor. Whisky? Ice cubes clinked as he raised the glass of amber liquid to his lips.

"So, Detective... Since you're here with more questions, I take it you're no closer to arresting Serenity's killer?"

In situations like this, Shep tended to play the good cop while I took the bad-cop role. Around Blane, I didn't need to act.

"On the contrary. We have some promising leads. Did you know Lyla was pregnant when she died?"

"Serenity. That was the name she chose for herself. And yes, I did."

"She told you?"

"No, Detective. If she had, I would have mentioned it during our first conversation."

"Then how did you find out? The autopsy results haven't been reported in the media."

"The officers of the LVMPD enjoy lecturing others on morality, but they're hypocrites. The department leaks like a sieve."

That motherfucker. Every time Lucian Blane opened his mouth, I disliked him more.

"We do *not* take bribes."

"Perhaps not you two. I realise Lieutenant Shepherd married into money, and as for you... I've met a lot of liars in my time. You tend towards honesty, except with yourself."

"What the hell is that supposed to mean?"

"The constant mating dance around Vee Pelletier. Either fuck her like you know you want to or back off and move on. You're confusing her."

My fists balled up at my sides, and Shep took a step

forward, putting himself between Blane and me. Inside, I was both seething and slightly nauseous. If Blane had noticed my feelings for Vee, who else might have?

Shep struggled with good cop today. "Mr. Blane, Detective Callahan's personal life has no relevance to this case."

"Au contraire. Not only is Vee a witness, but he's also preoccupied with his dick when he should be focusing on more important things."

"I'm not—"

Blane waved a hand, cutting me off. "I couldn't care less about the technicalities. Just get the man—or woman—who killed Serenity in prison where they belong."

"Why do you think it could be a woman?" Shep asked.

"Isn't poison a woman's weapon?"

"The victim was also stabbed in the neck."

"A poor imitation of a vampire bite. A panicked attempt to cover up the truth and frame somebody else."

"Frame who? Count Dracula? Lestat? Or...or... Who's that guy out of Twilight?"

"You don't think there are female vampires?"

Blane sounded so matter-of-fact, it was all I could do not to roll my eyes. Was the man cuckoo as well as cocky? Or just trying to distract from the issues at hand? One thing was for sure—I wasn't going to get sidetracked into a discussion on the supernatural, not when there was a murder to solve.

CHAPTER 35

Jack

"No, Mr. Blane," I said. "Nobody thinks there are vampires, female or otherwise. Can we get back to the subject we came here to discuss?"

Although at the mention of women, I was reminded of the blonde Serenity had stopped to talk to on the way to her death —the blonde we'd never identified. A loose end. Every case had them, and they bugged the hell out of me. As did Blane.

He smiled the superior little smile that made me want to knock his teeth out. "Of course. On balance, I'll agree the culprit's more likely to be a man. A deadbeat trying to avoid child support."

"Speaking of deadbeats... What exactly was your relationship with *Serenity*?"

Something flashed in Blane's eyes. Not fear, not anger... Irritation? Beauregard's face remained impassive as he relaxed on a leather couch on the side of the room.

"She worked for me. Perhaps you could call us friends. I looked out for her."

"And yet she ended up dead in your club."

"If you're trying to bait me into a confession, Detective, it won't work."

"Do you have something to confess?"

"How stupid do you think I am?" The answer? Too damn smart for his good and mine. "If I was going to kill someone, I wouldn't do it in my own club."

"Word on the street is that Saint Anthony's lucky to be alive."

A slight misrepresentation of the truth, but I was interested to see what Blane's reaction would be.

"Really? He always was prone to exaggeration. I'll admit he tripped and fell down the stairs here recently, but he was hardly at death's door."

Tripped and fell down the stairs? Yeah, right. I was beginning to see why Blane was reluctant to install more surveillance cameras.

"I don't suppose there were any witnesses?"

Beauregard spoke up from the couch. "It was a terrible accident. He should have looked where he was going."

"Which stairs did Saint Anthony 'fall' down?"

Blane gestured towards the set we'd climbed ten minutes ago. "I suspect he'd been testing his own products."

"Why did you feel the need to invite him up to your office?"

"I don't tolerate drugs in my club. The staff had warned him before, but he failed to get the message. I thought it might be more effective coming from me."

"This happened the night of Serenity's murder?"

I already knew the answer to that question, but if Blane confirmed Vee's story, I wouldn't have to admit that she'd told me.

But all I got was a wide-handed shrug. "I didn't make a note on my calendar."

Didn't want to get caught lying to the police, more like. "Have you seen him since that evening?"

"No, I have not."

"Did you see him talking to Serenity that night?"

"I never saw him talk to Serenity, period. She didn't take drugs. Why are you wasting your time here? Somebody poisoned her, and they're still walking free."

Interesting. He'd mentioned poison again. Blane knew about the pregnancy, and he knew Chavez had been killed by a substance she ingested rather than the wounds to her neck. But unless he was double-bluffing, he wasn't aware of her allergy to painkillers or the exact nature of her stomach contents. His police source was either someone on the periphery of the investigation or possibly an employee at the medical examiner's office.

"Let us decide how we spend our time. Did you ever sleep with Serenity?"

Blane's jaw tightened. "No, I didn't."

"Did you want to?"

Beauregard interrupted. "How is that relevant?"

"We're just trying to understand the background of each person involved," Shep explained. "It's a routine question."

"You mean did I find out she was pregnant, then snap and kill her out of jealousy?" Blane asked. "Again, the answer's no."

"I understand Serenity worked for you before," I said. "At a private casino? Can you tell me more about that?"

"What's to tell? She served drinks for five, maybe six months when the band was starting out."

"Served drinks? That was all?"

"What else do you expect a waitress to do, Detective?"

I'd never been to a private casino, but I'd heard enough about them to know that often, the waitresses were on the menu too.

"Did any of the clientele show a particular interest in her?"

"Not that I'm aware of."

"Do you have a list of members?"

Now Beauregard got to his feet. "Of course we do, but it's confidential. Our players value their privacy. We're not handing over anything without a warrant, and you won't get a warrant because you don't have probable cause. This is nothing more than a fishing expedition."

"This is a murder investigation," I snapped. "I'll ask whatever questions I need to ask to ensure Serenity's killer gets put behind bars. And if your client declines to answer those questions, I'm sure as hell going to wonder why."

Blane took a long swallow from his glass. Condensation dripped onto his polished wood desk—mahogany?—and he wiped it with a perfectly pressed handkerchief from his jacket pocket.

"I understand that. And if I thought her murder was in any way connected to her work at Tilt, I would tell you. But there were no issues during her time there, and I can't open all of my clients up to scrutiny. If you have a specific name, then I'll consider providing relevant information. Good enough?"

"No. You're asking us to do the investigation backwards."

"If you're as good a detective as your reputation suggests, then a little thing like that won't stop you."

Blane had been investigating *me*? That asshole.

"Look," he continued, "the men and women who play at Tilt wouldn't poison a woman in a busy nightclub, and they certainly wouldn't make a half-assed attempt to cover it up by stabbing her afterwards. These people hate drawing attention to themselves. With their resources, if they'd wanted Serenity gone, she would simply have disappeared."

All logical points. I still couldn't fathom out Blane. At that moment, I'd have liked nothing better than to march him through the club in handcuffs, but was he guilty? Of being an asshole, sure, but of murder? Time to lay a new card on the table. I wanted to see his reaction.

"But the person who caused Serenity's death wasn't trying to kill her. They only wanted her to lose the baby. Her passing was collateral damage."

How good of an actor was Blane? Could he be faking that look of total confusion?

"Explain, Detective."

"The culprit mixed a cocktail of drugs into Serenity's tea. Abortion pills and painkillers, which she was allergic to."

The glass flying past my ear caught me by surprise. Shep and I both ducked as it shattered against the wall opposite, splashing what was left of Blane's whisky over pale grey paint. Ice cubes skidded across the polished wood floor, coming to rest at the edge of a maroon-coloured rug.

"Son of a bitch," Blane cursed. "Painkillers killed her?"

Was that a guilty conscience speaking? Had he slipped her the pills without realising the most innocuous ingredient in the mix would cause a life-threatening reaction? Or was he just angry at her death in general and the person who'd killed her in particular? If nothing else, I'd gotten a glimpse of his temper. Could that same fuse have blown with Serenity the night she'd died? The wounds from the ice pick had been deep, fuelled by anger or fear or perhaps both.

"You didn't know? Perhaps you need a better mole."

"The baby's death alone would have been a tragedy, Mr. Blane," Shep said. "But two lives were lost. We don't believe that the person who slipped Serenity those pills meant for her to die as well, but the fact remains that if medical attention had been sought promptly, she might have survived. I'm sure you can understand that given the circumstances, we need to do everything we can to find out who fathered her baby."

"It wasn't me."

"Would you be willing to provide a DNA sample to confirm that?"

Beauregard practically catapulted in front of Blane. "Absolutely not."

"Mr. Blane?"

"Sorry, but I'll have to take my lawyer's advice."

An apology? Blane seemed unnerved. We'd blindsided him with the revelation about Chavez's cause of death, and now his facade had slipped. The question was, why?

"If you're as innocent as you claim, why wouldn't you want to clear your name?" I asked.

"Is that everything, Detectives?" He sagged back in the chair. When neither of us answered immediately, he waved a hand towards the door. "Joseph, can you show these men out?"

"Speaking of Joseph..." I turned to the man. "Will *you* take a DNA test?"

The jerk just laughed. "I'll take you downstairs."

Should I push for more answers? I decided to back off for now. With Beauregard moving into full-on asshole mode, it would be a wasted effort.

"No need. We can see ourselves out. Thanks for your time."

I added a hint of sarcasm to the last sentence. We hadn't gleaned an awful lot of new information from the discussion, but we did have the name of Blane's casino now. The best news? We'd rattled him. And when people were rattled, they made mistakes.

CHAPTER 36

Jack

Beauregard closed the office door behind Shep and me, leaving us alone in the hallway. That hadn't gone as well as I'd hoped or as badly as I'd expected. Blane had talked. Even with his lawyer there, he'd talked rather than hiding behind "no comment" the whole time. What would he do next? Whether he'd slipped his dick into Chavez or not, he'd still had a motive for giving her those pills. Serenity Strange and the Sinners had been one of his headline acts. Surely losing her would have hurt his bottom line? On impulse, I opened the glass door that led onto the balcony, only to get hit by a wall of sound. Bass made my insides vibrate, accompanied by the beat of drums and the higher pitch of a lead guitar. When Serenity had been alive, she'd played the keyboard too—I'd watched some of her old videos —but Keira, it appeared, was just a vocalist. There was no keyboard in sight.

"What do you think?" Shep asked.

I thought that if we came back, I'd bring earplugs. "I never heard Serenity sing live, but Keira doesn't seem to be on the same level."

Shep made a face. "No, she isn't. It's da Vinci versus paint-by-numbers. I'm sure Keira's a nice girl, but she doesn't put the same emotion into it."

"The crowd seems to be happy."

"If by 'happy,' you mean 'drunk'..."

A flash of pink caught my eye as Vee sashayed across the mezzanine. She'd dressed in skintight Lycra tonight, and honestly, I should have arrested myself for what ran through my mind. Maybe Blane had been right. Crude, but right. I couldn't dance around Vee forever. Perhaps she wouldn't feel the same way about me as I felt about her, but if I didn't even ask the question, then I'd lose her for sure.

Shep followed my gaze. "Blane's a first-class prick, but—"

I held up a hand to silence him. "Yeah, I know. Just stop there."

Vee leaned forward to place drinks on a table, and I caught myself mirroring the movement. Damn, I had it bad.

"You want to stay here for a while?"

I checked my watch. "Want to? Yes. But I've got a birthday party to attend. Reckon I should buy a gift?"

"You don't need a gift. You have a badge."

True. And if Keira really did lead us to the elusive dealer I'd spent weeks searching for, I'd have to buy *her* a gift instead. And a thank-you card. I dragged my gaze away from Vee and headed towards the stairs with Shep following.

"Are you—" I started, but I didn't get a chance to finish because a waitress walked out of the lounge right in front of me, teetering in four-inch heels, her tray piled high with glasses. Fuck! I made a grab for the tray while Shep plucked the girl right out of her shoes before she broke an ankle.

"Sorry! I'm so sorry," she squeaked, breathing hard. Her face twisted in a grimace when she tried to put weight on her right foot.

"Are you okay?"

"I should have been looking... I didn't expect..."

"No harm done." The glasses were still safely upright, all nine of them. Keira's—at least I presumed it was hers because of the pink lipstick on the rim—was still half-full. "Let me help you with this. The kitchen's downstairs, right? Did you hurt yourself?"

"Uh, my ankle... I think I twisted it. Yes, the kitchen's really close. I'm so sorry, it's my first day, and..."

"No problem, honestly."

I meant every word. This new development wasn't a problem at all. In fact, it could be a solution. I had no intention of dumping these glasses into the dishwasher. While Shep half carried our new friend into the break room, muttering about ice and swelling, I bypassed the kitchen and strode to the rear exit. Now it was my turn to be grateful for the lack of cameras. And also the waiting town car.

Thanks, Cece.

Blane had been drinking wine earlier, which meant there was a good chance he'd left traces of his DNA on one of these glasses. The situation wasn't perfect—firstly, I didn't know which glass, and secondly, this evidence wouldn't be admissible in court—but if he was as innocent as he claimed, then none of the DNA would be a match for Chavez's unborn baby. And I'd be able to bump Lucian Blane up or down the suspect list accordingly.

Five minutes later, Shep climbed into the car beside me, careful to avoid the tray on the floor. Another bonus of the town car? Generous legroom. Envy wasn't a trait I liked in myself, but sometimes, I saw the benefits of hooking up with a rich chick. Not that Cece's money defined her. But her trust fund was always there, lurking in the background along with her family.

Then I thought of Angie and quickly remembered that

when compared to love, wealth was insignificant. Lead beside platinum. Sackcloth beside silk.

"What are you gonna do with this lot?" Shep asked, nodding towards my prize.

"Let's take it straight to the forensics lab."

"It's nine p.m. on the Thursday before Christmas. Nobody's going to be there."

Well, I wasn't about to take it home and risk contaminating the evidence further. "I'll ask Brianne to help."

Shep snorted. "Brianne? Man, this'll be fun."

"She did say to call anytime."

"Pretty sure she was talking about a booty call, not a 'please come to the lab on your evening off to process my dubious DNA samples' call."

"Perhaps she should have been more specific."

I might have felt guiltier about interrupting the lab tech's evening if she hadn't interrupted mine a month ago by showing up unexpectedly with takeout from the Greek place along the street. Apparently, she'd thought I looked tired, so she decided to surprise me with dinner. In a cocktail dress. And heels. I'd also spotted candles in the bag—she really had thought of everything. And although Brianne was pretty and bubbly and permanently cheerful, I just wasn't attracted to her. My brain and dick concurred on that. So I'd been forced to activate the emergency system Shep had come up with when I moved to Vegas a year and a half ago, still hollow with grief and definitely not interested in dating or even in sex. One text, and he'd shown up twenty minutes later with beer and burritos, settled on the couch, and cheered on the Giants as they crushed the Dolphins.

Why didn't I man up and tell Brianne I wasn't interested, you ask? Believe me, I'd already tried that. Nine times, at the last count, but my responses fell on deaf ears. Daphne had overheard Brianne telling a girlfriend that I "just needed time."

You've heard the phrase "if you can't beat 'em, join 'em"? I figured I'd change it slightly: if you can't get rid of 'em, make use of 'em.

"At least the samples will get tested quickly," Shep conceded. "We might get the results this side of New Year's."

"Don't you dare leave me alone with her."

CHAPTER 37

Jack

If Keira's efforts at Club Dead had been uncomfortable, then the sounds leaking from Harmony were a rusty chainsaw to my guts. Was it a karaoke club or a slaughterhouse? A group of drunk co-eds spilled out onto the sidewalk, and I caught one of them under the armpits before she tumbled into the gutter.

"Nice save," Shep said.

"Thanks."

I set the girl back onto her feet, surprised we hadn't both ended up on our asses. At one a.m., I was running on empty. My head pounded harder as we walked into Harmony. Holy shit. If Hello Kitty had gotten beamed up by our friends from Roswell, this was where they'd crash-landed. A petite woman wearing a wet-look catsuit and tiger ears glided over, displaying the results of impressive dental work.

"Y'all here to sing?"

"We're here to see Jojo Hill."

The tigress looked us up and down, her expression a mix of boredom and disbelief. "Aren't you a bit late? She's been here for hours."

"We got held up."

"Where's your gift? Jojo left strict instructions—no present, no party. She's sick of freeloaders. Didn't you read the invite?"

Damn Shep and his "just use your badge." People were already staring at us, and this place was a warren of rooms. The last thing I wanted was for Saint Anthony to get word of our presence before we identified him and rabbit out of the fire exit. I needed to come up with an explanation. Hmm. Did I mention that I went to college with Shep? At Penn State, he'd supplemented his scholarship by stripping at bachelorette parties on the weekends. Thanks to his private gym, he still kept in shape.

I leaned forward, keeping my voice down. "Shh. He's the gift."

Now the tigress checked Shep out properly, giggling as her gaze paused in the crotch area. Which meant she missed his huffy glare.

"Ooh, okaaaaaaaaaay." Her eyes lit up, and she hooked a finger under his lapel. "Nice suit. I might stay for the show."

"You're a dead man," Shep muttered as we climbed the stairs to the next floor.

"Just distract the girls while I look for Saint Anthony."

"I'm too old for this. And I'm not even wearing the right clothes."

"So keep the pants on."

"It's not that simple," he said through gritted teeth.

He was right. It wasn't. The second we walked into Jojo's party room, the tigress yelled, "Stripper!" and women launched themselves at Shep like a pack of hungry wolves. I wasn't sure whether to be pleased or insulted when they completely ignored me. In the end, I decided to settle for "relieved."

As the opening bars to Tom Jones's "Sexbomb" played, I

scanned the room. If there was one piece of good news, it was that the human bait ball around Shep had left few people seated, and I spotted Saint Anthony without too much difficulty. He'd grown his hair, and his left ear sported a row of earrings, but it was unmistakably the same asshole. I dropped into the seat next to him. He half turned in my direction and gave his head a little shake.

"Women, huh? They be crazy."

"Rabid. Say, how's business?"

Now he turned fully, and I moved the edge of my jacket to show my badge. A second later, Saint Anthony was on his feet, ready to run, and a moment after that, he was handcuffed to his chair. Did he think this was my first rodeo?

"Chill, buddy. I'm not here to bust you." Not right away, anyhow. "I just have a few questions."

"'Bout what?" His expression had turned sullen, and he used his free hand to cover the bulge in his pants pocket. Cash? Drugs? Both?

"About your recent visit to Club Dead."

Every so often, one of the disco lights flashed on the side of his neck. Was that a shadow or the last remnants of a bruise?

"Don't know what you talkin' about. I ain't been there."

I sighed. "There are witnesses, Anton. I need to know what happened."

"I fell down the stairs."

"Are you sure about that?"

He looked me in the eye. "Yeah."

Had Blane somehow got to Anton tonight? Or did the businessman merely plan ahead and instil enough fear that Anton followed through?

"Fine. But that's not why I'm here. What happened before your chat with Lucian Blane? Who were you there to meet?"

"I only went to hear the band."

"What about casual conversation? Who did you talk to?"

"No one, man."

"You went to the club, and you didn't speak to a soul?"

"Nope."

"How about passing somebody a package? A prearranged deal?"

"Nuh-uh, I swear."

"You're telling me that you just walked into the club, headed straight to Mr. Blane's private offices, and then took a nosedive?"

"Yeah, that."

"Did you ever go to the club before that date?"

Anton Hardy squirmed in his seat. "Maybe."

"Maybe?"

"Okay, yeah."

"How many times?"

"Two? Three? I dunno. Four?"

"And on those occasions, did you visit Mr. Blane upstairs?"

Anton shook his head, and his eyeballs wobbled in their sockets. Was he high? Hard to see his pupils in this light. Also hard to see Shep, surrounded as he was by a herd of girls. What was the collective noun for squealing females? A pack? A horde? A plague? I glimpsed flesh. Damn, now I owed him a new shirt.

"Why did you go to his office this time but not last time?"

"'Cause last time, the assholes downstairs threw me out."

"Which assholes? I'm gonna need you to clarify."

"The security assholes. The stacked Black guy and that giant blonde bitch."

The Amazon. "And this time? The 'assholes' didn't approach you?"

"No, 'cause that lawyer got there first."

"What lawyer?"

"Blane's weasel. Discrimination, that's what it is. He was waiting for me by the bar."

"Discrimination?" Blane might have had many faults, but I hadn't figured him for a bigot. According to social media, the club had hosted a huge Pride event earlier in the year, and Vee once told me that when a bouncer got arrested for punching a prick who'd called him the N-word, Blane had personally paid the bouncer's bail and then given the man a raise. "What kind of discrimination?"

"Age discrimination. He kicked me out, but Miami Mike got to stay."

"Who the hell is Miami Mike?"

"Another de— Uh, a fellow entrepreneur."

"There was another dealer in the club that night?"

Anton shrugged.

"Look, I'm CAPERS, not Narcotics. I don't care about your business and I don't care about Mike's business. I'm interested in one particular transaction, and that's all."

"CAPERS?"

"Crimes Against Persons. A lady died at the club that night."

"The singer? Heard she got stabbed. What's that got to do with Mike? He ain't a man who gets his hands dirty."

"Drugs were involved."

"Yeah? What kinda drugs?"

"Abortion pills and painkillers."

"Abortion pills? What the fuck, man?" Even Saint Anthony looked genuinely horrified. "I don't sell none o' that shit."

"Does Miami Mike?"

"Probably. He's, like, a doctor."

"A doctor? A *medical* doctor?"

Anton's hand went to his pocket, and mine went to my gun on instinct. He just laughed.

"Chill, buddy." He echoed my earlier words back to me. "I'm getting my phone."

A minute later, I found myself looking at a website for the Hartsfield Clinic, a private rehab facility whose staff included Dr. Michael Klass, consultant psychiatrist. The "About Us" page showed a middle-aged white guy sitting at his desk, the picture carefully staged to show off his golf trophies in the background. I'd seen that motherfucker at Club Dead. He'd been sitting at the bar in the VIP area when I'd asked Vee to bring Cece's pita chips.

I bit out a curse. "You're certain about this?"

"One of the nurses from the clinic is a friend." Anton made a lewd gesture with his tongue. "Know what I mean? The dude can't even function without pharmaceutical help. Uppers, downers, shit to give him a boner. You should arrest that jerk."

"I might just do that."

"Addicts shouldn't be treating addicts, right?" Anton suddenly turned congenial, obsequious even. An effort to remove the competition? "You wanna know where he lives? That ugly pink house at the north end of Maple Canyon Avenue, the one with lions on the gateposts. Or he might be on his boat. He keeps a cabin cruiser on Lake Mead to impress women because his equipment sure don't do that. And he plays at the Royal Links Golf Club."

"Thanks for the information."

"You want me to write it down? Draw you a map? He'll be up in a few hours. I heard he takes speed and then goes jogging before work."

"Don't worry about that; I'll find him."

<h1 style="text-align:center">CHAPTER 38</h1>

<h1 style="text-align:center">Jack</h1>

The tigress reappeared, her lipstick smeared and her tail missing. "Oh, hey, you two know each other?"

"Sure. We're old friends."

Her gaze dropped, and her eyes widened when she spotted the handcuff around Saint Anthony's wrist. "What's that for? Ant, are you into kink?"

He smirked. "What would you do if I was?"

"Here, let me give you my number." She ran the tip of her tongue over her top lip, one hand on her hip. "That creepy lawyer's downstairs looking for you."

"Which creepy lawyer?"

He knew more than one?

"From Club Dead. Good suit, bad attitude."

That about summed up Beauregard, but what the hell was he doing here? Had he been talking to Keira as well? Anton tried to get up, but the cuff stopped him halfway.

"Let me out of here, man."

Did I need Anton Hardy? Not really, not anymore, and I also didn't need the paperwork that would come with arresting him. I unlocked the cuffs.

"Don't leave town."

"If that freak's after me, I'm leavin' the damn country."

He ran before I could respond, heading for the fire exit the way I'd feared he would earlier. The tigress reached out to cup my face.

"What're *you* doing later, sugar?"

Later? Sleeping. Right now? Rescuing Shep. I had to wade into a mass of writhing women and haul him out of the fray. He'd lost everything but his shoulder holster, his gun, and his boxers, although someone had thoughtfully clipped his police badge to his underwear. Half a dozen women chased us down the stairs, complaining that he hadn't done the full monty, although the crowd had still tipped well. I even spotted a couple of Benjamins tucked into his waistband.

"Good thing the car's right outside," I said as we burst through the doors. In the glare of the street lights, I noted the lipstick all over his face, neck, chest, ass...well, everywhere really.

"Laugh, and you're a dead man. I still have my Glock. My badge too, unless Captain Lindsay hears about this."

"You know I'll keep my mouth shut."

"Tell me the information you got was worth it."

The chauffeur held the back door open, lips twitching. "Where to, sir?"

"Home," Shep instructed. "Take me home." The door slammed behind us, and he leaned back in the seat and groaned. "I'll have to sneak in through the guest annex and take a shower. Fuck, I smell like the perfume counter at Bergdorf Goodman."

"Want my jacket?"

"What's the point? Just tell me what you got from Saint Anthony."

I ran him through the details, and when I got to the part about Dr. Mike, he gave a low whistle.

"So he's creating a stream of patients for his own clinic? Revenue generation times two?"

"I've only heard one side of the story, but it seems like a possibility."

"Damn. Talk about duplicitous."

"I need to talk with him. What are you doing tomorrow morning?"

Shep made a face. "Captain Lindsay's making me speak at a community event."

"Don't we have a whole PR department for that?"

"Yes, but I'm the only cop married to Maxwell Dorrington's daughter, and the audience is made up of corporate assholes. You'll have to take Daphne with you when you speak to Dr. Mike."

"Or maybe I'll just get up real early and catch him before he goes jogging."

"Actually, that's not the worst idea you've ever had."

"You sure are generous with the compliments today."

"If he's jacked up on speed, he might be more talkative. I arrested a guy on amphetamines once, and he didn't shut his mouth for three hours."

True, but on the other hand, speed could also make people aggressive. Did I really want the man lashing out at me? And then there was Vee to think about. I'd planned to pick her up at the club after work, but if I did that, I'd have to put off talking to Klass until later. I needed to fit in a couple of hours' sleep somewhere.

"An Adderall addict took a swing at me once," I said.

"But you ducked, right?"

"Yeah." The car turned into the driveway of Shep and Cece's mansion. Well, technically it was Maxwell Dorrington's mansion, a fact Shep hated, but he wasn't going to make Cece live in Sunset Tower just to give Maxwell the finger. The peach-coloured palace had seven bedrooms, eight bathrooms, a swimming pool, a tennis court, three garages, and at this moment, a pissed-off Cece standing on the front porch with her arms folded. Ah, shit. "Uh, speaking of ducking…"

Shep followed my line of sight and cursed under his breath. "Take the car. Escape while you can."

Tempting though that was, I couldn't leave my best buddy to face his wife alone. I swallowed hard.

"No, I'll back you up. Just so you know, I got a new couch."

"If I'm still alive in ten minutes, I might take you up on that offer."

"Hey, what if you borrowed my clothes?"

"The way Cece's standing, she knows there's a problem. And besides, a blonde wrote her number on my abs with a Sharpie. That's not coming off in a hurry."

We shuffled out of the car. Cece stared down at us from the top of the steps, her lips pressed together in a thin line.

"Honey, I can explain."

"Because this is you two, I know it's going to be good." She gave the chauffeur a friendly wave, and I realised who'd snitched on us. Traitor. "Sweetie, that lipstick really isn't your colour."

"So we went to this karaoke bar…"

I jumped in before Shep made the story sound even worse than it was already. "It was an undercover op. Shep was backing me up."

"In his boxer briefs?"

"He started off fully dressed, but as part of our cover, a group of girls somehow got the mistaken impression he was a stripper…"

"Because you *told* them I was a stripper, jackass."

"…and rather than blow the operation, he stayed in character. The girls got a little too enthusiastic. It was a totally necessary and very unfortunate incident, and I offer my deepest apologies."

"I'm sorry too," Shep mumbled.

Cece stared at us, eyes narrowed, for a full thirty seconds. Then one corner of her lips twitched. A cross between a snort and a giggle burst from her throat.

"Oh my gosh, I can't do this. I can't keep a straight face any longer." She doubled over holding her sides. "Move your hands."

"What?"

"Move your hands."

Shep dropped his arms to his sides, and Cece traced the digits on his stomach with a finger.

"You don't recognise the number?"

"Babe, I didn't even look at it."

"It's *my* number. My friend Heather wrote it right before she messaged me. She figured that if you tried calling, I'd know to kick your ass when you got home. Nice dance moves, by the way."

"She sent pictures?"

"No, a video. Do I get a private show later?"

"Anytime." Shep pulled Cece into a hug, getting lipstick all over her. "Love you, honey. I'd never do anything to hurt you."

"I know. But you might want to avoid Daddy for a few days. Massimo also gave me a heads-up, but he called my father before he called me."

I had to assume Massimo was the chauffeur.

"Shit."

"Don't worry, I told him it was a joke. But you know how overprotective he gets."

"How do you feel about spending Christmas in Europe?"

Cece giggled. "Too cold. Perhaps the Caribbean?"

And just like that, all was right in Shep and Cece's world.

Cece whispered something in Shep's ear, and although I didn't hear the words, his shit-eating grin gave me a hint.

"See you tomorrow, buddy. Massimo's yours for the rest of the night."

Which left me with a decision to make. Vee would finish her shift in an hour. Should I go to the club and wait for her? And her waitress friend too if she needed a ride home? Or should I focus on the case, take a nap, and then head to the "ugly pink house" to catch our local drug-peddling doctor by surprise? I could send Massimo to pick up Vee alone, but dammit, I wanted to see her. *Needed* to see her. I missed her. I was *drawn* to her.

Blane had been right, apart from one thing. I didn't just want to fuck Vee. I wanted to do everything with her. Take her out for dinner, go to movies, walk in the desert at night. Cook with her, buy groceries with her, watch her as she slept. The realisation hit me like an eighteen-wheeler. An impetuous, puzzling, pink-haired waitress had worked her way under my skin, and the only way to cure the affliction was to act on my feelings or walk away. And I couldn't walk away.

Would Vee be interested? Since the night at La Nostra Casa, since the almost-kiss outside her door, she'd pulled back. Built a wall between us. No, not a wall. More of a fence, a wire fence. Could I slip through one of the gaps? She'd obviously had a tough time lately—the break-up, the house move, the loss of her friend—and I didn't want to pile on any pressure. But at the same time, I needed to let her know I wanted more.

Time was ticking. Should I focus my efforts on clearing the Chavez case? That would remove one element of the barrier between Vee and me. Or should I give in to temptation and go to her now? Get a little fix to keep me going?

Hell, at this point, I was so tired, so confused, I might as well just flip a coin.

CHAPTER 39

Vee

"I could have taken a cab," I told Callahan.

He'd messaged me ten minutes before my shift finished to say he was waiting outside. Good thing I hadn't made dinner plans tonight. And while I felt guilty that he'd come to pick me up in the early hours, I was kind of glad too. I'd missed him.

"I had to drive past on my way home, more or less. Nice outfit."

Tonight, I'd dressed as a modern Harlequin—the pantomime character, not Batman's foe—in a white catsuit decorated with neon-green and hot-pink diamonds. I'd painted the mask myself, and as I climbed into Callahan's car, I unhooked it from over my ears and tossed it into the back seat.

"The mask seemed like a fun idea, but boy was it sweaty. Never again." I relaxed back into the leather seat of the town car. "Nice vehicle. The LVMPD must have a bigger budget than I thought."

"It comes courtesy of Cecily Shepherd. I was partnered with Shep tonight. Does your friend need a ride too?"

"My friend?"

"The waitress you shared a cab with the other morning."

"Oh, right. My friend." The fib I'd told when I needed to leave the club with a grotty stranger rather than a hot cop. "No, she doesn't need a ride. Her boyfriend already picked her up. You're only just going home? Have you been working the whole time?"

Callahan started to nod, but it turned into a yawn instead.

"Pretty much. I catnapped for ten minutes while I was waiting for you."

Why hadn't he gone straight home? Didn't he trust me to call a cab? Even if I'd walked, I was perfectly capable of looking after myself, although he clearly didn't know that. Next time, I'd say I was getting a ride with my imaginary friend and her significant other.

A low rumble sounded, and I glanced at the sky. "Was that thunder?"

Callahan chuckled. "No, my stomach."

"You haven't eaten either?"

"I'll make a sandwich when I get home."

"Why don't I buy us both dinner on the way? Or... breakfast, I guess."

I had to stop forgetting that normal people weren't nocturnal.

"I'll split the check with you."

"No, really, my treat. It's the least I can do after you saved me a cab fare, and I did well with tips tonight."

Plus my finance manager had called earlier. A biotech company I'd invested in six years ago had just listed on the New York Stock Exchange, and I'd cleared eight figures in that deal. I could afford to buy us both a pizza. Or perhaps something healthier? That was the trouble with being immortal—I didn't have to worry about my diet. My arteries basically de-furred themselves.

"But—"

"No buts. You look exhausted. I'll call ahead and order dinner. Any preferences?"

"Pizza?"

Wow, great minds and all that. I called the late-night takeout place near Berkshire Place, asked for two deep pans with everything plus a side order of potato wedges, then realised my mistake as soon as I hung up. Dammit. *Think, Vee!* Being around Callahan made me lose my freaking mind.

"Uh, we need to take a left here."

"Why?"

"Because I ordered from the Black Olive. It's near—"

"I know the place. What was wrong with Pizza Paradise? It's virtually next door to our apartment building."

"I just really like the tomato sauce at the Black Olive. Sorry."

Callahan let out a long sigh. "It's fine." He leaned forward and tapped the driver on the shoulder. "Massimo? We need to take a left here."

Back at Sunset Tower, Callahan broke the habit of a lifetime and headed straight for the elevator, only to groan at the sight of the *Out of Order* sign.

"Shit," he muttered.

"Want me to carry you?"

I was mostly joking. I mean, I could have carried him easily since I was at full strength right now, but he just laughed.

"Maybe I'll sleep down here in the stairwell."

"If you can make it to my apartment, I'll sort out plates and drinks."

"You eat your pizza off a plate?"

"Well, yes? I have a…" No, I didn't have a dishwasher. Not

in Sunset Tower. "I have a, uh, fondness for eating with cutlery."

And also sounding like a complete idiot. Luckily, Callahan was too tired to notice as he stumbled towards the first flight of stairs. If I had to guess, I'd say he hadn't been sleeping well for the past few weeks either. What had happened with the case? Perhaps I did have a tiny ulterior motive when I invited him over to my place. I was dying to find out whether there had been any progress, and he hadn't seemed too talkative in the car. When I'd tried asking if there was any news, he'd just glanced at the driver and put a finger to his lips, then wound up the privacy screen and promptly fallen asleep.

"I'm not sure I can hold a fork, but I guess drinking Coke out of a glass wouldn't be a bad idea."

"Coke? I have beer." Half a dozen bottles of craft beer, which I might have bought with Callahan in mind.

"Better not. After I've grabbed a couple hours' sleep, I need to go back out to work again."

"You have an early shift?"

"No, a lead."

Even through his tiredness, I heard the hint of excitement. A lead? In Serenity's case? I practically pulled Callahan up the last two flights of stairs, and he staggered into my apartment, then collapsed onto the sofa.

"What sort of a lead?"

"There was a dealer in Club Dead the night Lyla died. Two dealers, actually. And one of them sounds like the kind of guy who might have been able to source the pills she was given."

Callahan told me about his chat with Blane, the meeting with Keira, and his adventures at the karaoke club. I half wished I'd been there to see Shep's antics, but if I was being honest with myself—something I found harder and harder to do—I'd rather have seen a different detective without his shirt on.

This was why I avoided people, beyond superficial interactions and one-night stands, at least. Spending time with people led to feelings, to friendship and attraction and longing. On the rare occasions I did give in to those feelings, I only ended up getting hurt. And dating was out of the question. I could hardly have a relationship with one man while using others for their haemoglobin. It wouldn't be fair. Even if I did somehow manage it, I'd only end up with a broken heart when I moved on. And I always moved on. There were limits to the number of compliments about looking good for her age that a girl could brush off.

But sometimes, I had to live in the moment. So tonight, I ate pizza and drank wine and listened to Callahan's story.

"And that's why I have to get up early," he finished. "To catch Miami Mike before he goes to work."

"Do you need company?"

"Not from a civilian." Callahan closed his eyes for a second, then dragged them open again. "Sorry. That sounded harsh. What I meant was, Captain Lindsay would have my badge if he found out I invited you along. I messaged Daphne while I was waiting at the club. She'll come with me."

"It's okay; I understand."

Perhaps in another life, I'd have been a cop. I kind of liked the idea of getting justice for those who couldn't get it for themselves. But thanks to Voltaire being a *connard* of the highest order, I was stuck as a very rich cocktail waitress.

"I'll update you as soon as I can," Callahan promised. "But I don't want to wake you."

"You won't. I mean, you will, but I'd rather know what happens, and I can go right back to sleep again afterwards." Why was it getting more and more difficult to lie to this man? "Do you want a piece of cake?" I levered myself off the sofa in an attempt to change the subject. "Marianna's gone crazy with the baking again."

Callahan glanced at his watch. "Go on, then. I don't suppose five minutes less sleep is gonna make much of a difference."

Except his body had other ideas, it seemed. By the time I got back with a slice of chocolate cake on a plate—which took me less than two minutes—he'd keeled over sideways, his eyes firmly shut and his breathing steady. Should I wake him? Probably, but he looked so peaceful. Instead, I left him where he was, just fetched a throw from my bedroom and draped it over him. He didn't even stir when I took off his shoes. I watched him sleep for a moment, the rhythmical rise and fall of his chest hypnotic. Since I met him, I'd found myself looking forward to the afternoons. To the early evenings when he'd visit to chat and eat dinner. I didn't long for death anymore. Of course, the arrangement couldn't last forever, but if I took my own advice and lived in the moment, I might even consider myself happy. Yes, I definitely liked spending more time with this man than was healthy, even when he was more or less unconscious.

CHAPTER 40

Jack

"Hey, it's time to get up."

No way. My eyelids still felt like lead weights. Angie had always done this—crawled into bed in the middle of the night, then risen with the larks when a fresh wave of creativity hit. I loved the way her mind worked, but one of us still needed his beauty sleep. I reached out, and my arm hit bare legs.

"Come back to bed, baby," I mumbled.

"I'm not sure that's the best idea."

What the fuck? That wasn't Angie's voice. I forced one eye open, and my vision turned mustard yellow. Why the hell was I lying on Vee's couch? The events of last night came back in fits and starts, blurry vignettes dragged forth from a shattered mind. Blane's arrogant visage, Miami Mike, Shep covered in lipstick, pizza. Darkness.

Ah, crap. I struggled into a seated position and found Vee standing over me, perkier than should have been legal at that hour. It took an effort to force my gaze upwards, past the smooth, pale legs, past tiny shorts and a camisole, past the steaming mug of coffee she held in one hand, past the breasts I longed to caress, all the way up to her face.

"I must've fallen asleep."

Her expression said, "No shit, Sherlock," but she smiled and held out the mug.

"You said you needed to wake up by seven fifteen. I thought you might need this."

Keep your eyes on hers, asshole. I wished she'd put a robe on—a kaftan, a burka, anything—but my inappropriate thoughts were my problem, not hers. And when I shifted under the blanket she must have put over me, I realised I couldn't simply stroll to the door without my cock giving those thoughts away.

What was wrong with me? I'd dreamed of Vee, woken up thinking of Angie, and now I was back to Vee again. The person I should have been focusing on was Daphne because I'd promised to meet her at the coffee place near Miami Mike's at eight o'clock, and now I was late.

I closed my eyes for a moment, taking myself back to the morgue where Lyla Chavez's lifeless body lay on the steel table. My dick began to deflate, and I blew out a long breath of relief.

"Thanks." I took the mug of coffee from Vee. "And sorry for the intrusion."

"Hey, what are friends for?" She reached to the table behind her for a paper bag. "And I packed you a chocolate chip brioche to go."

Friends. That was all we should be, but I was finding it harder and harder to think of Vee that way.

"Thanks, babe. You're an angel."

Outside Cuppa Joe's, I alternated snatching bites of brioche with strapping on a bulletproof vest under my windbreaker and checking my gun. Daphne had been inside to fetch us both coffee, and she'd arrived already dressed for the occasion.

"Do you think Michael Klass is dangerous?" she asked. "I mean, I know he has no priors, well, apart from the car incident, but…"

Yes, Daphne had even found time to do some research, which she'd duly regurgitated to me the moment I arrived. If nothing else, this job had helped me to understand her better. Daphne's strengths lay in the scutwork, the paper-pushing, the stuff that most cops avoided. In that respect, I was lucky to have her. But in the field, she got nervous, like this morning.

The "car incident" she was referring to was the only interaction the LVMPD had on file with Miami Mike, although records showed he'd moved here from Florida a decade previously, hence the nickname. Five years ago, neighbours had called the cops because Mike and his wife were hurling obscenities at each other in the driveway, and when officers arrived, Mrs. Klass was accelerating towards the street with the good doctor spreadeagled across the hood. He'd landed at their feet when she slammed on the brakes. According to the file, both parties had sobered up and apologised, and no charges were ever brought.

"Honestly? I don't think he's dangerous. The man hawks prescription drugs, not guns. But vests are always a good idea in these situations."

"What if he shoots us in the head?"

I'd also discovered that Daphne could be a real pessimist on occasion.

"You can stand behind me. That way, he'll shoot me first."

With the last dregs of my coffee finished, I wadded up the paper cup and tossed it at the trash can. Missed. Stooped to pick up the cup and disposed of it properly. What I needed was six more hours of sleep, not more caffeine.

The two-minute drive to Miami Mike's mansion passed in a blur, and we pulled up outside a pair of ornate metal gates, black with gold-painted accents. Two lions regarded us haughtily from the tops of the gateposts, just the way Saint Anthony had described. Would Klass let us in? Time to find out. I pressed the buzzer. Nothing. Perhaps he was still out on his morning run? If so, that would give us an excellent opportunity to snoop around, with the added bonus that he'd probably be unarmed when he came back. Who took a gun jogging?

There was a pedestrian gate to the right of the main gates, and I hopped out to see if it was locked. Our lucky day—only a latch held it closed. I motioned Daphne to follow and set off up the driveway. Saint Anthony had said the house was ugly, and he'd sure been right about that. It was more salmon-coloured than pink, and nothing quite fit together properly. The front door, complete with oversized Doric columns, was slightly left of centre. The windows were different heights and mismatched sizes. The chimneys weren't symmetrical, and the two dormers in the roof didn't line up with the walls or the entryway. When I glanced across at Daphne, she had a pained look on her face.

"You think the architect was drunk?" I asked.

"Inside, my OCD is screaming."

The effect was worsened by the perfectly manicured yard. Trees pruned to within an inch of their lives sprouted from a lawn that would make golf courses weep. Sunlight reflected off water droplets left by the sprinklers. Birds twittered, and as we got closer to the house, I heard the faint strains of classical music coming from inside. Was somebody home after all?

"Should we knock?" Daphne asked.

I nodded. Despite my earlier bravado, I didn't want

someone rushing out with a gun because they thought we were up to no good.

The knocker matched the lions on top of the gateposts, and the *crack* of brass on brass echoed across the property. We waited. Knocked again. Nothing. The place felt still. Empty. But the music carried on playing in the background, Beethoven if I wasn't mistaken. Angie had been a fan.

Daphne stepped to the side to peer through one of the windows. "I can't see any movement."

"Let's take a walk around."

Had Klass left for work already? According to the website, psychiatry sessions at the Hartsfield Clinic didn't start until nine o'clock. There were no vehicles parked in the driveway, but the door was down on the double garage. And what about the wife? Was she home?

"This place gives me the creeps," Daphne said, shuddering. "I'd hate to live this way, surrounded by high walls. It feels like a prison."

More of a fortress. The place was grim, but the walls were designed to keep others out rather than the occupants in. Despite the bright day, a prickle of uneasiness crept up my spine. A prickle that turned to full-on foreboding when we rounded the side of the house and found the back door ajar. Instinct took over, and I drew my gun.

"What the...?" Daphne struggled to get her SIG out of her holster.

Shit. I really needed to take her to the range again.

"Stay behind me."

I pushed the door open farther with my foot and listened. Beethoven had turned into Tchaikovsky, and I heard the sound of running water coming from somewhere.

"Hello? Anybody home? It's the police."

Silence.

I stepped inside. Daphne stayed on my heels as I checked

each room, her breath rasping in my ear, robbing me of one of my senses. I was tempted to send her back to the car. The alarm panel in the hallway blinked green, and the place looked untouched. Not a burglary, then, but this wasn't right. Who turned their home into a fortress but left the damn door open?

I found out when we reached the kitchen. The smell hit me first, the stench of faeces, and beneath it, the faint metallic tang of blood. My own blood whooshed in my ears as my heart raced. Then I saw the foot. A hairy ankle, a white sport sock, and a bright blue sneaker.

Ah, fuck.

"Watch the door," I told Daphne.

My gut told me the guy was dead, but I had to check. As I got closer, I recognised Dr. Michael Klass, his milky eyes staring up at the white ceiling. And the worst part? Blood trickled into a congealed pool from two holes in his neck.

Chavez's killer had struck again.

Jack

"It's me," I said when Vee answered the phone.

I'd called her because I'd promised, even though it was a bad idea. This morning's distraction had already cost me a lead. If I hadn't fallen asleep in Vee's apartment, if I hadn't prioritised a woman over my job, if I'd gone straight to Miami Mike's abomination of a villa instead, then maybe he'd have been able to give me some clue to Lyla Chavez's killer. To *his* killer. The culprit had clearly decided to clean up loose ends.

"Took your time," Vee said. "I was starting to get worried. Is everything okay? Did you find the guy?"

"Yeah, we found him. Dead."

Her gasp matched Daphne's except Daphne had run outside to puke right afterwards. Although I hadn't known Vee for long, I couldn't imagine her losing her head at the sight of blood. Even when Lyla Chavez died, she'd stayed calm.

"How? What happened?"

"Our neighbourhood vampire struck again."

"Uh...what?"

"Klass had two holes in his neck. It looks as if the same person who killed your friend got to him."

"Ohmigosh! That's...that's terrible. When? When did it happen?"

"The ME reckons between five and six a.m. this morning."

It didn't take Vee long to do the math. "So when we were... Shit! I'm so sorry."

"Not your fault. Blame the person who killed him."

"At least I have an alibi." Vee laughed, but it was obviously forced. "Did you find any clues? Are you closer to catching the monster?"

"The forensic techs are still going over the scene. But as before, there wasn't much blood, so I don't think the neck wounds were the cause of death."

"Another anaphylactic shock?"

"No idea. The doc said he'd fit in the autopsy tomorrow, but if we have to wait for the toxicology results to come back, we won't get an answer this side of Christmas."

"So what happens now?"

"Well, we've been able to rule out one suspect. According to the sheriff's deputy in Heron's Rest, Jeb Moutree was in the drunk tank all night. Skeeter's another story, though. They haven't been able to locate him yet, and when Jeb tried to call him from jail, Skeeter didn't answer."

Which meant my trip west had been postponed. I couldn't say I was disappointed—after this morning's developments, I wanted to have another crack at Lucian Blane in any case. He'd been in town, and taking everything into account, I considered him the more likely suspect. If Skeeter was anything like his cousin, he might have succeeded in pulling off one fluke of a murder without leaving a trail of clues from Nevada to California, but I doubted he'd manage the feat twice. And whoever killed Klass had not only known his address, they'd also either been familiar enough with his morning routine to catch him unawares or friendly enough to be invited into his house. There'd been no sign of a break-in.

The first option seemed the most probable, firstly because it had been a two-bit dealer who'd given me the heads-up about Klass's jogging habit, so it was obviously common knowledge, and secondly because the man didn't seem to have many friends. How many other acquaintances were privy to his fitness routine? Would Skeeter have the right connections? I could see him arranging a drug pickup in the club, but having a deep and meaningful conversation with a man on the periphery of Las Vegas's underworld? I had my doubts.

No, Blane had leapfrogged Skeeter on the list of suspects. We knew for certain that Blane's sidekick had been looking for Saint Anthony last night. The question was, had Beauregard found him?

There was only one way to find out.

"Are you going to Heron's Rest this afternoon?" Vee asked.

"No, I'm going to Club Dead. I need to speak with your boss again."

"Blane? You don't think...?"

"At the moment, I don't know what to think. Just do me a favour and avoid spending time alone with him, okay?"

Vee paused to swallow. "Okay, I won't."

"Take a cab to work, and I'll pick you up after your shift again."

"I can—"

"You're not getting a cab. I'll pick you up."

"Let's get straight to the point, shall we?" I said. "Where were you between five a.m. and six a.m. this morning?"

Blane steepled his hands and leaned back in his chair.

Today, the only things on his desk were a blank blotter, an expensive-looking pen, and a mobile phone, face down. Did the man actually do any work?

"What's this about, Detective?"

"Why don't you tell me?"

"Because I don't have the faintest idea?"

Footsteps sounded, the door behind us clicked open, and I knew who it was without turning around. Beauregard. The man's slimy lawyer-aura preceded him, or perhaps that was his cologne. Either way, he was bad news. And why was he here? Did Blane have a panic button underneath his desk?

"Now, now, Detective. Have you been asking my client questions without me present?"

"Just one, and don't worry; he didn't answer. But now I have another—Mr. Blane, what do you have to hide?"

"Nothing that's pertinent to your case, seeing as I didn't kill Serenity."

"What about Michael Klass?"

"Who?"

"Miami Mike."

"Who?"

"Don't play games with me. He was in your club the night Ms. Chavez died."

"Wait, so you're saying *he* killed her?"

"No, I'm saying he's dead. Don't you watch the news?"

"Rarely. Are you going to tell me what happened, or should I guess?"

"Dr. Klass was found deceased at his home this morning. Preliminary evidence suggests that the person responsible for Ms. Chavez's death was involved."

"Preliminary evidence?"

"I'm not at liberty to disclose the details."

Blane shrugged. "No matter. I had nothing to do with it, so as usual, you're wasting your time here."

"Forgive me if I don't take your word for that."

"How about my word?" Beauregard asked. "Between five and six o'clock, you say? Lucian was with me. We were going over paperwork."

"Paperwork? At that time in the morning?"

"No rest for the wicked, Detective."

"And you'd be prepared to swear to that under oath?"

"Of course." Beauregard threw his arms wide. "I've got nothing to hide, and neither does my client."

"So he'll give us a DNA sample now?"

"You have a warrant?"

"Not yet."

"Well, come back when you do, and we'll talk."

I hated that man more every time he opened his mouth. Assholes like Beauregard made me doubt not only my sanity but my career too. How could I get justice for *my* clients with men like him obstructing me at every turn? Yes, I'd found a workaround to obtain Blane's DNA already, but that incident was just one example of Beauregard's interference.

"Since I'm here right now, perhaps the two of you could tell me if you recall seeing this gentleman in here?" I pulled up a photo of Klass on my phone, the one from the Hartsfield Clinic's website because it was either that or the morgue shot. "Late forties, and he's let his hair grow a little longer recently."

Beauregard made a non-committal noise, and Blane motioned for the phone.

"This is the man who got killed?"

"It is."

"Yes, I've seen him. He comes in from time to time. Sometimes with friends, sometimes alone. He was here last night, as a matter of fact, but only briefly. He left before it got busy."

"Always another party to get to in this town," Beauregard said.

"Is that unusual? A man coming to the club alone?"

Blane shrugged. "Unusual, but not unheard of. There are a lot of single women here. As long as he was spending money and staying out of trouble, I wasn't going to eject him."

"And by 'staying out of trouble,' you mean not doing his drug deals out in the open?"

"I'm sorry?"

"Dr. Klass was a dealer. Prescription pharmaceuticals."

In my interactions with Blane so far, he'd hopped between impassive boredom and cocky arrogance. There'd been the odd moment of annoyance or confusion, but not once had I seen him look shocked. Until now. Just for a second or two, but I was sure I hadn't imagined it, or the flash of anger in his eyes afterwards.

"You're sure about this?"

"Investigations are still ongoing, but the information came from a reputable source." Okay, so "reputable source" was stretching things, but Blane didn't know that. "You weren't aware?"

"Of course I wasn't aware. Do you think I'd sit back and allow drugs in my club? I've told you before—I don't tolerate them."

My turn to shrug.

Blane spoke through clenched teeth. "I'm not going to risk my licence so a two-bit criminal can make a profit at my expense."

Hmm. This was...unfortunate. If I'd had to pick out one good suspect, it would have been Blane. Everything fit—his evasiveness, his dubious alibi, the fact that he was familiar with both victims—but his surprise at Miami Mike's sideline seemed genuine. Now I wasn't sure what to think. This case had more twists than the lucky bamboo Daphne had bought me for my birthday three months ago. Which hadn't been lucky at all, and was probably dead now because I kept forgetting to water it.

My phone buzzed in Blane's hand, and he glanced at the screen. "Looks like your partner's trying to get ahold of you."

I snatched it back and opened my messages. Sure enough, there was one from Daphne. How did Blane know she was my partner? I was certain I'd never mentioned it. Had his research been that thorough?

Daphne: Found the wife. She's on a yoga retreat, heading back now. The local deputy says she's upset.

No kidding. A grieving widow was the last thing I wanted to deal with today, but I didn't have a choice.

Me: Just leaving Club Dead.

"Thank you for meeting with me today," I said to Blane, the words threatening to stick in my throat.

"As always, it's been a pleasure, Detective."

Liar. And that little untruth wasn't the only problem with Blane and his sidekick. When I'd first asked for Blane's alibi, there had been just the two of us in his office. So how had Beauregard known Klass's time of death? Even if Blane was innocent, that didn't mean his lawyer was too.

"Hey."

Just one word over the phone, but the warmth in Vee's voice made my heart swell. After the day from hell, I needed a dose of her sweetness.

Even though I'd fucked up this morning, even though there was an outside chance I could have apprehended Klass's killer if I'd gone to the salmon house instead of falling asleep in Vee's apartment, I couldn't bring myself to regret the time I'd spent with her. Part of me wanted to blurt it out, to spill the way I felt about her, but a tiny, niggly voice said, "What if she doesn't feel the same?" Friendship and uncertainty were better than rejection. I hated the thought of losing what we had.

"Hey yourself. I can't say much right now, but just watch your back around Beauregard too."

"You think he might be involved?"

"There's definitely something off about him, and Michael Klass was in Club Dead last night."

"Was he? I didn't see him."

Somebody had been watching the news, hadn't she? According to Daphne, Klass's picture had been on every local bulletin today.

"Blane said he wasn't there for long. He probably left before you arrived. Are you sure you have to work tonight?"

"Yes. And even if I called in sick today, what about tomorrow? Overmorrow?"

"Overmorrow? Is that even a word? Babe, you sound like you're a hundred years old."

"Uh, I meant the day after tomorrow. I've been reading a lot of classics lately."

I couldn't help chuckling. "What next? Overyesterday?"

"Ereyesterday, actually. Or nudiastertian if you want an alternative."

This was another reason I loved Vee—her quirkiness. And her knowledge. We never ran out of things to talk about.

"Because a man can never have too many words to describe the day before yesterday? *Nudiastertian.* I'm gonna put that in a report and watch Captain Lindsay pretend he knows what it means."

"He'll google it." A pause. "What's that noise?"

The sobs from the interview room were getting louder.

"Mrs. Klass."

"Oh, that poor lady."

Maybe. I wasn't so sure. According to Daphne, the first thing she'd asked the deputy was, "You're certain Mike's definitely dead?" Her hesitation over cancelling her yoga class hadn't gone unnoticed either. When I'd received the news of Angie's mugging, the fear and panic had hit me like a semi, my only thought to get to her. Grief had followed, a black shroud that dulled my senses, at least until the anger burst through me like an atom bomb.

Lettie Klass, on the other hand, had calmly packed her suitcase, fussed about a missing yoga mat, then gone to say goodbye to her instructor.

And now we had crocodile tears.

Shep had offered to sit in on the interview with me. He'd already spoken to the Sinners this afternoon, and they'd gone straight to a party after their gig at the club last night. Alcohol consumption meant they were hazy on how long they'd stayed, and Daphne was busy trying to track down the other guests. One small glimmer of hope was that the band members had all given DNA samples, so once Brianne had processed the glasses I'd borrowed from the club, we should be able to work out which was Blane's by process of elimination.

"Losing a loved one is never easy."

"*Merde*, I'm so sorry. I didn't think..."

"It's okay." And I was surprised to find that it was. Time healed. At first, I hadn't believed it was possible, but with every day that passed, the pain of Angie's loss receded just a little. The numbness faded and left room to feel again. And Vee... She'd filled that space. "I'll see you later tonight. Stay safe, beautiful."

CHAPTER 42

Vee

tay safe, beautiful. Four hours later, Callahan's words still echoed in my head. This...this could be a problem. Not because I didn't like him, but because I was starting to like him a tiny bit too much. Jack Callahan was easy to talk to, kind, and he understood that I was different. He just didn't know *how* different. Yes, he'd been remarkably accepting of my sunlight allergy, but going from that to, "By the way, *mon chéri*, I'm a two-hundred-year-old vampire who can't handle monogamy" was a thousand steps too far.

I should walk away, I knew I should, but I just couldn't bring myself to sever the invisible link that held us together.

"Where's Kristy?" Blane asked, and I forced myself back to reality.

"I don't know."

And right now, I didn't have time to think about it. She usually worked the bar while I handled the floor with Carlene, but today, she hadn't shown up. So Carlene was making the drinks while I ran around like a blue-arsed fly trying to keep the VIPs happy.

"Have you tried calling her?"

Even though HR wasn't part of my job description, I had. "She didn't answer."

I'd also left a voicemail that might have been slightly annoyed. This wasn't the first time Kristy had been a no-show, although it *was* the first time she'd flaked out on a Friday night. Usually, she picked Mondays or Tuesdays, evenings she knew would be quiet. And she always had an excuse. She'd gone to visit a girlfriend in Boulder City and missed the bus back. She'd had a row with her now ex-boyfriend and he'd locked her out of their apartment. She'd twisted an ankle and had to go to the emergency room. Kristy was a sweet girl, and I liked her, but sometimes I had to bite my tongue to keep from giving her a lecture on conscientiousness.

"Try asking Latisha," Carlene suggested, passing me a tray loaded with cocktails. "They're friends. Kristy might've messaged her."

As I hurried away, I heard Blane speaking into his phone. "Pandora, send Latisha to the VIP room. We need another waitress up here."

We? What was Blane doing to help? I was surprised he'd graced us with his presence at all. Usually, he hung out in his lair the whole night, spying on us from the balcony. But I had to be grateful Latisha was coming because the VIP area was heaving this evening, and although downstairs was busy too, the folks on the main floor weren't so demanding.

By the time I'd served drinks to a tipsy bachelorette party, answered their questions about the best cabaret shows, and apologised for the lack of strippers—apparently some members of the group had been to a karaoke bar yesterday and felt up a *very* hot cop—Latisha had arrived from the bar downstairs and Blane was drinking a glass of wine. A Californian Cabernet Sauvignon, not cheap but not extortionate either. Voltaire would have turned his nose up at it.

"Kristy sounded upset," Latisha was telling Blane. "Like she'd been crying. I think maybe her boyfriend died."

She had a new boyfriend?

"You *think* he died?" Blane asked. "Isn't that the kind of thing she might confirm one way or the other?"

Latisha leaned closer to our nosy boss, and once again, I was grateful for my enhanced hearing.

"Nobody was supposed to know he was her boyfriend. In case his wife found out. I mean, she never even told me, not officially, but he used to pick her up sometimes."

Oh my gosh. Kristy had been seeing a married man? I kept my face impassive and stepped behind the bar, ducking down as I pretended to rummage for the right flavour of chips on the bottom shelf. The guests would have to wait a moment because no way was I missing this.

"He picked her up from here?" Blane asked.

"Occasionally he came in for drinks too."

No. No way. I began to get a bad, bad feeling about this. Dr. Klass had been a patron—I recognised him from the news —and what's more, he always sat at the bar so Kristy served him. *Bordel de merde.* Had he come to see *her* on the night of Serenity's death? Or somebody else? Our murderer? I knew Kristy hadn't killed Serenity personally because she'd been upstairs with me the whole time, but what if Dr. Klass had mentioned a meeting to her? I needed to call Callahan. If Serenity's killer was tidying up loose ends, then Kristy could be next.

Blane took a sip of his wine. "And what makes you think this man's dead?"

"He was on the news this morning. That guy who got murdered in his house?"

"Mike Klass? Kristy was involved with Mike Klass?" Blane sounded interested. *Too* interested. Could *he* have been the person Klass came to meet?

"I forget the name. I think he was a doctor. Maybe the wife found out and did it?"

The news hadn't mentioned the puncture wounds. Callahan told me cops often withheld details from the media, little facts that only the killer and the police would know, so they could use them later in interviews. Which meant Blane couldn't know about the stab wounds to Klass's neck either, about the connection to Serenity, unless... Unless he'd been involved. I rose in time to see him hustling down the stairs like the fires of hell were behind him.

Why? Where was he going in such a hurry? *Did* he know about the connection?

"Just running to the bathroom," I told Carlene, patting my pockets to find my door pass. "And I need to grab some air. Back in five."

"Hurry, won't you? Do you need to borrow my pass?"

"I thought you lost it?"

"So the funniest thing happened. I was clearing out my closet to take a bunch of clothes to Goodwill, and I found it in the pocket of these really old red pants. Like, I don't even remember wearing them to work, but I guess I must have."

Brilliant. Another lead gone. "That's good news. I promise I'll be as quick as I can."

I kept an eye out for Blane as I hurried along the rear corridor, but he must have gone back to his top-floor crypt. Outside, the alley was empty and blessedly quiet after the noise of the club, and I took a deep breath. Then regretted it because the dumpsters smelled gross.

Callahan's photo flashed up on my phone as I dialled. I'd taken it when he wasn't looking, which left me feeling a little guilty, but not guilty enough to delete it. He was the first man in decades that I'd wanted to get to know. To spend time with. To wake up next to in my blacked-out bedroom. To burden with my secrets and my sins.

Arrête d'être si stupide, Genevieve. There was a reason I'd kept my heart caged for the last century, and I couldn't give the key to anyone, not even Jack.

"Answer the phone," I muttered, but he didn't. Instead, his brusque voice invited me to leave a message. *Merde.*

"It's Vee. Can you call me? It's urgent."

What if Serenity's killer was stalking Kristy at this very moment? He could be outside her apartment building, watching, waiting, biding his time for the perfect moment to shut her up for good. Or perhaps he'd done it already? An image of her lifeless body darkened my mind, blood trickling from two puncture wounds on her neck. A Hollywood vampire. Ridiculous. Even if I sucked someone almost dry, my saliva contained a clotting agent that helped to prevent unwanted mess afterwards. I tried Callahan again with the same result. What should I do?

After Serenity's death, I'd sworn that if I ever got my hands on the man who left her to die so cruelly, alone and fighting for breath, I'd choke the life out of him. The words had been born out of sadness and anger, spoken of an act I never thought for a moment I'd follow through on, but if that bastard went after another of my friends... I could fight a man and win. I'd done it before. Back in the nineteenth and early twentieth centuries, white knights like Callahan had been few and far between, while men who preyed on innocent young women had been all too common. But I wasn't as innocent as I looked, or as young, for that matter. If Voltaire had one redeeming feature, it was that he'd taught me to fight. He didn't like anyone to hurt me but himself.

I hunched my shoulders as I climbed the stairs to the VIP lounge, wrapping my arms around my stomach. Thankfully, my sun-starved skin left me looking pale on a good day. I staggered to the bar.

"Carlene, I'm so sorry. I'm sick."

"Sick? Like, puking?"

I nodded, and she quickly backed up until her ass hit the counter behind her.

"Don't come near me, okay? I'm going on vacation next week, and I don't want to hurl on the beach."

"I think maybe I should go home, but we're short-handed."

"Get the hell out of here. We'll manage."

"Have you seen Blane?"

"I'll explain to Blane. Go. Go!"

CHAPTER 43

Vee

Carlene didn't have to tell me twice. I kept up the act, clutching my stomach until I reached the far end of the line outside, then straightened to hail a cab. One stopped instantly, probably because I'd dressed as a schoolgirl tonight and my skirt barely came to mid-thigh. That outfit always got me tips. Hey, I might as well make the most of my assets, okay? Kristy lived a twenty-five-minute ride away, but I'd never drive my own car to that neighbourhood because I was rather fond of my alloy wheels. Luckily, I hadn't worn a nice watch to work.

I'd ride-shared with Kristy a few times over the past month, mostly because I knew money was tight for her and that way she'd only have to pay half. Tonight, a light glowed in her apartment window. To get to the door, I had to duck down a gloomy alley beside a run-down barbershop and climb a rusty metal staircase screwed to the side of the building. It creaked and groaned with every step, and for once, I was glad to be immortal. The whole way, I listened out for signs of company. A heartbeat. Breathing. As I neared the top, a single set of footsteps crossed the apartment, bare feet on wood. Light and unhurried. Kristy? I knocked softly, and the steps paused, then headed in my direction.

"Who is it?"

"It's Vee. From work?"

"Why are you here?"

"I just wanted to check you were okay."

"I'm fine."

"Do you want company?"

"No."

How could I get her to let me in? Breaking the door down wasn't exactly a viable option. Dammit, where was Callahan?

"I'm so sorry about Mike."

Silence. She was right behind the door, and I heard a quiet sniffle. Then—hallelujah—the sound of one, two, three bolts thunking back. Latisha had been absolutely right about the crying. Kristy's eyes were red and puffy. She opened the door just wide enough for me to slip inside, then quickly locked it behind me.

"You know about Mike?"

I mentally crossed my fingers and fibbed. "I saw the way he looked at you in the club, and then when I watched the news..."

Kristy burst into great racking sobs. *Fantastique.* Now what was I meant to do? Offering comfort wasn't one of my specialties. I pulled her into an awkward hug, sending silent thanks to Lola. That little girl gave the best hugs, and I'd gotten a lot of them over the past week.

"Things were serious between you two?" I asked.

Kristy nodded. "We loved each other. We were going to get a place together after he finished with his wife."

"His wife?" The words came out harsher than I'd intended. Yes, Latisha had let that little snippet slip earlier, but still... His freaking *wife*?

"They haven't been getting along for ages. He promised he'd leave her just as soon as he got his investments tied up."

Oh, sure, sure. They all said that. "It must have come as a real shock."

"He always said she had a bad temper." The tears were flowing freely now, and my shoulder was damp. "B-b-but I never thought she'd *kill* him."

"You suspect it was her?"

"Well, who else would it have been? Mike didn't have any enemies."

Wait. Was she even aware of his pharmaceutical sideline? "What about his clients?"

"At the clinic? Oh, no. No, no, no. They all *loved* him. He helped them so much."

"No, I meant at his other, uh, job?"

"Other job? What other job? He's on the social committee at his golf club, but he never mentioned any disputes there either."

Oh, shit. She really didn't know? Well, I wasn't gonna be the one to break the news. This was way, way above my pay grade.

"I guess I must've gotten him confused with another guy. Never mind. So... Uh, did you see him talking to anyone else in the club last night? I just wonder if maybe somebody followed him home from there?"

"He was always careful. His wife thought he was doing an emergency consult."

"What if she got suspicious? Hired a private detective or something?"

"Oh my gosh! That vindictive bitch!"

"I mean, I'm not saying she definitely did that. It's just me spitballing. Have you been in touch with the police?"

"I... No."

"You should probably call them."

"But... But what if... What if they think *I* did it?"

"You don't have a motive. If you were going to kill someone, it would be his wife, right?"

Kristy nodded, then her expression morphed into horror. "No! No, I wouldn't have killed anyone."

Oops. This was why I needed Callahan here. I wasn't a detective. Yes, I'd managed to bumble my way through the evening with Reuben, but now I had no idea what I was doing or which questions to ask.

"Of course not, you totally wouldn't. I wasn't suggesting that for a minute... So, yeah, uh, I was just wondering... Like, if somebody was stalking Mike, trying to work out the best place to, you know..."

Kristy started bawling again, and I bit my bottom lip. Thankfully I wasn't too hungry at the moment, which meant my canine teeth were safely retracted and I didn't do myself any damage. I'd snacked on an unconscious oil executive from Alberta the night before last, feeling horrendously guilty the whole time because I'd told Callahan I was sharing a ride home with Carlene.

"Sorry," I tried.

"Mike was so k-k-kind. We used to go sailing on his boat on the weekends, and he always brought me these stupid little gifts, like snow globes and teddy bears and... *Snow.* He promised to take me skiing."

"Is there anyone I could call to help you? Your parents? A sibling?"

Kristy shook her head. "It was just me and my mom growing up, and three years ago, she joined this weird religious sect and moved to Argentina. She doesn't even have a phone. I-I-I don't know what to do. I didn't even call in sick to the club. Do you think I'll get fired?"

"I can talk to Blane." Even if I had absolutely no idea what to say. "But I really think you should consider speaking to the police. You were one of the last people to see Mike alive."

"I don't want to go to prison."

"If you're innocent, you won't go to prison."

"Do you have any idea how many innocent people go to prison every day? A guy I went to school with, Jeremiah, he got framed by the cops and served six years before a lawyer got him out."

"The detective who's investigating Serenity's death lives in the same building as me, and he seems nice. Maybe you could talk with him?"

"I'm not sure..."

"Mike was at the club last night, wasn't he? I can tell Detective Callahan what I saw..." Which honestly wasn't an awful lot. "But you worked an earlier shift than me yesterday. They'll want to build up a picture of Mike's evening. Of everyone he interacted with. *Did* you see him speak to anyone?"

"Last night? He was there for, like, five minutes. He brought me a pair of e-e-earrings for our four-month anniversary. I'm telling you, it was his wife who killed him. Or maybe she, like, hired a hitman?"

"Why didn't he stick around last night?"

"Because he had notes to write up."

"On a Friday evening?"

"Usually he did it over the weekend, but we were meant to be going out on his b-b-boat tomorrow."

I handed Kristy another tissue. "Are you sure Mike didn't speak to anyone else last night?"

"I... I..."

"Think hard. It could be important."

"Uh, no, nobody. Well, not like strangers. Just Carlene. And Trayvon. And Blane right after he walked into the club. But I doubt his wife hired any of *them* to kill him. H-h-how do you think he died?" The tears flowed again. "W-w-what if it was slow? I can't bear to think...to think..."

"Don't think, okay? It won't help. Let's focus on the future, on making sure whoever did this gets locked up for a really long time."

"She deserves to rot."

Kristy might have thought the culprit was Mrs. Klass, but I knew better. It was someone connected to the club. It *had* to be. Why else would those puncture marks have been on Miami Mike's neck? For one brief, horrifying second, Voltaire's smirking face popped into my head, but I quickly discounted the possibility. He'd never have been that sloppy. Voltaire timed the moment of death perfectly, so the fang marks healed a beat before the victim's heart gave out. Who did that leave?

"Mike was in the club the evening Serenity died too."

Kristy narrowed her eyes and took half a step back. "So? What are you saying?"

"Nothing," I said hastily. "Just thinking out loud. What if he saw something that night?"

"Like what? He was sitting at the VIP bar when she died. You know that because you were there too. And besides, we talked about it the next day. He was as horrified by her death as I was."

"Who else did he speak to while he was there?"

"I don't know! It was weeks ago. Why are you asking these questions?"

"Because two deaths connected to the club in the same month is really weird, don't you think? And we still work there. What if somebody comes after us next? I just want to help the police solve these murders, don't you?"

At the word "murders," Kristy started weeping again. I fished around in my purse until I found a tissue. How did Callahan do this every day? Deal with emotional witnesses, I mean. One evening of playing therapist and I was feeling quite drained myself.

"Mike came to see *me* that evening. He always came to see *me*."

"But you were busy working. It stands to reason that he would have chatted. I saw..." Funny how seemingly unimportant things could suddenly come back to you, wasn't it? "I saw him say a few words to Dalton Cooper when he came to the bar."

And Dalton had been sitting with Serenity. Could he have been the one who...? No, Callahan had said the pills were mixed into Serenity's tea, and when she was speaking with Dalton, I'd given her sparkling grape juice and she'd left it untouched.

"He only asked Dalton when his new album would be coming out. Mike is—was—a big country music fan. H-h-he was going to take me to a concert."

"Did he talk to anyone else?"

"No, he was by the bar the whole time. Oh, except when he went to the main bar to get a bottle of White Zinfandel. I don't understand why Blane doesn't stock that in the VIP area."

I did. White Zinfandel was one small step above corn syrup and rubbing alcohol, an overly sweet abomination only good for a cheap buzz. Not something VIPs made a habit of ordering.

"He complained about it to Blane," Kristy continued. "But Blane said it was a downstairs wine, whatever that means."

"He talked to Blane? That night?"

"I guess so. When Mike got back upstairs, he told me what Blane said."

"That was it? Nobody else?"

"I guess he must have spoken to whoever was behind the main bar. And also Trist."

"Trist?"

"You know, from the Sinners?" Yes, I knew who he was. "'Rob Me Blind' is my favourite song of theirs, and he promised Mike they'd play it for me."

Of course they would—it had been Serenity's favourite song too, and she'd sung it in every set.

"Just those four people? He didn't speak with anyone else?"

"Not that he mentioned. And the main floor of Club Dead isn't exactly a place for conversation, is it? But why does this matter? Mike's wife was the one who did it. She wanted his money."

"You should tell this to the police."

"But what if she hears I snitched and comes after me next?"

"Do you want me to contact Detective Callahan? He can come to your apartment. I'll ask him to be discreet."

"W-w-would you do that?"

Oh, great. Now we were back to sniffing. "Sure I will. Keep your door bolted, and don't let anyone else in tonight. I'll call Callahan in the morning, I promise."

"Okay." She gave me another tearful hug. "I know I shouldn't have fallen for Mike, but I couldn't help it, and now...now..."

"Now you have all this grief to bear, but you don't have to do it alone. Kristy, I'm always here if you want to talk."

"Th-th-thank you."

"What are friends for?"

I made a hasty exit. No way could I wait until morning to update Callahan. I dialled his number as soon as I got to the bottom of Kristy's stairs, but the phone rang and rang. Voicemail again. Where was he?

"Could you call me? It's—"

Then I heard it. The quiet metallic *snick* of a revolver being cocked. Voltaire used to carry one in the old days, a heavy silver thing with a polished walnut grip. Russian roulette was his favourite drinking game, and of course, he never lost. Ever seen a man's head regenerate? It was freaky as hell.

"Uh, I'll call back."

Vee

M*erde*. There were three of them. Skinny youths wearing baggy jeans, tight T-shirts, and expensive tennis shoes. Two of them carried guns—both pointed at my chest—and the third had wildly staring eyes and a knife. I figured they weren't looking for directions.

"Gimme the phone," one of them demanded.

Most of the time, I hated being a vampire. *Hated* it. But just occasionally, in moments like this, the fact that I was immortal could be quite satisfying.

"No."

His look of puzzlement left me struggling to keep a straight face.

"No?"

"Buy your own phone."

"Lady, I have a gun."

"Yes, I see that. Perhaps you could trade it in?"

The asshole tried to grab the phone, but I sidestepped in a heartbeat, and then I had the gun and the phone. Which ordinarily would have been a good thing, but as we grappled, the second guy panicked and started shooting. *Merde*, that stung. In my peripheral vision, I saw the third guy, the one with the knife, launch himself in my direction. I braced for impact, but it...never came.

I didn't have time to dwell on that as I pried the first guy's hand from around my wrist. Which took less effort than it should have as his life slowly leaked out of the hole in his chest. Dammit. Dammit! Why did people always have to act like such idiots? The second guy had taken a few steps back, and his hands were shaking worse than leaves in a hurricane.

"Don't shoot me again, *con*."

Then I realised he wasn't looking at me but past me, and I became aware of another presence. Not the jacked-up third guy, but something altogether more sinister. There was a weird energy in the air, a tangible thing that pressed on my chest and made it difficult to breathe. An *evil*. Voltaire was the only man who'd ever made me feel that way. I didn't want to turn around, but I knew I had to.

The third guy was in the gutter, his knife lying beside one outstretched hand as a dark figure crouched over him. As I watched, the faintest shadow rose from his body and faded away, and then his hand went limp.

Run, Vee!

I tried to turn, but the first guy gave one last death stagger and slumped into me, taking me to the ground. The second guy dropped his gun and sprinted into the gloom, disappearing into the night with a wail that could have been pain or grief or sheer terror. Me? I couldn't speak. This...this thing...it wasn't human. Instinctively, I understood that much.

The first guy rolled to the side as I kicked him off me, a dead weight. I scooted backwards on my ass as the thing straightened.

And turned.

Oh, holy fuck.

I could do nothing but stare open-mouthed while Blane peered down at me, watching with mild curiosity as my injured shoulder turned from hamburger into smooth white skin.

"Get away from me!" I finally found my voice.

Blane arched an eyebrow. "Don't you mean 'thank you'?"

"Did you follow me? W-w-what the hell are you?"

"Shouldn't that be my question? That's a cool trick with the arm."

"You just killed a man!"

"Not killed, exactly. I merely relocated his soul to a different cosmic plane." Blane held out a hand. "Come. We should leave."

Was he serious?

"I'm not going anywhere with you."

"I won't hurt you, Vee. I'm not even sure that I can."

The darkness was receding now, almost as if Blane was sucking it back into his body. Was that even possible? Malevolence turned into the same vague feeling of discomfort that always afflicted me around my boss. Or should I say former boss? How on earth could I carry on working for him now?

"What are you?" I asked again, my voice stronger this time.

"I'll explain that later." He glanced at his watch. "Let's go. Police response times aren't the best in this area, but they'll show up sooner or later."

Yes, because Kristy had probably called them. At least she hadn't poked her head out the door.

"What about all of..." I gestured at the bodies. "All of this? And there's a witness."

"Oh, please. That coward was on drugs. And the cops won't care about these two. Gang violence? They'll just tick a few boxes, hose down the sidewalk, and go back to their coffee." Blane poked the first dead guy with one polished leather shoe and tutted. "You should learn to fight better."

"Really? And I suppose if *you'd* been mugged, you'd have delivered the culprits gift-wrapped to the nearest police station?"

"No, but I wouldn't have gotten shot either."

"Screw you." I bent to pick up my phone, keeping one eye on Blane. He didn't move. *Merde*, the screen was cracked. "I'm going home."

"I'll give you a ride."

"I'll take a cab."

"Tsk-tsk-tsk. You want *another* witness? Perhaps you could confess on Twitter as well? Here, you want me to take a picture of you with the bodies?"

"Shut up. I'll walk."

"Vee, you're covered in blood."

Dammit, I was. Wine-red splatters covered my white shirt, and it wasn't just the colour, it was the smell. The coppery tang of fresh haemoglobin. That was like the bouquet of a fine wine to me, but mortals tended to take a different view. Even in the dump that was Sunset Tower, I'd get some strange looks if anyone saw me walking to the elevator. And what if Callahan happened to be there? He'd been around a lot lately.

But what were the alternatives? Strip off my top and parade through the city in my bra? Perhaps Blane would enjoy that? His intense gaze was creeping me out, and my skin prickled with goosebumps. He studied me with the lazy intensity of a crocodile sizing up its prey—one snap, and I'd be gone. A shudder ran through me. Voltaire used to watch me the same way. Could he and Blane... No. No way. Blane wasn't a vampire.

Was he?

Movement caught my eye as a sleek black Mercedes pulled up to the kerb. Beauregard turned his head to look out of the driver's window. If the sight of the bodies disturbed him, he didn't show it.

"I'd rather walk through Vegas naked than go anywhere with you and your creepy lawyer."

Especially after Callahan had warned me about the pair of them.

"Try that, and I'll have to send Beauregard to bail you out when you get picked up for solicitation, and I don't suppose you'd like that either. Look, Vee, I promise I'm not here to harm you. Quite the opposite, in fact. I followed you to keep you safe."

A siren sounded in the distance. I heard it before Blane. Interesting. As it got closer, his lips flickered up in the faintest smile because he knew it would force my hand. He opened the car door. Waited.

Did I truly think he would hurt me? Honestly, I had no idea, but I had to chuckle at the irony. All of those decades I'd spent wishing I were dead, and the moment I decided that living might not be so bad, Blane came into my life, and he might be the one thing that could actually kill me.

But if that was his plan, wouldn't he have tried it already? This was the perfect opportunity—a quiet, dark street with two dead punks ready and waiting to take the blame.

Blane was a mystery. A conundrum. While he exuded power in unguarded moments the same way Voltaire did, he'd never exhibited the same cruel streak. I'd worked at Club Dead for months. Nobody knew Blane all that well, but I also hadn't heard any horror stories. Far from it. He went out of his way to make the girls at the club feel safe.

But then there was Serenity. Blane had lied to Callahan about his presence on the night of her death, plus Kristy said he'd been talking to Miami Mike. *Could* Blane have been involved? Again, I had no clue, but if Callahan kept pushing for answers and Blane was guilty, was there a possibility Blane might decide to relocate *him* to a different cosmic freaking plane as well?

I didn't want to take that chance. If anyone was going to dig, it had to be me.

Plus, I'll admit, I was the tiniest bit curious. For over two centuries, I'd thought it was only mortals and vampires who walked the earth in humanoid form, but now it seemed that there might be a hitherto unknown third category of being. And if the aura I'd felt from Blane gave a hint, then maybe, just maybe, Voltaire might have competition.

With one last backwards glance at the mess on the sidewalk, I climbed into the car.

CHAPTER 45

Vee

"Drink?" Blane asked, holding up a bottle of expensive Scotch.

We'd arrived back at Club Dead ten minutes ago, creeping in through Blane's private entrance at the rear. He had an apartment above his office suite, and now I was sitting in an armchair wearing a set of sweats that were far too big for me. My underwear still reeked of blood where it had soaked through my shirt, and the smell was making me hungry. Damn that man—if he hadn't shown up, I could have indulged earlier.

"Not Scotch. Do you have wine?"

"Red or white?"

"Rosé?"

In the corner, Beauregard snorted. Blane merely shook his head.

"You're not a rosé drinker, Vee." He disappeared for a moment, then returned holding a bottle. "Try this. The 2016 Sassicaia. I think you'll appreciate it."

Well, this was creepy. "What makes you think that?"

Blane didn't answer right away, just focused on pouring

me a generous measure of a wine that admittedly had a very pleasant nose. But how did he know I was a fan of Italian reds? He handed me the glass, then took a seat on the couch opposite. Cool, calm, confident. Everything I wasn't at that particular moment. It took every ounce of concentration to maintain the impassive mask I'd practised wearing so many times for Voltaire.

"You intrigue me, Vee. I knew the moment you stepped into my office for your interview that you were different. So I might have done some digging. Berkshire Place? You have good taste."

Shit.

"What did you do? Send your lapdog after me?"

Out of the corner of my eye, I saw Beauregard's jaw clench, but Blane merely shrugged one shoulder. Was that an admission?

"Joseph isn't a lapdog. He's a colleague. And what are you, Vee? I've been trying to puzzle it out. Why, when you're so obviously wealthy, did you show up here looking for a job? Joseph thinks you're a spy for the Celestial Council."

"The what?"

"Exactly."

"She could be lying," Beauregard muttered.

"No, I don't think so. I've met a *lot* of liars in my time." Blane paused to take a sip of Scotch. "You've been twenty-six for at least a century, you have a penchant for taking advantage of drunk men, and your soul has a dead quality to it. Like a shadow. It's there, but it's not. I'm going to go out on a limb here and say you're a vampire?"

"No comment."

"A vampire." Blane rose to circle me, glass in hand. "Fascinating. Tell me, are you the only one of your kind here in Vegas? Or are the others just better at hiding it?"

What an asshole. I got to my feet too. "Thanks for the ride, but I should get home."

Instinct took over. It was time to implement my escape plan. I *always* had an escape plan. Every time I moved to a new place, the first thing I did was work out ways to leave. I'd done it so often that it was a matter of routine, but this time...this time, something was different. The pang of sorrow in my chest...that was new.

And I knew why. Callahan. Marianna too. For the first time in years, I had friends who understood me just a little. They'd taken the edge off the loneliness that had plagued me for the last century. And then there was Serenity's funeral. I'd started organising it since nobody else had come forward to do so, but it couldn't take place until the morgue released her body. What would happen to her if I left? Would Callahan finish what I'd started, wondering the whole time where I was? I wouldn't be able to tell him where I'd gone or why, and despite my immortality, that killed me inside. At least I'd paid the caterers up front.

"Technically, you're still on the clock, Vee."

"I quit."

"Really? You never struck me as a quitter."

"Then you don't know me very well at all, do you?"

"I want to get to know you. That's why I invited you up here tonight."

Blane wanted to "get to know me"? Oh, hell no.

"Now you're hitting on me? What, you don't think my evening's been bad enough already?"

I wasn't sure whether to be relieved or insulted by his look of absolute horror. Beauregard's laughter didn't help either.

"I meant in a spiritual sense."

"Do you have any idea how many assholes have used that line on me? Over two freaking centuries? More than I can count. So you can take your spiritual bullshit and shove it up your derrière."

"You know, I'm actually starting to like her," Beauregard said.

Blane glared at him. "Shut up." He poured the rest of the Scotch down his throat, and I resisted the urge to do the same with the wine. "Vee, that's not what I meant. Aren't you curious? There are seven billion humans on the planet, and then there's us."

"Yes, there's 'us,' but I still have no idea who or what *you* are."

At the sleek wooden sideboard, Blane poured himself another two fingers of whisky. Then he sighed and filled the glass halfway.

"Sure you don't want something stronger?" he asked.

"Why? Do I need it?"

"That depends on how open-minded you are."

"I'm a freaking vampire."

"Yes, but you still seem quite human, what with your cat and your crush on Detective Callahan."

A chill ran through me. "Don't you dare bring him into this."

"Fine." Blane took another mouthful of Scotch. Did he get drunk like regular men? Or were his inner workings dulled to alcohol's charms in the same manner as mine? "Fine. Before I came to Las Vegas six years ago, I oversaw Earth's third cosmic plane."

"You what?"

"Project planning, sorting out personnel issues, managing capacity, organising pest control, that kind of thing."

"I meant the 'third cosmic plane' part."

"It's something of an abstract concept to people on earth, but—"

"He was Lord of the Underworld," Beauregard told me. "But he got fired."

"What the hell?" I meant that question quite literally.

"Hell is more of a human creation, and technically, it's not 'the underworld' either. Think of it as more parallel."

"Did you spike that wine?"

"You watched me open the bottle."

Was I dreaming? Hallucinating? Had I died and gone to a parallel universe myself?

"I don't understand."

"It's really not a difficult notion," Beauregard told me. "Try to keep up."

This time, Blane and I both glared at him.

"Where do you think souls go when they die?" Blane asked.

"I haven't spent much time considering it. I suppose they just...vanish?"

"No, they don't. Nor do they hang around on earth. Well, some do, but that's a separate issue. Souls go to one of three places. Humans would call them heaven, hell, and limbo, but officially, they're cosmic planes two through four."

"What about plane one?"

I scarcely believed I'd just asked that. Surely there couldn't be any truth to this story?

"That's head office. Management has access, plus it operates as a sort of clearing house for newcomers."

"This...this is impossible."

"On the contrary," Beauregard said. "It's not only possible, it's logical. Are you familiar with dark matter?"

"I might have heard the term."

"Plane Five scientists—this is Plane Five, by the way—they've worked out that seventy percent of the universe is made up of dark matter, but so far, they don't have much of an idea what dark matter consists of. Voila—the other planes."

"Where...where do I fit in?"

"We're not sure," Blane admitted. "That's why you're so intriguing. It's as if your soul got modified and stuck on earth. We think that possibly your kind was an early prototype, here to protect humanity from themselves. There were rumours."

Protect humanity? If Voltaire was any indication, that idea had gone very, very wrong.

"A prototype for what? This is too weird."

Beauregard snorted. "That's rich, coming from a woman who drinks blood to survive."

"It's not my fault I have an unusual digestive system."

"Stop bickering. Please," Blane added, as if he wasn't accustomed to being polite. "I know your secrets and you know mine, so can't we focus on the more important things? Why did you go to visit Kristy tonight?"

"Oh, no. No way. You're not changing the subject that easily. I'm straightforward—I got bitten by a self-centred asshole in the eighteenth century, and I've been allergic to sunlight ever since—but we haven't even scratched the surface with you. And what about him?" I pointed at Beauregard. "What's he?"

"My assistant."

"Think of me as a demon," Beauregard added. "A demon who's passed the bar exam."

"You didn't pass the bar exam. You stole a lawyer's body, read a few textbooks, and watched every single episode of *The Good Wife*."

"That chick was hot. In an uptight sorta way."

Putain de merde. "You stole a body?"

"The lawyer was a terrible guy," Blane said. "Quite frankly, he deserved to go straight to Plane Three. If I could have sent him there, I would have."

"Wait, wait, wait. You ran hell, but you can't send people there?"

"Not my job."

"Then whose job is it?"

"That's a long story."

Blane's private study followed the same theme as his office downstairs, except with more alcohol. Leather-and-wood furniture graced a thick grey carpet, and an ornate grandfather clock kept time against the far wall. *Tock, tock, tock.* Was it really only midnight?

"As you so kindly pointed out, I'm on the clock for four more hours, so you've got plenty of time to tell me the details."

"Does that mean you're not quitting? Good staff are hard to find."

"Are you kidding me? How can I stay?"

"Simple. You keep showing up for your shifts, and I keep signing your paychecks."

"I get paid by direct deposit."

"That wasn't my point and you know it." Blane sighed. "Look at it this way: why would you leave? You're different, I'm different—the only thing that's changed is that we're privy to each other's secrets."

He did have a point. If I left, I'd just be running again. And it might be nice to have someone I could talk to—really talk to—who wasn't Voltaire. And then there was Callahan...

Was I honestly considering staying? Perhaps. I did need a job that allowed me to find dinner unnoticed, and if I fled Las Vegas right now, I'd also leave my heart behind.

"Maybe I'll stay. It depends."

"On what?"

"On whether you had any involvement in Serenity's death."

For once, Beauregard had no smart quip. The atmosphere chilled a degree as Blane knelt in front of me, one hand on each side of my knees.

"Vee, I swear to you I didn't kill her. Serenity was a...as close to a friend as I had. I liked her. No, not in *that* way, but I admired her determination to get what she wanted. If she'd told me she was in any kind of trouble, I'd have helped her."

Blane looked me in the eye as he spoke, and I believed him. Yes, he was dark as hell and grimly powerful, overwhelmingly so at times, but I believed him. It was just possible that I'd lost my mind.

"Okay," I said to Blane.

"Okay?"

"Okay, I'll keep working here." I managed a wan smile. "At least for a while. Where else am I going to find such a varied dinner menu?"

"Does your detective know about your dietary requirements?"

"Are you serious? Of course not."

Another chuckle from Beauregard. "Well, this should be interesting."

"How do you put up with him?" I asked Blane. "Don't you want to toss him into the Grand Canyon?"

"Every hour of every day."

"Hey, I have my uses."

"Yes, you do. Go and get us something to eat."

"Please, Joseph, would you mind fetching supper," Beauregard mimicked.

Blane closed his eyes and took one long, deep breath. "*Please* get us something to eat."

Beauregard kept grumbling, but he did get up and head

towards the doorway. Before he walked through it, he turned to grin at me, and his eyes flashed red. Aw, *merde*, I truly had crossed onto the dark side, hadn't I?

"Enough with the parlour tricks, Joseph," Blane warned, but Beauregard had already left the room.

"So, he really is a demon."

"He wears contacts that hide the redness in his eyes. The flashy thing... I have no idea how he does that."

"You can't do it?"

Blane shook his head.

"Then what's your party trick?"

"You saw it earlier."

"The soul-sucking thing?"

"It's not so much soul-sucking, more the ability to move them around. It's certainly advantageous in the third plane. Things can get rowdy over there. Plus, like you, I'm pretty hard to kill, and I can also travel between cosmic planes and play the guitar. Oh, and..." He clicked his fingers, and a flame appeared on the end of his thumb. "This. But I don't usually go in for all that drama."

"I guess that's impressive." At least, it was if one wanted to become a pyromaniac. "Did that guy whose soul you 'moved' go to the third plane? I thought you said you couldn't send people there?"

"I can't. And the answer is, I don't know where he went. Probably to the fourth plane. That's the default. Souls wait there for new bodies."

"Like reincarnation?"

"If that's the word you prefer."

"And the second plane is, what? Heaven?"

"Something like that. There are a lot of golf courses."

I choked into my wine. "Golf courses?"

"My father's favourite pastime."

"And he runs the second plane?"

"No, my mother does, but my father spends much of his time there."

"This is insane," I murmured under my breath. Either Blane was certifiable, or my entire understanding of the universe had been turned on its head. "So if you can't send people to the second and third planes, how do they get there?"

Rather than answering, Blane took a seat on the sofa again, this time more relaxed with his legs stretched out and ankles crossed.

"Everyone has that one weird relative, right? The strange uncle that's into trainspotting or birdwatching or collecting teaspoons."

"I suppose. Back when I was alive, my uncle Eduard used to paint sheep."

"Is that...legal?"

Huh? Why wouldn't painting be legal? Then I realised where Blane's twisted mind had gone and burst out laughing. He was so serious most of the time, but occasionally, he could be a real goof.

"He didn't paint the actual sheep, you idiot. What, did you think he drew eyebrows on them?"

"It's not something I've ever considered before."

"Uncle used oil paint on canvas, but he did give all the sheep names. Henrietta was his favourite."

Bless Uncle Eduard. He'd helped me to hold a paintbrush before I learned to walk, and I'd painted sheep too, although mine turned out more like dirty clouds. It'd been those Sunday-afternoon sessions that led to my lifelong love of art.

"Henrietta the sheep? That makes Great-Uncle Tiberius seem almost normal."

"Define 'normal.'"

"He ran the earth realm before my father did. Things were busier in those days. Souls arriving constantly, judgements being made twenty-four seven. Tiberius was lazy at heart, but he also had a creative brain. So he started tinkering with metaphysics in his spare moments—the few he had—and came up with a solution that gave his entire team more time off."

"What solution?"

"He decentralised the decision-making process. Prior to that, the fate of every soul was decided by a council—Ad Tabulam—and sent to Plane Two, Three, or Four accordingly. Ad Tabulam rarely agreed on anything, and the five members wasted days arguing from dawn until dusk, dusk until dawn. Plus some of the old ideas of sin were misguided, to say the least. Did you know that in the United Kingdom, it's illegal to lead a cow while drunk? In Minnesota, you can be punished for chasing a greased pig, and in France, you're not allowed to land a flying saucer in Châteauneuf-du-Pape. Plus it was illegal to marry a dead person there until the nineteenth century."

"Oops. Guess I broke that last rule."

"You were married?"

"I tied the knot in seventeen ninety-six. I suppose technically, I still am married."

"Your husband's a vampire?"

"Unfortunately."

"What happened to him?"

"Are you always this nosy?"

"I rarely get the chance to speak candidly. It's refreshing."

"I suppose that's one way of looking at it. My husband... I left him years ago, and our paths haven't crossed since." I gave a careless shrug to suggest I didn't know where he was, which wasn't entirely true. "Were you ever married?"

"It's not really a thing on the third plane."

The door flew open, and Blane gave a sigh as it crashed against the wall. Beauregard was back, a tray of food balanced on each hand. He'd selected a whole variety of tapas dishes, the ones that made my mouth water every time I served them to other people. Snacking from the Club Dead kitchen myself would be a pleasant change.

"Blane does hook-ups," Beauregard announced. "The same way you do, but without sucking his dates dry at the end of it."

"Too much information," Blane said through clenched teeth.

"What happened to speaking candidly?"

Mental note: Beauregard had enhanced hearing. "I do not suck my dates dry, thank you very much."

He completely ignored me. "Here, try one of these olives. They came from Blane's Italian vineyard."

"You have a vineyard?"

"It's an investment."

Was it anywhere near *my* vineyard? Wouldn't that be weird, if we were vineyard neighbours? *No. No, Vee, that wouldn't be weird.* Sitting down and discussing the afterlife over wine and olives—that was weird. And Great-Uncle Tiberius? I had a feeling this would be beyond bizarre.

"Investments are always a good idea. You were telling me about your great-uncle?"

"Ah, yes. I was. Tiberius travelled more than your average celestial guardian, which meant he had a greater knowledge of science than the mortals on this planet, and that let him create three earth-based teams to assist Ad Tabulam." Blane rolled his eyes. "Tiberius and his damned experiments."

"Tell her about the werewolves," Beauregard said.

"I don't even want to think about the werewolves."

"And those mutant plants... Wonder what happened with them?"

"The coco du ciel trees?"

"Unless he created another triffid I don't know about?"

Dare I ask? "What's a coco du ciel tree?"

"Tiberius decided to experiment with cloning, and he

created a machine that was basically a cross between a palm tree and a photocopier."

"Except it photocopied humans," Beauregard said.

"What the...?"

"And technically, I'm not sure it was a palm tree," the fake lawyer continued. "It had branches as well as fronds."

Seriously? Fronds? That was his takeaway? "It *photocopied humans*?"

"Don't. Just don't. The end product turned out to be somewhat unpredictable. Thankfully, they only grew in one particular spot, and he made sure they were well-guarded. Now, where were we? Oh, yes, rather than every soul getting sent for evaluation on the first plane, the members of Factora Angelus tag potential entrants to the second plane, and Opus Vi suggests guests for the third. Those souls appear before Ad Tabulam for final judgement. The other souls bypass the permanent-residency planes and get sent straight to the fourth for reassignment."

"Wow. That all sounds very organised."

"It is and it isn't. FA and OV seem to have been slacking somewhat in recent years, and by 'years,' I mean centuries. Very few people arrive on the first plane nowadays, and those who do show up are completely unfit for purpose. One interviewee for Plane Two turned out to be a serial killer, for goodness' sake. It's as if the earth-based teams can't be bothered anymore."

"Can't someone have a word with them?"

"Sure, if we knew who they were. When I said Great-Uncle decentralised the process, I mean he decentralised it. The team members can identify each other, but we can't identify them."

"What about the other team? You said there were three?"

"Ah, yes, the Electi. Tiberius's crowning achievement, or so he said. Officially, they're the only people who can send souls directly to the third plane—do not pass go, do not collect two hundred dollars. And guess what?"

"They don't do their job either?"

"Got it in one. Every so often, a group of Middle Eastern terrorists shows up, and we get the occasional European backpacker, but beyond that? Crickets. Ever wondered where the phrase 'boring as hell' comes from? Because I can tell you."

European backpackers? Boy, that was some wrong turn.

"Have you tried asking your great-uncle where these people are?"

"No, because he vanished two millennia ago. Said he was taking a vacation and never came back. The Celestial Council opened an investigation, but they couldn't find him either. It's possible he slipped through to another dimension."

Dare I ask? "The Celestial Council?"

"Plane Zero. The big bosses."

"What about asking the terrorists? Or the backpackers?"

"Anyone dispatched by a celestial being has no memory of their death. But shhh. I'm probably not meant to be telling you any of this."

"Did you sign an NDA or something?"

"No, but mainly because if I explained these things to a mortal, they'd have me committed."

I knew that all too well. Except as a vampire, I'd probably be sent to a lab instead because if I wasn't careful, the physical manifestations of my affliction became glaringly obvious. I had nightmares about it. Being locked in a cage while people tested how long I was able to survive without food, or having my skin exposed to sunlight so scientists could watch it blister and smoke within seconds.

A tiny kernel of fear gnawed away at me—what if Blane spilled my secret? Would he? Or was that why he'd told me his story? To gain my trust? To show me that I could ruin him as easily as he could ruin me? I had a feeling the answer to that last question was yes.

Was it odd that I found myself liking him?

Beauregard, not so much, but Blane—now that he'd dropped the grim-and-grouchy mask he wore—was surprisingly easy to talk with.

"None of that explains how you ended up running a nightclub in Las Vegas. Did you really get fired?"

"I got sent here for remedial training."

"No, he definitely got fired," Beauregard told me, crunching on a breadstick. "Plane Three isn't supposed to be fun, son," he said in a gruff voice. "Where did this swimming pool come from?"

"It was hot," Blane muttered.

"You built a swimming pool? In *hell*?"

"I didn't abdicate my duties completely. I made the Category M guests dig the hole, and we filled it with their tears."

Wow.

"The Cat Ms are bad dudes," Beauregard told me. "And dudettes, of course. The Cat Bs are generally all right."

"The Category Bs should never have been sent to Plane Three in the first place."

"One guy's only crime was visiting a strip club. Who hasn't visited a strip club? And the greased-pig wrestler is hilarious."

"So you got fired for the pool?" I asked. "That seems a little harsh. Couldn't your father have just made you fill it in?"

Blane grimaced. "The pool was only one part of the problem. Mom and Dad arrived to visit while we were holding a fire-walking party, some of the flames got slightly high..."

"What with it being hell and everything," Beauregard interjected.

"And it turned out that whatever Mom had put on her hair that day was highly flammable."

My hands flew to my mouth. "You set your mom on fire? Was she okay?"

"Good thing the pool was there," Beauregard said.

Oh my gosh.

Blane emptied his glass and looked longingly at the bottle on the sideboard. Should I offer to pour him another? That was my job, after all.

"Mom was fine. Her hairstyle was not. She was forced to get a pixie cut while I got sent here because my father thought that if I saw earthly sins with my own eyes, I might take my role more seriously. Meanwhile, my older sister finally got her claws on the job she'd wanted ever since we moved to earth."

"Decima is perfectly suited to running Plane Three," Beauregard told me. "A total bitch. *Total.*"

"I can't disagree there. So, here I am. Exiled." A slow smile spread over Blane's face. A proper grin. "And loving it."

CHAPTER 47

Vee

It turned out that Blane's alcohol tolerance was on a par with mine. Beauregard and his borrowed human body? That was a whole other story. I'd barely finished my fourth glass of wine before he was snoring softly on the third sofa.

"I think I prefer him like that," I said to Blane. "Even if he fetches and carries, I still don't understand how you put up with him."

"He has his good points."

"Name them."

"He's loyal. Reasonably clever. Organised. And he's an excellent bullshitter, which comes in useful for his lawyerly activities."

I needed one of those abilities in particular right now. How the hell—no pun intended—was I supposed to explain any of this to Callahan? I'd managed to get an excellent lead on Serenity's killer from Kristy, but I could hardly tell Jack that I'd been to see her, not when there were two dead bodies lying outside her apartment, and what about all the blood? He was a freaking detective. He'd ask questions. It was literally his job,

338

and I had no answers that wouldn't see me headed straight for the nearest asylum.

"Another drink?" Blane asked.

"Why not?"

If I drank enough, I might get tipsy at least. Either that or I'd spend the rest of the night peeing. What time was it? One a.m., according to Blane's fancy clock. Only three hours until I needed to lie my ass off to the man I loved.

Wait a minute...

Loved? Putain de merde, I *had* lost my mind, and in every possible way. I wasn't meant to develop feelings for mortals. It only led to heartache, to awkward moments and decades of disappointment. In the early twentieth century, I'd made the mistake of growing a little too fond of a French artist during my time in New Orleans. Ulysse had been the first man in a hundred years to make me smile. But my lack of ageing caught up with me, and when he turned forty-five and I was still twenty-six, it'd been time for me to leave, both Ulysse and Louisiana. I'd spent the next thirty years mourning in New York, vowing never to get close to another man as long as I existed.

And then Callahan came into my life.

I was screwed.

Blane handed me a glass of red, full almost to the brim. I couldn't swirl it, but out of habit, I brought it to my nose.

"Floral," I murmured. "Violet, cedar, a hint of caramel."

Blane rolled his eyes. "It's all grapes to me."

"Heathen." I inhaled again, then took a long sip. "You should learn to appreciate a good wine."

"Then perhaps you could teach me?"

Did I want to do that? Spend time with Blane? He was being friendly enough now, but I couldn't forget the sinister vibes that had made my skin crawl earlier. I suppressed a shudder and shrugged non-committally.

"I'd buy the wine, of course," he added.

"Why are you doing this?"

"Doing what?"

"Being nice."

"You'd rather I was an asshole?"

"At least then I'd know where I stood."

"Where you stand? Well, you're in a rather unique position, Madame Pelletier."

"Not Madame," I told him. I hated being reminded that I was married, even if I'd gotten hitched under duress. "Pelletier is my surname, not my husband's, and as far as I'm concerned, he's dead to me."

"Possibly to everyone else too. The jury's still out on whether a vampire's corrupted soul is alive."

"Can we not discuss this? Alive or not, I have feelings."

Blane sighed. "Can you blame me for being curious? It's not every day a celestial being comes across somebody who doesn't fit into any of the planes as we understand them. And as for where you stand... You still work for me, but I appreciate that you're in it for the menu rather than the money. So maybe we could share the occasional drink?" He reached out to poke Beauregard with a foot. The red-eyed rogue didn't stir. "You're better company than some people I know."

"I guess we could do that."

If I cared to admit it, I was curious too.

"Splendid. And while we're chewing the fat, so to speak, let's talk about Serenity. As I'm sure you're aware, the Las Vegas police don't seem to have made much headway in finding the person who killed her. In fact, your boyfriend seems convinced that I had something to do with it."

"Because you're pretty damn sketchy, Blane."

"True. But since I didn't kill her, that doesn't get us any further towards justice."

"What about your pet demon?"

"Joseph?"

"Unless there's another one you forgot to mention?"

"Not on this plane. What about him?"

"Could he have been involved in Serenity's death?"

"No, Joseph had nothing to do with it either. He can lie to you, but he can't lie to me. So who does that leave?"

One deadly sinner. Thanks to Kristy, I was almost sure I'd worked out who the culprit was. *Trist.* Miami Mike had spoken to him that fateful night, and I already knew from Callahan that Trist had been the last of the Sinners to speak with Serenity. He'd admitted as much—so he had some balls at least—but he claimed it had been the briefest of conversations, a reminder from her not to be late for the show. But now? Now, I suspected there'd been more, that he'd handed her a drink too, a drink that had proven to be oh so deadly. And she'd have taken it. Of course she would—who wouldn't accept a drink from a friend?

Trist the traitor. But who should I share that information with? Blane? Or Callahan?

With Blane, it would be easy. All I'd need to do would be to repeat the conversation. But what would Blane do? I couldn't see him sitting on the information until Callahan followed the breadcrumbs and pulled Trist in for questioning himself. What kind of punishment would the devil dish out? I dreaded to think, but at the same time, if Trist *had* killed my friend then rotting in hell was too good for him.

How would I pass the information to Callahan? An anonymous tip? Would that be taken seriously? Or should I come clean about visiting Kristy and deny all knowledge of what happened afterwards? She didn't live in a good area. A double homicide wouldn't be entirely unexpected. Right?

Dammit all to hell. What should I do?

CHAPTER 48

Vee

I so, so nearly blurted out my suspicions to Blane, but before I spilled even more secrets, his phone rang. He nodded a couple of times, then stood.

"There's a problem downstairs. I need to go and deal with it."

"What kind of a problem?"

"The usual—drunk assholes with more money than sense. Two of them had an altercation, and Carlene ended up in the middle of it."

"Is she okay?"

"That's what I need to find out."

"Want a hand? I mean, I should probably finish my shift."

Blane was already out on the landing. "On any other day, I'd tell you to stay up here and relax, but if Carlene's hurt... There're spare women's clothes in the guest room closet."

Of course there were, although "clothes" was being generous. I quickly changed into the least risqué of the outfits and followed him down the stairs, and I have to say, he showed remarkable restraint in dealing with the belligerent jerk in the VIP area. Trayvon had him in a bear

342

hug when we got there, but that didn't stop the guy from yelling.

"Don't you know who I am?"

Blane stopped in front of him, arms folded. "No, and nor do I care."

"Well, I don't know who you are either."

"I'm the owner of this place, and if you want to walk out rather than crawl, I suggest you do it now."

"Are you threatening me?"

"Absolutely."

Carlene was sitting on a sofa beside the loser of the fight, a small man with a blood-covered shirt and a fistful of wadded-up napkins pressed against his nose.

"You okay?" I asked her.

"They were fighting over a woman. I don't even know where she went."

"Probably saw sense and legged it. Did you get hurt?"

"I just tripped over when one of them pushed me. Wait, I thought you were sick?"

"I'm feeling much better now."

A truly miraculous recovery, although I did feel slightly queasy when I thought about the bodies outside Kristy's apartment. But in some ways, the dead men were a good thing. Not only were there two fewer idiots on the street, but with the police on the scene, Trist wouldn't risk paying Kristy a visit at the moment. Callahan could question him before he got the chance.

Callahan... I still hadn't quite worked out what to say to him. Perhaps I could claim that I'd visited Kristy earlier in the evening? Deny all knowledge of the wannabe muggers? Or should I say I got scared and ran? No, because then he'd want to know why I hadn't called 911.

"Hey, can we get some drinks here?"

I turned to find a blonde woman waving at Carlene and

me. Blane had won his stare-off with the jerk, and now Trayvon was escorting the man to the door, the excitement over. Just another night at Club Dead. And despite the ups and downs, I'd miss the place if I left.

"Sure, coming right up."

I cruised through the rest of the shift on autopilot, my mind on other things. Well, one other thing. Of all the men in all the world, why did I have to get involved with a detective? Since that night in the bathroom, my life had become infinitely more complicated.

And then...things got worse.

At half past three, my phone rang. Callahan. Was it time for him to pick me up again? It was sweet the way he did that, although I wouldn't have minded putting the Trist/Kristy discussion off for a little longer.

"Hey."

"Vee, fuck, are you okay?"

"Uh, yes? Why wouldn't I be?"

"Where are you?"

"At work." Why did he sound so anxious? "What's the problem?"

"I'll be there in ten minutes. Better that we talk in person."

"My shift doesn't finish until four."

"Then I'll be waiting."

At five to four, I slipped out of the rear door. Blane had let me leave a few minutes early, and I found Callahan parked in the alley at the side of the club. What was wrong? Why had he sounded so on edge?

The instant I got in the car, he grabbed my hand and squeezed it.

"You're really okay."

"I said I was. Now will you tell me what happened?"

He hesitated long enough to take a deep breath. "Vee, you almost walked right into the middle of a double homicide earlier this evening. And then I listened to your voicemail, and you never called me back, and I just...panicked. I'm sorry if I worried you, but..."

Callahan let the word hang as I tried to gather my thoughts. He already knew about the dead guys? How?

All my carefully planned explanations flew out the window. When in doubt, act dumb.

"A double homicide?"

"You visited Kristina Halliday earlier this evening. Over in Sunrise?"

A statement, not a question.

"She called in sick. Carlene covered for me while I went to check she was okay. Uh, you spoke to Kristy?"

"A colleague did. Your name came up in the squad room as a possible witness."

"Oh."

"Well?"

"Well what?"

"Did you see anything? Hear anything?"

"Not really. I mean, there were three men loitering outside as I left, so I didn't wait around."

"Three men? Can you describe them? Or better still, could you draw them?"

Okay, this was turning out to be a lot easier than I thought.

"Sure. I'll do it this morning. They were young, late teens or early twenties." All I had to do was make accurate sketches of the two dead guys and change the third enough that the cops would never find him. "But there's something else I need to talk to you about."

Callahan was still holding my hand. Was that weird? I

came to the conclusion that it probably was, but also that I kind of liked it.

"You can talk to me about anything, babe."

Yup, definitely weird.

But nice weird.

"So, I found out that Kristy was having an affair with Miami Mike…"

"*What*?"

"Exactly. She's convinced his wife killed him, but I'm not so sure." I ran through everything Kristy had told me, finishing with my suspicions about Trist. "So he had it all—the motive, the opportunity, and possibly the means. If Serenity quit the band, his career would have taken a nosedive."

"It would."

"And the gig with Keira at the club finished by midnight." I'd checked with Blane. "He could have gotten to Mike too."

"The Sinners went to a party after the gig, but so far, we haven't found anyone who saw them after three a.m."

"Would he have had enough time to…?"

"Yes."

"Will you question him?"

"I'll have to speak to Kristy first. Probable cause, you know? And I desperately need a nap."

I wanted him to drive to Kristy's place straight away, but he was right. There were procedures to follow, and mortals couldn't function without sleep. An hour or two wouldn't make much difference.

"If you let me know when you get up, I'll make you coffee and breakfast to go."

Callahan brought my hand to his lips, just for the merest second, but I didn't imagine the kiss. My skin burned from his touch, and my stomach did a backflip. What did it mean? I was afraid to think about it.

But as quickly as it had flared, the heat in his eyes turned to puzzlement as he focused on the rear-view mirror.

"What was that?"

"What was what?"

"I thought I saw something." Callahan twisted in his seat to look out the back window.

"Saw what?"

"Dots of light. Like maybe two people were smoking, but I can't see anyone."

Two dots of orangey light? Oh, fuck.

Callahan shrugged and started the engine. "Damn. I need to sleep. I'm probably hallucinating."

I wanted to run inside and sew Beauregard's mouth shut. How much of our conversation had he overheard? And more to the point, what did he plan to do with the information?

"I think I forgot my scarf."

Callahan reached into the back seat. "Here, borrow mine. You can pick yours up tomorrow."

Double fuck.

"Thanks, I really appreciate it."

He put the car into gear. "You and me, we make a good team."

Yes, we did, but now there was a good possibility we'd added a pair of uninvited players into the game.

CHAPTER 49

Jack

"You have Trist in custody?" Vee asked when she opened her door. "That's good, right? It's over?"

It *was* good news. Not only was a double murderer in custody, but in what had to rate as the strangest conversation of my career, he'd freely admitted his guilt. Never before had a suspect been so nervous that he'd blurted out a confession before we even made it to the interview room. But confess he had, and he'd even signed a statement to that effect. Daphne was elated, Shep was happy, and even Captain Lindsay had cracked a smile. So why did I feel downbeat?

"Yes, it's good news."

"But..."

"It's all such a waste. Lyla Chavez's life got cut short, Michael Klass is dead"—although I couldn't bring myself to be devastated by that particular loss—"and Trist's just a scared kid who did something monumentally stupid."

And "scared" was an understatement. The boy was terrified. When he'd answered my knock at his apartment door, I thought he was going to shit himself.

"A scared kid who killed two people. The evidence fits?"

It did. Trist—Chad—had explained in detail how he'd slipped the pills into Chavez's drink, and when she began struggling to breathe, he'd convinced her to go outside for some air rather than calling an ambulance. After a few minutes, panic had set in as her throat swelled, and he'd led her back inside, only to shove her into the storeroom and keep her there while she gasped and clawed at her throat. She'd told him she was allergic to painkillers, and still he'd blocked the door. He thought she was overreacting, or so he claimed. Didn't women always exaggerate? If she'd gone to the hospital, they'd have missed the gig and the crowd would have been *pissed*.

Then she'd stopped breathing, and it'd been his turn to freak out. He'd grabbed the ice pick from the break room and stabbed her in the neck in a vain attempt to pin her death on an unknown psycho.

And Klass... He *had* been the one to supply the pills for Serenity, so Trist decided to ensure his silence. He'd called the doctor in the early hours, claiming to be desperate for a fix because his regular dealer was out of town. Miami Mike would do anything if the price was right. Chad had injected him with enough fentanyl to knock him out fast, then replicated the marks he'd left on Chavez. The use of fentanyl fit with the ME's preliminary findings that Klass had been drugged before he was stabbed. The ice pick? Chad had tossed that into a dumpster somewhere between Maple Canyon Avenue and his place—he couldn't quite remember where.

Vee was right. Chad didn't deserve my sympathy.

"Yes, the evidence fits. It's just hard to be satisfied with the outcome when two people are dead and a third's gonna be in prison for twenty years at least."

If Chad had stopped after Chavez died, he might have been able to plead it down to a year or two for involuntary manslaughter. Not that I agreed with that sentence after the way he'd trapped her in the storeroom, but at least Miami

Mike would be alive. Yes, he'd still be an asshole, but he'd also be the narcotics squad's problem, not mine.

"Want to come in?" Vee asked. "I can order dinner."

After the week I'd had, the only thing I wanted was a quiet evening with Genevieve Pelletier. Her smile could fix a thousand ills, and her dark little cave of an apartment had become a haven. A sanctuary. A place I could escape to when the outside world brought me down. I used to feel a sense of elation when I solved a murder, but now all I got was fleeting satisfaction before I moved on to the next crime. It never stopped. At times, I regretted rejoining the police. I could have become a cab driver or a grocery store clerk or a barber, anything that didn't involve taking my work home at the end of the day. Or death. Avoiding that would be good too. Sometimes, I envied Vee. Sure, she had to wear uncomfortable shoes the whole night, but she seemed to enjoy her job.

"I'd love to come in, but it's my turn to buy dinner."

She shrugged and stepped back, giving me room to enter. "I won't say no to that offer."

"Chinese? Mexican? Cheeseburgers?"

"Wong Fu's?"

"Same order as usual?"

Vee nodded. "And Marianna made another cake. Banana and coconut this time. Muse is obsessed with the coconut. Every time Marianna turned her back, Muse tried to swipe another piece."

Muse... If only I'd known that the cat would prove to be my downfall.

The evening passed like any other with Vee, which was to say far too quickly as we talked and laughed about everything and nothing. Every time she smiled, my dick twitched. And I began to consider switching to the night shift so I'd be able to spend more time hanging out with the girl I wanted to eat dinner with *every* evening. If we slept in the daytime, would that make it breakfast?

"So, if the case is closed, does that mean you get time off over Christmas?" Vee asked, forking a mouthful of pineapple fritter and satay pork into her mouth. She liked weird food combinations, I'd noticed. Peanuts and pineapple seemed to be acceptable accompaniments to any meal.

"No, I get paperwork. And I still have other open cases. Crime rates just keep going up and up."

"What about Christmas dinner? I realise it's a bit last-minute, but Marianna offered to cook, and..."

"Christmas dinner? Here?"

"I'll understand if you're busy."

"I'll be there."

That damn cat...

It happened after I'd finished my glass of wine. Liquid courage, they called it. More like liquid stupidity. Vee was fussing around with dessert while I cleared the takeout cartons into the trash, just two friends who'd gotten used to sharing space with each other, the pair of us dodging around the tiny kitchen as if we'd been practising for months. Then Muse decided to join the party. What was it about cats and legs? Were they genetically programmed to weave in and out of them? I narrowly avoided tripping over her, but Vee wasn't so lucky. The cake in her hands went flying, half a frosted sponge that hit the counter with a heavy squelch. Vee nearly followed, but I caught her, and for only the second time, she was in my arms. Delicate yet strong, sensitive yet fiery, innocent and yet so, so seductive.

Our gazes locked, her green eyes to my blue ones, and I kissed her.

And she kissed me back.

For five seconds, ten, she gave me all I'd imagined and more. Her racing heart beat against my chest, and her breathy little gasps turned me hard in the blink of an eye. Vee was everything I'd never set out to look for, and I drank her in, each atom of herself she gave me as our tongues tangled. For the first time since Angie died, I felt whole again, and the future turned from dark to bright as it unrolled in front of me. Evenings chilling with Vee, days spent lying beside her. Shared secrets, promises, our lives entwined. Vacations, a shared home, kids...who knew?

Then she pushed me away.

"Sorry! I can't... This isn't... I'm so sorry."

My heart went from a hundred to zero in the time it took me to curse myself. Shit! I'd pushed too far, too fast, and now Vee was backing away towards the living room, arms out as though she was warding me off. And the damn cat was already on the counter, licking the remains of the cake. From that moment on, I was definitely going to be a dog person.

"Vee, I'm the one who's sorry."

I had to try and salvage something out of the mess I'd created. Vee's friendship had come to mean so much, and if I lost that too...

"No, no, it's not you, it's me." She giggled hysterically. "*Merde*, that sounds like such a cliché."

Both of her hands tore through her hair, my easy-going Vee gripped by despair. No, *no*, not *my* Vee. She'd made that part quite clear.

"It was my fault. I fucked up, misread the signs. Some detective I am." Should I try to talk to her? Or leave? Neither would fix things, but which would be better for Vee? "Do you want me to go?"

Instead of answering, she slumped back onto the couch, the same couch I'd slept on just thirty-six hours ago when she'd covered me with a blanket and left me to rest. She cared. Even if she didn't feel the same way about me as I felt about her, I knew she cared. When she didn't reply, I skirted around the edge of the living room, heading for the door. Since I had no idea what to say, leaving seemed like the sensible option. Back off, regroup, work out what the hell I could say to mitigate the damage.

"It *is* my fault," she whispered as my fingers closed around the door handle. "I like you, I do, but I can't give you what you want. What you deserve."

"And what do you think I want?"

"A partner. A soulmate. You've got a beautiful soul, Jack Callahan, but all I can offer is the superficial. The rest, the emotional stuff... I can't. I just can't. And that's what you need, I understand that. You're not a one-night stand kind of guy."

She was right; I wasn't. But even so, if she was offering... Only a saint wouldn't be tempted. And I was no saint.

No. *No.* I wouldn't. Couldn't. My chest physically hurt as I sucked in a breath and tried to shake off the metaphorical bucket of cold water Vee had thrown over me.

"Sometimes, I think you know me better than I know myself."

It was then that it struck me—Vee had wormed her way into my psyche, but I didn't know her nearly so well. What made her tick? How had she become the woman before me today? She never mentioned her past or even her hopes for the future. Vee lived in the present. She was passionate about art, fond of the four-legged fiend currently gorging itself on cake in the kitchen, and sociable at work. But beyond that...a mystery.

I'd spent my whole damn life solving mysteries, but Vee gave few clues away.

Once, that might have bothered me, but she'd cast her spell, and living in the present didn't seem like such a bad idea. The past sucked, and fate already had designs on the future.

"That's not true." Now Vee struggled to her feet. "Jack,

you're a good man. But I've been burned before, and I don't want to hurt either of us."

The ex-boyfriend? I should have guessed by the way Vee refused to speak about him that it had been bad. And I'd pushed her too soon. How long had it taken me to consider moving on after Angie? Almost two years. Vee needed time and space, not an idiot who thought only of himself.

"I understand." My hand closed around the door handle again. "I think it's better for both of us if I leave."

This time, she didn't try to stop me.

CHAPTER 50

Vee

"Cheer up," Beauregard said, holding up the corners of his mouth with his forefingers. "You're not still hungry, are you?"

With Trist in jail and a festering cloud of awkwardness hanging over us, Callahan hadn't felt the need to pick me up from work this morning—in fact, he hadn't uttered a peep since I hurt him yesterday afternoon—so I'd taken the opportunity to eat and left the club with a slimeball instead. The pig had been all over me from the moment the cab door closed, but as soon as we got back to his hotel, I'd raided the minibar and poured half a dozen vodka miniatures down his throat, which meant he passed out before he could get it up. I drank my fill, then left him a note scrawled in lipstick that thanked him for being fantastic. I figured that stroking his ego was the least I could do.

And I'd needed that meal. Healing after an injury took a lot of energy, and I'd been exhausted for the whole of last night. But now? Now, I felt fine physically. Mentally, it was a different story.

"No, I'm not hungry. Not in that way."

"So why do you look as if you've been sucking a hornet? You were miserable as sin yesterday too. We already apologised for interfering in police business, so what's the problem?"

Yes, Blane and Beauregard had paid Trist a visit before Callahan got there. Blane wouldn't tell me exactly what he'd said to the ultimate sinner, but his words had made Trist choose a definite prison sentence over fighting for his freedom. I was slightly peeved that they'd gone behind my back, but I couldn't be mad about the outcome. Trist deserved to rot in jail.

"Will you just stop?"

"Wait, wait, let me guess... You hit on the detective, and he turned you down?"

"No."

"Okay, he hit on you, and *you* turned *him* down?"

"Shut up."

"Oh, so I'm right? Awkward."

I turned to Blane. "Out of all the demons in hell—Plane Three, whatever—this was the best assistant you could find?"

"Joseph, make yourself useful and fetch us a bottle of champagne."

Blane was growing on me. Last night during my break, he'd invited me up to his apartment again. His living room was a surprisingly tasteful space filled with eclectic furniture from every corner of the world, plus a cat named Khaki. Apparently, she'd just walked in one day and refused to leave. Now she had a canopy bed and six kinds of kitty treats, and her eyes followed me around the room like they did in those creepy old paintings. But weirdly, seeing Blane with Khaki made me feel more comfortable around him. Animals were good judges of character, and she obviously adored her chosen guardian, even if he pretended to grumble every time she shed hair on his lap. Beauregard told me Blane had invested in a company that made lint rollers, and I think he was actually serious.

Now he grumbled about modern-day slavery as he headed for the elevator.

"You okay?" Blane asked, leaning back on the sofa with his legs crossed at the ankles as seemed to be his habit.

"Yes, perfectly. Why wouldn't I be?"

He kept those dark eyes fixed on mine, his gaze boring into me until I squirmed in my seat. I'd perched on the edge of an overstuffed Chesterfield upholstered in grey velvet.

"Fine, I'm not. What are you, my therapist?"

"If you like. Joseph was right?"

"There was a difficult moment."

"The detective made a move?"

My silence obviously answered Blane's question.

"You should go with your feelings. It's obvious that the two of you like each other."

"How can I?" I stood and walked to the far end of the room. Floor-to-ceiling windows looked out over the street, pedestrians scurrying below like inebriated ants. "I hurt him."

"Apologise. He'll forgive you."

"Oh, sure. Just apologise. I'm a freaking vampire."

"Yes, but he's not to know that. Sure, your teeth are pointier than normal, but apart from that, you look human."

"If I don't drink fresh blood every week, my skin turns grey and my eyes go yellow."

Blane waved a hand. "A minor inconvenience. Just be discreet."

"Are you crazy? You're telling me to not only get involved with a human, but also cheat on him once I've gained his trust?"

"It's not really cheating, though, is it? It's the vampire equivalent of popping out for a burrito."

I began pacing. "And you're forgetting the other tiny issue: I don't age. Callahan's already five years older than me. What happens when he's forty? Fifty?"

"The average American marriage lasts eight years, so statistically speaking, it's unlikely to be a problem."

"Marriage? Now you're suggesting bigamy?" I marched back to the seating area and snatched my glass of wine off the coffee table. "Some therapist you are."

"I doubt there are any records from the seventeen-whatevers. Why do I get the impression that you're making this deliberately hard for yourself?" He thought for a moment, then snapped his fingers. A small flame flared between them. "Oops." He blew it out. "Are you scared?"

Was I? Deep down, if I cared to admit it, the answer was yes. My affair with Ulysse had been more of an informal thing. No dates, no deep and meaningful conversations, just friendship, a shared love of art, and good sex. We'd lived in separate homes, and he'd often become so engrossed in his painting that it was easy for me to slip away and sate my appetite. Callahan, well, I already knew it would be different with him. Firstly, the way my blood blazed in my veins whenever he came near told me that my feelings were so much stronger. With Ulysse, it had been more of a smoulder. And then there was the fact that Callahan was trained to observe. He'd notice if I kept disappearing.

But even with all that, even with the impossible odds our relationship would be up against, I still wanted him.

"Maybe I'm a tiny bit scared," I conceded. "But you've got no right to lecture me. I don't see *you* getting tangled up with a human. Isn't this just one big case of 'do as I say, not as I do'?"

In a heartbeat, the smirk vanished from Blane's face, replaced by... Was that sadness? He looked away, breaking the connection, and I wished I could take the words back.

"Sorry," I muttered.

"No, it's a fair question." He gave a long sigh. "There was a girl once. Soon after I first came to earth."

"What...what happened to her?"

"An overdose." Blane spoke matter-of-factly, still refusing to look at me. "She went to Plane Four."

"I'm so sorry."

"That's life, isn't it? Fleeting, fragile. Nevaeh will be back on earth now—population growth means souls don't stick around in Plane Four for long. My little sister keeps an eye on these things. The average stay is five weeks."

"Can't you look for Nevaeh here?"

"For what purpose? She'd be three years old, and I'd probably get arrested."

Okay, so that was a fair point. Blane looked so heartbroken that I tried to shift to an easier subject.

"You have another sister?"

Finally, I got a smile. "Aurelia. She's the sunshine to Decima's perpetual drizzle."

"What does she do? In the planes, I mean."

"Aura can be a little scatterbrained, so my parents put her in charge of managing the spirit guides. They visit recently departed souls trapped on earth to inform them about the Electi. Really, it's just a sinecure. The spirit guides organise themselves, and the Electi don't do their jobs anyway. So Aurelia gets bored. Mostly she hangs out in the library, but the last time I went home, she was learning to play the piano. You know, if you ever met, I think you'd like her." Blane topped off my glass. If there was one good thing to come out of this unlikely...friendship?...it was that I'd met someone who could match me in the drinking stakes. "But we're digressing. My problems are in the past, and yours is very much current."

"You truly think I should get more involved with Callahan than I am already? What about my living arrangements? I've moved from a six-thousand-square-foot penthouse to a shoebox of an apartment, and my cat hates it."

"Do *you* hate it?"

"Not as much as I thought I was going to." Yes, the space was tiny, but filled with friends and laughter, it didn't feel quite so small. Callahan, Marianna, Lola, Pablo... They made Sunset Tower feel like a home. "Okay, no, I don't hate it."

"Then stay there."

Really? Could it be that simple?

The elevator dinged, and Beauregard waltzed back into the great room, a bottle of champagne in each hand. Sometimes, I envied the way nothing ever seemed to faze him. I suspected it was down to a lack of a conscience, but it sure did make his existence easier.

"Since you're both lushes, I brought two kinds. Happy Christmas."

Happy Christmas... Would it be? After my conversation with Blane, I had an awful lot of thinking to do between now and tomorrow.

CHAPTER 51

Jack

L ast night, I'd gone to the mall. The place had been almost deserted, the only patrons men who'd left everything to the last minute just like me. First, I picked up an indoor herb garden for Marianna, a doll for Lola, and a toy car for Pablo, and then I paid homage to Saint Jude and scoured the stores until I found a gift for Vee. Damn, it'd been difficult. I mean, what did an idiot buy the woman he loved as a sorry-I-screwed-up-slash-Christmas-present? A department-store assistant tried to help, but after I'd explained the whole depressing story, she'd just given me a pitying look and suggested candy.

Candy? No, not unless it was pineapple and peanut butter flavour.

In the end, inspiration came from a tiny Japanese store hidden away in a corner, a shiny black facade framing a colourful window display. The owner had just locked the door, but she must have felt sorry for me because ten minutes later, I walked out with a stack of ornate paper squares and a book on origami. Plus a pair of hand-painted chopsticks, an

361

incense burner, and pink Hello Kitty slippers the lady swore any woman would absolutely love.

Then I headed to the grocery store and bought a microwave meal for one.

I'd planned to knock on Vee's door, hand over her gifts, and leave, but at nine a.m., my phone buzzed.

Vee: Marianna says dinner will be ready at two o'clock.

I was still invited? When I hadn't heard from Vee yesterday, I'd assumed she'd changed her mind, not that I would have blamed her. Christmas was meant to be a time for joy and celebration, not fidgeting and wishing you were somewhere else.

Should I go? Was Vee just inviting me out of politeness?

Oh, who was I kidding? If I had a chance—no matter how slim—to stay in her life, I'd grab it with both hands. I was on my way to the shower before my phone screen dimmed, beyond relieved that I hadn't drowned my sorrows last night the way I'd been tempted to.

Two o'clock, and I wouldn't be late.

"Please could you pass the gravy?"

Vee had also found the time to go shopping, and she'd bought new cutlery, a whole set of dinnerware, and even one of those fancy little jugs. I picked it up and held it out to her, our fingers brushing as she fumbled for the tiny handle.

Our gazes locked.

Electricity zapped through my veins.

Whatever there was between us, it hadn't gone away just because she wanted it to. But I'd never act on it, not again. Friendship was all we could have, and Vee was making an effort to be cordial. We both were. Only time would tell whether that effort would be enough.

"Could I have more gravy too?" Marianna asked.

She'd really pushed the boat out with dinner. A roast goose, mashed potatoes, and roast vegetables, plus Lola proudly showed me the plate of snickerdoodles she'd made for dessert. Judging by the state of the kitchen, I suspected she'd actually made more mess than anything else, but it was Christmas, so nobody cared. She was happy, and so was Marianna, which was a Christmas miracle in itself considering how downtrodden she'd been when she first moved in next door. Vee had been a good friend to her, and that was another thing to be grateful for.

Christmas...it was actually okay. And at least I wasn't Shep. He'd flown to California with Cecily yesterday evening, and now he was stuck on a yacht with Maxwell Dorrington and his third or fourth wife—I forgot which. Shep had actually been hoping for a nice juicy murder so he'd have an excuse not to go, but all that had come in this week was the two punks who'd met their maker outside Kristina Halliday's apartment. Looked like a mugging gone wrong, and since the muggers had come off worst, nobody was about to interrupt their holiday plans to hunt for clues. The ME was still hazy on the cause of death for one of the punks in any case.

"You have no idea how grateful I am that you cooked," Vee said, handing the gravy jug to Marianna. "Usually, I eat one of those pre-packaged roast dinners."

"You couldn't go to a restaurant?"

"I tried that one year, but it turns out that eating Christmas dinner alone in a restaurant is worse than dining alone at home. People kept staring at me. The staff at La Nostra Casa sent us a panettone this year, though. Being a frequent customer does have its benefits."

"Last year, I spent Christmas with my children's father," Marianna said. "His family said I was a terrible cock, so I wasn't allowed to help, and then his abuela set fire to the kitchen."

Three could play at this game. "I was on the Dorrington family's yacht. Cecily's brother drank too much and fell overboard, and we ended up sharing dessert with the coastguard."

Everybody laughed, even Lola, although she didn't understand what was going on. And I began to hope the friendship thing might work out. I didn't want Vee to spend any more Christmases alone, and no way was I setting foot on that damn boat again.

The new-found lightness in my soul lasted until after dessert. I slumped onto the couch beside Vee while Marianna sat on the floor with the kids, who were both fascinated by the pile of gifts in front of the TV. Someone had gone overboard with curly gift ribbon, and I suspected it was Vee. Overboard seemed to be something of a theme for her. She'd bought Lola a Gourmet Kiddie Kitchen that even had a dishwasher, which was more than my own kitchen did. Pablo got a brightly coloured ride-on llama, and Marianna received a set of Le Creuset pans. I understood that if men gave a girl bakeware as a gift, it was A Very Bad Thing, but the rule didn't seem to apply to women because Marianna was overjoyed.

And me? I got a coffee machine, and I knew from eyeing them up on the internet myself that it had set Vee back a thousand bucks at least. Holy fuck.

"I can't accept this," I whispered under my breath, barely audible over Lola's excited squeals.

"It's just a gift."

"It's too much. I got you slippers."

Vee's eyes lit up. "And I love them." She straightened her legs so her kitty-clad feet stuck out in front of her. "Aren't they the cutest?"

Score one to the old Japanese lady. But whether Vee liked the slippers or not, that didn't change the fact that she'd spent four figures on my Christmas gift. Yes, I didn't doubt that she took home a lot in tips, but she must have worked for a month to afford this.

"My first comment still stands."

She folded her arms. "I lost the receipt."

"Vee..."

Rather than answering, she joined Marianna on the floor to help assemble Lola's pretend microwave. Vee could be impossible, but deep down, I liked her rebellious streak. Why had she bought me the coffee machine? Because she was sick of me acting like a zombie in the mornings? Out of guilt? As an overblown effort to show we were still friends? Because honestly, socks would have been fine.

My knees cracked as I slid off the couch and picked up the side of... Was that a washer-dryer combo? Sometimes, the easiest thing was to smile and go with the flow.

We soon realised the error of our ways. Lola had fallen asleep on the couch, and now we had to get a small but remarkably complete kitchen into Marianna's apartment. Thank goodness she didn't have much furniture. This was going to take up half of her living room.

"Should we leave it until tomorrow?" Marianna asked. "I still have the kitchen to clean up."

Vee snorted. "No, you don't. After you spent all morning cooking, the least I can do is wash the dishes. And with Jack helping, it won't take long to move this stuff."

Upstairs, Marianna settled Pablo and Lola into their new beds—which I suspected had also come courtesy of Vee—

while Vee and I rearranged the living room to make space for Lola's gift. Vee was strong, surprisingly so, and I figured we could fetch everything in only two more trips. But not everyone was having such a great Christmas, it seemed. The hallway smelled of burned turkey and two of our neighbours were having a fight. Most of the words were too muffled to make out, but the sentiment was there. Something about a gold bracelet?

"Why is she complaining if he bought her jewellery?" I whispered. "Don't women like that?"

"He didn't buy her jewellery. That's her point. He bought someone else jewellery, and she found the receipt."

Huh. Vee clearly had better hearing than I did.

"What an asshole."

"Well, fifty percent of American marriages end in divorce, so I guess it's not all that surprising."

"That's a cheery observation."

"Sorry."

We reached the elevator for the second time. "After you. And there's no need to apologise. I'm just old and bitter now."

The doors closed behind us, and Vee leaned against the wall opposite me. Someone had scrawled *Happy Christmas bro's and ho ho ho's* in Sharpie, and I suppose I had to give them credit for the effort if not for the punctuation.

"If you're bitter, then that makes me grapefruit with a sprinkling of Bitrex. And I *am* sorry. Not only for being insensitive tonight, but for the way I acted the other night too."

"Vee, I just got my wires crossed."

"And I was too hasty."

"Too hasty?"

"I acted on instinct without thinking things through. I've been hurt in the past, and I don't know what my future holds, but..."

"But what?"

"The thought of you not being in it…"

"Vee, what are you saying?"

"Jack, I really like spending time with you. I want to spend more time with you." She gave me a dirty little smile. "Preferably naked."

It took a moment for my brain to catch up with my ears, and Vee was already on me, devouring my mouth with the plump lips I'd imagined around my cock far more times than was healthy. Time for *me* to act on instinct. I slid my arms around her waist and hoisted her up, and she returned the favour by wrapping her legs around my hips.

In my dreams, Vee had been wild and wanton, but even my filthiest fantasies came nowhere near the reality. Vee was an unbridled ball of energy intent on devouring me. Our tongues clashed, and Vee's hands tangled in my hair as she took everything she wanted, everything I willingly gave her because my heart had made its views on the subject quite clear over the last month.

"Fuck me," I choked out when we paused for breath.

"I plan to, but we have to move a tiny refrigerator first."

I leaned my forehead against hers, and then the laughter came. Yeah, we were a mess, but in the best possible way.

Back in Vee's apartment, I untucked my shirt to cover my raging hard-on, and we held ourselves together for long enough to carry the rest of the kitchen to Marianna's place. On our final elevator ride, we went all the way to the bottom of the building and shocked a middle-aged couple before riding back up to the sixteenth floor.

Once Vee's door slammed behind us, our clothes flew in every direction. There was a time for sweetness, but it wasn't now. Both of us felt it—the all-consuming need that blurred rational thought and let the senses take over. Vee was still fumbling with her bra when I carried her into her bedroom and followed her down onto her king-sized bed.

Which part of her should I feast on first? Those pebbled nipples peeking over black lace? Her sweet pussy? I could smell her arousal and that made up my mind, but she moved faster, tipping me sideways and crawling down the bed. When she sucked my cock into her mouth, I forgot everything but her. Nothing else mattered. Only Vee.

Those sweet lips almost destroyed me, but I'd been brought up well. *Ladies first.* Before I went over the edge, I flipped her onto her back and pinned her hands with mine.

"My turn," I practically growled. Growled? Fuck, I'd turned into a damn caveman.

She bucked against me as my tongue disappeared into her folds, and was it my imagination or did she taste of pineapple? Her protests turned to quiet mewls as I found the right spot, her thighs dropping open, her fingertips digging into my shoulders.

"Jack, I'm gonna..." She didn't finish the sentence before her back arched off the mattress, a long moan escaping from her lips. My Vee was a filthy little fox, and I loved every part of her.

I gave her a moment to get her breath back, but patience had never been my strong suit. I needed to get inside her, to bury my cock in her wet heat. Last week, before our aborted kiss, I'd bought condoms just in case, and now I thanked my lucky stars I hadn't taken them out of my wallet. Vee kissed me sweetly as I slid into her, that emerald gaze locked on mine, hot, intense, her eyes two liquid pools of lust.

The initial frantic desire was easing now, turning into something altogether deeper. A connection between two souls. Damn, could I sound any cornier?

But it was true. With every stroke in and out of my passionate little princess, my Vee, the knot holding us together tightened. I'd lost one woman I loved, but somebody up there had given me a second chance. A chance I didn't intend to squander. And when I came, Vee clenching around my cock and gripping my face with sweaty hands, I knew I'd do everything in my power to give us both the future we both deserved.

CHAPTER 52

Vee

The week after Christmas was the best of my life. I'd fallen fast, and I'd fallen hard. It was as if the stars had aligned, as if all the pieces of a jigsaw had finally slotted into place. I was the happiest I'd been in over two centuries. Of course, I should have known it was just the universe playing a cruel joke on me—or possibly Blane's Great-Uncle freaking Tiberius, wherever he was—but for that brief moment in time, I was content.

Callahan had been in my bed every evening, in my apartment in every spare minute. He had clothes in my closet and weird smoothies in my fridge. Every surface was covered in origami animals, and yesterday when I'd run out of paper, he'd gone to the mall and bought me more.

It'd taken Marianna three seconds to work out we were an item, probably because we couldn't keep the smiles off of our faces. She'd been almost as thrilled as I was and immediately made another cake to celebrate. I'd suggested she go into business, but she acted embarrassed and said she wasn't good enough.

I disagreed. If she wouldn't look into the logistics, then I would.

Next week. It could wait until next week.

Blane was also happy for us, but more in an "I told you so" sort of way. Better still, he'd agreed to me reducing the hours I worked—from six or seven days a week to five—so I could spend more time with Callahan. And Beauregard? He'd just made a lewd gesture with his tongue until Blane smacked him upside the head.

The only shadow hanging over us was the looming prospect of Serenity's funeral. The medical examiner had finally released her body, and the burial was scheduled to take place on Thursday, two days from now, The thought of having that wound torn open again preyed on my mind. Physical scars vanished, but the mental ones? Not so much. At least I had Callahan to help numb the pain, and Blane had turned out to be supportive too, albeit in a different way. Hell, he'd even started scouting out my dinner opportunities from his balcony.

Blane had also been right about Beauregard's organisational abilities. The demon might have been a prizewinning ass, but he'd helped me to finalise the arrangements for Serenity's final goodbye. Those little things I struggled with because of the pesky sunshine, like visiting the flower shop and liaising with the caterer, he'd taken them over. At least I'd been able to convince the priest to hold an evening service. A few invitees had commented on the unusual timing, but since I'd got off my butt and arranged the event and they hadn't, they'd have to deal with it.

The buzzing of the intercom snapped me out of my thoughts.

"Hello?"

"Genevieve!" It was one of the kitchen porters from La

Nostra Casa. If I tipped big enough, he'd deliver my food on his break. "Your dinner is served."

"*Grazie*, Matteo."

Callahan would be home any minute, and I'd bought his favourite pasta, a bottle of cheap wine, and yet another set of expensive lingerie. For years, I'd coveted the works of art on the Victoria's Secret runway, but I'd never been able to justify buying any of them. Now that I'd discovered how much *mon amour* liked to remove those lacy scraps with his teeth, I might have gone a teensy bit overboard with my credit card.

How far away was he? Perhaps I could skip the clothes and just wear the lingerie? Actually, no, because I knew exactly what would happen and then dinner would be ruined.

Although as it turned out, sex wasn't exactly uppermost on Callahan's mind for once.

"Penny for them?" I asked after he'd spent half of dinner staring blankly at the wall. "Did something happen at work?"

"It's probably nothing."

"But it's still bothering you."

"Yes." Callahan sighed and forked up another piece of pasta. "Sorry, I sometimes bring my work home with me. I guess I've been on my own for a while, and... I'll try not to."

"It's only because you care. Want to talk about it? I'm a good listener."

"I know you are, babe. But I don't want to worry you."

Worry me?

"Why should I be worried?"

Boy, that was a heavy sigh.

"We've been tying up loose ends on the Lyla Chavez case this week. Chad Bowen—Trist—says he left a party at a buddy's house around three a.m. and went straight to Mike Klass's place. But Daphne spoke to a girl who was at the party, and she reckons Chad went home."

"So, what? He went home and then went to Klass's?"

"No, that's just it. She swears he didn't go out again."

My spine stiffened. "You're saying he didn't kill Dr. Klass?"

"I don't know. I just don't know. I spoke to the girl myself, and she's a real groupie. Describes herself as Trist's biggest fan. There's a possibility she's lying in an attempt to keep her hero out of jail, but she claims she hung around outside for a while, waiting, in case he decided to go out to another party. Apparently, some members of the band are famous for their late-night drinking as well as their music."

"She *claims*. If she commits perjury, couldn't she go to jail herself?"

"Yes, and I explained that, but she's still sticking to her story. And she does know a lot of details about Trist's apartment. He lives on the first floor, and she must've been spying through his windows because she even described the pattern on his couch."

"Yikes. That's creepy."

"You're telling me."

"Is there any proof that she was at his place on the night Klass died and not another night?"

"Not yet."

"Not yet? So you're looking into it?"

"What choice do I have? I had the misfortune to be born with a conscience."

The ravioli congealed into a cold lump in the pit of my stomach. "What about Serenity?"

"Well, we know Chad was in the club that night."

"And so were hundreds of other people." My head hurt. None of this made any sense. "Why would he lie? Why would he confess to a murder he didn't commit?"

Had he been *that* scared of Blane?

"I can only think of one reason: to protect somebody else."

"You're saying there's another killer out there?"

"I'm saying there's an outside possibility. Vee, will you call in sick tonight?"

"What? Why? I'll be safe as long as I'm inside the club, and you'll pick me up, right?"

"Lyla died inside the club." There was a long pause. "And we never cleared Lucian Blane."

Ah, *merde*. Callahan thought Blane spiked Serenity's drink? No. No, I just couldn't see it. I'd gotten to know Blane better over the past couple of weeks, and I'd have bet my Leonardo da Vinci that he didn't kill her. He talked about her with a fondness that was hard to fake.

"I don't think Blane did it."

"I get that he's your boss, and the guy does seem to have some weird, enigmatic charm that makes women like him." Callahan gave his head a quick shake. "I just don't understand it myself. But please, babe, look at it objectively. There's something off about that man. His assistant too, and neither of them would provide a DNA sample."

"Beauregard?"

"Unless he has another sidekick?"

"No, just the one. He's been helping me with Serenity's funeral arrangements."

I'd told Callahan that Serenity's friends at the club had chipped in to help with the costs. They hadn't, but it was a more plausible explanation than the truth.

"I could have helped you with that."

"I know, but you needed a break, and he offered."

"Don't meet him anywhere alone. And after the funeral, steer clear of him until I can get to the bottom of this."

What should I do? Push back or take the easy way out? I didn't want Callahan wasting his time going after Blane, but how on Plane Five did I explain what I knew to my... boyfriend? Things were certainly heading in that direction.

I needed to talk to Blane about all this, but dammit, I hated leaving Callahan in the dark. Hmm, Callahan... Now that we were together, perhaps I should start thinking of him as Jack? I wanted us to have a future together for as long as my ageless body would allow. When it came to sating my appetite for blood, I'd already started setting ground rules for myself, the most important being "no getting naked with dinner." In future, I planned to pick the drunkest of men and back away if it looked as though they might cross that line.

"I'll be careful, I promise."

~

"And? What happened?"

Wednesday, and I'd been on tenterhooks all day, waiting for Jack to get home. *Home.* That's how Sunset Tower was starting to feel. The penthouse at Berkshire Place was covered in a layer of dust, and the concierge had probably forgotten my name. I needed to arrange for the hot tub to be drained. And clear out the kitchen cupboards.

Callahan—Jack—grimaced. Shit.

"I sat down with Chad for three hours today, and the more we speak, the less inclined I am to believe he's our man. Not only is there a witness who says he wasn't at Mike Klass's home at the time of the murder, but he also doesn't know the details of the crime scene. I asked where he hid outside—was it behind the brick grill or by the games-room window? He said behind the grill."

"And Klass didn't have a grill?" I guessed.

"Or a games room."

"That's crazy. Crazy that he'd give up his own freedom to allow a murderer to walk free."

"He'll have a reason, and I think I know what it is."

"You do?"

"His sister's sick. Really sick. Cancer, and mental health issues too. Her medical care costs a fortune, and somebody's paying him to take the fall."

I almost groaned out loud. Blane's visit had acted as a warning, hadn't it? Trist had known Jack was coming, that he'd be arrested, and he'd used the time to make arrangements with his accomplice.

"Do you know who?"

Jack shook his head. "And when I filled out the paperwork for a warrant to look at his finances, Captain Lindsay wouldn't let me file it."

"Why the hell not?"

"Because as far as he's concerned, we closed the case. Reopening it would mess with his statistics."

"But what if the psycho kills again?"

"He said we'd cross that bridge when we came to it." Jack threw his jacket down on the couch, angry. "Welcome to policing by the numbers. How do you feel about me quitting to become a PI?"

Jack was mostly joking but also a tiny bit serious.

"Whatever you want to do, I'll support you. But if you leave the LVMPD, even fewer victims will get justice."

He sighed. "I know. But that doesn't make this any less frustrating."

"Do you have any suspects? Other than Blane, I mean."

"No, but I have an appointment to speak with Blane again on Friday."

I wanted to sigh too, but I swallowed it down.

When I'd mentioned Jack's suspicions to Blane last night, I'd gotten another glimpse of that darkness he kept locked up inside, and I had a strong inkling that if a viable suspect was found, Jack wouldn't have to worry about paperwork or Captain Lindsay in order to get justice for Serenity. Blane would do the job for him. He said he'd let Trist live because

Trist was just a dumb, selfish kid who'd let things spiral out of control, but cold-blooded blackmail? That was a whole other level. As it was, Blane had insisted on arranging cabs to take all the female members of staff home at the end of the night shift, and he'd promised to carry on doing so until the culprit was off the streets. Beauregard had been tasked with installing a security camera over the back door, although I had a suspicion there would be occasional gaps in the footage when it suited Blane's purposes.

"You won't ignore other potential leads, though, will you?"

"Of course not," Jack assured me. "But medical bills aren't cheap, so our mastermind has money. According to Cecily, Lucian Blane has pockets deeper than the Grand Canyon."

I had to concede that much was true. Where had Blane's wealth come from? Mine had been built up over the best part of a century, initially from some lucky art purchases and then by careful investment in property and start-up enterprises. But Blane said he'd only been in Las Vegas for six years. Had he come to earth before that? Or did they print hundred-dollar bills in Plane One?

"And we need to note who attends Lyla's funeral tomorrow," Jack continued. "Including anyone watching proceedings from a distance."

"You honestly think her killer will come?"

"Some sick fucks like to see the final results of their handiwork. Blane's reading the eulogy, isn't he?"

This time, I couldn't hold back my sigh. It promised to be a really long week.

CHAPTER 53

Vee

When I'd attended funerals in the past, my sadness had always been tinged with envy. Envy that other people could die and I couldn't. But today as I watched Serenity's casket being lowered into the cold ground, lit by the moon and a few strategically placed floodlights, all I felt was overwhelming grief.

With several of Jack's colleagues also in attendance, we couldn't stand together, and nor could I accompany Blane. Instead, I huddled with a group of girls from Club Dead, listening to the priest over the sound of sniffles. It was a good turnout. Almost two hundred people had shown up, although that number did include several ghouls from the media and a YouTuber who'd been crass enough to record a vlog at the gates of the cemetery. And I'd finally caught up with Shelby, Serenity's old roommate, and we'd shed a few tears about our lost friend before the service started.

Earlier, Jack had introduced me to Daphne, his partner, and she was taking notes in a quiet corner. Both of them were wearing lapel cameras to record the attendees, just in case our culprit showed. Blane had worn one too. Yesterday evening,

378

he'd been reading the instruction manual, packaging and cables all over the coffee table as I shared a drink with him and Beauregard. Were they planning to hunt down the person who killed Serenity themselves? Secretly, I kind of hoped they were.

So many people... I focused on each face in turn, memorising, wondering whose grief was a sham. Some mourners I recognised, while others looked vaguely familiar and I wasn't sure whether I truly knew them or if my mind was playing tricks. Everyone looked so different in formal clothes, so uniform and sombre.

In the near stillness, I ran through the list of suspects. Whoever killed Serenity must have been close to both her and Trist. Invi and Lux, the two remaining band members, huddled under a leafless oak tree with Keira Michaels and their manager—Sidney Harber, according to Jack. No wonder he'd shortened it to Sid. Had one of them been involved? The only member of the quartet who'd benefited from her death had been Keira, and hadn't she given Jack a tip on Saint Anthony? If she was friendly with one drug dealer, perhaps she'd known a second?

But Keira was small. Could she really have killed a man so much bigger than her? Could she have trapped Serenity in that room while she fought for breath? Or had she and Trist split the workload? No, no, it didn't make sense—Serenity was never meant to die, only her baby.

The crowd shifted, and I saw two more familiar faces: Jeb and Skeeter Moutree. What the hell were they doing there? I hadn't invited them, and they most certainly weren't welcome. What kind of asshole gatecrashed a funeral?

Calm, Vee.

I closed my eyes for a moment, remembering Serenity, so determined and full of life. She'd once told me that when she stepped on stage, she felt free, and I pictured her striding in front of the band, microphone in hand, rocking yet another of her crazy costumes. Where was she now? Stuck in the fourth plane? Or back on earth, ready to embark on another journey?

Perhaps when the moment was right, I'd ask Blane whether he knew.

The attendants released the ropes on the casket, and a handful of people stepped forward to toss items into the grave. Folded notes, flowers, a teddy bear... I stayed put. Those gestures soothed the living, not the dead, and Serenity's soul had long since departed.

Jack caught my eye. Offered a hint of a smile. I returned it, feeling the blush creep up my cheeks as the final song played —"Every Last Breath," one of Serenity's. Even though it wasn't typical music for a funeral, I'd thought it fitting, and I was sure Serenity and her rebellious streak would have agreed.

The room I'd hired for the wake was at a hotel a short drive away, and I hitched a ride with Pandora, Carlene, and Latisha, thinking wistfully of my Porsche sitting in the garage at Berkshire Place. Would I ever drive it again? Perhaps I should just sell it and buy a cheap compact instead.

"I still can't believe Trist killed Serenity," Latisha said. "I mean, they were friends."

Carlene nodded her agreement. "And by aborting her baby? That's sick."

Oh, great. I'd ended up in the gossip car.

"Do you think the band'll split? Keira's okay, but she ain't no Serenity. Even if Trist wasn't in jail, that move totally screwed his career. Serenity was going places, and she'd have taken the Sinners with her."

"But what about the baby? She couldn't bring it on stage."

"She could've afforded a nanny."

"Keira won't stay," Pandora said. "Lux can't stand her."

Latisha checked her hair in a tiny mirror. "Is it his decision?"

"Technically, Sid gets the final say, but Lux will quit if Sid picks Keira."

"He told you this?"

Pandora shrugged as she signalled to make a left turn. "We talk."

"Can he just leave like that?"

"I don't think he cares. Lux is in it for the music, not the money. He has a trust fund."

My ears pricked up. A trust fund? Really? Certainly Lux had never flaunted his money. Yes, he always dressed well, but I'd figured that was part of his stage persona. Did he have enough cash to pay a hefty medical bill? I needed to talk to Jack.

But when we got to the hotel, Jack and Daphne were engrossed in conversation, speaking with one attendee after another as they moved around the room. Blane was doing the same. I saw him with the Sinners, and I couldn't resist sidling over to join them.

"A lovely service, Miss...Pelletier?" Sid said, and I was surprised he remembered my name. "I hear you organised it."

"With a little help."

"My wife and I will of course be making a donation to the Music in the Community project."

I'd asked for donations in lieu of flowers. Music in the Community had been a cause dear to Serenity's heart. She'd taught workshops there for as long as I'd known her.

"That's very kind of you."

Sid reached out to grasp my hand. "Without nurturing new talent, how will we find the next Serenity?" He checked his watch in one smooth movement as he let go. "Alas, I need to leave. I have a plane to catch."

"Going somewhere nice?" Making small talk was a reflex now, a skill learned at a century of gatherings just like this one.

"The Maldives. There's a beachfront villa calling my name. I had planned to fly out yesterday, but I could hardly miss Serenity's send-off."

"I appreciate you coming."

With Sid out of the way, I was able to turn my attention to Lux. Now that I was looking for them, I saw those little signs of wealth that I'd skimmed over before. He wore no designer labels today, but the cut of his suit said it was custom made. His shirt too, and his shoes were worn but still stylish. His teeth were perfect. And the way he spoke to the waitstaff, polite yet indifferent, said he was used to people serving him. I'd seen that same attitude in my parents, many, many years ago.

"Yeah, it was a great funeral," Invi said, then cut his eyes sideways to Lux. "Shit, not like, *great*, great, but you know..."

Lux nodded. "The night-time theme was an interesting twist. Serenity always preferred to forge her own path in life."

"And you?" I asked.

"It was one of our similarities. 'It is not death that a man should fear, but never beginning to live.' Marcus Aurelius."

"'Time is short for one who thinks, endless for one who yearns,'" Blane said. "Émile Chartier."

Oh, good grief. Were they going to try and outquote each other? I'd met Chartier several times, and in my opinion, he'd thought too much. He'd also lived to the grand old age of eighty-three, which somewhat discredited his own theory.

"You were close, then?" I asked. "Outside the band, I mean."

"Friends as well as colleagues. To know Serenity was to love her."

Invi raised his glass. "Amen to that."

Wine slopped onto the floor. Was he drunk? Yes. Lux

seemed to come to the same conclusion because he took hold of his bandmate's arm.

"We should get some water."

"Water? Who needs water? Party's just getting started."

"Sorry," Lux mouthed over his shoulder as he led Invi away.

Blane stared after them. "Invi might be a good drummer, but his personality came from the Plane Four reject pile."

"What about Lux?"

"Not quite so insufferable."

"Do you think there's a whiff of old money about him?"

"A whiff? He stinks of it, no matter how he tries to hide it."

"Why would he hide it?"

"Because he can't stand his family. Joseph did some digging a while ago—Lux's ancestors were slave traders, and their beliefs about class and status have passed down through the generations. Lux has all but disowned them, although he still seems to spend their money when it suits him."

"Blood money," I whispered.

"If you like. Why so many questions, Genevieve? Do you think Lux was involved in Serenity's death?"

I gave him a brief précis of Jack's suspicions. "So you see, we're looking for someone with money."

"And your boyfriend's still focused on me?"

"You have money, don't you?"

"I have enough."

"Is its origin of any concern?"

"*La curiosité a tué le chat*, Mademoiselle Pelletier."

"So it *is* of concern?"

Blane just laughed. "I admire your tenacity, *mon amie*." He steered me to a quiet corner. "One advantage of my Plane Three parties was the networking. And do you know who got sent to Plane Three? Thieves and pirates, Vikings and plutocrats. When they heard I was being banished to earth, a number of them offered me access to the loot they'd squirrelled away over the years. Ancient treasures. You know, to make my stay here a little more bearable. Returning the favour, so to speak. The old saying's true—you can't take it with you."

"I'll try to steer Jack towards Lux."

"I'd appreciate that. And I'll ask Joseph to take another look at his background as well."

"Where is Joseph?"

"He went back to the club. Somebody needs to keep an eye on the place since most of the staff are here." Blane's gaze shifted over my shoulder. "Your boyfriend is watching us."

Merde.

"I should go."

CHAPTER 54

Jack

"What did Blane want?"

I knew he was Vee's boss, so it was logical that she'd speak to him on occasion, but I couldn't lie—seeing them with their heads together like that made my blood boil. Crazy how far Vee had worked her way into my heart in such a short time. I'd wanted to stride over there and claim her as mine, but self-control had won, and I'd carried on with the job at hand.

"We were just discussing mutual acquaintances. Did you know Lux comes from money?"

The two of us were in my car now, sitting at a traffic light. Since Daphne had promised to go to a friend's place for dinner right after the wake, she'd brought her own vehicle and stuck to soft drinks and the occasional canapé so she could drive it. Vee must have bankrupted herself to pay for that spread. I only hoped Lucian Blane had tossed a few bucks into the kitty.

"Lux told me he was estranged from his family."

"Maybe so, but he's not estranged from their money."

This was news. "Where did you hear that?"

"Pandora, and Blane confirmed it."

Shit. My mind whirred as I pulled away. Had another suspect just thrown his hat into the ring? Lux and Invi had been somewhere near the bottom of the list with no obvious motive or means. But now it seemed Lux had the means. What about a motive?

And then there was Skeeter. Why the hell had he been at the funeral with Jeb?

My phone trilled in its cradle on the dash, and I swallowed a groan when I saw the name on the screen. Brianne. Just what I needed after a difficult day.

"I have to take this," I told Vee. "Work."

Her wave of the hand said, "Go right ahead."

"Callahan."

I put the phone on speaker. Vee was already privy to most of the facts about this case, and I didn't want any secrets between us.

"Jack! It's Brianne."

"I know. Caller ID, remember?"

A giggle. "Oh, yeah, right. So, I got those DNA results? All the wine glasses? Man, that was some party."

My stomach tensed. Would this help or hinder the investigation?

"And?"

"You said there were five results? But there were actually six. Well, maybe. One sample was really weird. Like, the machine kept coming back with an error, and I ran it three times."

"Contamination?"

"Maybe, I guess. But I've never seen the machine go all bananas before."

"What happened with the other five results?"

"Here's where it gets interesting. One of the samples was female, so we can rule her out?"

Keira. "For now. A male's more likely."

"Which leaves four. And I, like, did some detective work and three of them match the samples Lieutenant Shepherd brought in. You know, the band members?"

"Any hits on the fourth one?"

"Oh, yes." Brianne's tone said something big was coming. My knuckles were white where my hands gripped the wheel, and I noticed Vee had tensed too. "The fourth sample matches the father of Lyla Chavez's unborn child."

"Fuck."

Blane. He'd lied. Lied to my face, and then he had the gall to show up at Chavez's funeral to play the grieving friend.

"I thought that was good news?"

"Yeah, Brianne, it is. You did well."

"Really?" I could practically feel her preening. "Awesome. Say, what are you doing on Saturday? Wanna go out for drinks?"

"Sorry, I'm taking my girlfriend to a show at the Venetian."

"Your...girlfriend?"

I couldn't help smiling to myself. "I figured it was time to move on. Thanks for the DNA info, Brianne. Talk soon, okay?"

I hung up before she could say anything else. Tonight was going to be busy. Although I had a meeting set up with Blane tomorrow, I didn't want to wait until then. Every hour he was free meant another possibility for him to harm somebody. I needed to call Shep. Daphne. Probably the captain too, although I'd rather avoid that.

"I'll drop you off at home, and then I need to go to the office."

I brought Vee's palm to my lips, but she felt stiff. Unyielding.

"To do what?"

"It's time to have another chat with Blane."

"Why? I mean, why now? And what was all that about DNA? I thought he wouldn't take a test?"

"Sometimes we have to get creative. Cut a few corners."

"So, you what? Stole his freaking blood?"

"His saliva."

Why was Vee so upset? She didn't always play by the rules herself. Her renegade visit to Reuben was a case in point.

"How?"

"There was a meeting at the club. He and the band were there. I offered the waitress a hand with cleaning up and took the glasses to the lab instead of the kitchen. Why is that such a problem? We've both got the same objective here: to catch Lyla's killer."

"But only one of us is chasing after a person who didn't do it. Brianne..." Vee said her name as if it left a bad taste in her mouth. "Brianne said there were two unknown samples, and one of them gave an error."

"Yes, but it could have been a mistake. A fly that drowned in Cabernet Sauvignon or something."

"No, that was Blane's sample. Trust me. He can be a bit of a jerk, but he didn't kill Serenity."

"How do you know?"

Vee huffed out a sigh. "You'd never believe me if I told you. Trust me on that as well."

"Who are you calling?" Now she had her own phone in her hand.

"Blane. He can clear this whole mystery up."

"Vee, don't—"

"Blane, you recently had a meeting with the three remaining Sinners and Keira. There was someone else at the meeting. Who was it?" A pause. "Wait a second." She turned to me. "What date?"

I spoke through gritted teeth. "December twenty-first."

"Blane, did you hear that?" Vee covered the microphone with her hand. "He's checking his calendar."

Brilliant. Not only had Vee tipped off my prime suspect, but she'd also given away the fact that we were working together.

"Okay, thanks." My darling girlfriend tucked her phone into her purse. "It was Sid Harber. You know, the band's manager? He was there for most of the meeting, but apparently he left just before you arrived. Do you think...?"

Sid Harber? Did that fit? He hadn't been in town for Serenity's murder—thanks to Shep's efforts, we knew that much—but he had money. Or at least, his wife did. Fuck. *His wife.* If she'd found out he'd gotten Chavez pregnant, she surely wouldn't have been too happy about that. Could he have paid Trist to do his dirty work? Possibly... Plus Harber was a golfer, and according to Saint Anthony, so was Miami Mike. Had the pair been acquainted?

"Yes. I do think."

And more importantly, I trusted Vee's judgement. On paper, Blane made an excellent suspect, but she knew him better than I did.

"Ugh. Seriously? Serenity slept with *him*? He's old enough to be her father, and he's married." She suddenly clapped both hands to her cheeks. "And he's on his way to the Maldives."

"He's *what*?"

"That's why he left the wake early—because he had a flight to catch."

This just got better and better. Guess which island nation didn't have an extradition treaty with the US? There was no time to talk. I punched speed dial on my phone and prayed.

"Daphne? I need you to locate somebody. Yes, right away."

CHAPTER 55

Jack

"Stay in the car."

"But—" Vee started.

Now wasn't the time to argue. "Stay. In. The. Car."

Shep and Daphne were both on the way, but we didn't have a moment to spare. Daphne's research had found that Harber and his wife owned homes in New York, Las Vegas, and the Cayman Islands, and right now, he was getting ready to leave an impressive two-storey mansion in Summerlin. If Harber got into the Escalade parked outside the two-car garage, we could end up chasing him all over Vegas, endangering countless lives as we went. I needed to go in. Stall him. I checked my gun and racked a round into the chamber, just in case. If I had to use it, things would already have gone to shit, but it gave an added layer of comfort. I wished I had my ballistic vest as well, but who wore body armour to a funeral?

Harber's home was the same size as Mike Klass's, but a tasteful shade of cream and designed by an architect who hadn't been testing his client's products. Lights were on both

390

upstairs and downstairs, and I took that as a good sign. A shadow passed across the window to my right. Somebody was definitely home.

I started the voice recorder on my phone, then knocked on the door.

Come on, you asshole. Open it.

"Detective Callahan? Is this a social call?"

Harber looked happy, relaxed, a far cry from the grieving man I'd spoken to less than two hours ago. He'd changed into linen pants, a pink shirt, and sandals. With socks. If nothing else, I was tempted to arrest him for crimes against fashion.

"Business, I'm afraid."

"I didn't realise you worked this late."

"The LVMPD never sleeps. May I come in?"

"Certainly, certainly. What's this all about? You'll have to excuse the mess—I'm heading off on vacation this evening."

A vacation. With seven suitcases?

"I just have a few quick questions. About Ms. Chavez's contract, mainly. I'm sure you've seen Jeb Moutree on the news recently?"

"That redneck who claims he was married to Serenity? He was at the funeral today as well."

"Yes, I'm aware of that. At the moment, I'm trying to ascertain what he might have to gain from her death. Whether he might receive an income from her record sales. Can you shed any light on that?"

"I'm no lawyer, but I would think the royalties would go to her estate."

"Do you have a copy of the contract? We've had trouble locating one."

"I believe I do. In my study, if you'd like to follow me?"

I fucked up. There was no other way of putting it. I let my guard down, swayed by Harber's easy-going manner and apparent willingness to cooperate. One second, I was plotting out the next chapter in my cover story, and the next, I was staring down the barrel of a revolver. A .38 by the looks of it. A small gun for a small man.

"Hands in the air, please, Detective Callahan. Apologies, that sounds like a line from a bad movie."

To quote Vee, *putain de merde*.

I did as I was told, and as sweat trickled down my spine, I racked my brain for a way to get out of the hellish situation I'd landed myself in through my own stupidity. *I should have waited.*

"What are you doing, Sid? I just came here to ask about Serenity's contract."

"Do you think I was born yesterday? That you showed up here five minutes before I was due to leave is no coincidence, and I'm afraid I can't let you stop me."

"You killed Serenity?"

"As I understand it, an allergy killed Serenity."

"But you administered the pills?"

"No, no, I didn't. I wasn't even there." Harber shook his head, tutting. "That was Chad Bowen, the idiot. Too compassionate for his own good with those painkillers, and even then he would have gotten away with it if he hadn't lost his mind and tried to blame his stupidity on a vampire. A *vampire*." Harber chuckled, the uneven laugh of a madman. "As if those exist. I blame the alcohol. That boy always did drink too much."

"So if it was all Chad's fault, why threaten me with the gun?"

"This isn't the movies, Detective. I don't owe you a confession." He glanced at his watch, an oversized silver thing. "And now I'm running late."

My ears rang and my thigh burned as a bullet tore through my flesh. Harber barely hesitated, just huffed and aimed again.

"I never was so good with this thing."

"No!" I choked out.

I had to survive, if not for myself then for Vee. I couldn't put her through the agony I'd suffered after Angie's death. My strength ebbed as I sprang for the gun, but Harber fired once more, a punch to the chest. Now I knew what hell felt like. My legs buckled, and Harber loomed over me, a wraith of a man, this time pointing his gun at my head. The edges of my vision dimmed, my whole focus on the finger that squeezed the trigger. Then Harber disappeared in a blur of black and pink as he fired for a third time.

Was this the end?

A siren sounded in the distance, and Harber ran, his sandals slapping on the tile floor as he bolted through the house.

My brain began to function again.

I wished it hadn't.

Vee lay beside me on the floor, half of her neck missing, her lifeblood pumping from what had to be an artery and mixing with mine. A slick red pool spread wider with every gasping breath.

Fuck, I'd killed her. My Vee, my love. I might not have pulled the trigger myself, but I was responsible for her death.

"I'm s-s-s..." Every word was an effort. "S-s-orry."

She smiled. A beautiful smile beside such horror.

"Save your strength," she whispered.

There was no point. Because I knew what that bullet had hit. My heart. A red rosette of blood spread out from a hole below my left pec, and my life was ebbing away with every second, all the love and laughter that I still had left to give. Gone. Wasted. Wasn't there supposed to be a light to walk into or something? Because right now, all I saw was darkness. All I *felt* was darkness. A heavy foreboding as if the whole universe had shifted into another dimension.

"Vee, I..." *Breathe. Focus. Breathe.* "I love you."

That smile grew wider, but her eyes brimmed with sadness. Twice I'd loved, and twice I'd lost.

"I love you too. I always will."

Her words came easier than mine, and for that I was grateful. Small mercies. I glanced at her neck again. Was there a chance...?

No. *No, no, no.* My eyes were playing tricks. Her wound, that gaping hole, it was getting smaller. The flow of blood had slowed to a trickle. Flesh was knitting back together, muscle growing, skin smoothing. And Vee was scrambling to her knees.

"I don't... I don't..."

"Shhh." Her smile was almost serene as she pressed down on my chest with both hands. "I want you to live."

A *thump* came from somewhere in the house. The sirens drew closer.

Everything went black.

CHAPTER 56

Jack

What was that smell? That acrid, antiseptic-y stink? I inhaled deeply, trying to work out where I was. I could hear beeping, and over that, the sound of a woman's voice.

"Air traffic controllers and physicists are tonight attempting to work out how an Airbus A318 that took off from BWI Marshall Airport at eleven p.m. local time got from Baltimore to Las Vegas in just forty-five minutes. The flight disappeared from radar over Indiana, only to reappear outside Harry Reid International Airport a quarter of an hour later. All passengers are unharmed, but scientists are stumped."

I'd died, hadn't I? Died and fallen into a parallel universe. Vague memories were coming back to me now. Sid Harber... A revolver... One shot, two, three... Three! Holy hell, Vee! What had happened to Vee? I tried to sit up, but blankets pinned me down, fleecy wool tucked tightly around me. I tore at them, only for hands to push at my shoulders.

"Easy, buddy."

That voice... It was familiar.

"Sh-Shep?"

"Good to have you back, Jack. You gave us one hell of a scare."

I forced my eyelids open, blinking in the glare from the ceiling lights. Shep was standing over me, stubble speckling his jaw, his eyes bloodshot. Behind him, Daphne and Cece were hovering with concern etched across their faces.

"Where's Vee?"

Shep and Daphne looked at each other.

"Vee?" he asked, a little sheepish. "At home, I guess. When the doctors decided you were gonna be fine, we figured it was better to wait so you could call her yourself rather than freaking her the hell out."

"Fine? How am I fine? I got shot in the damn chest."

Sheepishness turned to puzzlement. "No, you got shot in the thigh. A through-and-through. The doctors said you were lucky. An inch to the right and the bullet would've hit an artery."

"No, my chest... There was a hole." I clawed at the paper gown until it ripped, found unblemished skin underneath. What the hell? "A hole in my shirt..."

"Buddy, you weren't wearing a shirt. That was the weirdest part of the whole thing. What happened to it?"

The weirdest part? No, no, no. On a scale of one to what-the-fuck, a missing shirt barely rated as a blip.

"Where's Harber? Sid Harber? He ran..."

"You shot him, remember? One round through the head with your service pistol. There'll be an investigation, of course, but it seems fairly clear-cut. Did he kill Mike Klass? We found an ice pick in his desk drawer."

"I don't... I don't know."

I barely knew anything anymore. Nothing made sense. Vee, my injuries... But if I was certain of one thing, it was that I hadn't shot Sid Harber. Hell, I hadn't even drawn my gun.

The door to my room opened, and a nurse marched in. Exhaustion rimmed her eyes, but she still managed a smile.

"Good to see you awake, Mr. Callahan. How are you feeling?"

How *was* I feeling? Surprisingly human. Tired, and my leg stung like hell, but apart from that, not too bad.

"Okay. I'm okay. I thought it would hurt more than this."

"That'll be the painkillers."

"What time is it? How long since I got here?"

"It's one o'clock in the morning. The doctors gave you something to help you sleep while they cleaned up your wound."

"My chest? My heart?"

"There's nothing wrong with your heart, Mr. Callahan. You're strong as an ox." She turned to my trio of friends. "How about we let our patient get some rest now? You can speak again in the morning."

"But—"

"She's right, Jack. We just wanted to check you were okay. We'll be back in the morning with breakfast." Shep leaned forward to stage whisper, "The food isn't great in here."

The nurse chuckled. "I'm sorry to say your friend's right about that. But don't worry; if there are no complications, you'll be discharged in a day or two."

A day or two? No, that was too long. I needed to see Vee, and I needed to see her right now.

"I feel fine. Great! How do I discharge myself?"

"That's not a good idea, Mr. Callahan." She wagged a finger. "The doctor will be around to check on you first thing."

Daphne squeezed my hand, and Cecily bent to kiss me on the cheek before they left. I suspected my private room came courtesy of her influence because my medical coverage could best be described as mediocre. I had good friends—great friends—and I'd be grateful for that as long as I lived.

As long as I lived.

How was I still alive?

And where was Vee? She'd been in the car outside Harber's home, so even if I'd hallucinated everything that had happened inside, she'd still have seen the cavalry arriving. She wouldn't have left, would she? She'd said she loved me. Or had I imagined that too?

If I couldn't see her, I needed to speak with her at least. Get her side of the story. Where was my phone? I screwed my eyes shut, trying to recall where I'd left it. In my pants pocket? Yes! I'd slid it in there right after I'd started the voice recorder.

The voice recorder.

The damn voice recorder!

If I played the file, it would answer all my questions. Shed light on the gloomy recesses of my mind. But where were my pants? Shep had mentioned my lack of a shirt, but he hadn't said anything about pants. Should I call the nurse back? Before I hit the button, I opened the door of the nightstand and breathed a sigh of relief when I hit pay dirt. My phone was sitting in the cubby along with my wallet and my shield. The phone's screen was cracked, but when I pressed the button, it lit up.

Time to solve this mystery.

In all my years as a cop, I'd experienced the bizarre to the downright ridiculous. But nothing—*nothing*—would ever be as unsettling as listening to my own death. Harber luring me into his study... Holding me at gunpoint... Apologising... *That creepy laugh.* Then he'd shot me once, twice... That all jibed with my fuzzy memories. The third shot came, and then the "I love yous."

Five seconds passed. Ten.

Harber spoke, words I'd forgotten or never heard, his voice strangled. Ice ran through my veins.

"What are you?"

Then he ran.

I heard a muffled *thump*.

Voices.

"Your boyfriend surely screwed the pooch tonight, Genevieve."

Lucian Blane. What the hell was he doing there?

"Stop being a jerk! He's dying. He's freaking dying! Sid Harber shot him in the heart."

"Ouch."

"If you won't help, get out. Go after Sid."

"I already did. He's feeling a little sleepy."

"We need an ambulance. Call an ambulance!"

"Let me look." Fabric rustled. "We don't need an ambulance, we need a bloody miracle."

"Isn't that your department? Do miracles even exist?"

A pause. "Couldn't you...you know?"

"No! He'd hate me the way I hate Voltaire. Maybe not now, but in twenty years. I wouldn't wish that on anyone."

"Then perhaps I could...hmm...swap his soul into Sid's body?"

"Are you *freaking kidding me?*"

"It was just a thought."

"Sid's going to prison."

"Prison's one option."

"Jack's breathing's slowing." Vee was sobbing now. "Over two hundred years of misery, and I get one week of happiness? *One damn week*? I really, really hate your family."

Swap my soul into Sid's body? I'd thought the recording would help to clear things up, not make them even more confusing. None of this made any semblance of sense. Two hundred years of misery? Vee was twenty-six. What was she talking about? And who the hell was Voltaire?

"Okay, okay." Now even Blane sounded stressed. "Okay, I've got an idea. It might work. I don't know. You need to keep the detective breathing for two minutes."

"I'm not sure he's got that long."

"Then do CPR or something. Plug the hole. Haven't you read *Gray's Anatomy*?"

"*Grey's Anatomy*?" Wait, Beauregard was there as well? "That was a great show."

"Be quiet, Joseph."

The voices stopped. For a minute and forty-seven seconds, all I heard was Vee's quiet sobs and my own sucking breaths, becoming shallower and shallower.

Then nothing.

How the hell was I still alive?

Six a.m., and I snuck towards the hospital's fire exit wearing a set of green scrubs I'd liberated from a storage closet. My left thigh felt as though it'd been napalmed, but the pain paled into insignificance beside my worry for Vee. I'd called Blane to see if she'd gone to work, but he told me she'd called in sick. When I mentioned the events at Harber's house, he'd muttered something about a meeting and hung up on me. Then turned his phone off.

Vee was right—the man was a jerk.

Somehow, I made it to the sidewalk and flagged down the first cab to roll past. The driver gave me a dubious look when I limped towards him.

"Sir, are you okay?"

"It's been one hell of a night. Sunset Tower, please." I held up a fifty-dollar bill. "I *really* need to get some sleep."

Sleep? Sleep? What a joke. I might never sleep again. When I knocked on Vee's door, there was no answer. For a moment, I considered breaking it down, but some asshole would only call the police. Not because of the potential burglary, you understand—our neighbours just didn't like noise in the middle of the night.

I kicked the door in frustration. It swung open.

And I found that Vee had been expecting me.

The apartment was silent, still, stuck in a time warp waiting for Vee to come home, but I knew she never would because Muse was gone. And there was a single white envelope propped up against the vase on the dining table, my name written on the front in Vee's neat cursive. I slid out a single piece of paper.

Jack,

Where do I begin?

First, with an apology. I should have known better than to give in to temptation, but you were impossible to resist. A mind-blowing lover, but above all a friend, and the kindest soul I've ever met.

Secondly, I should offer an explanation, although I'll have to keep it vague. I'm sure you've realised by now that I'm different. Too different to stay. But know that leaving you will be the hardest move I've ever made. Once, I doubted I'd ever feel human again, but you've proven me wrong.

Finally, I offer you my love. It's yours, every last piece of it. Never will I gift it to another. When I see the heavens, I'll think of you and know that your heart still beats under the same stars as mine.

The sacrifice was worth it.

Your Vee.

. . .

Well, that cleared everything up, didn't it? *Bloody hell, Vee.* She sure knew how to kick a man to the kerb in style. I felt as if I'd been shot in the heart again. Actually, no, this was worse. If I didn't have Vee, I might as well not have a heart anymore. She'd torn it out and fed it to the damn wolves.

Different... Yes, I understood she was different. Perhaps not even human? If someone had told me this time yesterday that the supernatural might not be entirely fictitious, I'd have died laughing instead of from a bullet wound, but I was certain I hadn't imagined what I'd seen. Vee's neck regrowing, turning from a mangled mess of blood and bone into the alabaster skin I'd kissed so many times. I didn't know exactly what she was, but I knew whose she was.

Mine.

Genevieve Pelletier was mine.

And I also knew where to find her.

CHAPTER 57

Vee

Eight suitcases and two trunks sat in a row in my foyer. Two of the suitcases were Muse's, and I was sure she wouldn't be impressed about moving yet again, no matter how many kitty treats I bribed her with. Right now, she was stretched out on her favourite sofa, waiting for the sun to rise. I always left the blinds up in one room for her, with the door cracked open so she could come and go from my dark world as she pleased.

Less than twenty-four hours to go... I'd miss Las Vegas. My time here had been enjoyable for the most part, and all too brief. Perhaps I'd move back someday, in a future decade when another generation had lived and died. In the meantime, my penthouse would sit here untouched, a museum to a past existence.

Today I'd sleep, this evening I'd feed, and by midnight, I'd be on a private jet heading for my next adventure. My favourite paintings would be safe here for now, and one day, a day when I felt less fragile, I'd come back for them. A flying visit. My art collection was the only thing that travelled with me from place to place, and now Angelina Callahan's

403

hummingbird would join my other treasures. I'd considered leaving it for Jack, but would that be too weird?

Pour l'amour de la merde, Genevieve. He saw your freaking neck regenerate.

Perhaps I could courier the piece to him anonymously?

At least Blane had offered to visit me in San Francisco. I wouldn't be totally alone anymore, so my disaster of a winter had brought one small benefit. A friend. A slightly annoying, most definitely unconventional friend. A friend who'd gone, quite literally, above and beyond to save the man I loved.

Why San Francisco, you ask? Why not somewhere that wasn't quite so sunny? Been there, tried that. Moving to Rjukan, Norway, had seemed like a fantastic idea at the time—thanks to the surrounding mountains, the town spent six months of the year bathed in darkness. But do you know what else it was bathed in? Snow. It was freaking freezing. Even the grass froze. Locals took the cable car up the mountain to feel the sun on their faces while I stayed in the valley alone, and there was only so much snowshoe trekking a girl could take. It was a similar story in Alaska. The Northern Lights were pretty, but the nightlife was non-existent and my neighbours got all in my business. Plus my dinner options were limited. In New York and Vegas and San Francisco, I had to spend much of my time at home, but when I did go out, at least I could have fun.

I caught sight of myself in the mirror. Yes, I had a reflection—that was another unfounded rumour about vampires, no doubt created by the same people who thought Satan had horns and a pointy tail. Now I knew he wore charcoal suits and favoured Brioni shoes. Yeuch, my eyes were yellow. I could cover up the irises with contacts, but today, the whites looked jaundiced too. And my skin was grey and blotchy, as if I'd stepped out of a Victorian photograph. I flicked my freshly bleached hair forward to try and hide the worst parts. No, that really didn't help, and after two hundred years, I was sick of the sight of myself.

Shit.

I was a mess, and the nausea and stomach cramps didn't help either. As soon as it got dark, I'd head down to the tunnels—not my menu of choice, but needs must. By tunnels, I meant the labyrinth of sewage tunnels buried beneath the glitz of the Strip. They were meant to protect the city from flash flooding in the event of a storm, but hundreds of people called them home. There was a whole city under there, protected from sunlight, divided into individual residences citizens had furnished as best they could. The Mole People even had an art gallery.

And there was always an addict I could snack on.

I hated doing it, hated taking advantage of people who had so many challenges in life, but when I reached that desperate stage between human and animated corpse, I had no choice. With my hoodie and baggy coat, the Mole People paid no attention to me, and I always left my victims money as a sort of apology-slash-thank-you.

The intercom buzzed. It turned out the concierge at Berkshire Place *had* remembered my name, and I'd asked him to fetch me breakfast.

"George, could you leave my croissant outside the door?"

"Miss Pelletier, there's a gentleman on the way up to see you. I tried to stop him, but he said he was a police officer."

Merde!

How did he even know where I lived? I'd barely had time to take a breath before Jack hammered on my door.

"Vee, I know you're in there."

A pause. What if I stayed really, really quiet?

Muse shot past me to the foyer and scratched the door, miaowing. Traitor. I'd forgotten how much she'd grown to like Jack too.

"Vee, if you don't open the door, I'm breaking it down."

Unlikely, since it was reinforced with steel and the six-point locking system would withstand a backhoe, but I didn't want Jack to break his shoulder. Both of Blane's sisters had gone home now, so it wasn't as if I could get him fixed again.

I punched in the code, and the bolts shot back with a muffled *thunk*.

The door swung open, and Jack just stared at me.

"Go on, you can say it. I'm a freak. An ugly, inhuman freak."

"You'll always be beautiful to me, but…" He took one tentative step forward to examine my face. "Damn. What… I don't even know where to start. You saved me. You saved my life."

"Technically, I didn't."

"Vee, you took a bullet for me. Why?"

"Because I could. Because I knew I'd survive the shot and you wouldn't. Harber was aiming at your head, Jack."

"You healed. I saw you heal." Jack shook his head in disbelief. "What's wrong with your eyes? Am I allowed to ask that?"

"Regeneration takes a lot out of me."

He reached out to touch my cheek, but pulled his hand back when I flinched.

"Sorry, I didn't mean to…" He sucked in a ragged breath. "You said you loved me."

"I did. I do."

"Then why are you leaving?"

Did I honestly have to spell it out? "Because you're human and I'm…not."

"Yes, I worked that much out from the recording."

"What recording?"

"From Harber's house. I recorded my own murder, but somehow, here I am."

I'd been grey before, but now I imagined I'd gone quite white. "Y-y-you were recording us? How much did you hear?"

"I could bullshit you and say I heard the whole thing, but I'll be honest. And I want you to be honest with me, Vee. Will you promise me that much?"

"Some of the secrets aren't mine to tell."

Like the way Blane had disappeared and come back nearly two minutes later with his little sister in tow. Aurelia. He'd been right; I did like her. But she also freaked me the hell out. Apparently, her special skill was bending time and space, but she wasn't so good at it. She'd spent twenty minutes telling me how she once got distracted and created a tidal wave that had come perilously close to wiping out a nation, while outside Harber's house, Shep and Daphne had balanced in impossible positions, halfway out of Shep's car. And Jack? He'd frozen in the middle of his last breath, his face surprisingly peaceful. As if he'd accepted his fate.

After Aurelia arrived, Blane had vanished again, this time for longer, but eventually he came back with Decima. The bitch. Once more, he'd been spot-on with his character assessment, and she'd huffed and fidgeted while we worked out the best way to stage the scene. But I had to be grateful to her. She was the one with the ability to heal people—ironic, Aurelia said, because Decima mostly liked to destroy things— and she'd fixed the butchered flesh that had once been Jack's heart. Not his leg because we needed a plausible story, but she'd assessed the wound and tinkered with a few blood vessels around the edges.

Then Blane and Beauregard had manoeuvred Harber into position and shot him with Jack's gun, the two women left, and the rest of us ran out the back door while Shep and Daphne burst in the front.

"Okay," Jack said. "I understand."

"You do?"

"Well, no, but I guess I'll have to accept it. Tell me what you can." Jack closed his eyes for a moment. "I heard Blane arrive. You were panicking. Then he left, and all I heard was you crying as you tried to save me. Which clearly worked. Whatever secrets you have, Blane knows them?"

"Most of them."

"Is that because he's...like you?"

"No, he's very, very different. For years, I thought it was just my kind and humans coexisting, but now I know there are others. I don't know who they all are, but they're out there."

"Vee, what are you?"

I took a deep breath. "I'm a vampire."

"A...vampire?" Jack took a step back. "A *vampire?*"

"Not like in the movies. That's mostly lies. Yes, I drink blood, but I don't kill for it. I have a reflection. A stake to the heart is unlikely to harm me, and you know I love garlic. Sunlight's a problem, but I've learned to work around that."

"The whole..." He motioned towards my face. "That's from sunlight?"

"No, that's the lack of blood. I only need a little, but I can't go without. As best as I can ascertain, it's not so much sustenance that my body needs, more a top-up of life force. If I get that, I'm basically human." I tried to smile. "I'll just be twenty-six forever, kind of like Cher."

"How old are you really?"

"Uh, I was born in 1769."

"Fuck me." Jack blew out a long breath.

"I don't think you mean that," I said, trying to lighten the moment. He was taking this remarkably well. As in, he hadn't sprinted from the building, screaming.

"I'm not sure what I mean." Jack tore a hand through his hair. "Common sense tells me to run and never look back..." Tears pricked at my eyes. "But I can't. Underneath, you're still the same person I was in love with yesterday. I like spending time with you... Where do you get the blood from, Vee?"

"Drunk men at the club, mostly," I said in a small voice.

"Fuck." He raised his eyes to the ceiling. "You couldn't...I don't know, drink animal blood?"

"It doesn't have the same effect."

Plus it tasted disgusting. Which I could cope with if it sated me, but it didn't. It just made the stomach cramps worse.

"And what about this place? Is it yours?"

"I made good investments?"

Was this twenty questions? I suppose I owed Jack some answers.

"What about the apartment in Sunset Tower? It was just a temporary arrangement?"

"It was meant to be. I panicked when you wanted to interview me at home, and I rented a place more appropriate for a waitress, but after I got to know you, I decided to stay there permanently."

"And give up all this?"

"A home is only as beautiful as the people in it. I found I was happier in the tiny apartment."

"The ex-boyfriend? Does he exist?"

"I was involved with a guy about a hundred years ago, more of a friend-with-benefits arrangement, but it didn't last. He got older, and I didn't." I gritted my teeth and forced out my next words because they made me choke. "And another vampire forced me into marriage in 1796. I escaped in the late nineteenth century, and I haven't seen him since."

"Voltaire?"

I froze. "How do you know his name?"

"You mentioned it on the recording." Oh. Yes. "He's still alive? Undead, whatever you call it?"

"He thinks Americans are uncouth, so he stays in Europe. That's why I made the US my home."

Jack stepped over to the window and stared out at my beautiful view of the city. Ten minutes, and I wouldn't be able to look at it anymore.

"If people find out what I am, they'll lock me up, Jack. I don't want to spend eternity as a science project."

"I'm not going to tell anyone about this."

The knot of tension in my belly loosened a smidgen.

"Maybe...maybe we could stay in touch? I don't have many friends. Just Blane and perhaps Beauregard, although he's a bit of an idiot."

"The lawyer's not human either? Why doesn't that surprise me?"

"I think inhumanity's a prerequisite for sitting the bar exam."

Jack stayed silent for a full minute. I could see the horizon lightening, and I stepped back just in case. The blinds in this room were automatic. They'd lower as the sun rose.

"Where are you moving to?" he asked.

"San Francisco." A tear rolled down my cheek. This long goodbye was a hundred times harder than a clean break. "I've visited several times, but I've never lived there before. I think it'll be quieter, but I'm looking forward to walking on the beach. Will you... Please, will you say goodbye to Marianna for me? I'll miss her so much. I plan to send her some money too, enough to start a business and fund Lola's and Pablo's college educations." The blinds slid down a foot, and Jack jumped. "There's a sensor."

Muse stalked across the room, tail in the air, and sat on Jack's foot, gazing up at him adoringly. *You and me both, kitty.*

"Would you like a drink?" I offered. Anything to break the lengthening silence.

Jack shook his head, and I slumped onto a sofa. How had

things gone so wrong, so quickly? Two months ago, I'd been bobbing along, reasonably content. Then Serenity's death had set off a cataclysm. It was hard to miss something you'd never had, but now that I'd had Jack, the loss would stay with me forever.

"No," he finally said.

"No?"

"No, I won't say goodbye to Marianna for you."

CHAPTER 58

Vee

Well, Jack's answer stung, but I could write a letter to Marianna. Once upon a time, I'd been good at putting words onto paper. In the days before email and telephones, I hadn't had a lot of choice.

"That's okay. I understand."

"No, I won't say goodbye to her because you're not leaving, Vee. This is your home." Now Jack was striding towards me, and he held out his hand. No, not his hand; his wrist. "Will it heal?"

"Will what heal?"

"The wound when you drink."

Shock reverberated through me, a ripple that jolted every cell and sent my undead heart racing. Was he saying what I thought he was saying?

"You want me to drink? From you?"

"I hate the thought of you with other men. You said you only need small amounts of blood? So in that case, it stands to reason that I should be the person to provide it."

"Jack, I—"

"Will it heal?"

412

"Yes, but—"

"Then drink."

This was crazy. What he was offering... Could I truly accept it? This would change my entire existence.

"For fuck's sake, Vee... I owe this to you. I owe everything to you. If you're moving to San Francisco, then I'll have to move to San Francisco, and I'm really not a San Francisco kind of guy."

I choked out a laugh. "Too many hipster coffee shops?"

"Babe, I hate avocado toast."

Jack pulled me up into his arms, and this time when I cried, it was with relief. Relief that I didn't have to move again. Relief that my secret, although shared, was still safe. But most of all, relief that the man I loved accepted me for who and what I truly was.

"You're sure about this?" I whispered.

"Honestly? Not completely sure, but sure enough that I want to try. Let's call this relationship a work in progress."

I appreciated his honesty. And how could I turn him down? I'd be rejecting him all over again. Yes, I hated the thought of using the man I loved as a food source, but the alternatives were far, far worse. *Get it over with, Vee.* Heart thumping, I cradled his wrist in my hands and bit as gently as I could. Took a tiny taste. Jack's blood was richer than the finest vintage wine, sweeter than any treat from a Parisian patisserie.

"It doesn't hurt," he murmured.

Thank goodness.

I drank just enough to sate myself, no more, no less, and Jack watched in fascination as my eyes and skin returned to their normal colour. A weight of exhaustion rolled off my shoulders, and I rubbed saliva into the wound, then held his wrist as it scabbed over.

"You can heal me?" he asked. "Is that how you...?"

"I can fix tiny punctures, not a whole ventricle." Although

I had used my saliva to slow the bleeding when he was lying in Harber's McMansion. That had given Blane just enough time to find Aurelia and get back to Plane Five. "Somebody else helped. An acquaintance of Blane's."

"But still… I'll remember that trick next time I get a paper cut." Jack twirled a lock of my hair around one finger. "Will this go back to pink?"

"Do you want it to? I dyed it."

"The blonde suits you. And I'm learning that change isn't necessarily a bad thing." He glanced at his wrist again, then cupped my cheek in his hand. "So, that's it? That's all you need?"

"For a week or so. If I know where my next top-up's coming from, I can push the timings a little farther apart. I never like to get caught short."

"Then we'll just have to make sure I'm around. Are you planning to move back to Sunset Tower?"

I nodded. "I am now. For me, there's no such thing as an impromptu trip out. It's far easier if we live in the same building."

"Do you own this place? Or rent it?"

"Own it. I own the whole of Berkshire Place. If you'd prefer to live here, there's an empty unit on the third floor."

"Babe, I can't afford the rent on my salary."

Oh, please. "The price is your company, and I do miss my hot tub."

"You're sure?"

"In every possible way."

"In that case…"

Jack kissed me on the temple, on the cheek, on the corner of my lips. If this was a work in progress, then I'd toil for as long as it took to make it perfect. I sank into his arms again, his heart beating against mine, his life force pulsing through my veins.

"Do you have to work today?" I whispered.

"I'm on sick leave. Bullet wound. Apparently, I tagged the guy who did it. Who did shoot Harber?"

"Uh, Beauregard."

There'd been a tiny argument about that. Blane had wanted me to do it. Not because he was too chicken to shoot Harber himself—on the contrary, he'd said it would be a pleasure—but because he had some crackpot theory about my purpose here on earth. When we first shared our secrets, he'd mentioned that he thought vampires were a prototype. At the time, he hadn't elaborated on the details, but as Harber and Jack had lain motionless, he'd explained his idea—that Voltaire and his ancestors had been a trial run for the Electi. And if that was true, then he believed there was a possibility that vampires could send souls directly to Plane Three. There was nothing to that effect in the celestial rule book, apparently, but Great-Uncle Tiberius hadn't been the best at record-keeping, and when the vampires hadn't performed the way he'd hoped, he'd tried to brush the whole debacle under the carpet. Aurelia agreed that Blane's theory had merit, while Decima had just tutted and checked Jack's watch.

What evidence was there? Not much, just a bunch of rumours that had been floating around Plane One for millennia. Oh, and the European backpackers who showed up in Plane Three from time to time. Young ingénues, mostly blonde, always confused, and I had to admit that they sounded just Voltaire's type. None could recall their deaths, but several had memories of a grey-eyed Frenchman who'd started off charming before turning nasty. The pieces fit.

But even if I did have that power—a prospect that gave me chills—would shooting a man work? Or did I have to suck the life out of him? Voltaire had shot a number of drunken idiots in his games of Russian roulette, and Blane didn't remember seeing any of them. Decima got snippy and said that Blane's records were as inadequate as their great-uncle's—just one of Blane's many, many failings, it seemed—and they began bickering about the merits of computerisation. Aurelia rolled her eyes because clearly she'd seen all this before, and Beauregard got bored, picked up the gun, and shot Harber in the head.

"Should I thank him?" Jack asked. "Would that be weird?"

"Uh, perhaps I should talk to him and Blane first? About my change in plans. About *us*."

Us. My new favourite word in the English language.

"Then I'll wait."

"So, what should we do today?" Sex would be pushing things, wouldn't it? Too much, too soon and all that. "Want to watch a movie?"

"A movie?" Jack managed a tentative smile. "A movie sounds—"

My front door crashed against the wall, and I sprang in front of Jack. Who the hell was in my apartment? Not the concierge—he phoned first and knocked second.

"Vee!" Blane called. "Where are... Oh." He stopped short in the doorway, a bottle of champagne in each hand. Beauregard trailed behind him holding a bunch of Bon Voyage balloons and a cake. "We came to see you off. I didn't realise you had company."

"The concierge didn't tell you?"

"We just tippy-toed past him. Detective, how are you feeling? Rumour says you were involved in a nasty accident last night."

"He knows, Blane."

"Knows what?"

"He recorded our conversation at Harber's house. The app stopped when Aurelia arrived."

Due to some kind of electrical interference, I suspected. The house lights had flickered too. Aurelia seemed incredibly sweet, but I wouldn't want to get on the wrong side of her. One wrong move, and she could probably zap you onto a deserted island or age you into an early grave.

"Ah."

"He won't say anything."

"You can't be sure of that."

"My client denies everything," Beauregard said.

Jack pulled his phone out of his pocket and handed it to me. "Delete it. Delete the whole recording. I don't want anything to come between us."

"Between you?" Blane gave a low whistle. "You're still together?"

"We're working on it. I'm not leaving Las Vegas."

"Excellent. Should I add you back onto the schedule?"

Jack raised an eyebrow.

"I actually like working at Club Dead," I told him. "Maybe for three nights a week?"

"What about...?" Blane mimed drinking, from a glass rather than somebody's neck, but I still understood the question. When I pointed at Jack, Blane's eyebrows shot into his hairline.

"Boy, that must've been some conversation."

"Are you going to open that champagne? Or just stand there holding it?"

"My dear, I thought you'd never ask." Blane popped the cork, and Jack flinched as it whizzed past his ear. "This one's a Dom Pérignon 2009. I've been saving it for a special occasion."

Well, today certainly qualified. I had Jack Callahan, I had friends, I had a home, and for the first time in a century, I had hope.

Epilogue - Vee

A *month later...*

Jack lasted precisely two weeks in the apartment on the third floor. The other tenants gave him funny looks when he rode down in the elevator each morning, looking dishevelled, so we moved all his things into one of my never-used spare bedrooms and called it a compromise. Not that he slept in the spare bed, but at least we could say we'd paid lip service to the "let's take things slowly" agreement.

We paid lip service to plenty of other things too. And tongue service, and... You get the picture.

With my reduced working hours, we spent plenty of time together in the evenings, but I found myself missing Marianna in the daytime when Jack was at work. We'd kept the apartments in Sunset Tower so I could sneak over before sunrise to spend the occasional day with my new friends, but it wasn't enough. Not anymore. Not when I'd grown used to

418

being able to pop upstairs for a chat anytime. So, Blane brainstormed a solution. My lotto win was an unexpected but amazing surprise, and apart from a small party thrown by Beauregard, we kept it very hush-hush because who wanted all and sundry begging them for money? Of course, I sent Carlene, Latisha, Pandora, and Kristy on vacation, and I also paid Trist's sister's medical bills because none of this was her fault and I didn't want her to suffer more than she already had.

The "windfall" gave me an excuse to offer the third-floor apartment to Marianna, and although she'd been reluctant to accept it at first, I'd convinced her by pointing out that the move would be as beneficial for me as it was for her. And what good was a fortune if I couldn't share it with those I cared about? I'd spent decades being rich and miserable; now I could be slightly less rich and happy.

So now Marianna, Lola, and Pablo lived a short elevator ride away, and after she'd made cakes for every single resident of Berkshire Place as a sort of reverse house-warming gift, they'd started placing orders for more. The concierge had hung a framed price list on the wall in the lobby, and now Marianna baked for profit every morning. Beauregard had helped her with the paperwork to set up a business, and I hoped to goodness his sketchy fake-lawyer ass had done it right.

Tonight, Jack and I were holding our first official dinner party, and it was my turn to cook. Well, not cook, exactly. I'd cheated and ordered dinner from La Nostra Casa, but I'd chosen the wine to go with each course. Jack didn't really appreciate the nuances of wine—yet—but at least I didn't have to hide my purchases of Tenute Silvio Nardi Brunello di Montalcino anymore.

We'd decided to eat early so we could go out to a show afterwards, and also so Lola and Pablo would be awake to join us for the meal. Marianna was a bit unsure about the kids coming, worried that they'd get bored or fidgety, but as my grandma used to say, it was never too early to learn to appreciate the finer things in life.

Our friends started arriving at five thirty, starting with Shep and Cecily, who brought even more wine. Yes, I very much liked this group of people.

"What happened to your face?" Jack asked Shep when he spied the butterfly bandage across one eyebrow.

"A suspect threw an eyelash curler at me."

"You should've ducked."

"Gee, thanks for the advice."

"No shop talk tonight," Cecily announced. "Wow, this is a stunning view. I bet we can see our house from here."

No shop talk. I could live with that. Having spent weeks stuck in the middle of an investigation myself, the last thing I wanted to hear about was more crime.

The final threads of Serenity's case were wrapped up. Jack had been cleared for active duty again, and Harber's funeral had been held last week. I felt so sorry for his wife. She'd been at her sister's the weekend Sid tried to flee the country, completely unaware of both his affair and his attempts to cover it up.

With Harber out of the picture, Trist had begun talking. The whole sorry story had started when Serenity confided in him that she was pregnant. She'd been upset, worried about her future in the music industry, about the baby's health because she'd been drinking before she found out she was pregnant, and about the father's reaction. She'd sworn Trist to secrecy, but far more concerned about his own career than hers, he'd told Harber.

And Harber had put the pieces together, realised the baby was most likely his, and convinced Trist that there was an easy way out.

Jack described Trist as malleable and not particularly

bright. I considered him weak. Even if Serenity hadn't died, her baby still would have, and for what? She'd been talented, not just vocally but at marketing herself too. She could have taken a year off from performing live, and the Sinners would still have sold records. All Trist had needed to do was show an iota of courage and some basic morals and stand up to Harber.

Apparently, Harber had taken care of Michael Klass himself, having promised Trist that he'd do it while Trist was at the party. Why had he delayed? Was it because Klass had still been awake in the early hours? Or in order to invalidate Trist's alibi? That part, nobody was quite sure of.

At least Jeb Moutree had gone away now. Jack had threatened to investigate his green-card sham of a marriage if he didn't fade quietly into the shadows, and Skeeter, who'd only been at Club Dead to warn Serenity of his cousin's plans to leverage her future royalties, had convinced Jeb to accept Jack's proposal.

Serenity and her child had been laid to rest, and now the investigation had been too.

A quiet knock on the door announced Marianna's arrival with Pablo on one hip, Lola at her side, and a bag of toys in her other hand. I crouched to give Lola a hug. Over the past few months, I'd grown to love the little girl and her infectious giggles. For years, children had made me sad because I'd never have any myself, but now I realised there was no point in dwelling on what would never be. Far better to live in the moment.

"This is a treat, not having to cook tonight," Marianna said. "Not that I don't love being in the kitchen, but sometimes..."

"I know exactly what you mean. My job's fun, but occasionally, it's nice to have someone serve me drinks instead of the other way around."

As soon as the door was closed, Lola made a beeline for

Muse. Jack and Lola were my kitty's two favourite people in the world. Since they'd come on the scene, I'd been demoted to "okay," but I didn't mind. If Muse was content, then I was content.

Blane and Beauregard were the last to arrive, and this time, Blane had brought fresh flowers as well as champagne.

"Genevieve!" Blane flung his arms wide. "How's my favourite girl?"

Jack scowled, but it was in jest because he and Blane got on quite well now. And there was trust between us. All three of us. The jury was still out on Beauregard.

"Better than I ever thought possible. You've met Shep and Cecily, and this is Marianna."

"Marianna, I've heard about your cakes."

It was then that I realised Lola had joined us, Muse trailing behind. She looked up at Blane with big brown eyes.

"*Hola*, Lucian."

Lucian? Who called him Lucian? That expression on Lola's face... If I didn't know better, I'd say they'd met before. And Blane? He just looked plain startled. What the hell was going on?

Marianna didn't notice anything wrong, nor did she pick up on the fact that nobody had mentioned Blane's name in front of Lola. This was freaky as hell. But a moment later, Blane's mask was firmly in place again, the bland expression that had been his default for so long. It was only in the last two months that I'd started to see the real him. Whatever had happened, he didn't want to talk about it.

"There's a platter of amuse-bouche on the table." I tried to lighten the atmosphere. "Won't you sit down?"

Blane played the congenial guest all evening, more or less ignoring Lola as he chatted with everyone. Lola herself seemed more interested in her dolls and toy ponies than the overlord of Plane Three. Had I imagined what I'd seen earlier? I didn't think so, but when the babysitter arrived to take care of the children and the rest of us headed out to a new circus show on the Strip, I pushed it to the back of my mind.

Perhaps I'd ask Blane later.

Perhaps I wouldn't.

Live in the moment, Vee.

The circus was spectacular, although Beauregard pooh-poohed the fire-eaters. Child's play, he said. Everybody who wasn't a demon applauded, and as trapeze artists flew overhead, I sent a silent thank you to Great-Uncle Tiberius, wherever he was. The past centuries had been hard, but I'd finally found my happy place.

That joy lasted an hour.

I should have guessed, shouldn't I? Guessed that destiny had other plans for me.

Outside the hotel, a car door slammed. A limo. I glanced across instinctively, and my heart stopped. Dead.

"Vee, what's wrong?" Jack asked.

I couldn't speak. Instead, I buried my head against his shoulder, hiding my face, wishing that it was all a bad dream and I'd wake up soon. But I knew it wasn't and I wouldn't. Voltaire's laser gaze burned into my back.

Just for a second, and then he was gone.

"Vee? Are you okay? What did you see?"

I took a deep breath, then forced out words that grated against my throat.

"My husband. I saw...my husband."

What's Next?

**The next book in the Planes series will be Blane's story,
A Devil in the Dark.**

Watch this page for updates:
www.elise-noble.com/devil

**If you'd like to find out more about the Electi, they have
their own series, starting with *Cursed*...**

Rania Algafari never asked to be different, and when she
escaped the war in Syria and moved to the UK, her only goal
was to live her life in peace. Get up, go to work, avoid talking
to the dead—that sort of thing.

But not everyone dies quietly, and Rania's soon being
pestered by one ghost, blackmailed by another, and distracted
by a handsome private investigator who's got his own reasons
for wanting to solve a particularly gruesome murder.

While Will Lawson doesn't mind using unorthodox
methods to crack a case, he's never had to contact his witnesses
via a seance before. But the clock is ticking, and Will and his

unlikely sidekicks need to hunt down a killer before he's dispatched to join the spirit world himself.

For more details:
www.elise-noble.com/cursed

If you enjoyed *A Vampire in Vegas*, please consider leaving a review.

For an author, every review is incredibly important. Not only do they make us feel warm and fuzzy inside, readers consider them when making their decision whether or not to buy a book. Even a line saying you enjoyed the book or what your favourite part was helps a lot.

Want to Stalk Me?

For updates on my new releases, giveaways, and other random stuff, you can sign up for my newsletter on my website: www.elise-noble.com

If you're on Facebook, you might also like to join Team Blackwood for exclusive giveaways, sneak previews, and book-related chat. Be the first to find out about new stories, and you might even see your name or one of your suggestions make it into print!

And if you'd like to read my books for FREE, you can also find details of how to join my advance review team.

Would you like to join Team Blackwood?

www.elise-noble.com/team-blackwood

facebook.com/EliseNobleAuthor

twitter.com/EliseANoble

instagram.com/elise_noble

End-of-Book Stuff

Like *Copper*, *A Vampire in Vegas* started off life as a serialised story in my newsletter, and like with *Copper*, I didn't have the faintest freaking clue where the story was going to end up when I started it.

The initial seed of an idea came from a pre-made cover I bought, originally titled *Club Dead*. The temporary blurb that came along with it featured nightclub and a detective called Callahan—well, it was actually Callaghan with a "g," but after I'd misspelled it a bunch of times, I figured I'd stick with the way my head preferred. And I figured I'd include a vampire because, hey, I'd never written about a vampire before.

By a quarter of the way through, I'd decided that I wanted Blane to play a bigger part in the story, and by halfway, I'd begun to see the bigger world he lived in and linked it to the Electi (I was also writing *Demented* and *Judged* at the time). Plus it fitted (yes, "fitted" is correct because I'm British) in with *Coco du Ciel*, a book I drafted years ago and which has been languishing in my "re-write" pile forever.

Anyhow, *Judged* is written, *Coco* is re-written, and they'll be my next two releases of 2021. Blane will be getting a story, but it's a little further down my writing list, so I don't have a date yet.

If all goes according to plan—and that's a pretty big "if" because my plans always seem to change—my next books after *Coco* will be the first three instalments in a new romantic suspense series, then Hallie's story in the Blackwood Security series, followed by another book that links them all together.

I'm nothing if not ambitious, lol. Plus I'll be starting another story in my newsletter because that's fun for me :)

Maybe I'll even find time to sleep for an hour or two.

Fingers crossed that at some point in the middle of all that, the world will begin to get back to normal. I love my house, don't get me wrong, but even a trip to the supermarket would be a novelty at this point. Might I also recommend a vitamin D supplement? Don't be like Elise and stay indoors for so long that you end up with a deficiency and get all sorts of sick.

Here's hoping the second half of 2021 will be better than the first...

Thanks so much for reading *A Vampire in Vegas*, and thanks also to my awesome team: Nikki for editing, Abi for designing the cover, and John, Lisbeth, and Debi for proofreading. And thanks to Team Blackwood and all of my newsletter readers for your votes and encouragement and for helping me to turn a tiny idea into a (much longer than intended) finished book!

Elise

Secret Weapon (Crossover with Baldwin's Shore)

The Devil and the Deep Blue Sea (2023)

Blackwood Elements

Oxygen

Lithium

Carbon

Rhodium

Platinum

Lead

Copper

Bronze

Nickel

Hydrogen

Blackwood UK

Joker in the Pack

Cherry on Top

Roses are Dead

Shallow Graves

Indigo Rain

Pass the Parcel (TBA)

Blackwood Casefiles

Stolen Hearts

Burning Love (TBA)

Baldwin's Shore

Dirty Little Secrets

Secrets, Lies, and Family Ties

Buried Secrets

Secret Weapon (Crossover with Blackwood Security)

A Secret to Die For (2023)

Blackstone House

Hard Lines (2022)

Hard Tide (2022)

Hard Limits (2023)

The Electi

Cursed

Spooked

Possessed

Demented

Judged

The Planes

A Vampire in Vegas

A Devil in the Dark (TBA)

The Trouble Series

Trouble in Paradise

Nothing but Trouble

24 Hours of Trouble

Standalone

Life

Coco du Ciel

A Very Happy Christmas (novella)

Twisted (short stories)

Books with clean versions available (no swearing and no on-the-page sex)

Pitch Black

Into the Black

Forever Black

Gold Rush

Gray is My Heart

Audiobooks

Black is My Heart (Diamond & Snow - Prequel)

Pitch Black

Into the Black

Forever Black

Gold Rush

Gray is My Heart

Neon (novella)

www.ingramcontent.com/pod-product-compliance
Lightning Source LLC
Chambersburg PA
CBHW060726190726
48285CB00001B/91